Aftermath *of* Empire

Roy A.K. Heath

Aftermath *of* EMPIRE

THE NOVELS OF ROY A.K. HEATH

AMEENA GAFOOR

THE UNIVERSITY OF THE WEST INDIES PRESS
Jamaica • Barbados • Trinidad and Tobago

The University of the West Indies Press
7A Gibraltar Hall Road, Mona
Kingston 7, Jamaica
www.uwipress.com

A catalogue record of this book is available from the National Library of Jamaica.

ISBN: 978-976-640-636-3 (print)
978-976-640-637-0 (Kindle)
978-976-640-638-7 (ePub)

Cover illustration: Bernadette Indira Persaud, *Kali's Necklace* (acrylic on canvas, 56" x 36", 2013).
By kind permission of the artist. Photographed by Dwayne Hackett.
Cover and book design by Robert Harris.
Set in Scala 10.25/15 x 27.

Printed in the United States of America

THIS WORK IS DEDICATED TO
EMERITUS PROFESSOR KENNETH RAMCHAND

Every line we succeed in publishing today . . . is a victory wrested from the powers of darkness.
—Walter Benjamin, *Selected Writings*

Living in a borrowed culture, the West Indian, more than most, needs writers to tell him who he is and where he stands.
—V.S. Naipaul, *The Middle Passage*

CONTENTS

PREFACE

The first thing to notice about Roy Heath's novels is their aura of timelessness, a quality that, in Jeffrey Robinson's view, defines the Guyanese novel. Asked by A.J. Seymour whether there was a special quality discernible in Guyanese writing, Robinson replied, fumbling for a word to describe our literature, that it seemed "strangely mystical". Later, he writes, "I should now prefer to say that there is, in the major works by Guyanese writers, a similarity of theme and attitude. The theme is the relationship between the mind and the world and between both of these, considered as a dialectic, and time. The attitude is one that renders these relationships not so much as philosophy or theory, but as riddle or mystery."[1] In Heath's own words, "My preoccupation with time is, I believe, the exile's way of dealing with the separation from his roots."[2]

If proof were needed as to how far the literary imagination can take us into the minds and motivations of fictional subjects, then Heath's creative output provides rich and rewarding scope. Glimpses into the flawed psyches of irrational, illogical characters who lack self-knowledge and who people Heath's nine novels cause us to reflect on the words of Josef Conrad: "The only legitimate basis of creative work lies in the courageous recognition of all irreconcilable antagonisms that make our lives so enigmatic, so burdensome, so fascinating, so dangerous, so full of hope. This is the only fundamental truth of fiction."[3] Heath has practically refined the introspective Guyanese antihero, his quest for cultural identity and selfhood as tortured and elusive as society's quest for freedom and self-determination.

In *From the Heat of the Day*, Sonny Armstrong is an arrogant, intemperate husband and father, incapable of rising above the negatives in society;

Esther is warped by her desire for revenge; while Genetha's flawed bid for independence ends in her too easily yielding to society's vices. Rohan, in *One Generation*, rash and impetuous in his desire for freedom, the equivalent of the Nietzschean Superman, expends his life's energy in a reckless romantic affair. In *A Man Come Home*, Foster is a pathetic, naive character who allows his family to be shamelessly exploited; Bird, who wants instant wealth, depends on a mythological creature to save him from humiliating poverty. In *Orealla*, Schwartz is a cruel, blackmailing master and Ben is a thief, a rebellious servant and an impulsive murderer. Galton Flood in *The Murderer* and Mrs Singh in *The Shadow Bride*, wilful and disillusioned souls, in search of cultural identity but trapped within alien and irrelevant conventions, are driven to the point of derangement. Gladys Armstrong in *From the Heat of the Day* and Lathi in *The Shadow Bride* are two spineless women with weak egos who cannot break out of the stranglehold of custom and culture and fail to act to preserve the self. Trickster figures, such as Fingers, Bird, Gee, Kwaku and Pujaree are linked to the perverse society, and Ramjohn in *One Generation* is as much a villain as the nameless Minister of Hope. Heath's rebellious characters all pursue their fates to the point of heroic inversion, while it is left to a few minor characters to discover the possibilities of salvaging their lives (and the texts) from negative outcomes, at the same time offering a positive vision of renewal: in *From the Heat of the Day*, Doc extols the virtue of family even as he abandons his own family; in *One Generation*, Sidique thinks of making a new life in the sandhills away from society's corruption; in *A Man Come Home*, Stephanie, the artist, with the creative impulse necessary for survival, offers Christine an option to a truthful way of life through art; and in *Orealla*, Carl must return to his staid, predictable community life at Orealla after finding no accommodation in the upside-down world of Georgetown.

Heath has, however, found occasion to celebrate every one of his flawed fictional creatures: their humaneness, their eccentricities, their weaknesses, and their strengths, even if they are social misfits and psychological wrecks; we come to appreciate the negatives and the positives of every situation.

The texture of Heath's fictional world is worth noticing: it draws its raw material from a geographical setting where numerous waterfalls punctuate the landscape, among them the transcendental Kaieteur Falls, churning rivers and choppy rapids, kokers and trenches. The mighty Amazon in its back yard, the murky Atlantic Ocean at its front door, Heath's fictional world is dominated by powerful water images that serve to intensify the dread of already vulnerable characters. Abandoned on the seawalls by her moody husband, Gladys Armstrong considers suicide in the lashing waves of the Atlantic Ocean. An atmosphere of fear and vulnerability engulfs Genetha, who constantly listens for the menacing sounds of the Atlantic, "like a jaguar on the prowl . . . so silent is the night that she could hear the sea pounding the shore nearly a mile away".[4] The Georgetown ferry stelling is the scene of a brutal crime in *The Murderer*, and Galton Flood disposes of the body of his murdered wife in the murky Demerara River. When the Minister of Hope thinks of eliminating his antagonist, Correia, he lures him to the dark waters of the Conservancy Canal, the very canal that the truant, Kwaku, breaches in his idleness, causing flooding and economic havoc in nearby villages. The jealous Genetha, who finds herself on the Vreed-en-Hoop ferry only to catch sight of her brother's pagan lover, peers into the frothing, churning river that mirrors her own mind seething with tormented thoughts. Kwaku crosses the Berbice River backwards and forwards, wracked by his self-delusions that he is an important medicine man. When Ramjohn's wife, Deen, is weary of life, she plunges to the bottom of Rohan's well.

For Heath, landscape is an ambivalent metaphor for freedom and entrapment, deployed largely as a mechanism to reinforce his theme of existential distress in a suffocating society. His writing conveys an overwhelming sense of futility and failure to transcend the daunting physical realities of the colony he depicts in nine novels. Even though the population of this vast land is sparse, Guyanese society is cramped, crammed in the narrow coastal strip between seawall and backdam, ocean and jungle. A character in *One Generation* succinctly summarizes the unyielding landscape of coastal Guyana: "The ocean on one side and the forest on the other, threatening to crush us between them."[5]

Heath's estranged characters dwell on the margins of the landscape: waterfront sawmills and stellings, urban tenement yards, market cookshops, brothels and rum shops. In *Orealla*, Mabel lives in a muddy tenement yard where "coconut husk islands form stepping stones across the mud lakes". This is the 1920s and the yard remains in the very same state of dereliction, occupied by Gee and Muriel in *A Man Come Home*, Heath's novel of independence – a testimony to the chronic poverty bequeathed by colonialism. The congested city remains the focal point in Heath's novels, and a very few of his characters harbour no more than a subliminal attraction to an unknown jungle interior: Armstrong constantly thinks of "Bartica, the gateway to the vast hinterland, the hinterland which made Guyanese such odd people" (*One Generation*, 58), but he lacks the will to venture through that symbolic gateway to explore either the vast, unknown hinterland of country or his dense, unknowable self.

That these works end in tragedy and collapse and still leave us with a vision of the open-endedness of human experience is testimony that Heath has revolutionized the form of the regional novel. We notice in his corpus a longing for community, especially when society threatens to disintegrate around vulnerable characters. We come to see in the tragic end of old relationships the possibility of renewal, the liberation of characters from the victim status bequeathed to them by family and by history, and the anticipation of something new and inventive after foundering and failure. Heath's characters are imbued with a sense of self and identity, a desire for change, and a few of them with revolutionary ideas: one is convinced that the way to change and renewal is to "burn everything to the ground and start all over", while another character advises: "Throw out everything and start over." In *One Generation*, Sidique rejects his narrow ethnic enclave on the Essequibo coast and dreams about humanizing a space outside the village, among the sandhills, with the possibility of a fresh start, free of the shenanigans of family and a poisoned past. Ben dreams constantly of the idyllic life of an Amerindian reserve at Orealla on the Corentyne River, a dream that is, however, never fulfilled. Heath seeks to revise the premises of a flawed society, and while his characters may be expendable, the writer's vision endures – a vision of the necessity for a new and creative architecture of community.

Through the utterances Heath puts into the mouths of his imperfect characters, and through their relationships with each other, his vision of renewal and wholeness becomes clear. Both the alcoholic psychopath, Sukrum, and the progressive Dr Singh in *The Shadow Bride* possess an unmistakable sense of belonging as Guyanese; the trickster, Kwaku, and the criminal, Ben, both rebels against an unjust social order, remind their employers that humans are not (owned like) chattel; Genetha struggles for her humanity in the face of a wily lover, a vengeful servant, and an intolerant society; Foster plucks up the courage to strike out against his villainous friend, Gee; Ben goes to the gallows with an invincible human spirit intact; and Mrs Singh rebels against threats to her cultural certainty in a colonial backwater. These characters expend their life force in rebellion but also in quest of human dignity, of a new order of community, of reprieve from a bitter past and a devalued sense of self. One hopes that this work can manage to alter some mistaken impressions conveyed in the existing criticism about Heath's vision being one of failure and pessimism.

No Guyanese or regional writer before Heath has been so consistent in dismantling the class paradigm in the quest for a more democratic society. No non-Indian writer has displayed such remarkable cultural knowledge and such psychological depth in depicting East Indian experience in the West Indian novel. Heath's portrayal of the volatile nature of the multiracial, multicultural society, with a symbolic clash of the two major races, is convincing. His investigation into the institution of the family, community and traditional values by which a society coheres is admirable without neglecting the matter of the valid pursuit of individual freedom. Heath also dares to experiment with the integration of the Amerindian into mainstream society in *Orealla*. His vision of assimilation (in *One Generation*) in a society characterized by racial and cultural diversity needs to be pondered on in an age when cultural distinctiveness is a valid concept.

In almost every one of his novels we witness change in the social structure occurring almost imperceptibly. The fragility of class boundaries and the erosion of social barriers deepen the reader's understanding of a society in flux, of colonialism teetering to its end: a middle-class woman marries below her social class; a servant is in control of a middle-class Queenstown household where she would normally be "kept in her place"; a young woman from a comfortable middle-class home in Queenstown becomes a homeless prostitute seeking shelter in the hovels of Albouystown, while a destitute family is ensconced in her house through trickery; an unemployed idler with questionable wealth dares to acquire a prestigious Brickdam residence; a vagabond is temporarily master of a mansion on Vlissengen Road, and, later, a vagrant takes over.

The virtue of Heath's oeuvre lies in its presentation of a credible psychological realism together with its redeeming vision of man and society. It mediates a line of thought in the region that the damage done under colonialism, more especially in psychological terms, remains a permanent scar that is mirrored in the socio-economic and political structures of the post-independent society.

Analyses of the texts yield ample evidence to support the argument that Heath is an urban/coastal writer who seeks to revise the complex terms of existence of his people. They reveal Heath's vision of the need for fundamental change in the society after independence, even if so far only articulated via art forms, and his insistence that only a renewal of consciousness can bring about the psychic changes sought by independence. So far, he is the only Guyanese novelist with an entire corpus devoted exclusively to the city and its crippling arrangements: its brutal social differentiation, its relentless poverty and trope of dispossession, its squalid range-yards and slums, its brothels, its corrupt political culture and its power structures. His idiosyncratic novels all add up to a lacerating critique of Guyanese society and a broadside against the political establishment. It would be fair to argue that a body of work that investigates urban failure, human uncertainty, psychological frailty and a redeeming vision is Heath's unique contribution to both the Guyanese and the regional novel.

Heath's novels participate in a view of the cultural importance of art as a reservoir of society's values and beliefs. Heath explained that he "laid much store by cultural customs and mythology" and built his narratives around man's reliance on such phenomena, for instance, the Water Maid, obeah, white-table ritual, séance, Kali Mai puja, his trickster figures based on the fables of Reynard the fox, and so on. Such influences and allusions helped to illustrate the "inexplicable and the irrational in man and his condition of existence".[6]

The novels achieve two effects: deepening understanding of the evolving society and increasing self-knowledge. Heath is likely to be claimed by many communities for the universalism of his ideas, but this work will demonstrate that this novelist has first dealt patiently with the specifics of his society. Heath's novels go far in giving twenty-first-century Guyana a clearer idea of itself, in offering the individual a deeper understanding of self and, fundamentally, of what it means to be Guyanese. His works sit firmly within the West Indian literary canon. It is perhaps fitting to introduce some broad comments from Susan Fromberg Schaeffer:

Heath's novels are unlike any I have ever read. British reviewers have called them exotic, and they *are* exotic, although not because of their unfamiliar settings (all of them are set in British Guyana) or the extravagant behaviour of the characters who inhabit the world Heath creates. What makes these novels exotic – and intoxicating – is how wonderfully they accomplish what the Russian critic, Viktor Shklovsky, said all art must do: they make new rather than merely make known. Heath's world is no more exotic than that of Franz Kafka, but it is no less exotic, either. After some acquaintance with Heath's characters, the reader finds them not in the least strange, but so familiar as to be frightening, so that everything we know to be true of them – their sudden plunges into lunacy, their tendency to take a step and find that the ground beneath them is no longer solid – we come to suspect is also true of ourselves. Our view of ourselves is made new, is changed, by reading Roy Heath. His work is the best illustration I know of the axiom which holds that in order to be universal a character must first be portrayed in all his unique, even eccentric specificity. The shock of Heath's work – and it *is* a shock – comes, when we realize, not how different we are from his Guyanese, but that we are identical with them.7

Our aim is not to seek a comfortable critical position on which to rest. We can only hope that this work will serve to create an opening for other critical inquiries and for the discovery of more meanings in Heath's novels.

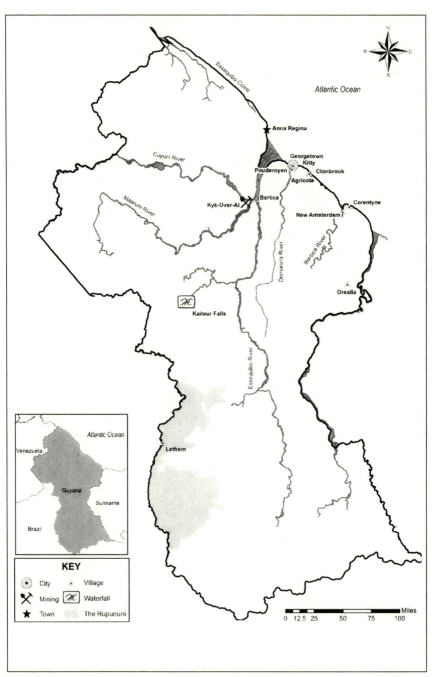

Map of Guyana. (Cartography by Thera Edwards.)

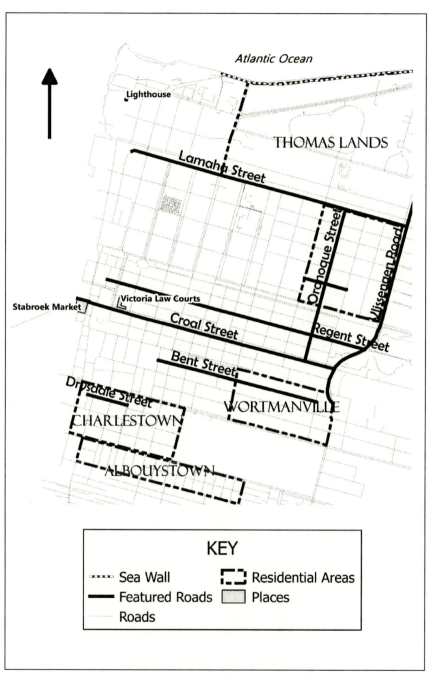

Map of Georgetown. (Cartography by Thera Edwards.)

INTRODUCTION

Roy A.K. Heath (born in Guyana 1926, died in London 2008) produced a significant body of writing that includes nine novels, a number of poems and short stories that appeared early in his writing career, one play and a handful of essays and lectures.[1] The novels were first published in the United Kingdom between 1974 and 1997 and only began to be issued in the United States in 1992. They were reviewed in most of the British newspapers, and the reviews were mostly favourable, but critical response has been limited to just a few essays in literary journals and one book-length work that examines seven of the novels.[2] Heath's novels have not had the sustained critical attention they deserve and he is only cited in passing in discussions on West Indian literature or of major West Indian writers. An incomplete autobiography, *Shadows Round the Moon: Caribbean Memoirs* (1990), recounts the writer's life up to the point of his departure for England in 1950. Very little is known about him in the years before his first novel was published, and even after his work began to appear not much information was forthcoming.[3] Heath remained self-effacing, his works are hardly ever mentioned in the United Kingdom and are not included in any educational syllabus in the Caribbean, and he is even less known in the land of his birth.[4]

There seems to be some difficulty in placing Heath as a "West Indian" writer: "Heath has received comparatively little notice as a West Indian writer. His novels are circulated worldwide . . . yet he does not fit into the established categories of Caribbean writing."[5] Some of the issues are clearly set out in the following remarks:

Roy Heath is a contemporary West Indian novelist whose work commands serious attention. It provokes interesting speculation about where he fits in the
tradition of the West Indian novel developed in the 1950's by writers such as
Edgar Mittelholzer, George Lamming, Samuel Selvon, V.S. Naipaul, and Wilson
Harris. . . . His trilogy of novels about Guyana does not deal with contemporary
issues in that country.

What, then, is the relationship of Heath's work to that of the previous generation? . . . Is he simply following paths in the West Indian novel that have been
worn down by others, or is he beating his own path? There are many ways in
which his fiction is significantly different from that of many other West Indian
novelists. . . . Heath's fiction is not overtly concerned with the theme of national-
ism, or of the search for a West Indian identity, or of the heritage of colonialism,
or of independence and its aftermath. He is not especially interested in history,
at least not in the manner of Mittelholzer.

On the one hand, this tendency to ignore so many of the themes that are
central to West Indian writing might suggest that Heath is out of touch with
the important issues in the life of the area, possibly because he is an expatriate.[6]

This introductory study of Heath's novels is an attempt to critically appraise
them as valid reinterpretations of a chronically dishevelled society from which
the author himself took flight. The landscape and the social reality of Heath's
fictional world are recognizably and uncompromisingly located in the city
of Georgetown and its suburbs, in Guyana, a former British colony on the
northeastern rim of the South American mainland and linked to the West
Indies by a shared history of slavery and indentureship. This work seeks to
trace the writer's vision of man and society; to relate the fictional world of the
texts to the social and cultural context that informs them; to examine Heath's
stylistic techniques; to enquire in what ways the novels might be "significantly
different" from those of other West Indian novelists; to enquire in what ways
the novels might have drawn from Guyanese writers before Heath; to correct
false critical impressions and broaden the scope of existing criticism; to place
the body of writing within a literary convention and, ultimately, to expand
the critical space.

In this chapter, we attempt to discuss extant critical views and interpretations of Heath's novels and to suggest a more coherent way of considering a body of writing that brings some of the arrangements, attitudes and
assumptions of post-colonial Guyana and its peculiar post-independence

history under critical scrutiny. A brief account of Heath's novels in the order in which they appeared may be useful at this stage.[7]

Heath's first published work, *A Man Come Home* (1974) is set in south Georgetown, in a Guyana that has newly gained political independence. At the centre of this work is the Foster family (Foster, his common-law wife, Christine, and their adolescent daughter, Melda). Foster, a cooper whose skills have become obsolete since the introduction of a pure water system to the city, supplements his meagre income as a lampshade-maker with regular remittances from Benjy, his son who lives in Canada. Another grown, permanently unemployed son, Bird, lives with his girlfriend, Stephanie, in a Broad Street range-yard close by his father's Princess Street cottage. These two families are linked by a friend named Gee, a baker's assistant who lives with his woman, Muriel, in a Bent Street range-yard. Gee is a leech who preys shamelessly on both families.

In Guyana, range-yards, derogatorily referred to as tenements or slums, evolved out of the migration of freed labourers and time-expired indentured labourers to the city, where they resorted to various menial jobs to survive. Over time, this movement intensified with the desire among the rural population to access better jobs and prestigious secondary schools for their children. Working-class people gravitated to the congested areas in south Georgetown (in the wards of Albouystown, Charlestown, Wortmanville), in the west of the city, in what is now known as Tiger Bay, and on Lombard Street, along the waterfront. Migration from villages to the margins of the city not only swelled the seams of the city but also severely tested its infrastructure. While not all émigrés headed for the poorer parts of the city, the range-yards are marked by human congestion, chronic poverty, underdevelopment, and neglect – harsh realities that reinforce a debilitating class divide.

The barrack-yard communities outside of Port of Spain, Trindad (for example, Laventille), and on the outskirts of Kingston, Jamaica (for example, Tivoli), have all the features of the Guyanese range-yard and often take on a more dramatic life of their own, with their own militancy and codes of conduct. C.L.R. James, arguably the first Caribbean novelist to portray the realism of the barrack-yard (in *Minty Alley*, 1936), depicts in an earlier short story: "Every street in Port-of-Spain proper can show you numerous examples of the type: a narrow gateway, leading into a fairly big yard on either side of which run long low buildings, consisting of anything from four to eighteen rooms, each about twelve feet square. In these live and have always lived the porters, the prostitutes, cart-men, washer women and domestic servants of the city."[8] Before James, Eric Walrond had published *Tropic Death* (1926), perhaps the first substantial collection of short stories set in Guyana and the Caribbean to have depicted the realism of the yard.

The alienation of the poor in socially and economically depressed areas provides raw material for the drama of the yard in several genres of literary expression. While the poet Martin Carter anguishes over "my strangled city", and Rooplall Monar has written amply about the lives of the East Indian indentured labourers on the sugar estates, Roy Heath remains the only Guyanese novelist who has a sustained body of work depicting the psyche of the range-yard dweller and how he negotiates survival and existence. It is the psychological more than the sociological that attracts the reader to Heath's novels. Heath said that he thought he had "much ground to cover" when he embarked on a writing career; at that time, no writer had yet consistently portrayed the realism of the range-yard: the poverty and the alienation of the slum-dweller as well as "the satiric vitality of the living language of the yard".[9] The geophysical features of the small island of Barbados do not seem to have encouraged such migration to the city; rather, the village movement took root in the island and later spread throughout the parishes, as famously played out in the fictions of George Lamming and Austin Clarke.

The best insight into yard communities across the Caribbean is to be found in early journalism, in early short stories in literary magazines[10] and in novels, notably (of Trinidad) James's *Minty Alley*; and (of Jamaica) Roger Mais's *The Hills Were Joyful Together* (1953) and *Brother Man* (1954); and Alecia McKenzie's *Satellite City and Other Stories* (1992) and *Stories from Yard* (2005).

A Man Come Home can be seen to have a double plot, and the action of the Bird plot is sparked off by news that Benjy has acquired a house in Canada. Eager not to be seen as a wastrel in light of his brother's reported success, Bird sets out in pursuit of instant wealth. His seeming connection with a Water Maid (a mythical female figure in Guyanese folklore that is said to hold men in thrall); his mercurial moods and irrational temperament; his frequent and unexplained absences from home; and his relationships with his family, his girlfriend, and his trickster friend, Gee, form one strand of the work. Gee's relationship with the Foster family and how he negotiates the wasteland he inhabits since it became a free state form the second strand.

The Murderer (1978), Heath's second published work, also set in the city of Georgetown in the post-independence period, depicts a central character, Galton Flood, whose self-image and perception of the world have been shaped by the entrenched morality that has been the measure of respectability in the colony for more than two centuries. Galton's parents die when he is a young man, leaving him free to chart his own destiny. He immediately flees the city, with its stifling rules, and finds love in the riverain town of Wismar. On their wedding night, Galton's wife discloses that she has had a previous lover, a revelation that does not square with the inbred Victorian upbringing rigidly ingrained by his mother. In anger, he subjects his wife to a humiliating existence in degraded tenement housing in the slums of the city, decides she is unfit to live, and then murders her, disposing of her body in the Demerara River before succumbing to madness. This work investigates the fractured psyche of the colonial and the damaging effects of an imposed Victorian morality through Galton's relationships with family and society, relationships that come to symbolize a divided consciousness inherent in the colonial condition.

The next three novels, *From the Heat of the Day* (1979), *One Generation* (1981) and *Genetha* (1981), form a trilogy that captures the lives of two generations of the Armstrong family and their struggle to negotiate survival in colonial Georgetown in the first half of the twentieth century. Together, the three works span a period of forty years, starting from 1922 and running up to the months just before independence (in 1966), and offer a picture of pervasive class schisms and isolation in a poverty-stricken backwater colony.

The first volume, *From the Heat of the Day*, recounts the experiences of Gladys Davis, a spinster from a middle-class Queenstown family, and her husband, Sonny Armstrong, a rural postal clerk from Agricola who is shunned as a social inferior by his wife's family. Rejected by the Davises, the couple cannot find a place in middle-class Georgetown and make their way to a rural village to raise a small family; there, Gladys is doubly victimized by a bitter and intemperate husband and by unfriendly neighbours. Armstrong cheats his sister of their father's property in Queenstown. When Gladys returns to the city, endemic poverty and rejection from her family guarantee her early demise.

In the second volume, *One Generation*, the Armstrong son, Rohan, a rash and restless young man, crosses racial and cultural boundaries in a romantic relationship with a married woman. He requests a job transfer from the Pouderoyen office where he is a clerk and pursues her as far as Suddie on the Essequibo Coast, where she lives with her husband and his extended family. The situation is further complicated by the arrival at Suddie of his sister-in-law, who entertains romantic notions about him. He misjudges the internecine nature of the society and transgresses its taboos in the conservative Indian enclave, with tragic results.

The third volume of the trilogy, *Genetha*, traces the social and emotional process of another Armstrong offspring, their daughter Genetha, whose socially inferior lover cheats her out of her family house in Queenstown and leaves her to scrounge on the margins of an indifferent society. Homeless and destitute, rejected by family and sexually exploited, Genetha allows herself to degenerate and is ultimately rescued by their erstwhile servant, Esther, and inducted into her brothel in the heart of Georgetown. Gladys had dismissed Esther on suspicion of sexual intimacy with her husband and thrown her out into the streets of Georgetown, and the servant has waited patiently through the years to take revenge on Genetha for her fall into prostitution.

Genetha concludes the trilogy, which turns out to be a study of flawed characters futilely struggling against a state of entrapment in a treacherous city of poverty and class prejudices. It examines in some detail the fate of the single woman seeking independence at a time when the colony itself is groping towards political independence.

Heath's next work, *Kwaku* (1982), is set in the post-independence period and begins in a rural village known only as "C", on the east coast of the county of Demerara. It recounts the experiences of Kwaku, the eponymous village buffoon and father of eight children, who makes disparaging remarks against the ruling party. Government thugs hound him and threaten him with harm, even though he has been paying his party dues faithfully to ensure a place in the village government school for his children. A locust plague is destroying crops along the coastland and causing massive unemployment and widespread poverty. Kwaku goes into hiding in the backdam, where he idly breaches the Conservancy Dam, causing flooding of crops and further hardships to villagers. His marriage to Miss Gwendoline is complicated by his liaisons with his lover, Blossom. To escape both his poverty and his wife's scorn, Kwaku absconds to the backwater town of New Amsterdam, where, unwittingly, he drifts into the role of a herbal healer preying upon credulous villagers. He finds himself in a lucrative trade and to clinch his newfound fame and image, outfits himself in expensive, well-tailored clothes and poses as a professional.

In addition to being a confidence trickster, Kwaku has another shortcoming, and it is that he cannot keep his mouth shut. He fails to keep a promise made to a village fisherman while visiting his own family in the village of "C", and the vengeful villager menaces his wife, who becomes blind from hysterical fear. This causes Kwaku to return home, as his teenage sons are becoming unruly. The villagers regard him not as a healer, but as the old village buffoon; unable to gain a clientele, he is reduced to poverty. He returns to New Amsterdam to find that his clients have deserted him; he ends up destitute and a stranger in the town, where his entire family has now accompanied him.

Orealla (1984), set in the 1920s, relates the story of Ben, a working-class black man who grooms horses and is a newspaper columnist and a known petty thief. Caught in an act of burglary, Ben takes the offer of indefinite indentureship with Schwartz, a coloured Treasury official, instead of a term of imprisonment, and goes to live in a servant's room under his master's mansion in Regent Street. This is a virtual recreation of the master/slave relationship, in the heart of what is recognizably twentieth-century Georgetown.

In addition to his childless middle-class wife, Tina, Ben keeps a common-law wife, Mabel, who bears him three children. Ben provides financial support for Mabel and their children out of his meagre salary and from fees earned from journalism. The triangular arrangement provides the grist for a study of the dynamics of class relationships and cultural mores in the colony. Ben happens to meet Carl, an Amerindian from the Orealla reservation on the Corentyne River (from which the work takes its name), at a street corner, examining birdcages, and invites him to share his servant's quarters. Ben devises ways of either cheating his master of additional rent due for Carl or of surreptitiously using his master's cab for hire to earn extra for Carl's rent.

Ben's relationship with his master is fraught with tensions and resentment that are reminiscent of acts of slave resistance. The work is devoted to the psychological power struggle between master and servant until Ben yields to a dark instinct for retaliation and revenge. It would seem that in contemplating the sequel to *Kwaku* Heath was moving to explore the twentieth-century relationship between employer and indentured worker (analogous to slavery and colonialism) as a way of understanding the dysfunction manifest in West Indian societies at independence.

The Shadow Bride (1988) covers most of the twentieth century, from the colonial 1920s up to the post-independence 1980s. The work recounts the experiences of an Indian woman, her dislodgement from India, and her struggle of adjustment and accommodation in a British colony. On the death of her wealthy Guianese-born husband, Mrs Singh begins to assert herself and plan the life of her son, employing a Muslim priest as a private tutor for the youth. Eventually, however, she clashes with her son, now a doctor, over issues of nationality and culture. Defying the wishes of his mother, Dr Singh chooses a bride for himself and sacrifices a successful private practice in Kitty to devote his service to the malaria-stricken, working-class poor on a rural sugar estate on the west coast of Demerara. Mrs Singh's tortuous relationships with her son and his wife, with her mentors and her servants and hangers-on at her suburban mansion, form the core of the work.

In *The Ministry of Hope* (1997), the sequel to *Kwaku*, the main character, Kwaku, now pitiably destitute and seeking any opportunity to re-establish himself financially, leaves New Amsterdam and travels to Georgetown in the hope of selling decorated chamber pots as souvenirs to gullible tourists. Kwaku connects with a youth he had met earlier on one of his healing excursions on the Corentyne coast and finds himself in the circle of a hardening political dictatorship. His young friend is now a minister without portfolio, but has risen rapidly to the office of Minister of Hope. The minister steals Kwaku's lucrative business venture in chamber pots and removes him from the scene for a while by sending him far away into the Rupununi to spy on a functionary who deals in illegal currency. Upon his return to the city, Kwaku is offered the lowly post of assistant to a messenger. Through a series of escapades, the work recounts Kwaku's encounter with the regime over a period of time, his intuitive negotiation of the political minefield and his struggle to avoid becoming one of its victims. This satire on dictatorship, also a testament to the wily ways of the confidence trickster, traces Kwaku's progress towards becoming a hardened impostor as he drifts into the role of professional herbal healer and talk therapist in a posh office with an impressive library on the outskirts of the city.

Marxist Influences

In his early novels, Heath examined the treacherous class gap and the ways in which the codes of middle-class respectability function to shape the private lives of ordinary people. His interest in reinterpreting the class-ordered society may have derived from his close association with Martin Carter (1927–1997), that inveterate Marxist revolutionary intellect, voice and co-founder of the People's Progressive Party (1950) led by the Marxist firebrand Cheddi Jagan.[11]

Heath found the moral seriousness of Marx's conviction pertinent to lingering questions about his own life as a colonial.[12] Karl Marx had extracted from French political life (the French Revolution; French revolutionaries stormed the Bastille on 14 July 1789) the notion of social reform through revolution. He believed that social growth and development hinged intimately upon the condition of the disadvantaged and the necessity of a consciously fostered clash between major interests and social classes. In Britain, also, the Industrial Revolution (from the 1760s) had ushered in a new era of human exploitation in dark and overcrowded factories in city centres, including the misery of child labour, providing fuel for writers such as Charles Dickens.

The Bolshevik Revolution, the Russian Classics and Other Influences

Heath came to a deeper understanding of the pervasive wretchedness of the human condition through his study of certain Russian classics, whether they depict the Gulag or Stalin's Russia. Heath was especially impressed by Gogol, Leskov, and the French writer Jean-Paul Sartre.[13] The Bolshevik Revolution of 1917 had a profound impact on the world and on the imagination of writers everywhere. The idea of the overthrow of the bourgeoisie in a class-driven society and the possibility of an ideal democratic/humanistic social order of the proletariat that would allow for a just society as well as the formation of an integrated human personality, in contrast to the alienation produced by capitalism and mercantilism, appealed to Heath.[14] He envisioned the reform of society and the renewal of man in a new moral order through the structures of art. In so doing, he locates himself through his writing and invites the society to know itself through art. It is not by accident that Heath chose the claustrophobic urban setting, with its wide class divide and its endemic poverty, as material for all his novels. He was, however, not satisfied with analysing society merely through social or ideological lenses.

Beyond Social Issues

His deeper interest in the complexity of the human mind and the human personality drove Heath to look beyond social issues in his writing and to delve into patterns of human behaviour, examining human relationships across race and class, and lending a new depth of psychological authenticity to character. Heath disclosed that he was obsessed with the idea of understanding the human mind, its irrationality, its illogicality, its collapse.[15] Edgar Mittelholzer (who was part-German) may have introduced the psychologically divided character in Guyana's seminal novel, *Corentyne Thunder* (1941) – "the mulatto divided by his racial angst",[16] while Wilson Harris (part-Amerindian) may have developed the fragmented character struggling towards a revolutionary change of consciousness in order to come to a sense of belonging in his novels set in the Guyana hinterland; but the Heathian character evolves as a fully developed, introspective creature, mired in poverty and cultural alienation, his sensibility irreparably fractured as much by the weight of the unjust system of colonialism as by his own flawed psyche.[17]

Heath's novels differ markedly in emphasis from those of his fellow West Indian writers. They are deemed to lack the nationalistic thrust of the pioneers: Claude McKay's *Banana Bottom* (1933), James's *Minty Alley* (1936), Mais's *The Hills Were Joyful Together* (1953). In their concern to express or discover a West Indian identity, these authors create characters with an innate will to be a part of a positive way of life and who exhibit an infectious *joie de vivre* in wretched "yard" communities. Mittelholzer's Guyana novels

(*Corentyne Thunder*; *The Life and Death of Sylvia*; *Shadows Move among Them*) seem concerned with the "split psyche", racial strength and superiority of European blood. The novels of Heath's contemporaries – Samuel Selvon, V.S. Naipaul, George Lamming, Jan Carew – are devoted to the themes of exile and alienation and the West Indian need for a sense of identity and belonging as a prerequisite to individual freedom.

Heath brings us to a more elemental point of departure in his novels: an enquiry into the ontological struggle of the ordinary man simply to *be* and the nature of *being* as a prelude to freedom and self-realization. It is the argument of this work that Heath's texts are only incidentally about class, colour and race, even though the class dichotomy is foregrounded in every novel. Heath's vulnerable characters struggle to maintain a toehold in a cruel, claustrophobic world for more complex reasons. The depth of psychological realism and the nuanced portrayal of the fragile architecture of the human consciousness achieved in the entire oeuvre are perhaps what guarantee its timelessness and are perhaps only matched in the regional novel in the works of Garth St Omer, who tries to work out in his novels a Caribbean version of existentialism.[18] Heath has crafted a coherent body of novels that speak directly to the psychosocial and psycho-cultural reality of what is identifiably twentieth-century Guyana in the post-colonial and post-independence periods.

Existing Criticism on Heath

The Ministry of Hope (1997),[19] the last of Heath's nine novels, had not yet appeared when a book-length study of seven of Heath's novels was published; the study *Colonialism and the Destruction of the Mind* (1996) did not include a consideration of Heath's arguably most accomplished work, *The Shadow Bride* (1988). In the study, Amon Saba Saakana makes the claim: "For too long non-western literature has suffered from the perspectives and vision of the Euro-American critic."[20] Yet this could not have been a serious claim in 1996. Book-length critical studies of the West Indian novel and of individual authors by regional critics exist;[21] there are several edited works in which appear critically illuminating essays, lectures and interviews about and with writers including Lamming, V.S. Naipaul, Harris, Braithwaite and Walcott.[22] In addition, there are critical articles in regional-based literary journals,[23]

but Saakana's work refuses to acknowledge the presence of a Caribbean critical tradition, and goes on to enunciate what he calls an "African-centred
approach . . . a way of seeing the world which is historically informed by
specific social and cultural conditions".[24] *Colonialism and the Destruction of
the Mind* selects certain themes running through Heath novels for analysis,
namely: mythology and orality, and female sexuality and intra-class violence,
with Christianity as the chief villain in the psychological fragmentation of
the typical Heathian character. Reading Heath's novels through "African-
centred" lenses offers only a partial sense of the multicultural and complex
psychosocial world the writer seeks to depict.

Even as Saakana purports to examine "psychosocial issues of race, class,
religion and sexuality" in Heath's fictional world, its analysis of the psychological dimension of character, the tour de force of Heath's writing, does not
go nearly far enough. Saakana does nothing to show this complexity in his
unoriginal conclusion:

> More than most novelists in the region, Heath has managed to portray the
> nature of the psychological make-up of his characters, and to explore the sub-
> conscious in a way which most writers have been unable to do. . . . This ability
> has distinguished him from most Caribbean novelists . . . his observation of
> personality and character development [lies] in a formidable knowledge of the
> multi-layered social differentiation and peculiarities among classes/races in
> Guyana.[25]

Saakana ends with a non sequitur: *"thus it is the social environment which is
principally responsible for the behaviour of all its people".*[26] Similar non sequi-
turs evidenced throughout the body of the work convince the reader that
Colonialism and the Destruction of the Mind is a self-referring work that falls
short of its promise of psychological analysis and can hardly be considered a
definitive or even satisfying critical study of Heath's texts.[27]

It is the aim of this study to broaden the scope of existing analysis beyond
a simplistic thesis about environment as the prime cause of human behaviour and to include the writer's engagement with issues such as the existential dilemma of the coloured middle class in twentieth-century Guyana;
the notion of family; the female condition; the quest for community; man's
inherently frail psychological condition; the recognition of a folk culture; and

a postmodern vision of society. Criticism has to look beyond environment, the antagonisms of ethnicity, class, religion, female victimization and the oppressive historical past to unlock Heath's fictional world. We find a humanistic approach relevant, a humanism that Edward Said defines as "a process of unending disclosure, discovery, self-criticism . . . a form of democratic freedom", with self-knowledge its chief characteristic.[28]

While Heath's works are not elegies on the theme of exile, even though he himself remained an exile in Britain,[29] they stand as testaments to the alienation of individuals from themselves and their ancestral cultures, and as indictments against society, including an entrenched middle-class hegemony and its imposed (Victorian) morality fostered by colonialism. It is possible to argue that even though Heath has set in motion a range of characters who have no doubt internalized the outer turbulence of their social environment, in all his novels there is the sense of a psyche not predictably determined by social and material circumstances. The choice of a mode of narration that catches the evanescence of thoughts and intervenes in the raw consciousness of characters allows the writer to reinterpret convincingly the complexity of human nature and the corruption of the quests of characters for freedom and survival in the post-colonial minefield. This aspect of the introspective character with his frail architecture of consciousness has been entirely overlooked in existing criticisms on Heath.

A Man Come Home (1974) was praised as a linguistic achievement: Heath's "grasp of the language behaviour of the range yard" allowed him to recreate the working class and the satiric vitality of the living language of the yard;[30] *The Murderer* (1978), winner of the Guardian Fiction Prize, has been hailed as "a concise, unsentimental masterpiece".[31] Heath's eighth published novel, *The Shadow Bride* (1988),[32] was adjudged "a massive work of fiction with its compelling narrative and engaging plot".[33]

The Ministry of Hope (1997) is arguably Heath's most overtly political novel, but critical comment on this work is almost non-existent. For all the positive ad hoc reviews, no substantial critical work has appeared that attempts to gather the novels and analyse their central thrust, their intrinsic unity, their intriguing form and their percipient vision or even to reconcile opposing critical views. Susan Fromberg Schaeffer remarks on the neglect: "Heath has now produced a remarkable body of work, yet is unknown in America.

He is virtually unknown in Britain where he has lived and written for the last twenty [*sic*] years."[34]

In addition, the critical issues raised in the body of existing criticism[35] remain largely ignored; perhaps most pressing of all is the question of Heath's place within the critical canon.

Heath's deceptive style has perhaps contributed to some unfavourable criticisms of his novels; for instance, one view has been proffered that they are devoid of social context: "They lack V.S. Naipaul's sense of a historically determined futility in the lives of the characters. . . . Heath never explains this the way Naipaul does, by reflecting on the society and the past and by dwelling at length on such historical causes as the failed myth of Eldorado."[36]

It has been argued that, for instance, the testimonies found in the poems of Edward Brathwaite on the "cyclic movements of history" are absent in Heath's texts: "There are no such affirmations to be found in Heath; rather, there is a sense in which his characters are victimized by the author himself, by his deliberate choice of a particular mode of writing . . . a fiction of victims and scapegoats, rather than heroes."[37]

While Jean D'Costa, meditating on characters mired in chronic poverty, determines that "Heath involves the reader in the hard reality of his world", other critics are hard pressed to find such realism: "Characters are victimized principally by large anonymous forces beyond their control . . . forces which are not named or described in any detail by the author but left deliberately vague or understated . . . there is no attempt to describe a historical context for the predicament of the characters in the way, for instance, that the specific date of Jean Rhys's *Wide Sargasso Sea* is crucial to an understanding of that novel."[38]

Whereas Heath was hailed as "a Man to Watch",[39] other critics were disenchanted with his craft, faulting him for "misusing plenty of rich raw material with the promise of life in them and producing only failure and tragedy". Heath has often been described as a psychological writer, yet criticism records, "but his is a psychology of despair and decline, as his characters confront the gap between their dreams and prevailing realities".[40]

At the same time there is praise for his convincing portrayal of a recognizable world, "strong interest in the details of daily Guyanese life and in the changing economic and social condition. Characters exist on the brink of economic disaster, amid intense cultural alienation, social conflicts and communal prejudice."[41] A few critics pinpoint but merely gloss over the social context: "We are aware, as it would seem that Heath intends us to be, that Rohan Armstrong's Guyana will soon be the Guyana of Forbes Burnham and Cheddi Jagan and, most recently, the notorious wasteland of [the] Reverend Jim Jones and his People's Temple."[42]

The Murderer has come in for ambivalent remarks: some critical opinions dismiss its introspective protagonist as "unlikeable" and fault the work for "technical misjudgment and clumsy writing",[43] while others claim: "its proportions are wrong, style is ungainly, and the reader feels little sympathy for the character . . . but the work is impressive",[44] and, again, "characters go almost undeveloped [and] in essence this can be seen as Heath's early wrestling with the fictional form".[45] A few reviews are simple expressions of doubt and wonder.

Heath's characters have been deemed contrived and unconvincing on the one hand, and psychologically fascinating on the other: "The psychological realism of the characters is as strong as the authenticity of their language behaviour",[46] and, again: "Ben's pained introspection, interrogating himself relentlessly, contrasts with Carl's ability to come to decisions with sudden arbitrariness that seems to preclude inner debate."[47] Heath's introspective characters do not seem to sit comfortably within the framework of Northrop Frye's structuralist theory, proposed in *Anatomy of Criticism* (1957), that fits all human behaviour into archetypal tropes.[48] Critics who rely on Frye's theory label character as either "victim" or "scapegoat", "unheroic on account of their ironic presentation by the writer and his choice of the ironic mode, a style which diminishes characters and qualifies their sense of tragedy. . . . Characters fail in an all-embracing external cause, rooted in the values bequeathed to the society by a bitter past – a past which other writers quickly bring to the fore, but which Heath hardly mentions."[49] Critical comments continue in the vein that where there appear to be "no sufficient or compelling reasons" for the tragic fall of main characters in novel after novel, the reader may be led to the view that the author is "manipulating" the character:

> All the characters, even the incidental ones, are somehow trapped – from the white director . . . to the servant girl, Esther. . . . This is because their worth has already been absolutely gauged and their roles definitively assigned by some

vague, impersonal force within the society for which they are all nevertheless responsible; their worth and their roles have to do with the location in
which they were born, the way they speak, the way they dress, the quality of
their possessions and the jobs they do. The inner self has nothing to do with
this . . . tragedy appears to be more mechanically contrived and less haunt-
ingly inevitable. . . . There is the same sense of relentless irony and [authorial]
victimization of the "hero".[50]

This work argues that the disparate comments made throughout the body
of criticism on the bizarre behaviour of Heath's characters only serve to allude
to the psychological realism of the novels which, at the moment, remains
undeveloped critically in scattered reviews and essays. In this critical introduction to Heath's novels an attempt is made to show that there is much more
interplay between character and circumstance than current interpretations
suggest.

The body of the criticism makes isolated references to instances of victimization and exploitation of women. We feel that Heath does more than
depict the victimization of women; he gives voice to the victimized woman
and, in spite of her marginalized condition, allows her to take centre place
in at least two of his novels, *Genetha* and *The Shadow Bride*. Both novels are
written from the female perspective and offer glimpses of the centrality of
female experience and the vulnerability of women in the regional novel that
seemingly only Mittelholzer before him had ventured to achieve in *The Life
and Death of Sylvia* (1953). Harold Ladoo's *No Pain Like This Body* (1972) is
possibly the first West Indian effort to depict psychological fragmentation in
an immigrant woman, but this tale is recounted through the innocent vision
of a child narrator. It is to Heath's credit that he allows us to view the world
of the exiled Hindu, his rituals, his fears, his quest for identity and selfhood,
and the creolization process at work among East Indians through the female
sensibility in *The Shadow Bride*.

In *One Generation*, Heath attempts to interrogate the potentially volatile
and internecine nature of the post-colonial society, offering an artistic solution to the dilemma of racial schisms in the plural society. Several regional
novelists have attempted to treat the African-Indian encounter in the Caribbean, but Heath's effort stands out: "It is the considerable, though still not
complete self-awareness of his own cultural perspective, not to say his vastly

superior skills as a writer which makes Heath's *One Generation* (1981) a much more rewarding portrayal of Afro-Indian relations. . . . [W]hereas in general Indo-Caribbean writers have been conscious of being part of a wider society, Afro-Creole writing has tended to ignore the Indian presence."[51]

The foregoing analysis of a selection of the more significant responses is intended to convey a sense of the general weakness of the existing body of criticism, its piecemeal and sporadic nature. If some of the verdicts seem unduly harsh, they only serve to underline the difficulty of placing Heath. While the foregoing comments may largely help to account for why no comprehensive examination of Heath's oeuvre has hitherto been undertaken, there is enough ambivalence in them to suggest the need for a close textual reading that would allow one to judge whether Heath can claim a place within the Guyanese literary tradition and that of the anglophone West Indies. Even though a close reading approach has been indicated, the work is informed by theoretical approaches to criticism without any self-conscious engagement of them.[52]

In this regard, Said's words are relevant:

> Thus a close reading of a literary text – a novel, poem, essay, or drama, say – in effect, will gradually locate the text in its time as part of a whole network of relationships whose outlines and influence play an informing role *in* the text. . . . Yet, [literary works] can never be reduced only to social, political, historical and economic forces but rather, are, antithetically, in an unresolved dialectical relationship with them, in a position that obviously depends on history but is not reducible to it.[53]

The works of some Caribbean intellectuals on social and economic development will no doubt also help to corroborate certain truths about the centrality of the modern human condition in Heath's novels. Heath is very much a social novelist, but whereas, overtly, he appears to ignore history, he is, in fact, attempting to chronicle a sense of a history that is steeped in a tragic legacy of colonialism while charting an alternative vision of renewal and regeneration of the individual and society. Heath's primary means of analysing a society where the tides of race, class, social values and cultures meet, and historically have always met, in a volatile confluence, has been not through overt dissection of political arrangements and events, but through probing the frail and fragile architecture of the consciousness of a range of vulnerable, introspective characters whose submerged experiences reveal the psychological scars of their encounters with history, their inner exile and damaged psyches.

Heath's idiosyncratic narratives all end with collapse of form, with bleakness and void. It is possible to read these brooding narratives of repression, fragmentation and frailty, separately or collectively, as a study of modern man at variance with self and society, floundering in failure and self-division. One may be tempted to conclude that Heath is embracing a tragic vision. Indeed, George Lamming had earlier warned: "To speak of the Negro writer is therefore to speak of a problem of Man . . . of man's direct inner experience of something missing . . . a condition which is essentially . . . tragic."[54] And yet, with their insistence on memorializing the traditional values of community and family, Heath's novels contain a redeeming vision of man, of possibilities for self-recovery and new beginnings from a fractured past.

Heath's novels are unequivocally steeped in the social and cultural reality of twentieth-century Guyana, evoking life in its urban and coastal communities, each narrative a work of art and an absolutely honest and subjective testament of man and society, of the chronic dispossession and psychic displacement of the colonial. Five novels study the colonial period, starting from the early 1920s, and run up to independence; two novels study the dramatic effects of independence; and two novels examine a sovereign state under native leadership. For this introductory study, we have chosen to conduct a textual analysis of the novels on a book-by-book basis or, where appropriate, in clusters of books, in preference to a thematic approach, so that the trajectory of the writing can be more effectively traced. The aim is that a close reading approach will reveal the unifying threads of Heath's concerns running through the novels and validate our argument that the writer has produced a cohesive body of fiction that deepens our understanding of man and society and belongs to the West Indian literary canon.

Arrangement of Chapters

Chapter 1 offers background information about the writer and his contemporaries and, in addition, an aerial survey of the Guyana novel. Chapter 2 examines a recurring theme in the trilogy, that is, the institution of the family, and attempts to situate the work in its social context. Chapter 3 analyses the first volume of the trilogy, *From the Heat of the Day*, and examines how the Armstrong family (fail to) manage in the colonial futility. Chapter 4 analyses the fate of the Armstrong son, Rohan, in the internecine society recounted in the second volume, *One Generation*. Chapter 5 is devoted to examining the experience of the Armstrongs' daughter in the eponymous third volume of the trilogy, *Genetha*. Chapter 6 leads naturally into an examination of two novels, *A Man Come Home* and *The Murderer*, as they each reinterpret the effects of decolonization and the implications of independence and freedom. Chapter 7 illuminates the master/slave relationship revisited in *Orealla*. Chapter 8 examines a sovereign state under native leadership in two novels through the character of a confidence trickster in *Kwaku* and *The Ministry of Hope*. Chapter 9 considers *The Shadow Bride*, a poignant account of female displacement and the struggle for place and cultural identity in the British Guianese society in the first half of the twentieth century.

1

A PORTRAIT OF THE ARTIST

Heath was born in 1926 in Georgetown, the capital of British Guiana, where his father was head teacher and his mother a teacher at St Andrew's Primary School. He was only one year old when his father died, leaving four children: two sisters and an older brother, Sonny, whom Heath describes as his "absent" brother.[1] Sonny had gone to live with his grandparents, a separation from his siblings that seems to have seriously affected the youth, who eventually suffered a nervous breakdown. This tragedy devastated the family, and Heath agonizes in his memoirs: "Sonny was the sacrificial lamb to the family's well-being."[2]

The premature loss of the head of the home made the young family cling tightly to the notion of family. Heath later recalls: "This feeling of belonging, the notion of the larger family, was very strong and, as I know now, a source of confidence in case of destitution" (*Shadows*, 13). The colony was at the time mired in the poverty of post-war stagnation, compounded by the onset of the Great Depression of 1929, with its pervasive mood of hopelessness and uncertainty. As a growing lad, Heath quickly detected that at the heart of colonial society lay a morbid preoccupation with social class that blighted human relationships and, from his mother, who regaled him with anecdotes of the social disparity created by differences in skin colour, he discovered the gulf between the classes, "as wide and often as profound as that between cultures" (32). He confesses: "The excessive snobbishness of my own mother was a flaw of which I would rather have remained in ignorance" (113). Issues of social differentiation and the implications for individual freedom and family life in the colony formed the themes of Heath's works, with one of the more devastating consequences of the class divide being recorded in *Orealla*.

When Heath was four years old, the family resettled in Jonestown, a stagnant little village, later renamed Agricola, about three miles from the capital, on the eastern bank of the Demerara River. Heath recalls his fascination with the network of waterways: canals, sluices, and the kokers associated with the mythical Water Maid figure of Guyanese folklore (*Shadows*, 24). The clogged-up trenches and bushy overgrowth found in the typical tropical village encouraged disease-carrying mosquitoes, and, after frequent bouts of malarial attacks, the family moved from Agricola when Heath was eight and went to share, with a bigoted aunt, the upper flat of a two-storey building at the corner of Camp and Regent Streets, in the bustling heart of Georgetown. Heath grew up in the grinding poverty of early twentieth-century British Guiana with its entrenched social prejudices and its cultural alienation of the colonial striving to be English. The old Georgetown of the 1930s that he knew so intimately, and recreated from every perspective in his novels, was a society in which poverty was endemic: "Even at the age of eight I was astonished [to witness] the most abject poverty. . . . The unemployed made up more than thirty per cent of the working population, social services were conspicuously slight, and threw up characteristic relationships of dependency" (49–56). This dilemma is poignantly recreated in the trilogy, Heath's first creative effort. The following year the family again moved, this time to Charlestown, a less affluent ward of the city, where Heath lived for fifteen years, until he migrated to England in 1950.

From early adolescence, Heath's consciousness was awakened to the nature of the heterogeneous society and the inherent cultural differences between the two major strands of the population, Indians and Africans: "There were two distinct working-class groups, East Indian and Creole, each with its own religious and secular practices. At that time I knew little about East Indians and had to wait until I worked on the West Bank of Demerara before I discovered the powerful undertow behind their passive conduct, their outward display of prayer flags and temple architecture" (31). At secondary school Heath struck up friendship with an (East) Indian pupil referred to in his memoirs only as "G". This connection opened a window onto the world of Indians. G's mother ran a cookshop amid the squalor of Lombard Street, and Heath observes: "The customers, many of them East Indian beggars, belonged to the wretched poor of Georgetown. . . . I used to sit in a corner taking in the unusual scene with an avidity that suggested an interest much deeper than mere curiosity, perhaps compounded of a fascination with the Indian community's life style" (115). G's paternal grandmother lived among the derelict tenements and range-yards of Albouystown and this association deepened Heath's awareness of the social disparities around him, so that he then began to take notice of wretchedness he would not normally have known from his middle-class upbringing. He came to see that, "generally, there existed a special urban deprivation, which hung around street corners, slept on pavements and spoke in a shrill distracted voice" (157). Heath's novels are powered by what Michael Gilkes terms an "urban angst".[3]

Heath graduated from high school, entered the civil service in 1942, and was assigned to the district commissioner's office at Pouderoyen, a virtual Indian enclave on the west bank of the Demerara River. There he came into direct contact with the rural Indians and "became initiated into East Indian society" (*Shadows*, 57). He doled out pensions to "haggard faces and open, wasted mouths which belonged to nearly all East Indians"; they inhabited a surreal space, "a terrifying other-worldly picture of destitution and suffering" (178). Once a week he witnessed the Crosby Courts[4] and heard the grievances of indentured Indians played out as living drama before his very eyes. Heath confessed that for him this was "a most remarkable thing" (178). He recalls that the Crosby hearings revealed the disadvantage of women in both the home and public institutions (179). Mohammed Umar, the Crosby agent at Pouderoyen, lived in Laluni Street in Queenstown, a stone's throw from Heath's grandparents. Heath was a regular visitor to Umar's home, where Umar and his two daughters were steeped in Indian arts, music and culture. This family left a profound effect upon Heath (181) and later became the raw material for some of his fictional characters in at least one novel depicting Indians.

Agricola was a racially mixed village, with each social strand displaying distinctive cultural traits. Heath recalls the Muslim Indians as "the most enigmatic Guyanese community . . . who have never deflected from their single-minded pursuit of an identity free of all outside influence" (36). As we shall see, these impressions have been transmuted into the portrait of the Ali family in *One Generation*, the second volume of the trilogy, in which Heath ventures into the thorny issue of Indian-African relations in the colony, depicting a failed encounter between a coloured middle-class youth and two Muslim families. The fictional character of Mohammed, the Crosby agent in *One Generation*, and that of the Mulvi in *The Shadow Bride* are drawn from Umar, a man of quiet dignity, while the musicians in *The Shadow Bride* are cast from Umar's talented daughters. Heath and this family enjoyed such close fellowship that *The Shadow Bride* is dedicated to Umar.[5] Heath struck up friendship with yet another Indian at his workplace at Pouderoyen: "Mr Ramoo and I became close friends, with a friendship different from that between myself and Mr U. . . . I felt my life inextricably bound to theirs, but in what manner I did not know. . . . It may be that I saw in them a humanity so profound I stood astonished at my own good fortune. They became for me . . . hooks on which to hang my projections of manhood" (*Shadows*, 186).

However, it was not the Indian vein that Heath mined at the beginning of his writing career. Possessing an abiding curiosity in the underside of the coloured middle-class world – "the forbidding places full of secrets" and "those among his relatives who were unfit subjects for conversation about whom he would question his mother closely" (*Shadows*, 55) – Heath had "no idea that he was storing up potent tales for his fiction that grew on a well dug in those formative years" (146). In 1950, the year when the colony's first nationalist political party, the People's Progressive Party, was formed to oppose British planter-class ambitions and challenge the social inequalities, Heath rejected the narrowness of his middle-class existence, and the chronic poverty and stagnation in the land of his birth, and migrated to England,[6] where he studied modern languages, read law, and lived for almost five decades, a teacher by profession, a lawyer by training, a writer by conscience.[7]

As a Guyanese, Heath belongs to both the pre-Columbian civilization of the Guianas and to the historical experience of the West Indies. Through inter-territory migration encouraged at the time, Heath's father, born in St Kitts, found his way to British Guiana, while his maternal line comes from the Dutch possession of St Maarten and from Barbados. Heath's conscious-ness of himself as part of a continental culture, of a psyche shaped by the vast hinterland of Guyana, where the Amerindian presence is living reality and not memory, and of a traumatic history that gave birth to a place called the West Indies, adds complexity to his writings.

Heath and His Contemporaries

The Guyana literary tradition was properly consolidated around the middle of the twentieth century. Heath was in the age group of the first wave of West Indian writers, but his is a relatively "newer" voice, appearing among the second wave. By the time he had intervened in the literary conversation with his first published work in 1974, three outstanding Guyanese novelists (Edgar Mittelholzer, Wilson Harris, and Jan Carew) and two poets (A.J. Seymour and Martin Carter) had already laid the foundations of the Guyanese literary tradition with their imaginative reinterpretations of the post-colonial society. This is not to deny the importance of three seminal novels, *Lutchmee and Dilloo* (1877) by Edward Jenkins, an Englishman born in India;[8] *Those That Be in Bondage* (1917) by A.R.F. Webber, a Trinidadian;[9] and *Green Mansions* (1904), by an expatriate writer, W.H. Hudson;[10] or the lesser-known pioneering short fictions of Sheik Sadeek and a full-length novel, *Guiana Boy* (1960), by Peter Kempadoo.[11]

Guyana participates in the tradition of the contemporary novel of the West Indies and Gilkes confirms the place of the Guyana novel within the regional canon:

> Although the attempt in the novel to assert a positive Caribbean way of life – a Caribbean identity and culture – began with earlier writers like Claude McKay, C.L.R. James and Alfred Mendes in the 1930's, it was Edgar Mittelholzer [with *Corentyne Thunder* (1941)] who first raised the question of the role of heredity itself: the phenomenon of racial admixture and cultural disorientation which is beneath the Caribbean writer's deep psychological need to define racial and cultural identity in an attempt to heal a division of consciousness (a peculiarly Caribbean theme).[12]

Heath arrived in England in 1950 in the same wave of émigré writers as George Lamming (of Barbados), V.S. Naipaul and Samuel Selvon (of Trinidad). Selvon's *A Brighter Sun* was published in 1952, followed by *An Island Is a World* (1955), and then by his linguistic masterpiece, *The Lonely Londoners* (1956). Lamming's semi-autobiographical work *In the Castle of My Skin* appeared in 1953, and Naipaul's *The Mystic Masseur* in 1957. Mittelholzer arrived in England in 1948 and altogether produced twenty-three novels in twenty-four years – including *Corentyne Thunder* (1941), Guyana's seminal novel, published while he was still in Guyana – up to his tragic demise in 1965. Carew's *The Wild Coast* and *Black Midas* both appeared in 1958. Carter's *Poems of Resistance from Guyana* (1954) became the *cri de coeur* of the struggle for political independence. Harris had published at least twelve novels between 1960 and 1974, when Heath appeared on the literary scene.

Heath confides: "In the period leading up to my fortieth birthday, I began to experience a sort of panic because I had not yet written anything. I wanted to write a dramatic chronicle of twentieth-century Guyana. I was conscious of the fact that the Guyana novel had much ground to cover and I just wanted to write fine novels."[13] With this urge to sketch in the gaps in the evolving literary movement, Heath set out to recreate a largely neglected area in Guyanese fiction: the psycho-cultural dilemma of the coloured middle class stranded in a crumbling city at the end of empire.[14] Eight of Heath's nine novels are devoted to this subject, while his eighth published novel, *The Shadow Bride*, is as much a portrait of female alienation under colonialism as it is a concession to the multicultural society that shaped his artistic sensibility. Whereas some of his London-based contemporaries switched their fiction from West Indian settings to London and the English countryside, Heath uncompromisingly grounded his novels in the Guyana landscape. If he lived continuously in England for half a century, he adamantly denied it any place in his novels. Heath's autobiography remains incomplete, since he refused "to bring in England",[15] thus maintaining his stance as a colonial writer, the writer as exile who refused to adopt a hyphenated or hybrid identity, but retained the right to interrogate the society whose futility he had fled, and to revise its assumptions and premises. Heath explains in part: "My preoccupation with Time [in my work] is, I believe, the exile's way of dealing with the separation from his roots."[16]

An Aerial Survey of the Guyana Novel

It is hardly a surprise that the Guyana novel sprang up from among the coloured middle class, they being men of means (however modest), education, time to indulge their creative impulses, and the urge to explore the dilemma of their mixed blood, with its implications for identity. However, it is a coincidence that the progenitors of the Guyana novel, Edgar Mittelholzer (1909–1965), Jan Carew (1920–2013), and Wilson Harris (b. 1921) all have roots in New Amsterdam, a former Dutch township at the mouth of the Berbice River.[17]

The old Dutch town of New Amsterdam comprised, at the turn of the twentieth century when Mittelholzer, Guiana's seminal novelist, was born, residues of Dutch and old German families who maintained their puritan attitude however much their offspring's lineage may have been diluted by intermarriage or liaisons with Africans. This attitude caused the township to be severely stratified, so that the following testimony is credible: "New Amsterdam was known to be very segmented, very conservative, with very narrow vision, an enclave in which twelve prominent coloured families constituted a *Kingdom* and upheld a morality of supreme snobbery and contempt based on the prevailing divisions of race and class."[18] Guyanese who have sprung out of the New Amsterdam township and its environs, such as Canje, would endorse this view: "Truth be told, New Amsterdam's coloured middle class feared the degradation of being subsumed by the teeming black population and, conversely, the 'mulatto syndrome' was highly suspect among blacks."[19]

A sense of strength and superiority in the town is best exemplified by Mr von Ravensburg, a pure German but a naturalized British subject who had married a near-white creole woman, as he empathises with Mittelholzer's father: "Just *one* drop of the great blood. Just one drop in your veins, and it makes you different from everyone else. German blood!"[20]

Mittelholzer's own account of the drastic social differentiation in the township in his autobiography, *A Swarthy Boy* (1963), is testimony to enduring middle-class prejudices in a narrow, suffocating society that would provide fuel for his novels:

> Indeed, sad to relate, it was my own class – people of coloured admixture, of fair or olive complexions – who dispensed any colour snobbery that it was possible to dispense. It was my class which looked down upon the East Indian sugar plantation labourers ("coolies" we called them . . .). It was my class which considered the Portuguese social inferiors. . . . We, too, treated the Chinese

sweet-sellers and shopkeepers with condescension. . . . We even looked with a
certain distinct aloofness upon the young Englishmen who came out to serve
as sugar-plantation overseers. We deemed them "white riff-raff". And as for
the negroes, it goes without saying that they were serving people. (155)

Herr C. Mittelholzer, so far as anyone knows, was the first Mittelholzer to
come to this part of the world. He was Swiss-German and worked as manager of Plantation de Vreede, some fifty miles up the Berbice River, on whose
eastern bank New Amsterdam sits at its estuary. Jan Vincent, who became
Edgar Mittelholzer's great-grandfather, was manager over some few hundred
acres of sugar cane and the unfreed labour at another plantation at least eight
miles from New Amsterdam. It is thought that Jan Vincent

> dropped the pebble that started the ripple of black blood in the family. I have
> seen a photograph of him, and the picture was clear enough to show that he
> was pure European. . . . My grandfather, John Robert, the Lutheran pastor, was
> definitely a man of colour . . . of olive complexion and features that revealed his
> admixture; his hair, while not frizzy like a negro's, was far too curly and dark
> to be entirely European. (*Swarthy Boy*, 11)

Edgar Mittelholzer explains in his autobiography: "For my father, [my birth]
was an occasion of momentous disappointment. I turned out a swarthy baby!
Himself fair complexioned with hair of European texture, as were his brothers and sisters, and his wife also fair complexioned and European in appearance, he had, naturally, assumed that the chances were heavy in favour of a
fair complexioned baby. I was a confirmed Negrophobe" (17).

We have searched Mittelholzer's autobiography for evidence of a split consciousness arising out of rejection or out of hankering for European blood
and have found that in spite of a father whom he feared, an overly protective
mother, and the severity of his early upbringing and the terrors of the learning methods in the primary years, Edgar ostensibly came into his own and
did all the things boys did when he entered secondary school. There is no
evidence of psychological setbacks. If anything, Edgar inherited his father's
literary bent: "He wrote a long account of his trip to Europe [1901]. . . . His
literary style, as in everything he has written – short stories and letters to the
Press – was Gibbon-like and sonorous, and lavishly besprinkled with Latin
phrases" (*Swarthy Boy*, 15).

Nonetheless, critics have found that an inner conflict between his perception of himself as a descendant of the powerful Germanic line and the reality of being tainted with the blood of Africa – the two halves of himself that did not seem to make a whole – becomes a morbid obsession mirrored in his works, and that, consequently, psychic division forms the *raison d'être* of almost all his works:

> a serious conflict of loyalties, a consistent and conscious wish to identify with the European side of his ancestry while recognizing, at the same time, his individuality as a West Indian. . . . This attitude undoubtedly led to the psychological disunity which became, in turn, not only the chief cause of his unhappiness as a man, but also the main theme of his work as a novelist. . . . The division between urban and rural, self and society, gives way to a more disturbing, though related, *malaise*: the *mulatto angst*.[21]

Mittelholzer's first published work, *Corentyne Thunder* (1941), may support this theory if one holds the view that the author is projecting his own experience rather than recreating the society he knows. While offering a glimpse of the world of the East Indian peasantry in the post-indentureship period and the dilemma of cross-relationships in a class-structured society, *Corentyne Thunder* establishes the underlying theme of "divided consciousness". The dilemma is captured in an unlikely romantic relationship between Kattree, the young East Indian daughter of an indentured labourer, and Geoffry Weldon, a fickle mulatto youth from the city, and forms the emotional centre of the work. Prevailing criticism of it proffers that "the protagonist [is] a prototype of the psychologically flawed character, racially divided and inclined to brooding and pessimism, whose drift towards emotional frustration, self-loathing and death" powers many of Mittelholzer's novels.[22]

More than a decade later, Mittelholzer published *The Life and Death of Sylvia* (1953), a novel that draws heavily on the fractured sensibility of a mixed-race adolescent girl, trying to maintain a toe-hold in the entrapment of the stratified society of colonial Georgetown. Mittelholzer was attempting to portray the experiences of marooned Europeans: those who chose wives from the local population, whether openly or secretly, and those who could not immerse themselves in the creole society but who could not return home: hence their fractured psyche. His early novels are set in Guiana; of these,

Shadows Move among Them attempts to recreate a utopia, the perfect isolated society of European mores in the Guiana jungle.

The three books that comprise his *Children of Kaywana* trilogy are deemed to be of national importance: "In a very special sense, the preparation and composition of these three novels completed Edgar. He was able to allow his own love of the Mittelholzer ancestry to run coincidental with the history of Guyana, and in this manner, he was able successfully to project the image of his nation . . . this series puts him fully in the national tradition."[23] This work is, on one level, an important chronicle of the sojourn of several generations of a Dutch planter family, the van Groenwegels, and their courage in the face of successive slave uprisings in Guiana, including the historic 1763 rebellion in the upper reaches of the Berbice River; on another level, it is an ironic affirmation of the supremacy of European blood with which Mittelholzer's identity and creative energy are said to be integral. It is possible to argue that Mittelholzer is a coastal writer whose imaginative excursions into the "ancient county" (Berbice) served in some ways to celebrate his German ancestry and to memorialize the pioneering Dutch colonial plantations. All Mittelholzer's later works are set in Trinidad, Barbados and Britain.

Further, the physical landscape of the country has had a profound impact on the imagination and seems to have played a compelling role in shaping and defining the Guyanese novel. The long, narrow strip of flat mudland facing the Atlantic and a huge, haunting, myth-making interior rainforest together provide a perfect geographical metaphor for the two contrasting kinds of writing the country has produced: "urban" and "interior".

> These two schools of writing emerging out of two contrasting emotional and literary impulses, are also seen in Guyanese painting and other creative arts. . . . This contrast of "styles" operates within the Guyanese psyche and goes far beyond the superficial dualism of urban and rural, coastal and interior, and so on, achieving mythopoeic force in the work of Wilson Harris and Aubrey Williams . . . the interior becomes a world-creating jungle of tremendous aboriginal possibilities.[24]

Arguably, the fictional narratives of Wilson Harris reinterpret the Guyanese reality more dramatically than any of his contemporaries. Harris envisaged a radical break with the form of the conventional English novel as a necessity for the imperial/slave experiences to be reflected more truthfully and for new definitions of identity and self to evolve. Jeffrey Robinson states: "Few writers in English have mounted as concerted an attack on the traditional form of the novel as Wilson Harris has done."[25] Harris also shaped a new language as dense as the Guyana jungle he surveyed, as disjointed as the fractured Guyanese psyche. Where one gets a sense of a breakdown in language, this might really be a desire, as Gilkes puts it, "to dislocate the conventional habit of perception".[26]

Landscape forms a mystical part of the psyche of Harris's characters who inhabit the Canje and the Pomeroon Rivers, the Rupununi Savannahs and the waterways of the Essequibo River, characters who traverse the interior of Guyana, physically in some novels and imaginatively in others, seeking lost dimensions of history and culture and new meanings of self and community. Imagery becomes highly symbolic rather than realistic or literal, offering new possibilities of self-awareness. The motif of the journey into the hinterland, a metaphor for the journey into an unknown (and, perhaps, unknowable) self, gives structure to the Harrisian novel. One runs the risk of being simplistic in trying to discuss Harris, his style, his language or the authenticity of his vision in a few sentences; this survey merely seeks to mark his place in the literary canon.

Jan Carew's *The Wild Coast* (1958) and *Black Midas* (1958) both appeared before Harris began to propose a reconstructive art associated with the heartland, beginning with *The Palace of the Peacock* (1960). It has been remarked that Carew exploits the Guyana landscape less as a metaphor for the exploration of self than as the background of his canvas,[27] and this view is borne out in *Black Midas*, a work that exposes the spiritual void of the double-edged mineral-rich interior that awaits the working-class man in pursuit of gold as a means of self-fulfilment. *The Wild Coast* draws upon the rustic world of Tarlogie village on the Corentyne coast, and examines the plight of a young black male protagonist whose initiation into manhood takes place in the context of the shenanigans of the adult world. This is the same landscape as Kempadoo's *Guiana Boy* – Port Mourant estate with its open, idyllic savannahs beyond.

Heath intervenes in a literary conversation in which the Guyana narrative has been shared up by writers with certain attitudes to the country's history. Mittelholzer recreates life in coastal Guyana, while Harris gropes in the unknown hinterland and the pre-Columbian cultural systems for an innovative art form of freedom from a bitter colonial past. Carew provides the bridge between coastland and jungle interior. Seymour's poems straddle the divide and are in a sense utopian as they celebrate the great aboriginal spirits; memorialize the Dutch plantations on the Canje river; and question the drama of life among the struggling masses: the "Comrade" who falls in the Enmore struggle, the fruit-seller at "Bourda Market", the proletariat in "Tomorrow Belongs to the People". Mark McWatt's entry into imaginative literature came long after Heath's, but it is worth mentioning that McWatt's two volumes of poems, *Interiors* (1988) and *The Language of Eldorado* (1994), reaffirm the "urban and interior" dichotomy in artistic attitudes to the Guyana landscape.

Ultimately, Heath's prose narratives, all set in the festering city, are devoted to exploring the terrain of physical and the social landscape as well as, and perhaps most importantly, the hinterland of the human psyche, the dark and flawed architecture of the human consciousness.

One is left in little doubt that Heath was primed to be an urban writer. In his autobiography he states: "The wasted wrecks who frequented Georgetown rum shops contributed to my impression of the capital as being special, a repository of the eccentric and exciting . . . left a mark on me" (*Shadows*, 43). His fabricated characters, all totally convincing, are not all financially poor; rather, they range from the power-wielding bourgeois to the civil servant and further to the tenement-dweller existing among the dereliction of old tyres, debris and coconut shells that form stepping-stones through muddy slush to their hovels. His tricksters, bold villains and Anancy figures, directly linked to the perversity of the social order, all thrive in the congested slums of the city. Heath's urban prosaic voice complements Carter's poetic anguish on his "strangled city":

> Here, right at my feet
> My strangled city lies
> My father's city and my mother's heart.[28]

Occasionally, a character ventures into the Mazaruni goldfields or as far as Lethem on the Brazilian border; he makes a fleeting dash to Morawhanna or dreams of the idyllic freedom of Orealla along the Corentyne River;[29] but on the whole, Heath's characters do not have sustained engagement with the hinterland, which remains a subliminal force in each consciousness. Homi Bhabha remarks: "Heath's characters are not the demonic agents of Harris's magical narratives, but Guyanians [*sic*] with easily recognizable aspirations."[30] Characters lead ordinary, uninspiring lives, mostly converging in the cloying city of Georgetown, the centre or heart of failure and futility.

2

AN INTRODUCTION TO THE TRILOGY
The Notion of Family

Heath's first attempt to write prose fiction was in the 1960s. It came in the form of a massive novel whose task was to reinterpret the nature of existence of British Guiana's urban coloured middle class in the first half of the twentieth century. The notion of the family gives structure to Heath's narratives, and his first work focuses on two generations of the Armstrong family, on characters whose lives coincide with fluctuations and changes in the social history of the colony, and whose fragile relationships with each other mirror the malaise in the society and emphasize their tenuous place in its social evolution. This critical introduction to Heath's *oeuvre* examines the novels on a book-by-book basis; however, this chapter will examine the three novels that form the trilogy as one work, as it was originally conceived. It seeks to examine two main features running through the trilogy: the notion of the family and the social and cultural contexts in which Heath's characters survive or flounder.

The work traverses the years between the early 1920s and the mid-1960s, the dying years of colonialism in the British West Indies, and is distilled through the consciousness of the Armstrongs, who embody the vulnerability of the coloured middle class stranded in a no-man's-land. Their drama of survival and existence takes place in a colony with a background of slavery and plantation culture; the decimation and displacement of its original inhabitants;

the large-scale introduction of indentured labour; and the beginnings of the struggle for political independence and self-determination.

Initially, Heath met with rejection, for he could not find a London publisher willing to take a risk on a lengthy work from an unknown writer.[1] He was encouraged to write a shorter novel that was published as *A Man Come Home* in 1974.[2] This was followed, in 1978, by *The Murderer*;[3] both these novels are set in a newly independent country recognizable as Guyana. Success inspired Heath to return to the long work he had put aside. He divided it into three blocks before it was accepted and published as three separate novels: *From the Heat of the Day* (1979), *One Generation* (1981), and *Genetha* (1981).[4] The break-up of the original novel had the positive effect of allowing the experiences of two generations of the Armstrong family to be scrutinized separately. In the absence of manuscript evidence it can only be a matter of speculation that returning to the earlier novel after publication of *A Man Come Home* and *The Murderer* could have caused Heath to make significant revisions.

The main character's reflection on her past in the opening pages of the third volume, *Genetha*, is a device for linking the three novels, while the presence of epilogues to the first and third books, and the sustaining of a single narrative voice throughout the three volumes convince the reader that Heath intended the books to be read as a trilogy. The three novels are now widely referred to as "the trilogy", and were published in one volume in America in 1994 under the title *The Armstrong Trilogy*.[5]

The trilogy can be read as a springboard for the entire oeuvre, providing a point of departure for an exploration of man and society in nine novels that span twentieth-century Guyana in the pre- and post-independence periods. Heath's voice and vision are established in this seminal work and elaborated in succeeding novels through a range of themes, among them colonialism, of course; the polarization of the society along the lines of race, class and colour consciousness; "otherness", rejection and exclusion; the institution of marriage; the attitude of men in the patriarchy; the quest for individual freedom and independence; the quest for community; entrapment; power and powerlessness; the master-and-servant relationship, sexual exploitation and the victimization of women; alienation; poverty and homelessness; madness, love and death; and, not least, the pervasive trickster figure thriving in a decaying society. To trace the trajectory of Heath's vision and his point of entry into prevailing philosophical and ideological underpinnings that the texts confront or respond to, this study will begin with the trilogy.

The trilogy and all Heath's novels that follow are set within two narrative frames: the individual (his place within the home and family unit) and the society (with a history of displacement and dispossession). The next chapter of this book analyses the first volume of the trilogy, *From the Heat of the Day*, and focuses on a web of relationships of which Sonny Armstrong, head of the Armstrong family, is at the centre. Chapter 4 takes up an examination of the growth to manhood of the Armstrongs' son, Rohan, and the relationships he cultivates in his quest for freedom and identity depicted in the second volume, *One Generation*. Chapter 5 discusses the social and emotional progress of their daughter and how she manages her relationships recounted in *Genetha*, devoted to her.

As the fundamental unit of society and indicator of its wholeness and stability, the family absorbs society's changes, its fractures and its convulsions. Yet it remains one of the most complex social institutions in existence and, possibly, the least understood.

This chapter will first examine the notion of the family across the social spectrum of the trilogy: the Davises encapsulate an irredeemably prejudiced middle-class morality that undermines the unity of the family; Armstrong, who, with no sense of family, brutalizes his wife and cheats his sister out of the family home in Queenstown; Esther, an East Indian servant girl from a wretched sugar estate, is betrayed and victimized by a family whom she has served with loyalty and love; Doc, a retired schoolteacher, abandons his family in a rural village but continues to advocate the value of family; Fingers, Genetha's wily lover and unemployed billiards expert, exploits her to support his family and cheats her out of her home; Zara, a restaurant assistant, financially supports her rough and uncaring family in the slums of Georgetown; Mr Mohammed, a liberal-minded civil servant, heads a family of adolescent girls and a carefree wife; the Alis, wealthy Indian rice-millers, are garrisoned in a cultural enclave at Suddie; and Ramjohn, a rancorous Indian clerk, heads a destitute family on the Essequibo coast and exacts revenge for the tragic loss of his overburdened wife.

From the Heat of the Day recreates a sense of life in a financially bankrupt colony in the post-war period, of which A.R.F. Webber writes: "Depression caused by sugar slump was at its greatest depth in 1922 . . . a crisis unparalleled in the memory or experience of any colonist."[6] The brutalization of labour in the colony has been documented by historians,[7] but perhaps the most devastating consequences of colonialism and its plantation culture has been the alienation caused by the social divide, so that, in addition to economic and material inequalities, the quest for individual freedom is subverted by race, colour and class differentiation. At a time when the colony is floundering in labour unrest, with sugar on the verge of collapse, a major preoccupation among the privileged class is with issues of social status and social boundaries. The opening image of the work reveals the sharp social dichotomy:

> It was February 1922, the year Georgetown witnessed the rise of a brilliant young newspaper columnist writing under the name of Uncle Stapie.[8]
>
> "Georgetonians," he wrote in one Sunday article, "are of two kinds: those who live in Queenstown and their unfortunate neighbours who inhabit the remaining part of our garden city."
>
> From that Sunday the circulation of *The Argosy* – Uncle Stapie's paper – shot up while its rival *The Daily Chronicle* fell. (*From the Heat*, 9)

The Davises, a coloured middle-class family, ensconced in "a recently built cottage" (9) in the exclusive Queenstown ward of the city, are brought into dramatic conflict with Sonny Armstrong, a rural postal clerk with middle-class aspirations. Very early in the work, the patriarch, Davis, pontificates to his hopeful son-in-law, Armstrong, on notions of family: "Family. The root of everything, I always say" (12). The desire for family name as prestige and security is a principle that powers Mittelholzer's saga of the van Groenwegel family in the *Children of Kaywana* (1952), but whereas in the three-century Guyana epic, the van Groenwegels and Kaywana stock display outstanding strength of character and struggle fiercely to perpetuate the family name for the next generation, in Heath's trilogy both the Davis and Armstrong families are almost nondescript, with an unheroic presence, and no vision or legacy for the next generation. The Armstrongs in particular bear the collective grief of the poor coloureds in the colony and form the emotional centre of the work.

The desire of the coloured middle class to be co-opted into the morality of the colonizer speaks to the polarities of colonial society. Davis, a bourgeois mimic of diluted Victorian manners, is scandalized by his youngest daughter's betrayal of her middle-class upbringing in her choice of a socially inferior husband. Ironically, Gladys's two older sisters join their father in rejecting Armstrong while they themselves remain trapped within incapacitating class rules – both sisters remain unmarried, for their suitors never gain the approval of their class-conscious father, mortified at losing his family's place on the social ladder. So as to escape a similar fate of spinsterhood in the imprisoning middle class, Gladys takes a chance with a man below her social class in the hope of co-opting him into the middle class, but instead, the idealism of these two characters clashes with the imperatives of rigid social classification. They incur the unmitigated wrath of her family and are rejected from the middle class. Davis, incorrigibly flawed by inbred prejudices, when he speaks of "family" refers to "respectable" middle-class names, but Armstrong, an "unfortunate" and unknown rural dweller, does not fit the middle-class pretensions of the Davises.

Unlike Davis, a salaried man in a city commercial concern, Armstrong's father was a successful wheelwright who bequeathed his children several properties, including one in Queenstown, but the family appears unknown in social circles. Nonetheless, Davis is contemptuous of a virtual nonentity stumbling into bourgeois space and threatening his social image. Heath, in his autobiography, alludes to the fears and insecurities of the likes of Davis: "Experience of coloured middle-class life taught me that coming down in the world was a kind of death" (*Shadows*, 50), and Armstrong, for all his prospects of promotion in the postal service, is deemed an unlikely suitor. Ironically, Davis strikes at the very heart of the ideal of family he purports to defend with the cruel injunction to his daughter: "Obey or get out!" (*From the Heat*, 45).

Heath presents in Davis a character who finds himself challenged by imperceptible social change, for whereas customarily, the bonds within the patriarchal family are defined by obedience (his two older daughters comply without question), the society has evolved such that the old morality is being tested by the "conflicting desires and frustrations that define the inner life" of the youngest daughter.9 The temporal setting of this tale and its exploration of submerged areas of the human psyche coincide with the development in psychoanalysis pioneered by Sigmund Freud. As a result, Gladys is led by emotions and desires to break free from hegemonic familial bonds and seek freedom and fulfilment. However, the work has deeper resonances of the mythical tale of disobedience and fall. The couple, after the briefest of courtships and a hasty marriage, is cast out from the family fold. Instead of Armstrong's being co-opted into the urban middle class, Gladys falls from privilege and is exiled to the misery of a rural working-class existence. Rejection rankles in the form of a subtle rebellion between Armstrong and his wife's family, inevitably impairing relations between the protagonist and his wife, as well as his two children, Genetha and Rohan; his servants, Esther and Marion; his unnamed sister and his friend, Doc.

The Davis family is cemented by the illogic of blind prejudice and by false notions of respectability and superiority. In their household, their son's name is never mentioned – he who took his freedom, made off to the bush with "a gun and a dog, married an aboriginal Indian", and remains an outcast (*Genetha*, 147). The arrival of Gladys's eldest sister, Deborah, at the Armstrong home in rural Agricola, with the intention of being a support to Gladys, who is expecting her second child, only serves to widen the chasm, for she not only keeps her social distance from the "inferior" Armstrong, but does nothing to conceal her hostility, despite his respectful attentions to her with lavish gifts. The attempt of this uncompromising spinster to impose the order of "a civilized household" upon her sister's village life, an interference Armstrong duly resists, precipitates crisis; and in the event, Deborah brusquely abandons the family. Furthermore, Gladys's plea to her inflexible sister – "the contempt in your eyes . . . and your silence whenever he speaks or I speak of him" (17) – only serves to heighten tensions within the family, for within the recesses of Deborah's unvoiced thoughts (conveyed in italics), the reader gleans the inbred disdain and intolerance towards the "outsider", Armstrong. At this point in the text the narrator is able psychologically to penetrate Deborah's consciousness. Consequently, there is a blurring at this point between the narrator's voice and Deborah's. Some of the thoughts are clearly Deborah's. This makes the reader feel close to the character and provides an intimate voice (in the style of Jane Austen): "As she stood and re-enacted in her mind the quarrel of the evening before, *the feeling gradually came over her that yesterday was probably the beginning of a permanent estrangement. . . . What had been responsible for his fit of temper? . . . What's done is done! He lacked breeding, and there was nothing she could do about that*" (*From the Heat*, 18–19; my italics).

Davis exhibits no twinge of emotion as he expels Gladys and Armstrong from the family fold, precipitating his daughter's tragic isolation and early demise; neither does it square with his earlier provoking injunction to Armstrong: "Family. The root of everything. . . . We have to treat the women right" (12). His open endorsement of Deborah's scorn is a symptom of the pervasive prejudice in the family and in the wider society: "Great pity she didn't marry someone with backbone – and background. Without background you're nowhere" (20). Heath's skill in developing his narrative by milking the raw consciousness of characters is perhaps the greatest virtue of his writing, for years later, the Armstrongs' faithful servant, Esther, would reflect upon the irreparable fracture in the family relationship – "the visit to Agricola . . . Deborah's contempt for her brother-in-law's words and her conviction that even in his own house he should know his place" (*Genetha*, 173).

Rejection by the family is final, so that when Gladys and Armstrong ultimately acquire a house and return to Queenstown years later, they feel nothing but a profound sense of estrangement: "although much had not changed since she was married and went away, she felt like a stranger rather than someone who was coming back to the district in which she was born and spent her youth" (58). A disillusioned Gladys questions the logic of middle-class morality as it pertains to family life: "According to her mother, women obeyed and loved; the man dispensed security and affection", but her chauvinist father curtly placed the burden of the family squarely upon the shoulders of the woman: "happiness in the home depended on the women" (99). The colonial world is a man's world and this novel restates the patriarchal authority over the family. It has to be said that Mrs Davis displays none of the family's contempt of Armstrong and, with a show of feminine logic, rightly states: "the better Armstrong gets on, the better it would be for Gladys" (30). In the event, Davis's wife is a passive cardboard creature, overshadowed by her tyrannical husband and, virtually invisible, exerts no influence on the tide of family affairs.

The most trenchant evidence of Davis's indifference to family and his remorselessness, and perhaps the most memorable scene in the novel, is drawn from Armstrong's consciousness and comes in the epilogue to the first volume of the trilogy. Gladys's untimely death after only fourteen years of marriage causes Armstrong to reflect with bitterness and rage upon his estrangement from the Davis family, where he longs to belong:

Armstrong recalled his father-in-law's manner when he asked Genetha in his presence why she thought he had not visited them all these years. He did not smile, did not seem put out in the least, did not even offer any reason for the neglect of his daughter or grandchildren. Could he not at least have said, "I thought that you disliked us, so we didn't come?" Nothing, not the slightest twitching in his features. And the renewed proof of his superciliousness, that certainty of status that was capable of overcoming even a crippled body or a devastating stammer, had driven Armstrong to distraction. (*From the Heat,* 155–56)

As the embodiment of "that savage breed of middle-class men" (*Shadows,* 32) that seeks refuge in the outward trappings of class, and terrified of losing face socially, Davis remains a metaphor for a skewed middle-class morality that Heath rejects.

If Armstrong's cruelty to his wife and neglect of his family can be read as his flawed response to the prejudice of his in-laws and to the domineering role of the male in a patriarchal society, his fractured relationship with his unnamed sister exposes the fragility of his psychological endowments. Dissatisfied with the two income-bearing cottages he has inherited from his father, he begrudges his sister the thriving wheelwright business bequeathed her: "Bitter at [what he perceives as] the inequitable distribution of the estate, Armstrong found little consolation in his promotion to Postmaster of a Georgetown post office" (*From the Heat,* 28). During the sugar crisis, instead of offering the financial advice his sister comes to seek, he seizes the chance to defraud her of her substantial Queenstown property, but not before humiliating her and reopening old emotional wounds festering within him:

He took the lamp . . . and laid it on the floor near to his sister, so that it lit up her face in a grotesque fashion. . . . Armstrong was almost frothing at the mouth with rage . . . He sat down, hardly able to contain his anger . . . all the old hatreds that lay dormant in him were flaring up. . . . One more provocative word out of her and he would chase her out of the house. . . . Every time Armstrong spoke she seemed to shrink in her chair, like a nail in a hole, under the blows of a hammer. (51–52)

Gladys, for her part, eager to return to Queenstown, to the community of family and friends, dares not question her husband's wicked deed while the relationship between brother and sister is irrevocably destroyed: "Armstrong's stubbornness and his uncompromising attitude had come between them, more than any selfishness on her part . . . if only he had realised what a lonely woman his sister was, and that, with tactful handling, she would have been willing, on their father's death, to accede to any reasonable arrangement . . . his manner would have softened towards her" (52).

Stung by her brother's perversity, Armstrong's sister takes a malicious pleasure in the deterioration of his family: "She watched the progressive decline in the family's living standards with satisfaction" (94), and, preferring the solace of strangers, refuses to be reconciled with her contentious brother even in his grief on Gladys's passing.

A glimpse of Esther's family, "her parents, her brothers and sisters and a house of endless births" (36) on the estate at Little Diamond, reveals people conditioned by the cruelty and violence of the plantation culture and the pain and poverty bred by colonialism. Heath understates Esther's racial identity, but the reader can safely deduce that she is from an (East) Indian family:

> Her two uncles stripped her brother and held him down in the yard while her father flogged him with the cow-whip until blood came and the neighbour's wife shouted in protest. The power of those men – in a village where there were women bringing up a family single-handed – the helplessness of her mother, revolted her. And from then on she dreamt of going away from the village, her hut and the cloying stench of asafoetida. (*From the Heat*, 36)

Bitter memories make return to the family fold impossible for the young servant-girl, Esther, the more senior of the two Armstrong servants, the other being Marion. A seemingly minor character but a major force in the saga of the Armstrongs with whom she seeks family having been alienated from her own family on the sugar estate, Esther is more than their servant. She is the emotional anchor to the distraught Armstrong children who cling closer to her as their parents' union unravels, certain that *she* embodies the traditional values of home and family:

> What indeed was family? Marion with her flamboyant dress, her men friends, her independence, had been, as a servant, as much a part of the family as Esther. But no one would have described her as *family*. Esther, [though] never close to her mother, had an essential place in that web of relationships that bind groups together, and if her parents would never have included her in the term "family" Genetha and Boyie had had no doubt as to her position. (*Genetha*, 66)

Armstrong's sexual depredation of Esther undermines the family, since Gladys duly evicts her into the streets, the "cauldron of Georgetown" (*Genetha*, 22). Rejected and alienated from all family, including those she left on the estate, Esther finds community of a sort in a brothel and bides her time to wreak revenge on Genetha.

Armstrong's friend, the schoolmaster Doc, offers another perspective of family. Recounting an anecdotal tale, he clarifies the notion that home for the colonial is, in reality, not the solid base it is thought to be, but as shifting and liminal a space as the relationships themselves:

> And you'd think he was happy! Nothing of the sort. He used to live with his mother and father sometimes and at other times with his grandmother. When he was at his grandmother he used to pine away and think of home and when he was at home he used to threaten to run away to his grandmother. But you should hear this man talking about jamoon trees by Clay and the bananas he and his brother used to steal from the farmer. (115)

Doc himself has deserted his family, fleeing an overbearing mother-in-law and an indifferent wife, and is now closeted with a concubine in Plaisance; yet, in an ironically post-modern vision, it is the imperfect, unfaithful Doc who is the author's mouthpiece on the ideals of home and family. Doc exhorts Rohan about the continuity of the family as the foundation of society: "Never let the lack of money stop you from having children" (*One Generation*, 91). Yet, as some of the myths surrounding the institutions of marriage, home and family are being dismantled in the trilogy, Armstrong recounts his favourite tale that exposes the fragility of the family unit as a virtual facade: "a Minister, a man of God. He practically lives in God's house, as you call it. But it's common knowledge that he hasn't spoken to his wife for years" (105).

We turn to the Mohammeds, a Muslim Guianese family admirably versed in Indian arts and culture and sufficiently integrated into the racially mixed society. Mohammed is a liberal who places no restraint on his wife's movement and free spirit and simply allows her to wander off freely "like a bird without a nest" (34) between his home and her parents, never trying to yoke her to the responsibilities of family. Left to themselves, he and his three adolescent daughters are simply concerned with *being*. One would imagine that this virtue would stand the family in good stead, but, ironically, they offer a no less troubled picture of family life in the second volume, *One Generation*.

Their sense of racial and cultural openness in the creole society leads to tragedy when the headstrong Rohan freely enters their home and becomes romantically involved with Mohammed's married daughter, Indrani. He pursues her to her marital home at Suddie on the Essequibo Coast, where a more pervasive picture of the cultural bindings and taboos that define family begins to unfold.

In the Alis' household at Suddie in *One Generation*, Mrs Ali is the typical Indian matriarch, wielding authority over her husband, a wealthy rice-miller, her two grown sons and their wives. This extended family is barricaded within the tacit boundaries of an Indian enclave, all conducting themselves in keeping with Ali's vision of racial and cultural purity: "Like to like! We Mohammedans don't go round hob-nobbing weself" (131). Rohan's pursuit of the Alis' daughter-in-law threatens the respectability of their family, and, like his father Sonny Armstrong, who was seen as a threat to social status and respectability and remained unaccommodated in the Davises' paradisiac space, Rohan is considered an intruder who can find no accommodation in a community defined by race and ethnicity. Increasingly, in Heath's novels, in addition to a sense of man unaccommodated socially and psychically, the reader gets a sense of the family in crisis, and Indrani's husband, Sidique pro-vides a good example of the dysfunction within the Indian family: "fancying that his wife no longer loved him, [Sidique] went out of his way to humiliate her while Indrani reacted by withdrawing even further into herself, and this was the beginning of a long period of bitterness that was to afflict the couple. They did their best to hide their unhappiness from others." Sidique is also at odds with his influential parents over their plotting and scheming to eject Rohan from the village; feeling trapped, he moves around "like a jaguar in a cage" (154), ironically, never freer than when he is in prison on suspicion of murdering his wife and her lover. In *One Generation*, Heath takes a stab at the monied Indian family with its materialist instinct, its racial insecurities and its resistance to assimilation into the creole process.

The trilogy explodes the fallacy of the Indian woman as an invisible and dutiful victim indentured to the family, since, for all Ali's material success and ostensible authority, it is his tyrannical wife who wields the real power, the very opposite of what we have noticed in the coloured middle-class fam-ily. The work debunks the myth of family across race and class as a haven of love and security and suggests that it is a facade that endures in the face of internal convulsions and self-deceptions, as evidenced in Mrs Ali's gloating following the brutal murders of her daughter-in-law and her lover: "Indrani gone, like we did want. Armstrong and Dada gone, like we did want. And the family together again" (200).

This chapter argues that the family is in reality a myth sustained by the illogic of blind faith and by social conventions and expectations, of which Ramjohn, his wife, Deen, and their five girl-children, in their abject poverty in *One Generation*, must be the ultimate exemplification. Like Armstrong, who eats and dresses well in the teeth of poverty to conform to tacit middle-class expectations, Ramjohn carefully maintains a "glistening exterior in his only suit", struggling to be counted in mainstream society, while his children are put to bed without any food. Deen, ravished by malaria, exhausted by the burdens of marriage and child-bearing, tired of life and reduced to helplessness by grinding poverty, is found one day at the bottom of Armstrong's well after she discovers that she is pregnant with yet another child. Even with the loss of wife and mother, the family will continue to cling together, as Deen had forewarned the wily Ramjohn: "If I go and dead you'd buy a bottle o' rum and go under the house and cry like a child. An' the nex' day you'd make Asha do all the work an' say how good she is" (141). The burdens and suffering within the family are met with blind indifference by society, as articulated by Rohan: "What the hell's it got to do with me?" (143). The family itself remains an enigma even as Ali philosophically reminds us of the enigma of life itself: "We're like grass in the fields. We lie down and stan' up and don't know why" (132).

Across the social spectrum, Genetha's workmate, Zara, lives with her contentious family in an overcrowded tenement building in the squalor of Albouystown, her life marked by duty and repression, an enduring symptom of the plantation culture. In a scene where she must ask her parents' permission to attend a New Year's Eve party after working long hours as a waitress in a dingy restaurant, the reader is left in little doubt as to the violence and dysfunction endemic in the family unit: "Zara's father got up, climbed over his fat wife and, taking no notice of Genetha, cuffed his daughter on the side of her head. Thereupon he climbed back over his fat wife and lay down again. In a few moments he was snoring more loudly than ever. Zara's mother turned her head away from her daughter, who stood motionless next to her friend. She was consumed with chagrin and humiliation" (*Genetha*, 118).

Genetha's lover, Fingers, must come under scrutiny. An unemployed billiards expert and trickster, he exploits Genetha shamelessly in order to provide for a household comprising his grandmother, his unemployed father and a handful of siblings, all with no income.

The Armstrong trilogy is about the Armstrong family, but there is no family, and all evidence points to the illogic of its unity. All around them other families are just a shell, similarly cracked and tainted with internal dissensions, human frailties and uncertainties and held together by slender threads. By the end of *One Generation*, the family is breaking up: all that is left of the Armstrong family is Genetha, alone in the world, while Sidique must raise a young child without a mother and Dada must fend for her fatherless newborn. Both Genetha and her brother, Rohan, are ironic figures whose separate and tragic quests for freedom and independence are in harmony with the human need for individuality, but conflict with the traditional values of community and loyalty to home and family. Heath's advocacy of community in his novels is a substitute for the traditional family life and the values left behind in the ancestral lands, a suggestion first implied in regional literature in McKay's *Banana Bottom* (1933).

As *Genetha* takes the reader to mid-century and into the pre-independence period, the picture of the fragmented family is crystallized. Genetha is by this time a solitary figure: her parents are dead, her brother abandons her, and her lover, scorning her middle-class status, cheats her of the family home, which he then occupies, an act that symbolizes the displacement of the Queenstown middle-class family and the depiction of a society in flux. In contradiction of all evidence in the text, Heath reaffirms the inviolacy of home and family, ironically, through Genetha's aunts, who have remained unmarried and are themselves unsupportive of her, her brother, her father or her mother, with their moralizing: "The family before everything else. The individual is nothing. The family's everything" (6). Genetha struggles to reconcile these conflicts within the cruel polarities of an indifferent society. The stability of society is grounded on marriage, home, and family, but Genetha's attitude to the institutions of marriage and family is tainted by bitter memories of the experience of her mother, who, "having acted like a doormat all her married life, had not achieved any worthwhile stability either for herself or for the rest of the family" (43). When, years after her mother's death, Genetha overhears a man speaking with admiration of his family, she wonders "why things could not be so in their family where present and past deeds conspired to corrupt their relations and their words, to rise up and threaten even in the midst of brief periods of contentment" (*One Generation*, 72–73). If the reader learns anything from Heath's penetration of society in the trilogy, it must be the internecine nature of the society and, fundamentally, that family relationships are brittle and fragile, in spite of outward appearances.

The end of the Second World War brings demographic changes that shift social boundaries in the colony as the seams of the city range-yards and slums are stretched to accommodate the flow of peasants from the rural areas seeking employment in the city. By mid-century, agitation for independence anticipates the erosion of sharp class lines and change to an egalitarian society with a native government which occurs in 1964. Heath does not mention the post-war exodus from the colony, beginning in 1948 with the SS *Windrush*, bound for Britain. Significantly, Davis, the "once all-powerful" patriarch, who in his cultural confusion did nothing to mould the family as one, is "dying a slow death" (*Genetha*, 139), symbolically signalling not only the decline of colonialism but also existential change for the coloured middle class with their fine graces, their exquisite gardens and their imitation Victorian morality.

The trilogy is a powerful evocation of despair and desolation at the level of the family unit. The rest of this chapter attempts to set the work in its historical and cultural contexts and offer a sense of the peculiarities behind the existential plight of characters studied in the chapters that follow. The population comprising the planter class and the freed men and women must also include indentured immigrants from Madeira, China, West Africa, the West Indies and finally India, from where workers were imported as a cheap source of labour after emancipation in 1834. The inevitability of a racially and culturally complex society evolving and the reality of racial admixtures produced by intermarriage and cross-relationships define the colony. The indentureship scheme came to an end in 1917 in British Guiana.

The failed union of Gladys and Armstrong takes place against a background of endemic poverty and chronic crisis:

> The foreboding in the air about sugar's future was echoed by the newspapers. *The Daily Argosy* warned against the dangers of panic and when, the same day, it was announced over the radio that sugar sales on many foreign markets were suspended those who held sugar shares tried to sell them at whatever price they could get. There was talk of suicides and a rumour that there would be a budget deficit. Several sugar estates were in danger of closing down and the government had drawn up plans of retrenchment and suspended recruitment to the Civil Service. (*From the Heat*, 49)

The 1918 worldwide influenza epidemic had devastated the East Indian indentured population shortly after the indentureship scheme came to a halt. Approximately twelve thousand immigrants perished that year, causing a crisis in labour that only exacerbated the grim prospects of the sugar industry, already said to be "a subject of considerable embarrassment" to the British government.[10] Social historians and economists have noted the state of impoverishment and dependency that characterized the existence of colonized people in the West Indies in this period,[11] while the chronic situation was earlier summarized thus: "Any socio-economic study of the West Indies is necessarily a study in poverty."[12] Cheddi Jagan writes of the period:

> At about this time, the political situation was at simmering point. The Great Depression of the 1930's and falling sugar prices on the world market had left their mark. . . . Protective duties had to be imposed and other forms of assistance given to save the sugar industry, the sheet anchor of the Caribbean, from ruin. Living standards had deteriorated. Social discontent had erupted in widespread strikes and disturbances in Trinidad in 1934; in St. Kitts in 1935; in British Guiana in 1935 and 1936; in Barbados, Trinidad and Jamaica in 1938 and 1939. In many cases sugarcane fields had been set on fire. In Trinidad fires had lit up the oil belt. . . . In Guiana, at Leonora, [colonial] police had opened fire on demonstrating workers in 1939, resulting in 4 killed and 4 wounded.[13]

Britain responded to the worsening situation in her West Indian colonies, including British Guiana, by appointing parliamentary commissions[14] to investigate social and economic conditions, but each time, rescue, in the form of a paltry increase in subvention, did nothing to alleviate poverty. The end of the war and closure of the American airbase compounded the pervasive poverty, unemployment and general discontent in the colony.

The indentureship system bolstered economic prospects for the planters at emancipation, but contributed to the emergence of a racially divided and internecine society. The coloured element of the society, stranded between colonizing planter and colonized slave, clung to the ambitions of the planter class and to the culture of the distant Western metropolis while shunning its black heritage. Gilkes sees this psychic alienation as a form of "cultural schizophrenia",[15] while Frantz Fanon describes it as self-doubt, "the most damaging legacy of colonization . . . that wrestling contradiction of a white mind in a black body".[16] Up to the granting of political independence to the colony in 1966, a social hierarchy operated within the coloured strand itself along the lines of wealth, fine distinctions and gradations of skin colour and other physiological features. Derek Walcott's famous poem poignantly articulates the dilemma of the mulatto: "I who am poisoned with the blood of both / Where shall I turn, divided to the vein . . . ?"[17] Heath himself comes from the coloured strand of the Guyanese society, "the world which shaped my perceptions and inspired my writings".[18]

Anthropologist Eric R. Wolfe comments on the cultural deprivation of plantation society: "Wherever the plantation has arisen, it always destroyed antecedent cultural norms, imposed its own dictates and set the pattern" of social relationships.[19] Raymond Smith examines the fragmented nature of the society and questions whether "there was such a thing as a Guianese society in the nineteenth and early twentieth century since each plantation constituted a separate unit and a segmentary society with plantations made up of a simple linear series of units" with little or no organic interrelation.[20] Jay Mandle argues that "by 1921, British Guiana had a population of 288,541 whose existences were controlled by a white elite minority numbering no more than 3,271 and that, under the circumstances, the majority was socialized to mimic the antics of the minority. By the early 1960s when the colony was on the verge of independence, the total population of the country stood at a little over half a million."[21] Webber closes his famous study of a colony in perpetual crisis and poverty with these words: "British Guiana cannot be said to have progressed in the 350 years since it was brought into contact with Europe . . . it is to be feared that B.G. will ever be haunted by the ghosts of strangled opportunities and the cry of what might have been."[22] If poverty forms the subtext of Heath's trilogy, then race, class and colour disposition add to its complexity.

It is worth noting that Heath's *From the Heat of the Day* (1974) covers the same ground as Edgar Mittelholzer's *The Life and Death of Sylvia* (1953)[23] and vividly supplements the picture of its workings and conceits. In *Sylvia* (which runs from 1920 to 1942), Grantley Russell, an expatriate engineer, ostracized by the small local white community for marrying the half-Arawak, half-Negro (a *buffiander*, in local parlance) Charlotte, enlightens his daughter, Sylvia, about the society in which she is growing up:

> I've never seen a more complicated social set-up. Such a tangled mass of cliques and clans and sub-cliques and sub-clans. . . . There are the whites in an exclusive little corner of their own. Then the high-coloured in various little compartments, according to good, better and best families, with money and quality of hair and shade of complexion playing no small part in the general scheme of grading. Take two steps aside and you're up against the East Indians in another cluster, with a hierarchy of their own, ranging from rice-miller to barrister-at-law and doctor and then down to bus-driver, chauffeur, provision shop-keeper or businessman. Stagger off a pace or two and you're sniffing at the Portuguese, split up into rum-shop-pawn-shop class and professional man class and big-businessman class. My God! If it isn't bewildering! (*Sylvia*, 38)

Rebuked by his wife for omitting blacks in his reckoning, Russell hastens to further elaborate on the nature of the polyglot colony:

> "By God, the black man! . . . Now, where does he come in?" He began to reckon with his fingers. "Shovel-man-scavenger. Schoolteacher. Policeman, fireman. Newspaper-reporter-lawyer's-clerk-bank-messenger-office-boy ambitious type who hopes to become an editor or a lawyer or get into the Government service. And, last of all, the imposing figures of the few who Have Got There. Doctors and barristers and solicitors whose one aim is to crash into coloured middle-class society!"
>
> He suddenly swept Sylvia up into his arms. . . . "Where do you come into the picture? What's your rating? Money, but no family background. Good hair, light olive complexion, European features. How will you end up, Goo-goo?" (38–39)

The education system serves to reinforce the rifts in the colony, as exemplified in Miss Jenkins's private school – a bastion of snobbery and middle-class conceit. Miss Jenkins is "coloured but passed for white" and moves among whites exclusively – the desire of the colonial to move up the colour scale remains an obsession. Because too few white children enrol, she is obliged to admit coloured children to set her off financially, but "only coloured children of good family and light complexion". Sylvia fails on the grounds of family, "but she had the approved shade of complexion . . . her father was English and a man of means, so Miss Jenkins had seen it fit to waive the family question" (27).

Russell's advice to his middle-class teenage daughter on the implications of marriage in a class-driven society is instructive; it is also the crucial issue that sparks off the crisis in Heath's trilogy, realistic advice that Davis neglected to offer his daughter:

> "If I were you I'd give the Portuguese, the Chinese, the East Indians and the blacks a wide berth where choosing a husband is concerned . . . stick to the coloured. . . . I'm telling you what sort of world you're growing up in. . . . The coloured middle-class have Background. In the far past, their ancestors were Dutch and English and Scottish planters. . . . It's true, slave-blood made a most annoying mess of their hair and complexion, but that is overlooked in the face of Blood – genteel Blood. Respectability. They have a trail of refinement and good breeding behind them. They are snobs. They lack unity, too. They're split up into cliques. . . . They live above their means in their efforts to keep up a certain standard of dignity. They'd rather starve than not be properly dressed . . . the coloured gentlemen always had to live, or at least make an attempt to live, as well as their planter ancestor. . . . [He] would be able to sympathise with your desire to possess a car and a radio and two big houses." (63–66)

Sylvia is a work of tragic realism. Whereas Sylvia's cruel and schizoid city of endemic prejudice is the very society in which the Armstrongs live and eventually perish, her tragedy may lie more in the fact of a predatory society and its attitude to women than in her mixed race. In Heath's trilogy, class and colour are undermining factors and Genetha is constantly reminded of some four decades earlier, when "money alone couldn't get you in" to the convent school that her maternal grandmother attended. However, the reader detects in Heath's work certain redeeming features.

3

FROM THE HEAT OF THE DAY
In Search of Community

A proper understanding of ourselves as individuals depends on our relationship to our community. If that relationship is lost, we are lost.
—Roy Heath, *Art and Experience*

As head of a family, Armstrong's problems are threefold: a social problem caused by marrying into a different tier of the social hierarchy; the economic instability and chronic poverty in the colony in the decades following the world war;[1] and an inherent personality flaw evidenced in the protagonist's unpredictable temperament and his lack of a moral compass. Through Armstrong's idealism and his confused response to his complex predicament (which begins with his brief courtship and hasty marriage to Gladys Davis, a spinster from the Queenstown middle class), Heath broadly explores the colonial experience and the neuroses that complicate the struggle for self-realization. Heath shows a native middle class in the dying years of colonialism imperceptibly replacing the colonialists and perpetuating a society of clichéd relationships amid upheaval and change. Short chapters afford alternating points of view from the main characters, while the male point of view predominates in the representation of a colonial world of patriarchal authority.

This chapter will examine the influence of the social and cultural environment upon the psyche by following the fate of Armstrong and his relationships with other characters in the suffocating city of Georgetown. In psychologically revealing moments, the reader shares Armstrong's rejection and exclusion by the Davis family; his fears of dismissal from the post office; his ensuing neglect of his wife and their two children, Genetha and Rohan; his exploitative relationships with his unnamed sister and his two servants, Esther and Marion; his association with a prostitute; his moral degeneration; and the loyalty of his friend Doc.

The absence in the trilogy of institutions around which community is built and from which the individual psyche might take strength seems to have been grasped by John Sutherland: "The three principal characters of the trilogy are racked by passions whose unchannelled forces can only destroy them. They have no sense of history, no religion, no tradition, no myth, no poetry to sustain them."[2] The trilogy illustrates the social void and the cultural impoverishment of the colonized that Sutherland notices, as well as the gulf between what Wilson Harris deems "the idealism of the world, its optimism and illusion" and "the actual state of the world, its process, its changes, its needs . . . the wide difference between human passion and destiny on the one hand, and order and morality on the other".[3] In the colonial sterility of the trilogy, characters struggle against contradictory impulses and impossible ideals and this discussion embraces Heath's observations of the internal conflicts of his characters, many of which are exacerbated by external realities. This opening book has all the features of the trilogy.

Even though Heath does not employ a first-person narrating character, there is a wealth of first-person testimony in this episodic work, achieved through dialogue and direct speech that give the work its immediacy. In addition, Heath's strategy of employing a third-person omniscient narrator using the indirect-speech technique that allows him the versatility to mediate the raw consciousness of characters, their evanescent flow of thoughts, feelings and subjective responses, achieves a depth of psychological realism that has become the strength of his novels. The narrator is thus invested with the latitude of a "voyeur" and achieves the illusion of being inside the minds of several characters instead of a single perspective, of having more knowledge about characters than they could possibly have of themselves and of eavesdropping on unguarded lives instead of possessing a single consciousness, a technique that places the text squarely in the modern realist tradition. Heath's manipulation of the linguistic register – the Guyanese Standard English (of his narrator) and the creole dialect (of his working-class characters) – is not for the purpose of lending a comical tone to his works, but to give a sense of realism. It has to be said that Heath's art is equal to the dual task he has set himself of describing the external world and its symbiotic relationship to the interior consciousness of his characters.

It is useful to begin the account of Armstrong's life with an utterance by a character, Doc, who is often a foil to Armstrong. It is ironic that this comes from Doc, who has deserted his family, but the statement is nonetheless valid for looking at Armstrong in his pursuit of freedom and identity: "Nobody understands himself or his own troubles. Everybody's making frantic efforts to get out of some deep pit. If it's not a husband or a wife or a mother-in-law behind them it's a boss or a neighbour or a father or son. There's always a tormentor kicking you back into the pit" (*From the Heat*, 117).

It is perhaps the dream of every colonial who has had to exist in a stagnant backwater village where "pigs root for food in the mud" to escape to a world of charm and difference such as that inhabited by the coloured middle class of the Queenstown ward of the city. This desire had taken root in Armstrong since he was a youth and had had brief glimpses into the well-furnished home of another villager in Agricola, "a woman from town with a superior manner . . . everything there was from a different world – the furniture, the window blinds, the lamps, the bed – everything" – an impression that had caused Armstrong to "tremble with excitement". Seeking social mobility through the trappings of a pseudo-metropolitan exoticism as a panacea to his colonial impoverishment, Armstrong attempts the impossible leap into the forbidden and forbidding middle class. He confides in another character: "Something did draw me to those houses in Queenstown"; but Armstrong lacks the instinct of a ruthless social climber. Possessing a weak ego, this colonial is enthralled by "even the men who went around the well-maintained alleyways [in Queenstown] with cisterns of oil which they sprayed on the gutter-wall to kill the larvae of malaria-carrying mosquitoes" (81). His intrusion into bourgeois space is an affront to the Davis family; it disrupts the social dynamics of the class-conscious Queenstown society and sparks off the crisis of the work.

While Gladys's outraged sisters taunt her with "disparaging remarks about his [country] manners and his dress . . . their laughter like barbed wire drawn across her skin" (9), the protagonist is equally vulnerable, his sense of security undermined by the formality he is unaccustomed to: "On the whole he never felt happy in Gladys's house. The piano-playing, the embroidery, the sketching, the genteel talk made him feel an intruder in a world to which he could never belong" (11). He shies away from their invitation for breakfast, "knowing full well that at their table he would be on test. The mention of forks and fish knives, napkins and serviettes would put him in a panic" (11). As his daughter would later recount, for the remainder of his life Armstrong's mind remains poisoned by their hypocrisy and "their constant talk of superior things like saffron and potted orchids" (*Genetha*, 4) that served to alienate him and emphasize his felt sense of inferiority.

Despite his dread of a social class whose internal logic he imperfectly understands, Armstrong is led by passion and idealism and hastens into marriage with Gladys. Neither of them knows the world of the "other" in the discrete society, but both venture into the unknown, where they inevitably lose their way and founder in the treacherous undercurrents of class prejudice. Gladys, tyrannized by unyielding family conventions and reduced to abject poverty by an intemperate husband, succumbs to an early death after only fourteen years of marriage, leaving two adolescent children. The work runs to the early 1940s, by which time the Second World War has added to the economic depression in the colony, social stagnation and unremitting poverty lead to labour unrest, and calls for political independence from Britain become insistent in British Guiana and in Britain's West Indian colonies.

The defining moment in the protagonist's experiences comes early in the work, when he arrives one evening at the Queenstown cottage to receive formal approval for Gladys's hand in marriage and is treated to a sample of middle-class hypocrisy: "the family assembled in the gallery to greet him" (*From the Heat*, 11) in a mock welcome by Davis, who has already issued his daughter with an ultimatum to "Obey or get out!" What gives the semblance of a celebration with "all the lights blazing" takes the form of a subtle cross-examination by Davis of Armstrong's lineage, or lack thereof, with "Davis trying his best to draw Armstrong out, but with little success" (12). In this "duel", Armstrong becomes enraged by Davis's pointed enquiry, "without warning, looking him straight in the eye" (12), as to whether he intends to engage a servant – a symbol of middle-class status – a move he considers a strategic assault on his self-esteem. Armstrong's dilemma is captured in his unvoiced thoughts and reflections and illuminated by the narrator:

> The gesture was not lost on Armstrong. Davis who had always treated him with deference had shown his hand. . . . *You only had to cross these people,* thought Armstrong, *and they expressed disapproval. . . . He was in the lion's den and he would fight. A quick submission for the sake of peace, followed by a lifetime of misery? Oh, no! He was not going to run his home in consultation with a father-in-law.* (12; emphasis added, to denote the protagonist's thoughts as distinct from the narrator's account)

Armstrong, an outsider eager to be co-opted into the ranks of privilege, rejects its pseudo-formalities and rebels against its morality. One strategy of the work is its deceiving moments of optimism and the knack of the suave middle class for masking its prejudice behind an unruffled surface of near-innocent language. For instance, in response to Armstrong's feeble murmur to his question, Davis subtly answers, "'Oh well,' stretching his legs in the pretence that they had gone to sleep. . . . [However] by the time Armstrong got up to leave, Davis's talk [of his own courting days and of the nineties] had set his mind completely at ease" (12). Heath's narrative style in the trilogy is deceptively simple, his dialogue spare and almost Pinteresque. Heath explains: "The writing in these early novels is very succinct, the compression extraordinary. . . . I abandoned this style later with *Kwaku* when I began to use far more details in the later works."[4] But, as we shall see, it is with *Genetha* that Heath adopted a full-bodied prose style that filters the society through the eyes of subjective female experience.

The wedding between Armstrong and Gladys is "a modest affair", reduced to insignificance by its insertion as a footnote to the emotionless first chapter of the work, a technical ploy that prefigures the marginalization and alienation of the couple. The moment of truth comes when, instead of Armstrong's inclusion into his wife's middle-class fold, both he and Gladys are expelled from it, forcing him to start a new life, ironically, in the very village of Agricola he had sought to flee, where "the trench that ran along their street with its green moss-like growth" (14) serves as a motif of the general stagnation of colonial existence and a metaphor of their own enveloping entrapment. Gladys's vulnerability, precipitated by displacement from the accoutrements of her privileged life – her piano, needlework, lace and polished silver –

to the bareness of rural existence, is compounded by a morbid change in Armstrong's moods and his habit of going out at nights, leaving his new bride to face the loneliness, "to stare out of a window into an empty street, where no one passed by and nothing ever happened" (47).

Through the conflicting points of view of Armstrong and the Davises, who together encapsulate the class dichotomy, the novel parts the curtain on the insecurities and fears of a crumbling middle class. Armstrong's encounter with this family highlights the impossibility of accommodation and integration between the segregated racial and cultural elements of colonial society; his plight measures the wide gap between desire and reality. While Gladys remains a study in isolation, from here onward the reader is gathered into society's paranoia and Armstrong's futile rebellion against subtle forces he least understands.

Rejection awakens the irrational in the protagonist and underscores his sense of inferiority. When his haughty sister-in-law deserts them in Agricola, Armstrong "fell into a surly mood" (20) and his attitude to his wife undergoes a morbid transformation. In plantation cultures such as this one, the ready resort to alcohol, drinking as a pastime and especially as a palliative for one's problems, is a well-known social phenomenon/disease that is marked by violence and destruction of the personality, an evil that continues to plague the society to the present day. To compensate for his injured pride, he flees the home, but returns under the influence of alcohol to vent his frustration and to humiliate Gladys with snide remarks: "He shouted at her for lying in bed like a 'fat sow'" (20–21), lashing out at the "uselessness" of her genteel upbringing, and physically brutalizing her for the snobbishness and intolerance of her "superior" family. Ironically, Armstrong is as chauvinistic as his prejudiced father-in-law and helps to widen the class gap he hopes to bridge.

The emotionally unstable nature of the main character, his mercurial temperament and his lack of understanding of his inner motivations add complexity to his dilemma and undermine his quest for a secure place in the social order: "He wanted to throw himself at his wife's feet and say he was sorry. How could he explain he did not mean a single word he had spoken and that all he wanted was to provide a happy home for his family? What force within him drove him to do the very thing he did not want to do?" (21).

Armstrong's unexpected virulence towards Gladys shatters her inner sense of security and partially unhinges her. In exchanging one repression for another she comes to a rude awakening that home, glamorized as a place of love and security, is in reality a repressive place of violence and victimization:

> She walked around as in a dream, wiping her hand on the corner of her dress as some people wash their hands, without any reason, except to relieve the tension in their minds. . . . Tonight she would find it impossible to sleep, but he would sleep like a log. He always did, no matter how badly they quarrelled. Whenever he got up to drink a glass of water or to urinate and found her sitting at the open window, he became angry and asked her if she was studying the stars. (22)

Lacking the inner resources to creatively transcend the entrenched prejudice of the colonial society, Armstrong allows himself to be reduced to a remote spectator of his own helpless drift into a dysfunctional shadow. Through his fractured consciousness the reader gets a sense of his inner despair:

> It was as if a cancer were growing in his body and gaining control so effectively that he was no longer master of his own actions. He knew how to achieve peace in his house, but as soon as things were going well, as soon as Gladys began to talk a little the cancer would grope into the brain that ordered his actions and would dictate an outburst without cause. . . . And he knew that with every outburst, with every quarrel, her silences lasted longer, so that the time might come when the gulf between them became so great that no penitence, no sustained act of indulgence could bridge it. (23)

Armstrong deserves the reader's sympathy in his flawed struggle for social mobility, and the reader might consider him one of society's scapegoats but for his own psychological frailty. In a scene where he hires a cab and takes Gladys for an afternoon's outing to the sea wall, an irascible mood overwhelms him and "the slender thread of his composure snapped" (32), causing him to abandon her there: "Suddenly he found himself struggling with a wave of irritability that seemed to have no cause. The presence of his wife, the strong wind, the noise of the surf, like the breathing of some leviathan, the money spent on the journey, everything seemed designed to put him out of sorts" (32–33).

Left alone on the beach, "as if rooted to the spot, Gladys looked out to the sea and for the first time the idea of suicide came to her" (33). Vulnerable though she is, Gladys does not yield to self-destruction, for such an act would too readily affirm the notion of the meaninglessness of life, an ethical and a philosophical position that Heath does not intend us to embrace in this work, even though her attempt to say something conciliatory proves an exercise in futility in the face of Armstrong's irreconcilable moods: "He uttered a sound of impatience that brooked no further talk" (34).

Dreams form a potent metaphor for the existential dread of Heath's characters, whose lived experiences are defined by anxiety and crisis.[5] Gladys relives her tragic estrangement from her husband and her relatives in her dreams – "little lights in front of me and it was as if I was floating, above and away, over the houses" (*From the Heat*, 67) – while Armstrong, in his declining years, has dreams of his dissipated life that comes to him in the form of "grains of sand falling from a man's head, like sugar from a punctured bag" (*One Generation*, 58). Many years later, Genetha, burdened with the family's guilt, is constantly persecuted in her dreams by their wrongfully dismissed servant. Even when the erstwhile servant, Esther, comes to visit her, the feeling of guilt is dominant in their exchange: "You think that fifteen dollars can pay me for all I did for your family? After I worked myself to the bone for you, your mother put me out on the street. Your Christian mother" (*Genetha*, 23).

Rather than face the harsh reality of a disintegrating family, Armstrong escapes to the invitation of a prostitute, another of society's outcasts, with whom he shares an affinity. Agonizing over his perceived inferiority, "harping on his inadequate background, his in-laws' aloofness and matters that cut deep into his heart . . . of the isolation in marriage that breeds unhappiness, and of the guilt he felt on account of the lack of contact with his children" (*From the Heat*, 81), he finds relief in confiding in her: "At times I wish for something to happen so that I can show my wife how much I care for her, that everything I do is because of this unutterable love. And yet I treat her worse than a dog sometimes. If I did tell you the things I did and especially the things I'd like to do to her, the humiliation I'd like to heap on her" (82).

Still craving acceptance within the middle-class fold, Armstrong is overjoyed to see his in-laws on the occasion of his son's christening. He had invited them by letter, "as formality only, since he was certain that they would not come", but is enthralled by "the aura created by their very presence" and awed at "his father-in-law's eloquence. . . . He had never got to know him well and regretted it. He spoke as Armstrong always dreamed of speaking" (26). Of course, Armstrong's optimism is misplaced, since his incorrigible father-in-law resorts to his seasoned indifference and narrow-mindedness immediately after the christening, and maintains his aloofness even up to the time of his daughter's untimely demise. Armstrong's intransigence hardens with constant rejection and he responds to the malice of his in-laws with equal vehemence, forbidding Gladys to visit her family when they move back to Queenstown: "After all, it might be a good idea to permit her to go home to her parents from time to time. But he would never do that" (32). In this sense, he gains a pyrrhic victory over his in-laws.

Optimism again assuages a fragile ego and the anticipated arrival of a third child holds hope for reconciliation, but the child dies soon after birth, and with it dies his illusion, for no shred of the marriage is left to be salvaged: "In time, they found little to say to each other" (30). At this stage in the novel the union is at its lowest ebb, the point where Gladys would speak to her husband through their servant, Esther, who might have been considered the moral centre of the trilogy but for her thirst for revenge, as we shall see in the third volume. The embattled protagonist totally shuns his family, and instead seeks gratification in his friends, who fill the void in his existence: "On the slightest pretext he went out and often returned in the early hours of the morning" (30), frequenting a grimy cake shop where he whiles away the time playing draughts. In Agricola, Gladys is not only faced with the bleakness of village life and its lack of basic amenities, but also with a lack of accommodation within the community, doubly victimized by hostile villagers, who deem her an outsider, "a mad woman who fed bats", and who report her every move to Armstrong. Meanwhile, Armstrong drifts "further and further away", as Gladys sees it, "like a flock of dark birds" (71) – a brooding image that deepens the moroseness of the work.

Even though the plots of Heath's novels follow linear arrangements, time is both specific and fluid in the narratives. Typical opening phrases, such as: "One night, on returning home", or "Four months later", or "One morning Armstrong received a letter", or "The following night he arrived at the house", or "A couple of weeks later Ben was lying in bed on a Saturday morning" not only lend a tenor of oral storytelling to the works but also reassert man's place in a timeless sphere of being. Heath's technique for handling time in the trilogy bears directly on his vision of man's alienation, inner despair and existential dread, and reinforces a sense of the impermanence of man vis-à-vis the permanence of the cosmic universe.

With little self-esteem left, Armstrong moves from Agricola by night. His basic pieces of furniture seem to him items of shame. Their move to Queenstown, into the house that Armstrong cheats his sister of, brings neither the desired social mobility nor inner security, for Gladys is now so completely alienated from her intractable family that she feels "like a stranger rather than someone who was coming back to the district in which she was born and spent her youth" (58). Sandwiched between resentful husband and proud family, her spirit broken by the cruel psychological bludgeoning on both sides, Gladys is unable to recuperate in the familiar city of her youth and becomes a virtual recluse: "People look at you and say, 'How you're lucky! . . .' And they fail to understand how pathetic and vulnerable you are. . . . I dread meeting people I used to know, because I've forgotten how to make conversation and would only make a fool of myself" (70).

If Armstrong is paralysed by a sense of inadequacy since his dislocation to the city, the squalor of the waterfront establishments offers him a vicarious freedom denied him in the staid atmosphere of Queenstown. As displaced in Queenstown as his wife was in Agricola, Armstrong haunts rum shops across rickety bridges, market cookshops, cake-shops in the Kitty back streets, and brothels on Lombard Street, on the fringe of the city and in the heart of the slums of Tiger Bay, while "his estrangement from his wife seemed to take a decisive turn" (66). Without a moral conscience for guide, he degenerates to the point where he neglects the basic "formalities of polite conversation he had maintained for the children's benefit" (66), going "on the binge" with his friends on Saturday nights and perversely looking on "his sorties into depravity as outings into some forbidden but beautiful well of sin" (76).

The central problem of the work is Armstrong's flawed personality, his rebellious spirit that brooks no compromise, an inner tyranny that he himself can least understand. The lack of self-knowledge and the unpredictability and illogicality of human behaviour are facets of human nature Heath would continuously grapple with throughout his novels. Freudian inquiry into the instinctive compulsions of the human mind helps to clarify a suggestion in Heath's novels that man's nature is in some ways alien to him and out of his control.[6] Gilkes's view that "Heath's work seems to mine the old seam of the personality versus urban society with a coldly observing force and directness that is, in a sense, existentialist"[7] is instructive, but Heath's characters challenge Western existentialist theories that propose that man is endowed with free will and free choice and "is nothing else but what he makes of himself".[8] Beginning with Armstrong, Heath brings onto the stage of his novels a range of characters who defy the notion that the individual is an entirely free and responsible agent determining his own development. They defy the notion that man is the rational, Cartesian being he is thought to be (the Enlightenment's assumption that man is fundamentally reasonable and governable). Heath's characters demonstrate in novel after novel that man is constrained by biological imperatives and his psychological endowments, and lacks ultimate choice in the terms of his existence.[9] This adds complexity to the motivations in the world of Heath's novels, but it does not prevent us from recognizing certain social determination.

Armstrong's confusion – that of a castrated colonial who inhabits a prison defined by class – is captured largely in the flow of his tortured consciousness: "Was it true what her family thought of him? That he was coarse? Was it really his fault that Deborah had left? Was he wrong about her and her arrogance?" (*From the Heat,* 23). The first volume of the trilogy is devoted to the grief of two psychologically damaged characters trapped in the cracks of conventional morality of a decadent and self-indulgent British Guianese middle class. Yet, however much Armstrong squanders his life, he remains protected by the ambivalence of the patriarchal society: "Why could he not recognize the failure of their marriage? . . . He needed only go on as if he were happy as the way things were. She would be the sufferer, since he went out and met people and saw his friends on the evening" (32).

As sugar prices tumble on the world market and the economic crisis in the colony deepens, setting off fears of widespread dismissals, Armstrong and his family are reduced to a precarious survival. He almost weeps with relief at the offer of a reduced salary instead of total dismissal from the post office, but selfishly decides that "cuts . . . would have to be made in the home" (61) while he maintains the obligatory semblance of a middle-class lifestyle.

This necessitates the dismissal of one of their servants; the tragedy is that the more trusted servant, the one who loves and nurtures the children, is severed. Armstrong's retrenchment three months later plunges the family into abject poverty. Bitterness compounded by lack of purpose fuels Armstrong's sustained rebellion and degeneracy: "If in Agricola he sometimes came home at ten or eleven at night, he now did so regularly; and on Fridays he invariably crossed his bridge at midnight, tottering uncertainly as he put his bicycle under the house" (75–76), while his frightened wife pretends to be asleep in order to avoid his drunken wrath.

Notions of class and respectability assume paranoid dimensions among the urban middle class in the teeth of the sugar crisis. Fears of losing face socially, of "coming down in the world", prompt Armstrong "to dress as well and eat as well as he had always done. He could not walk into his post office looking like a pork-knocker . . . neither did he wish to suffer the fate of a colleague whose pension "could not feed an estate mule" (75), echoing an entrenched awareness in the colonial world of human existence defined and (de)valued in terms of the plantation, its goods and chattels, and its estate culture. Disdain for the brash commercial spirit embodied in his bourgeois father-in-law, coupled with the daunting prospect of entering a world dominated by light-skinned middle-class Portuguese, causes Armstrong to shun a job offer in the business sector and to opt to exist on his meagre savings, while ignoring the implications of his children's educational development being severely hindered. In Queenstown, Armstrong stands face to face with all that he had desired – "fine houses with large gardens in which flourished roses and dahlias . . . fixed jalousies and wrought-iron grill" (136) – yet this unheroic character lacks the will to salvage his life. Wracked by self-doubt – "the most damaging legacy of colonialism"[10] – which dampens his aspirations, he could only see "the obstacles, the hard work and the pains he would have to take" (136).

Poverty levels the Armstrong family socially and erases the distinction between them and their remaining servant: "Armstrong reduced his wife's allowance . . . the butter was now carefully rationed. Even Marion's white headdress, insignia of her status as servant, was not replaced when it began to suffer from constant laundering so that the last evidence of rank that distinguished her from her employer was removed" (75).

Social relationships in the Armstrong household become corrupted under his seeming indifference as his wife slides into neurosis and the family slides numbly into poverty. An inversion of the social order then occurs imperceptibly as the servant displaces the now dysfunctional Gladys, usurps her authority, and virtually becomes the lady of the house, even though her middle-class upbringing had taught Gladys that "you had to keep servants at arm's length" (70). The myth of middle-class superiority is being dismantled in this work with great compassion. The knowledge of his ruthless sexual exploitation of their servant, Marion, in their very home, devastates Gladys: "humiliated, she believed herself incapable of living any longer"; but the reality of economic dependency within marriage forces her to "accept it as she accepts everything else because she relied entirely on him for support" (94). On the day the servant absconds from her duties and Gladys confronts Armstrong with his depravity, she is physically abused: "Armstrong lost his temper . . . and, with a swift movement of his arm, struck her a blow across the face" (104). Whereas Armstrong always complained "she was too submissive", ironically, any display of independence "put him in an indescribable fury" (106). Armstrong, failed husband and father, nevertheless continues to assert his male power and authority in the home, while his wife, the homemaker and nurturer, remains powerless and neglected. The work offers a picture of isolation within isolation, of the woman behind a crumbling middle-class façade beset by pervasive poverty in early twentieth-century colonial society. The protagonist and his wife represent opposing attitudes to the colonial condition: one rebelling against its inequities, the other quietly accepting its entrapment as duty.

A no less troubled picture emerges of Armstrong's relationship with his children. Having neglected them in their tender, formative years, he now agonizes over the emotional distance that separates them: "How could he come close to his children when he did not know what to do? Could he stroke Genetha's head? When? On what pretext?" (107). Armstrong's cultivated indifference to life produces cynicism and negativity even at the good news that his son has won a government scholarship to high school: "They must be crazy. He's never had a good report in his life" (128). The possibility of Rohan's (fondly called Boyie by his parents) education being cut short because they could not afford to keep him in shoes and shirts "was the least of my worries . . . if we can't afford to buy books he can always sponge on his friends" (135). Armstrong's pessimism underlines the Sisyphean task of the colonial rising out of poverty and blind prejudice, even though he must know that education is one means of closing the social gap. Where he himself is on a slippery slope, he is content for his son to slide with him and to perpetuate the cycle of impoverishment. Typically, when asked about his daughter's education and prospects, Armstrong replies with a "deprecating" gesture: "She's a girl . . . we can buy a sewing machine for her" (135). Upon his dismissal from the post office, "there was no doubt now that Genetha would have to leave school and relieve her mother of some of the housework" (139) in the absence of servants. Genetha is set to fail through her father's scornful attitude to family, his betrayal of family ideals and values, and his indifference to the colonial society and its institutions at a time when the education of women is limited, across the social spectrum, to the domestic arts. Armstrong is, in equal measure, a creature of social circumstances which he has not the will to rise above, challenge or creatively alter.

Armstrong's relationship with his wife is poisoned by class inequities as much as his relationship with his children is tainted by his own intransigence and depravity. This somewhat lengthy interiorization of the consciousness of his son, Rohan, reveals his father's wickedness and the emotional scars borne by the family:

> Boyie recalled the night when he saw his father and Marion embracing in the dark. He had never told anyone; he had never felt like telling anyone. But the secret was painful, and early the next morning, when everyone was asleep, he got up and searched for Marion's dress in the dark. He tried to rip a hole in it, but could not manage to undo the seam. And while he was looking around for something else of hers to destroy she woke up and asked him what he was doing.
>
> From then on he went to any lengths to inconvenience and annoy her, and he once told a boy at school that he wanted to die because he did not like their servant.
>
> St Barnabas school, with its dingy walls and anxious teachers, had no idea what an impression it had made on young Armstrong who often had been condemned as a delinquent and caned as a rebellious spirit. (133)

Throughout the trilogy, home and family, traditionally perceived as havens of love and security, are exposed as repressive places of violence and victimization, especially for women and children, and this is forcefully depicted in the Armstrong household. Young Rohan keenly feels the absence of his father's love: he "often wished his father would take him out kite-flying or to cock-fights, as his friends' fathers did", but the truth is that Armstrong "was hardly at home" (132). Perhaps the best portrait of Armstrong as head of a family is offered by the couple's grown daughter: "Her father, a depraved, good-for-nothing, had lied, cheated and frequented the house of prostitutes. . . . He had taken no interest in the family except to revile them" (Genetha, 20).

The reader simultaneously feels sympathy and anger towards Armstrong, but accepts that a combination of factors contributes to his deformed will, including a lack of self-knowledge that hinders him from recognizing his moral degeneration or his part in the breakdown of the family. An analysis of the protagonist's relationship with his servants completes the picture of the depths to which he has fallen in his lack of self-restraint. When the hand of fate brings Esther and Genetha together again years later, the reader discovers what has remained an enigma in the first volume – whether Armstrong was sexually exploiting the young servant – since Gladys's motivation for dismissing her, the more loyal of the two servants, remains suppressed in the first novel. The adult Genetha accuses Esther, now proprietor of a brothel: "You've changed. You're coarse", to which the erstwhile servant retorts, "I was coarse in Agricola when your mother wasn't looking. And your father was coarse when your mother wasn't looking too" (101). The reader is left to deduce that Armstrong had been sexually exploiting her, causing her to be thrown onto the streets of Georgetown, a seething "cauldron" of vice.

Esther's expulsion from the Armstrong home coincides with the unravelling of the family unit, for in every sense she is the emotional anchor of the Armstrong children. She nurtures Boyie's tender imagination with "stories from newspapers and magazines, and fed his taste for fantasy . . . and loved him as if he were her own" (From the Heat, 64), and while Gladys loses her grip on her role of mothering, Esther resourcefully manages the home in the economic crisis. Esther seeks community with the Armstrong family – but there is no family, and rejection prompts within her a desire for revenge. The family's guilt thereafter and Esther's determination to exact revenge on Genetha both have their provenance in Armstrong's perversity and shame-lessness: "The first experience in Marion's arms had excited him, but with time he found her less and less desirable, knowing that everything she had to offer was his for the asking" (92).

Yet Heath asks the reader to recognize the multilayeredness of human nature and to consider Armstrong's humanity: that he is not entirely the victim, abuser nor predator we have so far deemed him to be. Even though he is unable to bridge the irreconcilable gulf at the family level, he nonetheless craves to be counted a valid member of the human community, even if that community is one of misfits and outcasts like himself; and Heath grants him his humanity: "His friends and acquaintances knew him as a restrained person who never raised his voice, and the harlots he met in the Water Street brothel saw him as a considerate type, a gentleman" (107).

In this respect, Armstrong's friendship with Doc, with whom he frequents the brothels, is ironic. These two friends are like two cracked mirrors looking at each other. Armstrong, always seeking gratification outside of home and family, is jealous of Doc and his concubine – "he had never experienced such envy in all his life" (114) – while Doc, in turn, envies the possibilities he sees in Armstrong's home as anchor: "In that kind of house and with that sort of woman, who was capable of maintaining such a home, his ambitions in the teaching profession would surely have been realized" (137). In a very basic sense, the friendship between Armstrong and Doc represents an ideal sense of community and human relationship that Heath attempts to restore through the structures of art: "The two men swam as in an effort to reach the limits of their understanding of each other, the secret behind their gestures, their affected carriage and guarded words" (142).

Unlike Doc, who possessed the courage to desert his family, Armstrong is afraid to be cut adrift and remains securely anchored to the emotional desert he has created. He is the first in a range of Heath's flawed characters for whom the Socratic injunction to "Know thyself" is meaningless. Armstrong is a tortured character tyrannized by the inner passions and compulsions Freud suggests. We may also wish to consider the protagonist by the light of a statement by Sir Isaiah Berlin, that no good can come of "the crooked timber of humanity"[11] – a suggestion that an inherent flaw lies at the heart of man's psychological attributes, one that Claude McKay, C.L.R. James and Roger Mais possibly did not make allowance for when proposing a wholly positive spirit and a community of feeling and wholeness in their artistic vision of a West Indian identity.

The possibility of a moral awakening comes to Armstrong rather late in life, through an epiphany he experiences, ironically, on his way from a brothel. In this trance, the Davises ingratiate themselves to him, in fulfilment of his wish for acceptance, and he remembers a snatch of conversation about the uncertainty of life, words that "aroused something slumbering deep" within him, bringing a new awareness of himself as a spiritual being rather than simply a social animal:

> It was as if someone inside him had spoken, uttering hidden feelings . . . far from frightening him, had comforted him, reassuring him, as it were, of the continued existence of an inward companion, who was still capable of asserting his presence. . . . The streets appeared new and clothed in a wondrous, diaphanous material. . . . From now on he would march through life with firm steps, confident of his strength. (126–27)

Armstrong has enough humanity left in him to reflect regretfully on his actions: "Surely with a few more years his voyage of self-knowledge would have been complete and he would have been able to take her out into the bright afternoon sunlight . . . and over and over his thoughts travelled the same round of his past mistakes, as if by recalling them he could bring his wife back to life" (144). Paradoxically, Armstrong's self-awakening coincides with his wife's death, and although he is unable to fulfil the promise of the epiphany, it is nonetheless a vision of self-renewal, for by the end of the work he comes to the realization that it was she "who gave birth to their children, who had anchored him as a family man, supported him through the anguish of his dismissal and presented to him a mirror in which he discovered himself so painfully" (145). In a scene after Gladys's funeral, he stands by her bedside remorsefully: "He must have loved her after all for how else could he explain the feeling of desolation in his breast? He flayed himself with remorse and in a fit of despair he began to weep silently" (148).

On his way to his wife's funeral in a carriage, an emotional dam bursts and he is flooded with memories of his idealism, regretful of the missed opportunities to mould his family as one. This is a changed Armstrong from the character who has just prevented his children from attending their mother's funeral and who shuts his door to keep out sympathizers. Too late, he agonizes over his cultural alienation, his powerlessness to break free from the repressions and inhibitions of society, including the irrelevance of an imposed (Eurocentric) Christian dogma,[12] or even to seek comfort in the warmth and vitality of a folk religion:

> His mind went back to the evening when, dressed in his best suit, he had stood on the edge of a crowd of people who were taking part in a Salvation Army meeting in Bourda. Carried away by the infectious singing and the sound of tambourines he forgot for a while that he was waiting to make his first visit to Gladys's house in Queenstown. He had set out too early and was obliged to wander around until he heard the music in the distance. No, her family would not have approved of tambourines or singing at street corners. Yet, such things stirred his heart. And these very things that separated them, these impulses, he suppressed for her sake, or perhaps for his own, believing that they were the signs of a defective upbringing. (147)

A romantic union that begins in conflict and alienation, and disintegrates under the strain of inbred prejudice, psychological weaknesses and endemic poverty during the years of the Depression, ends tragically with Armstrong's retrenchment from the civil service, Gladys's death and the fragmentation of the family, leaving the protagonist to face "black nights and mornings pale as clama-cherries, a kind of indefinable void" (153). Even as Armstrong comes to regret his marginal role in the family, he is nonetheless outraged when sympathizers treat him scantily, as though "Gladys had been married to a phantom which had managed to dress itself in mourning clothes" (148). Even though his marriage is poisoned by forces beyond his control and his quest for individual freedom fails, there is every suggestion in the novel that Armstrong instinctively longs for community and the fellowship of family, for after his wife's death, he "suppressed his old rage against Gladys's family in the interest of the children, who should cleave to their grandparents and aunts, as was the case in most families" (154). Consumed with a lifelong anguish at the obstacles he failed to conquer – the gulf between himself and her family, "an unbridgeable void that yawned between one way of life and another, like those mighty rivers that divide" (155), Armstrong withdraws from the world and barricades himself in the house, refusing to answer Doc's repeated knocking on his door. The truth is that he yearns for human community and connectedness: "Armstrong returned to his chair after bolting the door. . . . When he recovered he would seek Doc out to find again those brighter days . . . only remembering the need for companionship and hours of laughter. He wondered if his friend still went to Plaisance on Sundays, whether he would welcome an unexpected visit there as in the old days" (153).

In spite of the raw tensions between Gladys and her husband over the years and the intense alienation within the marriage, the myth of the family persists: "they had grown into each other like the hundred-year-old trees in the back yard, irrevocably intertwined" (145), though they seem more like two towers of silence chained to each other: "Separation from Armstrong was unthinkable, and when he fell into the abyss the chain that bound their lives would drag her with him. She searched for a reason for this terrible liaison, but could not find one. Things were just so. There was a sky and an earth; there was the wind and the sun; and there was marriage" (140). The Armstrongs are a classic example of tenuous and tortuous family relationships held together in an illogical, imperfect sense.[13] It is perhaps inevitable that Armstrong should experience moments of dis-ease, an overpowering sense of futility and the feeling that reality is absurd: "Wasn't everything absurd? . . . He did not choose to be born, just as he was unable to choose the moment he was going to die. The things he wanted most were beyond his grasp and whatever was within his reach was pale and insignificant" (125).

Heath uses the enigmatic character of Armstrong ironically to attempt to work out the dilemma of human existence in terms of some intellectual theories we have come to know. If the introspective Armstrong is perplexed by the absurdity of existence and the mystery of life, he never stirs himself to engage the notion of free choice nor to exercise the free will with which man is supposedly invested. Freud rejects the idea that man is a rational being, judging the human mind to be impulsive, irrational and unpredictable.[14] Certain European philosophers[15] go further and propose that rational man is irrelevant and free will is also irrelevant because existence is absurd and all human striving is useless in light of the impossibility of ever attaining one's ideals. In the final analysis, Armstrong, with his weak ego, diminished and crushed by the subtle power of the colonial middle class, does nothing but drift. If Heath's first creative effort teaches us anything, it is that human existence is open-ended and man can be certain of nothing but his own consciousness, however flawed. In his time and place, the anguished protagonist discovers that beneath the middle-class veneer lies a questionable morality.

He fails to find a place in a society constructed for predators and victims, and he progresses to a void of unmitigated loneliness. Armstrong is simply emblematic of the human struggle with all its limitations; his condition must be accepted as a valid version of the unending struggle in the Caribbean to transcend a bitter past and an unknowable self.

The lush landscape of Georgetown, the legendary "garden city", is totally obliterated from the setting of this work; what is portrayed are the stark streets of a soulless city, its rum shops and brothels, an impoverished and brooding atmosphere, where "the slaughter house with its familiar sight of a line of black vultures perched on its roof and the reek of blood" (143) closes the work and completes a bleak and macabre picture of a festering and decaying society in the dying light of colonialism. Carter offers a vivid sense of the urban deprivation in which Heath's wretched urban dwellers are trapped, and Carter's poetic voice contains immediacy equal to that of Heath's subtle prose:

> Do not stare at me from your window, lady!
> Stare at the wagon of prisoners!
> Stare at the hearse passing by your gate!
> Stare at the slums in the south of the city!
> Stare hard and reason, lady, where I came from
> And where I go.[16]

And, from "Run Shouting through the Town",

> See me? I would rip off my clothes
> run shouting through the town
> . . . .
> A black child in a kitchen
> searching in a black pot
> smoke – hanging on his head
> naked! naked! naked![17]

Unnoticed by society, the intransigent Armstrong allows himself to sink beyond redemption. At least half of the second volume of the trilogy is devoted to the final decline of the lonely and drunken recluse he has become, still frequenting the waterfront rum shops "solitary against the ravaged sky" (*One Generation*, 8), and still resenting the irrational prejudice and the "ill-concealed hostility" of the coloured middle class (13), until he falls off his porch to a swift end. At a time of the colony's agitation for independence from the mother country, the deaths of their parents liberate Genetha and Rohan to explore selfhood on their own terms, and it is hardly a surprise to the reader that Rohan seeks to flee the confusing values of his middle-class boyhood and adolescence in the city, where the only legacy bequeathed them is a memory of dysfunction and guilt.

4

ONE GENERATION
In Search of Self

Race and cultural polarities give structure to the second volume of the trilogy. Bereft of the anchor of family, Armstrong's son, Rohan, and his sister, Genetha, are left to drift in a dying social order. All of Rohan's relationships point to endemic racial and ethnic insecurities in the society as a whole. Heath continues in *One Generation* with the male point of view in recounting the fictional experiences of the character Rohan and his quest for integration in the heterogeneous society. Although this work recaptures the years from the 1940s to the early 1960s, it was composed much later (the trilogy was first written as a long novel somewhere between 1966 and the early 1970s and laid aside; one could speculate that it was revisited by Heath around the mid-1970s) with an appreciable consciousness of the social and political upheaval, the conflagrations and racial violence of the 1960s in the run-up to independence in the British colony.

With the establishment of an American military base in the colony during the Second World War, British Guianese rush to find employment and the city's brothels flourish, giving Lombard Street the "bright, brash appearance of a thriving red-light district" (*One Generation*, 6). The eighteen-year-old Rohan, however, commutes from the city to his posting at the local government office at Vreed-en-Hoop, on the west coast of Demerara. Indians form the majority in the district and through his friendship with an Indian officer named Mohammed, Rohan is exposed to Indian customs, dance and music, particularly the sounds of the sitar and violin, a world previously unknown to him in his middle-class Queenstown cocoon: "Accustomed to the urban world of Georgetown, he was fascinated by what he heard and saw in Vreed-en-Hoop, just across the river from town" (22). Rohan's growth to manhood and his quest for selfhood and identity are analysed through his relationships with an Indian woman and her family connections; with his sister Genetha; and with Ramjohn, a clerk at the commissary's office at Suddie.

Like his father, who had rushed into a hasty marriage hardly knowing the world of the "other", Rohan enters "forbidden" racial and cultural territory. Nothing in his psychosocial growth has prepared the young Armstrong for the encounter as he is drawn into a passionate relationship with Mohammed's eldest daughter, Indrani, "an attractive young woman in her early twenties" (22) who is already married to Sidique, the son of a wealthy Muslim Indian Essequibo rice miller.

The issue of people of mixed race seeking to mingle with the wider Guianese society was first broached in Mittelholzer's *Corentyne Thunder* (1941), through the brief love affair between a half-white college student, Geoffrey Weldon, and a young Indian cow-minder's daughter on the Corentyne Coast. In Heath's work, the encounter of the fair-skinned middle-class protagonist, Rohan, with the (East) Indian strand of the society, and a family that has its own internal tensions, is complicated by the fact of its illicit nature and his inability or unwillingness to manage his libidinous impulses: "How near he had come to doing what was absurd they would never know. He could not guarantee that in future he would behave" (*One Generation*, 23).

Rohan and Sidique are antagonists in a triangular love affair. A stereotype of the gauche, moneyed rural Indian, Sidique, with his provocative language, his chauvinism and his boorishness, rouses the city-bred Rohan to anger to the extent that they come to blows and their barely concealed antagonisms surface: "Rohan seized Sidique by the throat. The two men fell to the ground . . . Rohan managed to wrench himself free, his chest heaving and a streak of blood and spittle dripping from his lip. Sidique in turn got up with an expression of hate on his face. When he recovered sufficiently to speak he said, 'Get out, you beggar!'" (39). The conflict between the two individuals is reflective of the tensions between two polarized ethnic groups to which they each belong; it could be read as an analogy of the meeting of the Indian and the African in the segmented society and the suppressed hostility between the two major racial strands. The conflict dramatized in Heath's fiction looks forward to the racial disturbances of the 1960s in the colony, a pathology that continues to characterize the culturally complex society in post-independent Guyana.[1]

Even though Rohan belongs among the privileged few who, by virtue of colour and class, have permanent, well-paid jobs in the civil service, he nonetheless "saw himself drifting, careless, pilotless, like a boat whose destiny was to end on some mud-flat up-river" (98). He contemplates flight from the purposelessness of colonial existence: "He could no longer endure this clerking. Soon he would have to make up his mind about what his aim in life was" (98). Rohan is part of the drift C.L.R. James remarks upon, the limited opportunities available to the colonial, "except to be a civil servant and hand papers, take them from the men downstairs and hand them to the men upstairs".[2] As Rohan reflects, "The futility of writing down numbers on a coloured coupon and taking them to others was never more apparent than now" (41).

But Rohan's fate is pre-empted by Indrani's boldness in coming to the city to seek him out: "a feeling of elation came over him . . . he was beside himself with excitement. The desolation he had felt had gone without a trace" (44); all his thoughts of flight vanish on the day she pursues and seduces him at his home in Queenstown.

His sister's disapproval of Indrani, her condemnation of his "preoccupation with these country people" (25) and the sanctions she imposes on Rohan speak of middle-class prejudice and abhorrence of the racial "other". She judges the relationship between Rohan and Indrani to be "obscene and unpardonable" (26). Three factors drive Rohan closer to the Indian friends he has come to know: the lurking fear of taboo feelings for his sister; his disillusionment at the discovery of Genetha's affair with his friend Fingers, a gambler born in the slums of Kingston; and his conviction that a return to the Queenstown home is now impossible for him. Rohan pins his hope of a new life in his connection with the Indians, a haven in his drift, hesitating to sever the link for fear that "he would find himself in a wasteland of loneliness" (28).

Heath takes a dig at the dominant Christian faith depicted in Genetha's intolerance of the Indian woman. Just returned home after taking Holy

Communion one Sunday (42), she is in a far from Christian-like mood; she is outraged that a "common" woman would dare to intrude into their middle-class space and disturb their Sabbath: "Genetha could have choked with anger . . . harbouring her bitterness" (45). Her mother's valid relationship with her rural working-class father was similarly opposed by her prejudiced grandfather, a bias that lay at the root of all the grief in their family; now the circle of irony closes quietly as her own brother breaches invisible social boundaries and is set to suffer a far worse fate than their father.

Even though Genetha herself currently flouts the rigid social rules of her colonial middle-class upbringing and liaises with a slum-dweller, she reserves the right to make the journey to the backwater village at Vreed-en-Hoop to investigate the social standing of Indrani, "the mysterious woman" she deems an inferior: "The worlds of Vreed-en-Hoop and Georgetown, separated only by the expanse of a river, were far removed from one another in Genetha's eyes." Her mind churns in turmoil, like the murky waters of the Demerara River she contemplates from the ferry: "The prayer flags, the hedges, the dusty roads, represented a vaguely romantic but wretched world. Genetha knew that her brother had fallen into bad company . . . she knew that no good could come of such a relationship. She must do all she could to bring it to an end" (*One Generation*, 26).

Rohan's request for a transfer from Vreed-en-Hoop where he first meets Indrani, to Suddie on the Essequibo Coast, where she lives with her husband and his influential family in a seemingly self-sufficient Indian enclave, has little to do with his wish to be part of a larger society he did not know in his childhood. In Earl Lovelace's *The Dragon Can't Dance* (1979), the desire for social integration fuels the movement of the Indian peasant Pariag from a sugar estate to a mixed suburban community because "he wanted to be a man, to join the world, be part of a bigger something in a bigger somewhere, to stretch out, extend himself, be a man among people" in multicultural Trinidad.[3] Rohan's quest for integration in multiracial British Guiana and his inverse journey from city to village spring from unchecked passions that have more to do with instant self-gratification than with a desire to take his place in the society. Sheltered from the realities of racial undercurrents in the colony, and too rash to consider the illicit nature of his relationship with Indrani, let alone its cultural implications, he fails to heed the warning in Mohammed's knowing words: "Pity! . . . people will watch your every move. If you so much as look at Indrani they'll start gossiping; and when that happens God help her! Remember she's a Mohammedan. If his parents get to know of her association with you in Vreed-en-Hoop they'll carve her up! . . . My advice to you is to withdraw the application, in everybody's interest" (*One Generation*, 102).

To Rohan, "Everything now appeared in an absurd light. . . . What did he owe society which had foisted on him the participation in a daily ritual, devoid of meaning, a society that was unmindful of his own private aspirations?" (104). On the steamer to Adventure, he resolves to "spare no pains to see Indrani" (104), to exercise his free will, the will to act and follow his own instincts towards self-gratification. Ironically, the journey towards individual freedom is double-edged, for it marks the separation of brother and sister and the disintegration of the Armstrong family in the trilogy.

At Suddie, Rohan crosses the barriers of racial exclusivity zealously guarded by self-appointed custodians, such as the Alis, against seepage from the dominant creole culture in a conflicted colony.[4] As if this situation were not sufficiently volatile, the arrival of Indrani's younger sister, Dada, on the scene adds fuel; her presence severely tests Rohan's libidinous nature and his lack of self-restraint. Her rebellion against traditional Indian customs and values, including her defiance of the conservatism of the Alis, gives complexity to the plot: "Her very presence makes him feel unaccountably happy. She had tempted him too far. Ever since he watched her from the water that morning he realized that he desired her" (122). Faced with an impossible choice (between two sisters) and driven by unchecked passions that run counter to social and cultural conventions, Rohan scandalizes the village by openly cohabiting with Dada. In the exercise of his free will, Rohan is, ironically, overcome by feelings of entrapment: "he felt more like an animal in a cage . . . like a man who had built his own prison and locked himself in it" (145).[5]

Rohan's clash with the Alis opens a window to the creolization process at work in the colony, revealing the suppressed resistance within racial and cultural groups to assimilation into the wider society. Ali warns his son, Sidique, that the implications of Rohan's presence for their cultural traditions are greater than the social scandal of an errant wife: "Is not you, is us. You want to see our women smoking and drinking and going out to work?" (150). In Ali's question lies the suggestion that their opposition might have been less vehement if Indrani had had an affair with an Indian man. Ali's meeting with Rohan to negotiate to send Dada away and avoid scandal in the small coastal village where "everybody know everybody" (133) fails, for Rohan is indignant at Ali's offer of a monetary inducement, Ali being caricatured as the "bribe-making" Indian. Consumed by lustful passions and swollen with what might be interpreted as the arrogance of racial superiority, Rohan brashly ignores Ali's offer of an exit and does not heed his scarcely veiled warning: "The Mohammedans watching you like a chicken hawk . . . you offend our customs in full view of everybody" (133–34). Even if Rohan realizes that he has exchanged a decadent middle-class existence in Georgetown for the cultural inwardness in the deep rural community at Suddie, he displays no evidence of self-restraint or inclination towards self-reflection.

Rohan's encounter with the Indians at Suddie is a device for examining the dynamics of society and its conventional morality. Rohan comes from a socio-cultural milieu where the assumption is that Guyanese society, its morality, beliefs and values, are solely creole-European and that anything outside this circle is somehow inferior. The assumption of the Suddie Indians is that they and their cultural customs have a valid place in the society. This volume illuminates the racial paranoia of the society and the brittleness of interracial relationships, for when he unwittingly violates society's taboos, Rohan is dealt with swiftly and brutally in this artistic reinterpretation of the plural society.

Indrani, with a relatively liberal upbringing, may initially have seen Rohan as a means of escape from the imprisoning Indian enclave into which she is married, but, in the final analysis, finds herself bound to the deeper cultural traditions of her race: "Deep down . . . she was on the Alis' side. If people wanted to behave like this they should go and live in some isolated place" (165). The virtue of this work lies in its depiction of the quandary of both worlds in the 1940s: the disintegrating middle class and the Indians in various stages of acculturation.

Ali and Mohammed represent two sides of the Indian immigrant experience: the one clinging to the traditional values of his cultural heritage; the other yielding to the creolization process in his efforts at assimilation. Whereas Mohammed (with his generous human spirit ready to accept "the other") feels Rohan's departure from Pouderoyen for Suddie as a loss of human fellowship and "shudders to think that the office will be a wilderness again" (102), Ali, on the other hand, does everything, even to the point of corruption, to reject Rohan from the Essequibo village and maintain the fixed order. He bribes his son with a share in the Leguan rice mill to induce his wife, Indrani, to persuade the intruder, Rohan, to leave, although Indrani's visit has the opposite effect on the fickle Rohan – when he sees her, his desire for her only intensifies, he can apply no self-restraint, and all he knows is that he "loved Indrani more than ever [to the extent that] each time her name was pronounced by Ali he resented it as an impertinence" (137).

However, much of Heath's strength lies in his psychological insights, and while he is pursuing social and cultural themes, one cannot avoid noticing the psychological depth of his characters, of whom Ramjohn is a case of intractable warping. The most treacherous of Rohan's encounters with Indians in the community is not with the Alis, with their open fears and insecurities, their veiled threats or their determination to preserve their "respectability" and their cultural traditions, but with Ramjohn, a poor clerk in the commissary's office where Rohan is stationed. Ramjohn has reasons of his own to hate Rohan, and when Ramjohn's wife, Deen, is found at the bottom of Rohan's well, the tragedy spurs Ramjohn to vengeance: "humiliation that had been ripening in his heart for months was to grow into a cancerous hatred for Rohan and his mistress" (183). In a moment of insane anger and jealousy when he discovers Indrani in Rohan's arms, Ramjohn murders them both, as a kind of compensation for the tragic loss of his own wife.

The actions of this evil character can be deemed "motiveless malignity",[6] even if certain motivations are noticed in the work: as an Indian man, Ramjohn is outraged at the audacity of a coloured man so casually violating Indian womanhood; he is indignant at Rohan's disrespect for the taboos and implicit order of the society. Ramjohn feels betrayed by Rohan, and his act of revenge is a kind of protest against Rohan's extravagance and lavish social whirls in the face of the grinding poverty of the village: "Ramjohn was so bitter about the way Rohan has let him down that he could not bear to ask him . . . for money to pay the doctor to see his malaria-stricken wife. Incensed at all these contradictions, he avoids Rohan's eyes at the office" (139).

An additional factor fuels Ramjohn's discontent: he is jealous of Dada's claim on Rohan, deeming it a hindrance to his valued fraternizing with this officer, to their "games of draughts and their drinking bouts" (139).

Ultimately, Ramjohn's disillusionment with Rohan stems from the latter's arrogance and inbred class bias, which was only suspended to enable his lustful intentions: "Rohan, generous and broad-minded, nevertheless suffered from the limitations of all his class. Ramjohn was thrust into the background whenever there were guests, and although he found this only proper, Rohan was conscious-stricken over his own cowardice" (109). As it stands, Ramjohn is a study in perversity. Eager to rise above the popular stereotype image of the socially inferior Indian as voiced by another character – "You coolie people, if you not cutting somebody throat you licking their boots" (159–60) – he considered Rohan's coming "a blessing", an opportunity for him to upgrade his social standing through association with the creole officer. Little could anyone guess that an insane hatred lurked beneath the mask of respect for Rohan:

> All the chief clerks he had hitherto dealt with snubbed him as soon as they could fend for themselves. As he once remarked bitterly to his wife, he was good enough to show them the ropes, but not good enough for company. He worshipped the dirt Rohan walked on and, in spite of the fact that they had become friends, always treated him with the greatest deference. A life of boot-licking had left its mark on him. (109)

In this novel, no one is certain of anything and nothing is as it seems, and perhaps this is the closest portrayal of the human condition in Guyanese literature. The reader is unsure whether Dada, now pregnant with Rohan's child, is unwittingly implicated in the murders, as her thoughts would seem to suggest: "At the time she had laid her plans to have him watched she had been transported on the crest of a wave of hatred for him and her sister. Now she thought it would have been a thousand times preferable to have an unfaithful Boyie than be without him" (181). As Dada ponders Ramjohn's virulence towards her, uncertain what to make of it, and doubtful that he could be the murderer, many questions remain unanswered:

> But what was the significance of Ramjohn's remarks about seeing Boyie and Indrani together? When did he see them together? Had they been seeing each other at times she had not been aware of? Or did he see them the night of the murder? Was it he who . . .? That was impossible. Ramjohn lacked the courage to kill a rat. Besides, the person who had committed the murders must have been exceptionally cool. Ramjohn was nervous and excitable. (196)

When the police bring news of the crime, Ramjohn is "invaded with a feeling of immense satisfaction at the sight of Dada's suffering" (183) and on entering his consciousness the reader gleans the identity of the murderer: "Shooting Mrs Ali had also given him pleasure. His own wife had died before her time, why should someone else's life be spared? Life without his wife was not worth living and in killing Rohan he had . . . acquired a feeling of power" (183). The murderer is never apprehended and brought to justice, so that the horrific deaths of Rohan and Indrani are symbolic ritual sacrifices to a society steeped in racial and cultural insecurities. Rohan slips into the yawning gap that Wilson Harris refers to as "the wide difference between human passion and destiny on the one hand, and order and morality on the other".7 Rohan's idealism and passions drive him into forbidden areas of the diverse society, while Indrani too must die, because conventional morality condemns errant female sexuality. There is a vein of eroticism running through Heath's works which one can read as a kind of rebellion against the Victorian morality upheld by a "mimic" colony. Such scenes are not written for the sake of self-indulgence, but suggest the urgency of man emasculated by colonialism and reduced to his baser instincts.

Heath's strength lies in studying these flawed characters, who all seem to have an affinity to each other. Ramjohn, with a Manichaean psyche, acts swiftly to bring a violent end to Rohan and Indrani when he thinks he has enough justification. Rohan, insisting on his perverse right to act, even if it is contrary to his own good, fits the definition of the Nietzschean Superman. His flight to Suddie, "in his sister's eyes a callous abandonment of her", represents for him "an act of the utmost necessity" (128) – an act to dramatically transcend the paralysing ethos of the 1930s in which his parents were trapped and did not act to redeem themselves.

Rohan's rejection by society, culminating in his brutal death, is a cruel repetition of his father's life, but his tragic end must be read as the celebration of the free will to pursue individual freedom and to reject the fatalistic world view of the previous generation. In *One Generation*, passion is a prelude to tragedy, and despite the wish of the older Armstrong to shelter his son from the abyss into which he himself had slipped, an impulsive, anarchic will drives Rohan to expend his life force in death, as if in fulfilment of Herbert Marcuse's proposal that "the uncontrolled Eros [the love instinct] is just as fatal as its counterpart, Thanatos [the death instinct]". His destructive energy derives from the tragic fact that he strives for "a gratification that culture cannot grant".[8] In this context, Jeremy Poynting rightly sees sexual passion in Heath's unsentimental texts as "simply one force which collides with others: class, race and religious feelings".[9] Rohan's quest for individual freedom and integration into the wider community is corrupted by social factors, but more so by his own flawed ego, as it was for his father.

The first two volumes of the trilogy, through the tortured consciousness of father and son, suggest that reality is often too complex for the individual to understand and that man is certain of nothing but consciousness itself. Many things remain a mystery, as Heath himself notes: "Perhaps the greatest truth is the elusiveness of truth" (*Shadows*, 124).

One Generation is set in the period before independence, with its upsurge of racial conflict in the colony, and Heath explores the idea of assimilation (through miscegenation) as the means of integrating the polarized racial strands and artistically solving the interracial strife. The new life that Dada bears within her embodies the promise of racial unity in a historically divided society and this is the last image in the work – the eternal picture of mother and child, in which lies the world's hope.[10]

Out of the deaths of Rohan and Indrani comes the possibility of change and renewal. Indrani's death paradoxically frees Sidique to dream of a new community for himself and his son in a totally new space outside the crippling, clichéd relationships prefigured by colonialism. Added to Ali's philosophical view that life is an enigma – "We're like grass in the fields. We lie down and stan' up and don't know why" (*One Generation*, 132) – is his pragmatic approach, which leaves no room for open-endedness in human relationships. It takes a new generation, in the person of his son, to conceive a fresh vision of alternative models for the survival and existence of Caribbean peoples:

> A new life was germinating in him, he felt, for within the four walls of his confinement he dared to do more than he did when he was free; to challenge what was accepted in his father's house. Here he dreamed and he dared. . . . Should he ever leave this hole he would marry again and set up house among the sandhills and bring up his son as he wanted, even at the risk of being a pariah in the Mohammedan community. (192)

In this respect, Heath's redeeming vision of community is as valid as Harris's despite their vastly contrasting styles, settings and subject matter. In Harris's *The Whole Armour* (1962), Cristo tells Sharon: "And we have to start all over again. . . . We've got to pick up the seeds again where they left off. It's no use worshipping the rottenest tacouba and tree-trunk in the historic topsoil. There's a whole world of branches and sensation we've missed, and we've got to start again from the roots up even if they look like nothing."[11] Writers write in order to clear the past and find signposts to wholeness, and in *One Generation*, we find optimism for man and society and look to see if this open vision in human affairs has been sustained in the texts that follow.

5

GENETHA
Through the Eyes of a Woman

Genetha runs parallel in time with *One Generation*, the second volume of Heath's trilogy: both works span the period from the 1940s up to the mid-1960s. This is a strategic duplication, for in this volume, virtually the same events captured in *One Generation* are covered, this time from the perspective of a woman – a reflection of the growing recognition that too much of the history of these societies has excluded the female version. A shift in this work from the predominantly male point of view, perhaps indicating Heath's responsiveness to the feminist movement of our time, both deepens and enriches the trilogy. This is hardly a surprising development, as Heath's novels are all seen to include the woman's point of view, the submerged, subjective female experience, and her condition of survival and existence at a certain time and place.

The futile striving of the eponymous heroine, Genetha, for independence and selfhood can be read as the culmination of the failed struggles of all the women in the trilogy, including her mother, Gladys; her brother's lover, Indrani; and Deen, wife of an office assistant at Suddie, who all meet early and tragic deaths. Her experiences also cap those of her maternal and paternal aunts who, stifled and cheated in hegemonic relationships, have all stagnated socially and are hardly able to be in sympathy with Genetha's struggle for freedom and selfhood. Genetha is a metaphor of female isolation at a certain time and place, and all her social relationships point to the doom of the female.

The female struggle unfolds through Genetha's determined efforts to transcend the family's tortuous past and achieve self-realization in colonial Georgetown. This narrative can be read as an analogy to the colony's struggles for political independence from a suffocating historical past. In this concluding volume of the trilogy, all that remains of the Armstrong family is the lonely and desolate figure of their daughter, Genetha, "left to brood in the house in Queenstown" (*Genetha*, 1) after her father's death and her brother's departure for Suddie.

In this volume Heath comes at last to an exploration of the extent to which Genetha's psyche has been traumatized by the experiences of her family history – chiefly, how much she has internalized of her mother's isolation and the family's burden of guilt, accumulated through the years. The effect of past experiences on her social and psychological progress is now more fully told. It should be remembered that the trilogy was originally written as one work but later broken up into three books to find favour with the publishers. It is our argument that reading back through the trilogy to illuminate the events that have consequences for Genetha's psychosocial process is not only justified but also necessary. These events were not examined in our critique of the two earlier volumes, which chiefly throws light on the notion of the family, on Armstrong's relationship with Gladys and her family, and on the fate of Rohan in Suddie. We now seek to examine Genetha's relationships, including the truth concerning the eviction of Esther, their faithful servant, from their home, at a time when Genetha was too young to understand the underlying reasons, an event that becomes a reference point for the family and comes back to haunt her throughout her adult life.

In illuminating Genetha's course in the class-ordered patriarchal society, this chapter will chart the formation of her personality through those relationships and events that shaped her perception of the world and moulded her into the adult she becomes by the end of the narrative. These include: her early childhood experiences and lessons learned from her mother's life; her brother's abandonment of her after the death of their father; her strained relationships with both her mother's and her father's family; the eviction of their devoted servant from their home; later, the shock of discovering her father's depravity; and, crucially, the rancour of their erstwhile servant, Esther. In addition to her immediate family, relationships exist with her two lovers,

Michael and Fingers; with a priest of the established church; and with a co-worker, Zara. From Genetha's perspective the reader gains deeper insight into her mother's isolation within the prison of marriage and her early demise suppressed in the first volume of the trilogy.

The reader also gets a sighting of the urban impoverishment in which Genetha is trapped, a sense of the social and cultural disorder, and the dependency arrangements going back to colonialism under which individual freedom has proven elusive for the rest of her family. The social fabric is unravelling: the end of the war sees the closure of the American airbase and an increase in unemployment and poverty; labourers from ruined sugar estates are converging on the congested city in a vain search for work. Political agitation for constitutional independence intensifies.

Genetha lives through major historical upheavals in the colony, such as the Enmore riots of 1948;[1] the suspension of the constitution in 1953;[2] and political dissension turning into open race wars and naked tribalism in the period preceding the granting of political independence in 1966. In these turbulent times, Genetha struggles heroically for a secure place in society as external insecurity acts upon inner insecurity. Heath discards the clipped, unsentimental style employed in the first two volumes of the trilogy in favour of a more expansive, full-bodied style to explore the troubled female consciousness in a restless society.

At a tender age, Genetha's self-esteem is undermined by the sight of her mother's downtrodden condition, and by a belligerent and neglectful father whose irrational and savage outbursts left them all cowering in fear. Now an adult, she offers the most vivid portrait of her father, "a depraved, good-for-nothing who had lied, cheated and frequented the houses of prostitutes when he was alive. He had taken no interest in the family except to revile them" (*Genetha*, 20). As a child Genetha has no sense of belonging to a family unit that coheres or offers warmth or self-certainty or one that prepares her for life's possibilities.

A fierce sense of independence and rebelliousness is first noticed in Genetha when, still a young girl, she attempts to oppose the authority of a domestic in the household whose behaviours are determined by a practical understanding of the precariousness of the woman's place in colonial society. Deprived of motherly nurturing, her upbringing left to servants, Genetha somehow manages to stand up for herself and square off with the servant. Marion's resentful declaration foreshadows Genetha's eventual fate:

> Marion raised her hand, but Genetha stared at her without flinching.
> "Go on, hit me! I dare you to hit me. I'm not Mother, I don't care."
> "You li'l bastard!" shouted Marion. "You watch! You going end up a street woman. You goin' see where them fine airs going get you." (*From the Heat*, 67)

This spirit of independence and defiance is alive in Genetha as she faces crisis after crisis in her various relationships. When after her mother's early demise she is left to care for her irascible father and her unruly brother, who is pursuing a lover from another racial segment of the society, Genetha questions her blind filial devotion. She is defiant at what she considers her brother's betrayal and summons up the courage to resolve to break out of her prison:

> From now on, she thought, she would go out more often, rather than cultivate the bland acceptance of her lot as housekeeper to her father and brother. The idea of freedom filled her with uncertainty, even dread. . . . The intrusion of that shameless woman [Rohan's lover] from Vreed-en-Hoop into the household, like the irruption of a dormant idea, forced her to follow a course of action she had not, in normal circumstances, the courage to take. All the bells that once proclaimed her loyalty to her father and brother had fallen silent in her head and she sat in the broken light of afternoon inwardly cursing her past devotion. (*One Generation*, 45–46)

Even when, after a series of misfortunes, she is reduced to a state of homelessness and abject poverty, she still possesses a proud spirit, so much so that the Catholic priest who later sexually exploits her admits: "From the first I admired your defiance. It's a quality the early Christians had" (*Genetha*, 180).

Only when she is a teenager does Genetha come to appreciate the hard reality of her mother's predicament, her economic dependence and her lack of choices in the grinding poverty of the 1930s. She gains a better understanding of her mother's entrapment during a heated exchange with her brother:

> "Then what were you doing at this Mamus place [a brothel]?" she asks her brother.
> "And you think," he replied, "that if I went to church and listened to a minister stumble his way through a sermon I won't go to Mamus? And when you

talk about Mother being a saint why don't you ask yourself why? If she'd left Father, where could she have gone? Eh? What work would she have done?" (*One Generation*, 69–70)

Genetha is "*bewildered* and *confused* at what she had heard of her father" (*One Generation*, 70; emphasis added), including the surreptitious sexual encounters taking place under her very roof. What she hears makes her consider for the first time that no options exist for the married middle-class woman like her mother in colonial society in the first half of the twentieth century except to suffer silently in the secure prison of marriage.

As Armstrong badgers Genetha to give shelter in their home once more to Esther, the disclosure of Armstrong's continued depravity with the servant girl who turned to prostitution after having been expelled from their home "into the cauldron" (22) of the city of sin "stirred conflicts" (72) that Genetha is not emotionally equipped to handle. Esther is embedded in Genetha's consciousness from childhood and she is now burdened with simultaneous feelings of sympathy and guilt towards the servant. She fears that some day Esther will exact payment for the injustice done to her, and as a result, Genetha spends much of her time on anxious self-reflection:

> She had often thought of Esther. Since the servant's going away she could not think of her without a feeling of guilt and the belief that the family was bound to suffer for dismissing someone who, until then, had been an integral part of it. Her mother must have been right, but was she, Genetha, expected to forget Esther just because she no longer lived there? The disclosure of the servant's relations with her father stirred conflicts in her she was not prepared to face. (*One Generation*, 72)

Without a doubt the most devastating event in her young life has been the eviction of their faithful servant from their home. After her mother's death, Armstrong brought the erstwhile servant into their house to continue their liaison. This has the most traumatic impact on Genetha, for Esther has been their nurturing anchor. The image of Esther defiled by her father could not be easily dismissed and now, alone in the world, Genetha is panic-stricken and tormented at nights by these past events that do not square with her previously held image of morally upright parents:

> Night after night, on coming home from work, she went over the events since

> her family had come from Agricola to settle in the north of Georgetown . . . the dismissal of Esther, the servant who had all but suckled them . . . the discovery that he had brought the former servant to the house and paid her as other men did. . . . And every night the recollections brought the same panic fed by some demonic energy. (*Genetha*, 1)

Genetha resolves to break out of the cycle of female subjugation into which she has been conditioned since childhood. She rejects a repetition of her mother's life as she remembers it: "in the way her mother had been until her death, tied to the house, like a dog to a post". Finding her loneliness overwhelming, she is torn between social propriety and emotional needs: "The war between Genetha's loneliness and her vague fear of allowing an intrusion in the family home reduced her to tears on her waking up in an empty house. She came to dread the morning with its clamour of bells interspersed with the pounding of dray [cart] wheels" (1). Now that she is alone, she reflects upon the extent to which her actions have been regulated not only by her family but also by society: "The mask she wore on their account she still wore, but only when she was out of the house and her behaviour was subjected to the examination of others" (4).

Genetha is aware that the moral parameters of society are shifting, that the American military presence has left a negative mark on the moral fabric of the city: "all around her she saw the way other women had changed, how they smoked and drank, how they took advantage of their status as working women to go out with more than one man or to leave their men if they were married; how they flew in the face of convention with that aplomb of a youth who had drunk for the first time" (4). As a middle-class young woman, she is constrained to maintain "her show of propriety"; however, this restraint lasts only while the family coheres in a sort of fashion. Now alone, she is prompted by a neighbour to use her freedom from family to "entertain" (a word that carries sexual connotations), and when she allows her opportunistic lover into the house, the people she worked with "noticed the transformation" approvingly, as did the inquisitive neighbours and shopkeepers (15). Genetha's induction into the role of woman as sex symbol is inevitable, as McWatt remarks: "Genetha inhabits a sexist society in which a woman's worth depends upon a physical relationship with a man."[3]

Left alone in the house, Genetha develops a terrified consciousness;[4] turbulent memories, morbid fears and anxieties haunt her constantly:

> Genetha woke from a dream of Esther sweating. All her family had, at one
> time or another, dreamed of the servant, filled with guilt at her out-of-hand
> dismissal. She looked around, expecting to find Esther in the room with her.
> But there was only the furniture in the bedroom lit by an unusually bright
> moon. . . . The next morning Genetha tried to recall her dream but remem-
> bered only the anxious awakening. All day at work she was dogged by the
> image of Esther's face, so much so that her closest associates noticed how
> preoccupied she was. (22)

At the time of the servant's dismissal she was a child and did not understand the reason for it, for her parents pretended it was Esther's decision. But
later, after her father lost his job as a result of widespread retrenchment in the
government service, he became less discreet and reproached his wife openly
for choosing to send away the more loyal of the two maids:

> Side by side with the fond memories of Esther grew a fear of her because she
> had been wronged. . . . And after that night when she heard her father thun-
> dering at her mother on the same theme and accusing her of "throwing the
> servant out into the cauldron of Georgetown" although she was from the coun-
> try and knew no one in town, she spontaneously found herself calling to mind
> Esther's dilemma. . . . She would wake up sweating from dreams of Esther . . .
> dogged by the image of the servant's face grey and gaunt. (22)

It is a few weeks after her first dream that Esther appears again in another
dream, "grey and gaunt", and asking Genetha for a loan of money; Genetha,
in a perpetual state of fear, and anxious to give some form of compensation
and dispatch Esther, offers her fifteen dollars, "as a gift, for all you did for me
and Boyie . . . and the rest of the family", to which Esther retorts:

> *You think fifteen dollars can pay me for all I did for your family? After I worked myself*
> *to the bone for you, your mother put me out on the street. Your Christian mother. You*
> *don't know how I live these last few years.* . . .
> Genetha put out her hand to touch the servant but she had vanished. She
> jumped up from the chair by the window. Had she been sleeping? (23–24;
> emphasis added)

Genetha is so unnerved and frightened by that vision that she rushes out of the house and waits for Fingers, whom she impulsively invites to live with her, imploring him never to leave her. When Esther actually comes to meet Genetha a few days later, uncannily, the events and tenor of conversation are similar to the dream.

In the cultural wilderness of the colony, her interests are narrow: work, church and Sunday school, and when boredom settles upon her, "a healthy boredom that afflicted most of her class" (3), Genetha turns to Michael for companionship (*One Generation*, 94). She meets this "tall, slim and downright ugly" worshipper at religious meetings, a stranger to himself with "his mask well adjusted like the revellers of the twenties on the eve of a new year" (10), a person with whom she has little in common. Michael masks "his lack of spirit with blind religious fervour" which he displays at religious gatherings.

Michael does not approve of the clothes Genetha wears, "by most standards conservative", nor of her love of the cinema, "an incipient vice" he denies her after they have gone out together for a few weeks. Convinced she is unattractive, Genetha does her best to please her uninspiring partner. She mistrusts the "model of marriage her parents had presented her, now relying on her own ideas of what her role as a potential wife ought to be", but does no better than her mother. She is prepared to be subservient to Michael, "to conceal her revulsion and listen dutifully to his boasting" and to suffer all his restrictions (*Genetha*, 8). While recognizing the "apparent absurdity of friendship with him" (*One Generation*, 95), she believes that "his uprightness was the uprightness of her dead parents", convinces herself that he appeals to "the genteel side of her upbringing" (*Genetha*, 10), and so will not give him up despite all his "noticeable shortcomings" (8). Against her expectations she not only grows attached to her egotistical partner but also becomes aware that as soon as he was certain of her affection and loyalty, he exercised power over her, "imposing his will on her with unexpected ruthlessness" (8).

The pressures of family continue to regulate her life and Genetha is obliged to heed the wishes of her brother, the male authority figure in the home, who would prefer his sister to maintain her class status and contemplate marriage to the cold, bloodless Michael, whom he considers superior to the shiftless Fingers, from whom she has turned away. Genetha is inclined to commit herself to this passionless symbol of puritanical uprightness only for the sake of maintaining her middle-class status, until one day, when she glimpses Fingers passing in the street outside, stirring old passions and desires within her, she abandons Michael, despite his desperate pleadings (12). The suffering displayed by Michael on their parting leaves Genetha with a sudden awareness of female power. She finds the courage to defy her brother and the pressures he brings to bear to maintain their middle-class status, and she settles for a partner who is less inhibited. Rohan's attempt to control his sister's life is only one testimony of the crippling pressures of family relationships that Genetha endures.

Turning away from the passionless Michael, Genetha finds herself in front of the Astor cinema, where a queue has formed for the night show and where she feels the distinct exhilaration of mingling with the community: "There was a certain excitement in rubbing shoulders with the crowd that slowly gathered, as the queue started moving she was impatient with anticipation" (13). Genetha longs to be a part of the pleasures of life, to belong to its freedom and its possibilities. Heedless of the consequences, she renews her relationship with Fingers, exchanging the dubious stability of marriage to Michael for libertine pleasure with Fingers, cognizant of the compromise in her social status.

Genetha has a romantic sense of freedom, fired by stories of pork-knockers, "who, once they have tasted the freedom of the bush there's nothing to come back to" (148). She is impressed by the tale of her uncle, who renounces the rules of the city and "takes off in the bush with a gun and a dog". Genetha's pursuit of independence is an ironic device used by Heath to discuss the problem of the quest for female self-realization in the trilogy. Meantime, one of Genetha's unmarried aunts constantly voices the author's position, reminding Genetha that it is the institution of the family upon which society is founded, for it guarantees the perpetuity of things: "The family before everything else. The individual is nothing. The family's everything" (6). Genetha embodies the predicament of the woman at mid-twentieth century, hard pressed to choose between individual freedom and self-reliance or commitment to marriage and home and, in this sense, epitomizes the centrality of female experience:

her father and brother's conduct had goaded her into setting out on the road
to freedom; but soon afterwards her father had died and Rohan went away,
precisely because of her show of independence. Then came the discovery that
she had not yet learned to use her freedom. . . . She remembered how Michael
had nearly broken down when she confessed to having no love for him; how
she looked on, refusing to accept the reality of his weakness, and how, as his
vulnerability was exposed by the fear in his eyes and the way he twirled his hat
in his fingers, she quivered with elation. (14–15)

Even though Genetha is seen as a defiant young woman, she proves to be
gullible, her sense of power short-lived, when Fingers comes to dominate her
life; he undercuts her with the "brutal affirmation of her father's and brother's
egoism" (15). In pursuit of his goal, her lover bides his time and "yielded with
a docility that was not in his character" when she proceeds to tyrannize him
with "countless little rules she inflicted on him in order to foster the illusion
of her mastery over the household" (27). She tires of his "temperamental
behaviour, interminable silences" and drunken outbursts, and orders him
out of her house, but a few days later, "unable to bear the loneliness", she
weakens and begs him to return, even though "she foresaw the outcome: she
would relax her vigilance, inevitably, and he, predator that he was, would soon
be digging his claws into her, reducing her to a proper state of subservience"
even in his own state of dependency (31). What she could not foresee while
she experienced a period of immeasurable happiness with Fingers was that
he would reduce her not merely to a state of subservience but to a state of
homelessness and poverty.

Genetha is not "prepared for her brother's fury" (1) when she boldly
informs him that she is consorting with his friend Fingers, the shiftless
snooker expert. The vehemence of Rohan's rejection of the unemployed
slum-dweller as an unsuitable lover for his middle-class sister is ironic and
underlines the contradictions in the society. She naively believes that Finger's
poverty and his lower-class origins are "no impediment to their association",
since Fingers is good enough to be her brother's best friend, with whom he
roams the streets and plays billiards in the gambling salons. Her brother's
duplicity therefore surprises her, for it means that a man can move freely
in the society without staining his reputation, whereas a woman's is judged
by stereotypical images of sexuality, shame, and guilt. In his rejection of

Fingers, Rohan reinforces the treacherous gap in class relations. Driven by her passions to disregard the power of blind class prejudice, Genetha again defies her brother, causing Rohan to leave the Queenstown home in disgust.

Rohan's abandonment of the home leaves Genetha betrayed and bitter, vulnerable and distrustful of all men:

> If he knew how much she loved him. . . . She loved him for their dead mother and feckless father, for Esther who had doted on him, for his friend who had seduced her – he could just spread his wings and fly away. . . . Every man she had known was selfish. He, Michael, her dead father. . . . Their selfishness was like a force that swept everything out of their way. She could never marry. . . . Never! (*One Generation*, 103)

Her lack of trust is rooted in the traumatic experiences with her family in a turbulent home, as she knew it in her youth, a place of violence and insecurity. She is unable to dismiss a remark her mother had once made: "The stability of the family had always been bought at the expense of women." Genetha notes that her mother, "having acted as a doormat all her married life, had not attained any worthwhile stability, either for herself or for the rest of the family" (43). Throwing aside all restraint and all that experience had taught her, Genetha falls in the path of Fingers and becomes the reputed wife of her brother's best friend (*Genetha*, 38).

The maverick character Fingers is the forerunner of a range of trickster figures who thrive in Heath's fictional world. Neither the image of him as "the forbidden face of Georgetown and Agricola which surged up out of the alleyways and cook shops" (10) nor the fact of his "lack of breeding" in any way diminishes Genetha's fulfilment of the pleasure instinct: "I've tasted the fruit of depravity and enjoyed it" (20). She reflected, "Her love was strong and beautiful. If it was sinful then she would embrace this sin and be glad of her happiness" (20) – words reminiscent of her father's debauchery, his enjoyment of his "sorties into depravity" (*From the Heat*, 76) in the first volume of the trilogy. In this sense, Genetha joins the cast of Heath's flawed, remorseless characters.

Genetha reflected that even as a schoolgirl she had been good out of fear. For her, "this silent suffering had become a part of the fabric of her behaviour and, in fact, she had ceased to suffer, and moved about in the world of grown-ups like a ghost in a peopled room . . . [but now] Something had exploded in her first experience with Fingers" (*Genetha*, 20). Yet, despite her outward show of rebelliousness, Genetha is inwardly a vulnerable and tormented young woman, wracked by self-doubt and guilt, conscious of the judgemental eyes of the Christian society around her and their verdict that her depravity "is in the blood" (16) when she settles in with Fingers as if they were married:

> Did people not say that lust had killed her father? And was it not she herself who accused Rohan of lusting after that woman in Vreed-en-Hoop? Would people not say that her lust had driven her to take up with Fingers? What she was doing was a thousand times worse than what Rohan had done. Besides, she was a woman. She closed her eyes and listened to the rain drumming on the roof. Voices started whispering incoherently and as they became louder the sound of the rain grew softer. In the end the voices were thundering at her: "Lust! Slut! Lust! Slut!" . . . and as they came nearer and she could see the faces behind them they turned out to be all women with bared teeth and hateful faces. (21)

Deliriously happy, for Fingers "had given her flowers of wickedness in handfuls, black orchids that gleamed like pearls" (20), like the proverbial sin-bearing blossom, Genetha is defiant of the moral authority of the church and packs away her Bible in a bottom drawer "without the slightest twinge of conscience" (16).

Genetha returns to the spiritual drought of the city after a brief season of "ineffable contentment" (47) in Morawhanna, torn between her determination to be an independent woman and her more urgent desire to be enslaved by Fingers. Her inner turmoil is matched by the social unrest in the streets of Georgetown and the agitation for political freedom: "The streets were teeming with people . . . since the Enmore sugar-estate riots [in 1948] when several people were killed or hurt by police bullets, political meetings had become commonplace" (62); both Genetha and the Guianese society are caught up in a symbiotic struggle for freedom and selfhood from a suffocating past.

Little does Genetha suspect that a pervasive class consciousness lurks just beneath the surface of seemingly decent behaviour, or that Fingers bears "a latent hostility to her class deep within him" (27). Stung by his initial rejection by Rohan, Fingers, the villain given free range in a pernicious society, plans "to play a false role and to rob Genetha in some way and then leave her". He returns to her "thirsting for revenge", so that however willingly she gives herself to him, he "still considers her to be aloof" (40). Even when "at times her talk of servants and her past was so irksome that he was taken by the desire to injure her in some way", he yields "with a docility that was not in his character" and bides his time, a posture which Genetha mistakes for "sympathy for her and her family" (27). However, she soon senses a change in Fingers and fears that her entire security hinges on this unstable character who "had changed and she could not bear the uncertainty of her position" (63). She intuits that she is "peering into a gulf which she always knew had never been bridged", that is, the unbridgeable chasm of class (63).

Genetha's baptism in the Barima River has not been the occasion of any lasting self-awakening, and the "undeniable influence" of Sybil,[5] the embodiment of the free woman whom Genetha meets at Morawhanna, comes to nothing, since the measure of self-knowledge gained during her brief visit to the hinterland has been neutralized by the pressure of parasitic relationships in the city. Her plans to socialize Fingers are idealistic and impossible. Under her brave exterior shell lies a frightened, vulnerable woman who must defer to a man without question, and thus she allows him to cheat her by readily signing over the title of her Queenstown family house to him on the pretext that he will effect repairs. Genetha is powerless to alter the colonial order of male hegemony and exploitation. A similar tale of female victimization is told in Jean Rhys's *Wide Sargasso Sea* (1966) of a young heiress, uprooted from the solid world she has known, cheated and emotionally destroyed by a husband whose only motive is to gain her wealth. Mittelholzer's eponymous antiheroine, Sylvia, is another emblematic figure of the same colonial disorder who is cheated of property after her father dies.

The shiftless Fingers, "skilled at nothing except billiards", is a dysfunctional product of a poisoned society. His villainy is linked to the oppressive social order in which he can see no progress by legitimate means. He feels the need to cheat someone to compensate for his own lack of self-worth and to fill a spiritual void within himself through the fraudulent acquisition of property. His crabbed mentality is a symptom of the corrosive power of class divisions rankling deep within colonial society. It will be remembered that Genetha's father is victimized by superior class forces, her mother is ostracized from within her own class and doubly victimized by her socially inferior husband,

and now Genetha comes to bear this cross inversely, cheated by a social inferior in revenge against her class – an unending cycle of toxic relationships endemic within the structures of colonialism.

This is an ironic repetition of an earlier misdeed, for the reader will recall that Armstrong in his perversity had cleverly cheated his sister out of this very property. Whereas in a Wilson Harris novel, material dispossession may be the occasion for spiritual awakening in a character, Heath is anxious to show that certain fundamental social institutions, such as home and family, are anchors to the individual and that their breakdown renders the character displaced and vulnerable. In the event, the shock and distress caused by the loss of her home results in hysteria and Genetha's brief stay at the mental asylum in New Amsterdam. Dogged by the stigma of the asylum, from which she is unable to recover, she never regains her place in the stratified middle-class society.

Homeless, jobless, Genetha is driven to the margins of society to survive in abject poverty. She slides from hovel to brothel, shunting between her aunts, barely managing on a series of low-paid jobs no middle-class person would consider: selling sweets at the Empire Cinema, working as a cashier in a Chinese grocer's shop in a side street, selling in various Lombard Street cake shops, and serving as a waitress in a dingy restaurant where the only remaining evidence of her middle-class status is her refined speech, which "made an impression" (*Genetha*, 112). Genetha finds accommodation in a rooming house in the slums of Georgetown, among drunkards and misfits, in the dereliction of the urban wasteland: the infamous Tiger Bay with its prostitutes, the "range-yards wrapped in gloom" (81) and the Ramsaroop poor-house in Albouystown, where all derelicts, social outcasts and remnants from sugar estates sharing an affinity converge, an adjustment that causes her no little anguish over her loss of place in middle-class society: "The area she now lived in was as alien as the people she was now forced to associate with. Late at night and in the early hours of the morning there was often shouting and hammering on doors, and sometimes there was fighting among customers of the rum shops, who left at closing time, besotted with rum. It was the quarter of the damned" (89).

Even though now homeless and desolate, Genetha still longs to connect with human fellowship and community:

Genetha could not bear to be alone. She put on an extra blouse and went out into the chilly night. . . .

She found herself walking in the direction of the sea wall, past the dingy shop-fronts of Upper Water Street. Her life was in a haze, she reflected. Before, there were landmarks by which her thoughts could pause: mother, father, a steady job, Boyie, even Fingers who had treated her like dirt. Esther was only a shadow from the past. . . . The uncertainty of the future gnawed at her inside. If her mother had been alive she might have pulled the "strings" she and her father talked about as being indispensable in securing a job. Alone, and dogged by her confinement at the mental hospital, she felt helpless and frightened. (89)

Genetha's process will continue to be examined through her relationship with Esther. Her "tenuous connection" with her mother's family really began with "her long stay with them in the wake of her mother's death" (5), when her father grudgingly gave his consent for her to go and when their "constant talk of superior things, like saffron and potted orchids" only served to widen the gap between them. Armstrong had never permitted his wife or children to visit the Davises and now Genetha remains "on her guard" when she visits her mother's family, "carrying deep within her a residue of her dead father's resentment, of the gulf that separates him from her mother's family . . . and Boyie who hardly knew them": "her mother's two sisters never failed to remind him [her father] of his origins in a hundred and one little humiliations. And for that reason he did everything he could to keep their family and his apart after his marriage . . . after that she did not dare speak of those relations in her father's presence" (5–6). Even now, as a grown woman, Genetha is met with a "frigid silence" (6) from her aunts whenever she happens to speak of her father. She is disillusioned by their hardened prejudice in the face of her desperate need for the embrace of family.

But now, homeless, Genetha "is drawn to these two ageing women, their hair streaked with silver" (7) for she is terrified at the prospect of destitution. If she is tempted to confide in her two maternal aunts, in the hope of being rescued, without disclosing her (euphemistically put) "mistake" with Fingers, their ambivalence and lack of warmth, despite their ironical mouthing about the importance of family, render accommodation within their home impossible: "Genetha could never cut through the undergrowth of dissembling that surrounded the things her [older] aunt said and the things she did"

(96). Disturbed by such ambivalence, Genetha is overwhelmed with grief, "as though someone close to her had died" (96). She intuitively realizes that what is dying is the family and her place within its illusory façade. In his autobiography Heath alludes to the importance of clinging to family, however flawed or imperfect, but reveals the truth in fiction.

The reality is that the protection of her aunts' home has saved her from a life on the streets for several months when Genetha has escaped Esther's grasp and her brothel, during which time she begins to regain her self-respect; however, upon discovery of her association with Esther's brothel, her aunts callously close their door to her and banish her from their respectable middle-class home, thus sealing her fate. Cut adrift, Genetha senses that her options for independence and selfhood are narrow: she "struggled with sleep that night as if her life depended on it; for it seemed that the last chance of maintaining her status as a decent person lay in keeping awake" (97).

Genetha's relationship with her paternal aunt has been no less tenuous ever since her father fractured the bond with his sister by cheating her of her home in Queenstown, to which he relocated his family. Her visits to this aunt are "out of duty", for even though her aunt had continued to occupy a room on the ground floor of the very house for years, "that had brought her no closer to them" (7). This unnamed aunt maintains her bitterness towards Genetha and her brother, who are daunted by her resentment: "Her obsessive conversation, which consisted of little else save her opinion of the Queenstown aunts and her dead brother's injustice towards her, had the effect of reducing the frequency of Genetha's visits" (7–8). Ironically, when the worthless Fingers cheats Genetha of the very house, she turns to this wronged aunt, "the last blood relative whose home was open to her" (158), but finds that her aunt is unsympathetic, as she has never been able to climb out of her poverty since that falling-out with her brother.

This episode again points to the perpetuation of a vicious cycle of exploitation and poverty in the society and the desperation of predatory characters to acquire property by unfair means to fill the emptiness within themselves. Her aunt, content to drift, now lives in a dilapidated building with "leaking sewage pipes in a rat-infested yard" (159), hidden behind two other cottages, in the congestion of the slums, for "the city was growing not outwards, but in its backyards, in its bowels as it were, at the expense of fruit trees and yard space"

(174). The burgeoning of the slums, attributed to the post-war movement of desperate labourers in search of work, adds to the existing wretchedness in the city and Genetha now finds herself living in these very slums. It is this (paternal) aunt who, when Gladys discovered her husband in a liaison with their servant, crisply summed up the reality of the patriarchal society: "It's a man's world. Women were not in a position to change it and were therefore obliged to accept it" (*From the Heat*, 94). Nothing has changed for Genetha's generation.

Through the powerful device of dreams Genetha's subconscious fears are replayed, including her revulsion at the prospect of "soiling herself" in prostitution, now the only avenue open to her:

> Then she relived the night when she went out with Esther and her two friends and met the beggar with his peremptory manner and wagging finger. The paper that blew in from the pavement alighted on her table, a paper smeared with filth which the others did not seem to mind. She turned away to avoid looking at it, but Genetha's companion picked up the paper and deliberately thrust it in her face, to the amusement of everyone in the restaurant. Then her younger aunt, Alice, appeared and led her out of the eating-place, away from her companions. (*Genetha*, 97)

Genetha struggles to keep a toehold in society as a homeless, independent young woman with no sympathy from the collective family that has bequeathed her a legacy of psychic pain and insecurity. Her relationship with family as a child incapacitates her from sustaining relationships in her adult life and, with no tangible support from family to steady her, Genetha is vulnerable to the evils of society.

It is not by coincidence that Esther surfaces at the very moment when destitution and ill health fill Genetha with "the sensation of abandonment" (*Genetha*, 79). Watching her downfall with macabre delight, Esther's timely "rescue", ironically, takes the form of inducting her into the world of prostitution as "the steely, implacable sky stared" (80) at her inevitable fate. This is the fulfilment of the deepest fear of Esther that Genetha carried all through the years, whether consciously or unconsciously. Esther's resurfacing drags Genetha back to the bitter past she is struggling to escape. Seeking revenge for the injustice done to her years ago, Esther makes it impossible for Genetha to transcend her troubled childhood, when she floated around as a spectator in an adult world she never understood.

In the vendetta society of Georgetown, Genetha is doomed, as Esther's thirst for revenge is strong. Esther's indignation is aroused by Genetha's inbred arrogance and contempt for the servant's métier: "She was prompted to curse Genetha and her family, but restrained herself" (82), fearing that she might drive her away without achieving her "goal" of inducting her into prostitution. It is a moment of enlightenment for both Genetha and the reader, as no one was ever sure if Armstrong had been sexually exploiting Esther while she lived with them, and when Genetha hurls insults at Esther, calling her "coarse", the servant replies: "Your father was coarse when your mother wasn't looking." The following exchange reveals Esther's bottled-up bitterness for the Armstrongs and their bigoted middle-class values:

> "Money is everything to you, isn't it?" Genetha suddenly asked Esther.
>
> "You'll soon find out if it's not everything," declared Esther, maintaining her show of indifference.
>
> "No, but it's everything to you, isn't it?"
>
> "Yes, you –" replied Esther, losing her composure. "And if your sweet man didn't rob you, would you be waiting now for me to put bread in your mouth?"
>
> "You're right, you know. Money is everything," said Genetha.
>
> "You needn't be sarcastic. It's your parents that taught me that first. I worked my fingers to the bone for your mother and she kicked me out. Then I realized how important money was. More important than loyalty and trust and such. . . . When people like your mother talk about loyalty and trust they meant my loyalty and my trust, not theirs. It's she, when all is said and done, who taught me to sell my body for sixpence on the racecourse. You remember how people used to say what a good Christian woman your mother was and your father didn't deserve her." (102)

Whereas a struggle of wills deepens into a state of continual warfare between the two women, a "peculiar relationship seemed to bind them together".

Ultimately, Genetha, a desolate figure, walks to the seawall to contemplate the collapse of her life as reflected in the vast emptiness of the Atlantic Ocean stretching before her: "Her life was in a haze . . . the uncertainty of the future gnawed at her inside . . . her brother was the only person she had in the world, so that once and for all she wanted to know where she stood with him" (89).

Subsequent news of Rohan's brutal demise at Suddie completely devastates her, so that for months afterwards she "lay on the brothel floor, drunk and half-naked" (98). Esther, also shaken by the news of Boyie, whom she had nurtured, has become hardened to life's cruel realities: "the last years had drained her of all sentimentality. Life had to go on" (101). Incidentally, Esther's brothel is in the heart of the city, tantalizingly close to the halls of justice.

As in Mittelholzer's novel *Sylvia*, where the antiheroine futilely tramps through the streets of Georgetown trying to escape the human sharks with whom her father once associated, so Genetha frantically traverses the streets of the soulless city determined to escape Esther's vengeful grasp. She flees the brothel and retreats to a hovel in Albouystown, a temporary respite from her tormentor where, even in her fallen state, she finds a peculiar satisfaction in her lonely existence, "for her soul was her own at least" (*Genetha*, 112). However, her progress to selfhood is further complicated by a censorious society that will not allow her to transcend her troubled past. When a workmate's brother recognizes her and discloses her past link with the brothel, Genetha is stung by rejection and "seized by a kind of elated hatred" for the rest of the world: "There was no one she could trust and was glad of it. All those she loved had died and all those she trusted had spurned her trust. From then on she intended to make her way through life alone and resist anyone's attempt at forming an association with her" (121).

Setting aside the linear events of the plot, the reader is left with a complex emotional drama of a young woman with a dim understanding of herself: "She could not understand who she was . . . struggling against the perpetuity of things . . . only in her dreams did Genetha glimpse that swarming world within her and a partial understanding of her nature" (137–39). The novel attempts to address this deficit in self-knowledge by exposing Genetha to a form of magic theatre similar to that employed by Herman Hesse in *Steppenwolf* (1927), in which surreal scenes enable the confrontation of the many and various aspects of the self which comprise the human entity. Drawn again "like a magnet" to Esther's brothel, she finds herself in a room and "suddenly the wall ahead of her became animated with indistinct shapes which gradually became clearer" (*Genetha*, 127). Incredible phantasmagoric images unfold before her eyes, recalling familiar scenes of her childhood days and her family home. Genetha is confronted with an erotic scene of herself and her brother when they were younger (127–31). She "shuddered at what she beheld but kept telling herself that it was not possible", denying the suggestion of suppressed incestuous feelings between them. Although there is no evidence in the text that this artistic form of psychotherapy has any significance for the alleviation of Genetha's condition of displacement and dispossession, one may conclude that it at least contributes to her self-awakening, her self-knowledge and her general acceptance of her place in the social order.

In defiance of society's rules and its puritan institutions, just as her father had rebelled against them in his time, Genetha flouts social conventions with her nightly prowls on Palpree Dam, where she picks up strange men and flaunts her sexuality. She decides that all her hurts and disappointments have been caused by men and she resolves to avenge herself on them: "The problems of her freedom, of her depravity as well, were all reflections of her life with men. . . . What was certain, however, was her resolve never to be hurt again. Every month she would seek out a stranger and entice him to Palpree Dam to assuage her own longings" (139).

As her mother had done two decades earlier, Genetha now rejects the imprisoning lives of her aunts on the Davis side, "the desert-like bareness, on which their very lifestyle was grounded, an absence of joy, of quarrels and reconciliations" (154–55). From her experience of "knocking around" the city, she gathers enough courage once more to attempt to break away from the stranglehold of both dysfunctional family and vengeful servant: "Somehow she must travel another road and if this was not possible she now had the will to end her life" (155). In every sense, Genetha's existence is an ironic repetition of her mother's, as the reader will recall that similar thoughts of suicide come to Gladys when she is left stranded on the seashore in the first volume of the trilogy. To seal her fate, Genetha's maternal aunts banish her from their respectable middle-class home upon discovering her association with a brothel. And so, ironically, it is Genetha who is now thrown "into the cauldron" of Georgetown and comes to experience a cruel repetition of Esther's fate, the fate of the unmarried woman in a class-structured city. It is worth mentioning that Heath's tragic tales of fallen characters in the trilogy lack self-indulgent prurience.

Genetha is emblematic of the human condition and its uncertainties: "Like the land surveyor who is unable to see further than a few yards above his head, that, for Genetha, represented the state of her self-knowledge" (139). She is only one of Heath's characters for whom many things remain incomprehensible. If reality itself remains much too complex for the protagonist to unravel, all the same, she revels in her rebelliousness: "Had her life in the brothel made her depraved? Or did the brothel uncover what was already there? She felt no shame at her conduct, only curiosity that it was in contrast to the behaviour of the women from her social class. . . . But in retrospect there was something heady about the depravity, the wanton disregard for the regulated life of the family" (139).

Losing her footing irrevocably in Queenstown society, Genetha moves back and forth between Esther's brothel and the anonymity of the slums of Albouystown, left to find a more inconspicuous refuge "among the new wave of East Indians arriving from the sugar estates than among her own people, one of whom sooner or later would point a finger at her" (163). She walks the streets, a pitiable figure, "head down, haggard and overcome with an indescribable fatigue. . . . All her liaisons were strewn in the wake of the present like jetsam, becoming smaller and smaller with the increasing distance", with even the memory of Boyie receding now like "the swift flight of a small bird" (164). This paves the way for Esther to renew her efforts to claim her prey with "the sunken eyes and premature lines on her dried-out face", while Genetha vehemently rejects the servant's claim on her: "I have nothing, but I'm free" (172).

In the desperate struggle for self, Genetha rejects Esther and her gifts of food: "Put it all back in your dirty bag and get out of here! . . . Everything about you is vulgar . . . take your hatred and old resentments to the men you've gone with" (174). Esther, for her part, is outraged that "the enormity of Genetha's mother's conduct" should be trivialized in such a way and this only increases her determination to destroy Genetha.

Ironically, the Catholic Church, with "its scent of incense, its mysteries and, above all, its weeping candles" (165), where the battered young woman turns for rescue, executes the ultimate betrayal. Emotionally and physically frail and weary of life, Genetha is stalked and raped by the priest and, after this violation, she abandons her struggle for independence and concedes the impossibility of salvaging her life in the poisoned city.

When Genetha returns to the brothel, the erstwhile servant "could not conceal her astonishment" at her appearance: "The greyish white corners on her mouth, the thin, whip-like body and the slightly bent shoulders caused her to hesitate, as when, after an absence of several years, a man sees his mother again, ravaged by age, and draws back momentarily, believing he is mistaken, but on closer scrutiny discovers the features he knows and loves so well" (125).

This work is an indictment against the church, questioning its ambiguous role in the struggle of the colonized for freedom. It challenges religion to come up with a viable vision of society, a vision that is not egotistic, exploitative and dogmatic, but one that is compassionate to human ideals. The reader will recall that, in the first volume of the trilogy, Genetha's father is transported to a deeper awareness by "the infectious singing and the sound of tambourines" of the religious folk meetings held at the street corner: "such things stirred his heart. And these were the very things that separated them" (*From the Heat,* 147) and created schisms in society, so that in Heath's novels so far examined, the established Christian church has a strong presence but remains aloof to the spiritual needs of multicultural colonized peoples generation after generation.

Broken and battered on the wheel of a skewed Georgetown morality, and unaccommodated in society, Genetha yields to her inevitable fate in Esther's brothel, a pervasive feature in an independent Guyana where poverty continues to blight the souls of women and drive them into prostitution. Anaesthetized by disappointments and grief, Genetha finally comes to accept life's sleight of hand: "She felt she had come to the end of a long journey, arriving at a place where she was to be cleansed, to be freed from all notions of happiness and unhappiness, pain and exhilaration" (*Genetha,* 186).

The work ends with more ironic reversal of the class paradigm: a high-colour young woman from a middle-class family is now a prostitute and lives in complete anonymity in a brothel; a house of ill repute is now a place of refuge and a community of a sort, ironically, a safe haven for a woman levelled by a vindictive society. The supreme irony is that Esther, who had been Genetha and Rohan's emotional anchor in childhood, who sustained them "with her resourcefulness . . . and loved them as if they were her own" (*From the Heat,* 64), is now the agent of Genetha's final degradation.

All of Genetha's social relationships are based on the colonial pattern of exploitation, of male power and female subjugation, and this novel under-scores the impossibility of the single woman escaping its inevitable doom. Her avenues to freedom are all problematic. Genetha's story is given depth when seen against the background of her mother's failed aspirations exam-ined earlier. Her destiny proves to be a fulfilment of her mother's worst fears in the first volume of the trilogy: "Was that really all there was to life for women? To breed children and obey their husbands? Was little Genetha's life to be a repetition of her own? What would be her lot?" (*From the Heat*, 45). There is no doubt that Genetha hardly fares better than her mother, despite the fact that her status as a single woman allows her to exercise her free will. Her struggle for selfhood is heroic even if she does not present as a heroic figure in the end. Armstrong's lack of sympathy for his daughter, whom he perceives as the beneficiary of social change favouring women of her genera-tion – "she went out to work and met people, a privilege her mother never enjoyed" (*One Generation*, 61) – is misplaced in this patriarchal society.

Just as the death of his father brought Armstrong his freedom, but brought his sister "a kind of enslavement to his memory" (*From the Heat*, 158), so Genetha, in a cruel repetition of her aunt's life, is strapped to the bitter memo-ries of her parents and their dysfunctional lives. Genetha's life, then, is a deep-ening of her family's: that of her mother, who takes a chance with a husband below her social class, and of her brother, who steps outside his class and racial boundaries and heedlessly trespasses into forbidden space at Suddie. The Armstrongs and their children founder in the volatile, polyglot society, whose undercurrents and dynamics sweep them away in its immutable tide.

Moreover, the cruelties inflicted by slave masters under the colonial dis-pensation (including the church) are now perpetuated by fathers, husbands, brothers, boyfriends and other close relations in a callous society founded on the violence of plantation culture. Whereas the crux of Genetha's predicament is "freedom and the secret of a settled mind" (*Genetha*, 148), the novel seems to suggest that the real meaning of female independence in colonial Guiana is to be homeless, adrift and unanchored. Genetha struggles to reconcile herself to the notion that society can offer her nothing loftier than a place in a brothel, but this does not prevent her from appreciating the beauty of the natural world: "she woke up on the porch and saw the houses and offices opposite smeared with the colours of morning. . . . The sound of birdsong had awakened her, the warbling of canaries singing from their cages as if they were free" (185).

While *Genetha* deepens the burden of the trilogy, whose protagonists all rebel against the status quo and who are consumed by intense passions and unfulfilled desires, the trilogy recaptures the lives of the directionless Armstrongs, blowing like straws in the wind, trapped in crippling relationships with no possibility of escape except in death.

In spite of the palpable existential distress of Heath's antiheroes, it is possible to discern in the narratives glimpses of genuine community spirit at varying levels of the society and a wholesome feeling for the land, as evidenced on Genetha's release from the New Amsterdam mental asylum, when she passes through a succession of villages on her way back to the unwelcoming city:

> The swampy land and the lonely houses appealed to her. . . . On the steps of one house, which was leaning heavily to one side, about a dozen persons were sitting, ranging in age from about two or three to about seventy; and the harmony of the group had had a profound effect on her that she looked back and watched the house until it went out of sight behind a clump of trees.
>
> Two women, bent double in a large field, were collecting cow dung in baskets, while a herd of cows grazed placidly on the sparse grass. Then came the coconut plantation, an endless succession of palms along the border of which ran a trench overgrown with weeds and water hyacinth. Occasionally the road came close to the sea defence wall, so that the expanse of mud and sand could be seen, broken here and there by shimmering puddles or long stretches of courida bushes. Every now and then a koker rose from the flat, featureless landscape, its sluice gate raised to let out the drainage water. This was her country, this sprawling, sea-beleaguered land; the roar of the sea by night, the heat of the sun by day would follow her wherever she went, as would the trenches, the wild eddoes, the dark folk and the tamarind. (91–92)

Even though *Genetha* culminates in human defeat and failed relationships, in betrayal, revenge and unmitigated loneliness, the reader is enriched by the experience, by the humaneness of the antiheroine and by her courage in her pursuit of selfhood. The triumph of the entire work is its psychological realism and the integrity of individual experience. The texts of the trilogy offer a picture of flawed and vulnerable characters who fail to understand themselves, who are surprised by their own actions, and who fail to understand their place in the colonial disorder. Yet they offer a vision of the simultaneous quest for freedom and for community, and what must be praised in the third volume is Genetha's tireless and energetic struggle, however flawed, to find a place in society as a single and independent woman. Carol Rumens's statement that "The whole trilogy is a masterly piece of sustained narrative which by its unflinching focus on an ordinary family's hopes and struggles, quietly achieves political resonance too"[6] is relevant, considering that the trilogy looks forward to *A Man Come Home* and *The Murderer*, two novels that look to a new order of society, human relationships and cultural values in a newly independent state.

6

A MAN COME HOME AND *THE MURDERER*
The Novels of "Independence"

> Plantation – feudal coast!
> Who are the magnificent here?
> Not I with this torn shirt
> —Martin Carter, "Not I with This Torn Shirt"

Literary criticism has so far failed to grasp Heath's essential thrust in the Guyanese novel. This has caused all his novels, beginning with his first two published novels, *A Man Come Home* and *The Murderer*, to have been generally read and criticized in ways that hardly do justice to the depth of psychosocial realism that has come to characterize Heath's work. We attempt in this study to critically examine Heath's novels and offer readings of them in ways they have not been read before.

Jean D'Costa's review of Heath's first published work, *A Man Come Home*, alludes to its linguistic feats: "the writer's technique of deceptively simple language; his taut and economical style in developing characters as, 'Bird drifted in . . . as usual'; the use of dialogue in plot development; and a faithful representation of the language behaviour of the 'yard'". D'Costa also notices the psychologically fascinating characters the reader encounters in this work: "The psychological realism of the characters is as strong as the authenticity of their language behaviour." It is one of the rare perceptive interpretations of Heath's craft and even though the intervening years have seen Heath produce an entire oeuvre in the same mode, criticism has failed to follow up this rich lead.[1]

Heath's novels have attracted harsh critical comments: for instance, his second published novel, *The Murderer*, examined in this chapter, has received ambivalent remarks. One critical opinion dismisses its introspective protagonist as "unlikeable" and faults the work for "technical misjudgment and clumsy writing",[2] while another claims "its proportions are wrong, style is ungainly, and the reader feels little sympathy for the character . . . but the work is impressive"[3] and, again, "characters go almost undeveloped [and] in essence this can be seen as Heath's early wrestling with the fictional form".[4]

A Man Come Home and *The Murderer* are referred to in this work as novels of "independence" because both examine the viability of independence through the disorder created by the collapse of empire and the failure of the promise contained in the notion of independence. In this respect the texts cover similar ground to V.S. Naipaul's novel *In a Free State* (1971), which examines the implications of freedom in an African state and the resulting chaos when the old order is shattered at independence and the free man is led only by his own passions and instincts. In Heath's novels the social and cultural structures through which a free people might subsist psychically and define themselves as a society that coheres have not yet begun to take shape in the transition between the end of empire and the functioning of a new independence; thus they depict a people mired on the threshold of a new order that is yet to evolve. The dilemma of Guyanese society at the dawn of political independence unfolds through the consciousness of characters whose submerged experiences reveal the irony of "independence" at both the individual and the national levels.

What Elsa Goveia describes as the "white-black scale of dependence"[5] in colonial societies imposed a stable and predictable order, however unjust that order might have been, but the constitutional and legal dismantling of that scale has left the individual and the society in a void, trapped in postures and mental attitudes that indicate a malignant and crippling interiorization of the old order.

This chapter examines the experiences of psychologically convincing characters and their social relationships, caught on the threshold of independence, and how they negotiate the void in their quest for individual freedom. Heath relied on the institution of the family to structure his novels and to illustrate the symbiotic relationship between the lived lives of ordinary people and the formal structures of society. These two novels of "independence" recreate the euphoria that suffused the nation momentarily – in expectation of the possibilities promised by native leaders – as well as the tragic efforts to transcend the deep psychological scars inflicted on the psyche by slavery and the brutal plantation system, indentureship and colonialism.

In *A Man Come Home*, Egbert Foster was still a little boy when "his father had promised him that the country would one day be free" and thus he has waited "half a lifetime in anticipation" of this auspicious moment to celebrate his status as a free man (1). The opening imagery of the work finds Foster, now a fifty-year-old artisan, swelling with pride on Independence Day in Guyana (26 May 1966), credulously savouring the occasion, the new Guyana flag fluttering overhead in the wind and his heart fluttering within his sanguine frame as he raises, lowers and raises the symbol of freedom over the porch of his modest cottage, one degree above the tenements and range-yards occupied by the other characters in the work. The opening paragraph closes with anticlimax: "Foster's dog sat under the flag, scratching itself languidly as the afternoon light faded" (1) – an image that is absurdly unequal to the historic occasion and mocks the high note of optimism established in the opening line. Heath's playful satire, achieved through the skilful control of dialogue, also serves to emphasize the level of awareness (or lack of it) among ordinary people evolving to a state of self-determination:

> "I like it, man! I like it! Is what?" Foster's neighbour asked from the other side of the fence.
> "How you mean is what? Is the flag!"
> "We flag? The country flag?" the neighbour asked again.
> "Yes! You ignorant bad, you know. All my children and grandchildren know this flag." (1)

What differentiates Foster from his next-door neighbour, who lives in blissful unawareness of the new flag or its symbolism, his life filled with more mundane concerns such as keeping track of his "no good wife", is the vast gap between their expectations. However, even with his awareness of the historic change in the constitutional arrangements of the country, Foster is nonetheless woefully impotent to bring his idealisms to realization.

The Murderer also opens on a high note of optimism, with its antihero, Galton Flood, in pursuit of individual freedom in a colony that has recently been granted political independence. The Floods are an average middle-class family and all that is known of them is what is gleaned from the narrator in relation to the flawed social conditioning of their son, Galton, a character whose ego development is incomplete. The deaths, early in the work, of a long-suffering father and a domineering mother ostensibly free Galton from the confines of family. Intending to give definition to his newly found freedom, he flees the narrowness of his suburban Kitty existence "to begin life anew, as it were" (*Murderer*, 13), a parody of a newly independent country attempting to begin anew to chart its own terms for self-determination. Heath's notion of freedom is a renewal of the human spirit to underpin the promise of independence, but as Galton explores the possibilities for freedom and self-determination, he meets only contradictions and malignancies that necessitate brutal actions before dramatic changes can come to the individual and to society. *The Murderer* is a tale of just such a struggle for freedom and identity and Galton Flood is a metaphor for a dysfunctional society strapped to a deformed past.

Both works examine the vacuum created by the granting of independence and the flawed human relationships that mirror a society whose collective psychic failure is rooted in the conventional morality of the mother country, the borrowed images that persist from the old dispensation and subvert the process of the new nation.

Heath's portrayal of a fundamentally flawed independence is deepened by the picture of poverty sustained by Clive Thomas in *The Poor and the Powerless* (1988), a work whose central burden is to examine the trail of poverty left by colonialism and propose structural reform of the economy for self-sustaining growth.[6]

These two novels deepen the picture of social misery articulated by Carter in 1953, when British Guiana made its first attempt at self-government but had its constitution suspended by Britain:

> is the university of hunger the wide waste.
> is the pilgrimage of man the long march.
> The print of hunger wanders in the land . . .
> Twin bars of hunger mark their metal brows

twin seasons mock them
parching drought and flood[7]

The fictional world examined in this chapter, recognizably British Guiana, stands at the dawn of independence still bound to the old plantation culture and a repetition of old authoritarian relationships that make rising out of economic and spiritual impoverishment a daunting experience.

Heath's massive first novel, now known as the trilogy, was still unpublished when he embarked upon a new work that might find favour with his publishers. *A Man Come Home* appeared in 1974, the same year Carter addressed the eighth convocation ceremony at the University of Guyana (eight years after the country gained independence) and complained of a thwarted process that subverts society's quest for identity:

> Something seems to have gone awry with that process of metamorphosis, which, if we are to accept what our leaders tell us, should transform us from what we function as – an aggregation of begging, tricking, bluffing, cheating subsistence seekers and assorted hustlers – into a free community of valid persons, each of whom has existed in a way we have come to conceptualise as, at least one, among other, higher modes of being, where the essence of staying alive means fulfilment of self and self-realisation: which when achieved ceases to remain merely the accomplishment of a competence but goes onward to the acquisition of the status of a function of the personality; a function which consummates itself in the enrichment of every self that participates with it in the creation of a free community of valid persons.[8]

It is as if the two writers are speaking to each other, Heath with his ironic novel of "independence" and Carter questioning whether the granting of political freedom is matched by the psychic transformation necessary for a clichéd society of predators and victims to become a "free community of valid persons". Through one of his characters in *A Man Come Home*, Heath too questions whether a society newly emerging from colonialism can advance to freedom upon a defective morality and flawed self-image of the people:

> Muriel stopped listening and got tangled in the strands of her own reflections. There were times when she wished that Gee was a butcher, so that he would bring home meat instead of bread. Meat could be sold; but no one would give you anything for bread. What did not come from the baker was judged to be stale. Her next-door neighbour's children had that healthy, smooth appear-

ance of the meat eater. In addition to the scraps her father was given he managed to steal chunks of beef when his employer went home and left him in
charge of the stall. The whole yard knew what he was up to and though they
envied him, did not begrudge him his good luck. When he sold Muriel the
beef he had stolen she had to pay nearly as much for it as for the meat in
the market. . . . When people with money thief and build big house with the
money nobody can touch them; but when poor people thief a pound of beef
people throw their hands in the air and shout for he to go to prison. . . . If Gee
had taken her advice he would have stolen everything he could lay his hands
on in the baker shop. And the oven would have been left only because it could
not be dismantled. (102–3)

The characters who populate Heath's "independence" novels are all vainly
in search of Carter's "free community of valid persons". Heath shifts his
focus from the preoccupations of the trilogy – skin colour, race, social status
and coloured middle-class morality in Queenstown – to the depressed wards
of south Georgetown and the condition of the working-class coloureds at
the dawn of independence, successfully evoking a "yard realism" of raw and
riotous living.9

A Man Come Home reinterprets the experiences of two generations of the
Foster family: Foster and his son Bird grapple with the notion of independence and attempt to work out what freedom means to each of them. This
novel can be said to have a double plot: the first is built around Foster, his
younger and attractive common-law wife, Christine, and their adolescent
daughter, Melda, all of whom live on Princess Street, just around the corner
from where Heath grew up on Drysdale Street, a stone's throw from the koker
at Princess and Lombard Streets. It recounts Foster's efforts, or lack thereof,
to salvage his life from poverty and dependency in fulfilment of the promise
of independence. The high point of Foster's purposeless days is to leave his
home ritually at four o'clock every afternoon to commune with friends at the
barbershop.

The second plot centres on Bird, Foster's son by his first marriage, a
dreamer to whom work is anathema: "the sight of labour revolted him" (7).
Bird lives with his girlfriend, Stephanie, not far off in a tenement yard on
Broad Street, "among old bicycles, kerosene drums, baskets and old car tyres
that littered the yard", where, during the rainy season, "the stepping stones
are submerged and only the drums are visible" (31), an evocative image

that speaks to the precarious existence of the poor coloureds of the society. Another of Foster's five sons, Benjy, who has fled the colonial stagnation and lives in Canada, supplements Foster's meagre income with periodic remittances, of which Foster lives in constant anticipation. Benjy's supposed success in Canada awakens unrestrained jealousy in Bird. The crisis in the work is sparked off by news that Benjy has acquired a house in Canada, news that disturbs Foster, since the monthly remittances will cease, but not as much as it rankles deep within the shiftless Bird and sets off a train of events that change his life irrevocably.

The character Gee, a mutual friend perversely involved in the lives of both households, links the families of Foster and Bird. Gee lives with his wife, Muriel, in the squalor of a Bent Street range-yard, quite close to the city jail, in a one-room enclosure. It is worth noticing that within Gee's range-yard lives another shiftless, unnamed friend who, like Bird, has "hardly ever worked and was continually in and out of prison" (118). These characters encapsulate the issue of the invisible poor in the city and the impossibility of finding a way out of poverty at the dawn of independence. Always cash-strapped, Gee gives Foster a glimpse into his wretched existence of desperation and futility: "You lucky you got Bird to help you out. By Wednesday my money does run out and from Thursday till Saturday we live 'pon credit" (68). Through Gee's consciousness is filtered a dismal portrait of a new and hopeful nation left to work out its self-sufficiency from a position of pennilessness and utter hopelessness:

> "What else can a man do but drink, drink? . . . What kind of ass hole [sic] world is this, eh? Rain, liquor or the hot sun beating down 'pon you and eating you blood up. Shit! . . . I could'a gone to Canada and make money over there. I don't know. . . . If it in't Muriel sawing away at me balls, is worrying 'bout keeping you job."
>
> Gee was overwhelmed with bitterness at his wasted life . . . disgusted by the appearance of the range yard, with its row of rooms canting on crooked pillars. Once inside, he made up his mind to finish the bottle of rum alone . . . one by one the lights went out. (71–72)

Benjy's reported success shocks Bird into recognition of his own dysfunction, deftly captured in the flow of his reflections that mirrors his flawed perceptions of social mobility and selfhood:

No single incident or remark had ever brought home so forcibly the fact that he, Bird, had wasted his life. . . . He sat down by the river and thought over the bit of news he had just heard. Benjy rich? Benjy, of all people. If Benjy had got rich anybody could make money. Suppose he took it in his head to come to Guyana, he would see him floundering without a suit of clothes or a cent in the bank. . . . There was a shortcut to the acquisition of wealth and he would have to find it. (6–7)

There is a connective thread running deep between Bird and Gee, who have shared a life of abject poverty since boyhood and whose twisted lives bring to realization the theme of an "urban angst" that Heath is possibly intent on exposing. Barely schooled – Bird and Gee both "left school at the age of twelve, Gee to deliver bread on a carrier bicycle and Bird to devote his time to a life of sloth" (55) – these friends gravitate to the vicarious pleasures of rum and sex, with an eye on the "quick-fix" solution to easy wealth, escaping into the fantasy of tall tales of bravado and boasting of imaginary travels to foreign lands (58). A young generation is deemed to be the future of a nation, but Bird's band of youths is stagnated, with no capacity to contribute to nation-building. They have lost their way in this tale, still trapped in postures of dependency and lacking the self-knowledge necessary for achieving selfhood.

In this context, Bird's urgent desire for material possessions, as a measure of freedom and success, and his dependence upon the fantasy of a mythical Water Maid for escape from an embarrassingly crippling poverty become understandable. In a landscape of abundant rivers, creeks and trenches, water images pervade the canvas of Heath's fiction and, in plotting Bird's escape from poverty, Heath employs a cultural artefact whose stranglehold of Bird fuels the drama of this novel. Bird seeks the solitude of the riverbank to contemplate his plight and to be in communion with the mysterious and feared Water Maid, a jealous woman trapped in the body of a sea creature, who gains a central place in the plot. As Bird is a character who is not given to much self-examination, the reader is permitted no insight into his raw reflections.

Myth and folklore are powerful shaping influences on the human psyche, and Bird's version is built on the notion that the Water Maid, with her legendary powers, is the agent of the newly found wealth he exhibits after long and unexplained absences from his range-yard home: expensive clothes, gold jewellery, a new motorcar and a large house on residential Brickdam, the scene of lavish parties. He considers himself "married" to this magical river fantasy and wears around his neck a symbol of his betrothal: "a gold chain, from which hung what appeared to be a nugget which, on closer examination, was seen to be a representation of a skull with deeply gouged-out eye sockets" (42). Caught in a trap between the belief of a mythical wife and the reality of daily existence with a real woman, Bird becomes a divided and tormented man. Crisis develops when he defies the myth and proceeds to marry Stephanie, for fear of losing her, at a wedding that only a few guests are courageous enough to attend – "the little church was practically empty . . . the wedding reception a dismal affair" (97–98) – an indication that, by and large, society's response to myth is instinctively one of incomprehension and fear.

Foster's self-esteem has been severely compromised, ironically, by social progress – the Pure Water Supply Scheme has made his skills in vat-making and vat-repairing redundant, rendering Foster not only without income but emotionally choked, with "a lump in his throat" when he is reminiscing with friends and reliving the pride he once felt in his work. As a lampshade-maker, his creative spirit derives no fulfilment, "his heart was not in it . . . it lacked the warmth and poetry of wood. . . . Perfection required that the spirit should soar" (12). Foster's prospects of financial independence and self-fulfilment become more remote with the advent of independence.

Foster's fragile thoughts and feelings about self and self-fulfilment are complicated by his relationships in the home with his wife and his daughter, relationships which he can scarcely manage and which emphasize his ineffectualness in the sterile society. Heath's spare, dispassionate style, and the short, abrupt chapters of *A Man Come Home* and *The Murderer* frame the disjointed existences of his characters. Wilson Harris has aptly described Heath's style as one that "truncates emotion";[10] Heath discloses: "In these early works, the writing is very succinct, the compression extraordinary. I aimed for subtlety."[11] In this deft style, Foster's apathy is palpably brought home when his daughter announces a date with a sexual predator at the workplace:

> "You don't like the job?" Foster asked Melda.
> "No, but I can't do nothing else."
> "And what you school friends all doing?"

"Selling, most of them," Melda replied.

"This man, he nice?" Foster asked her.

"I don't know. Is the first time he going out with me. He go out with three of the girls already. Now is my turn."

"What? You mean . . ." Foster began.

"What's wrong?" Melda asked, her mouth falling open.

He hesitated, then said, "I didn't say nothing wrong."

Foster lifted the last mouthful of food to his mouth with less relish than the others. (*Man*, 3–4)

Unprepared for his daughter's emotional growth and burgeoning sexuality, even though clearly aware of the perniciousness of the society, Foster barely manages a feeble response – "I hope you know what you doing" – and fails to take a firm hand to prevent the sexual exploitation of his daughter: "he switched on the light, intending to read the newspaper he had brought from the barber shop. Instead, he lit a cigarette, sat down at the window . . . and gazed out on an empty street" (4). Foster is an emasculated colonial whose aspirations are undercut by his own deformed will and one of the triumphs of the text is the author's skill in executing a prose that is innocuous on the surface but mined with layers of meanings and compassion.

On the other hand, the unexpected happens in the mother-daughter relationship within this fictional family. Christine, initially elated that her daughter is able to attract a man and "settle" her future, is now shattered at her daughter's sneering announcement that she is expecting a baby. Apart from the social stigma an illegitimate child brings, there are consequences for their impecunious economic condition and, in a fit of uncontrolled anger, Christine brutalizes Melda, causing her to suffer a miscarriage and a nervous collapse: "If only Melda had not smiled. The bonds that connected them from the night of the girl's birth until then had snapped with that sneer. . . . Snatching the brush from Melda she brought it down on her head and back several times . . . until she fell to the floor at her mother's feet. Only then did Christine stop. . . . She looked down at her daughter's body, uncaring and unfrightened" (36).

The post-independence society is heir to a culture of violence that has been internalized across the society, of which Christine's savagery, ironically understated, is symptomatic: "Recalling Foster's words about her gentleness she let the brush drop to the floor" (36).

Even though Heath does not reproduce Foster's thoughts and feelings directly, he uses an omniscient narrator to keep the reader informed. Foster cuts a vulnerable figure, while the reader continues to draw a blank on his thoughts and must be content with the narrator's description of a frightened, isolated figure set against the eerie landscape of St Philip's churchyard, with its shadowy trees and the unearthly howling of dogs, as he suffers the consequences of his weakness:

> At three o'clock in the morning Foster left his house like a thief. In his right hand was a paper bag, in which Christine had put the afterbirth, wrapped up in brown paper. After making sure there was no one in the street he walked down to the koker and threw the bundle into the river. He then folded the bag, and dropped it into the murky water as well. . . . The water in Princess Street was lower than he had ever seen it. . . . On arriving home he realised that he was shivering. With trembling hands he poured himself a shot of X-M rum and downed it in one gulp. (39–40)

In his apathy, Foster continues to turn a blind eye to what is going on around him, essentially, to Gee molesting his half-demented daughter whenever Foster takes his daily escape to the barbershop. Foster is blind to this assault on his pride as a man. Gee is one of Heath's raw and sensuous creatures who use sex as just another means of depredation in a vulturous society. Heath's characters sport their sexuality unabashedly. Erotic scenes and passions, never prurient or self-indulgent, permeate the canvas of his grim tapestries as if in defiance of the dominant Victorian morality, but, as D'Costa observes, this never reduces the work to the banal:

> Significantly, the character's inner experience is authentic and central to the vision of the work even when scenes of sexuality and violence threaten to reduce the work to the banal. . . . The emphasis on character and on the character's interpretation of the experience rob these scenes of pornographic qualities . . . all gratuitous sensationalism is excluded. . . . Motivation and psychological reaction are the main goals: the mother's inchoate emotions exploding into action and gesture, the conflict in Christine's own personality.[12]

Melda, a victim of her parents' docility, "cooped up in the house all day and every day, except for visits to church", actually looks forward to Gee's predatory visits "with an avidity bordering on hysteria" (*Man*, 78). Christine, too, falls prey to the trickster Gee, as gleaned in this suggestive gesture: "Gee breaks off the end of the newly baked malt loaf [he has brought her], spread some butter on it and bit into its sweet, soft pulp" (81), a sensuous image that anticipates his lecherous intentions.

The following exchange between Foster's wife and his daughter-in-law, Stephanie attests to Foster's blindness to the welter of confused feelings welling up in his wife, feelings she can scarcely understand or control, including her desire to project herself as sexually marketable:

> "You see," Christine observed, "I can't even make conversation no more. I loss me discretion. . . . Gee say I don't got discretion."
> "Who?" asked Stephanie.
> "Gee," she repeated.
> "Bird friend?" asked Stephanie.
> "Yes," replied Christine, hesitantly.
> The two women looked at each other. Stephanie was more puzzled than interested. Christine tried desperately to find something to say in order to save the conversation. (124–25)

Trapped in a marriage with an older man, Christine is both angry and jealous of Gee's attentions to Melda, while Foster continues to delude himself that "he was lucky with his women" (15). The reader is not afforded more insight into Christine's consciousness and must conclude that this character has been used to illuminate the symptom of unawareness in the degraded society.

Foster's most abysmal failure is perhaps with his idle son Bird, whom he describes as a "dreamer, he did always want a good life. . . . Things did come to him so easy. He did prefer to hang round the men and listen to them talk big" (20). Foster is in self-denial about his role in Bird's stunted growth and dysfunctional adulthood, and at Bird's homecoming party Foster brashly associates himself with his son's success without questioning how Bird has come by such wealth: "Foster lost no opportunity to be by his side, so that guests would know that he was Bird's father" (42). Foster can best be described as a casualty of colonialism invested with a weak ego, but, to his credit, self-awakening comes to him, rather late in the work, and he ultimately breaks out of his apathy, hopefully to regain control of his life.

Bird's illusion about his place in society as a wealthy man is challenged by his relationship with Stephanie. When every rational explanation for his prolonged absences eludes her, she resorts to consulting a high-priced card-cutter, part of the subculture of Guyana with its unofficial healers and problem-solvers who perpetuate the colonial exploitation. The cultural tapestry of the work is enriched by a local version of an African survival: the folk figure of a nameless obeahwoman turned card-cutter and backstreet abortionist. This dubious character[13] inhabits a corner of the post-colonial wasteland, a "vast and gloomy" house on Adelaide Street in Georgetown, a cross-street near the gate of the cemetery "with its endless rows of gravestones which stretched as far as the eye could see" (30). Heath recreates not the vast, inscrutable land-scape of the country but a ghostly realism that deepens the picture of failure and doom with his directionless characters floundering in the urban void.

Bird returns to the city, seemingly as a result of the card-cutter's interven-tion, but with altered mood and circumstance, so that Stephanie's apprehen-sion that "his homecoming had brought with it pain and anxiety" (44) is justified, for, looking hale and hearty, "full of swank and money" (45), amid a blaze of music and partying, Bird announces glibly that he is buying a large house on residential Brickdam because "I couldn't stand being poor no more" (44). Stephanie, a would-be artist who believes in the work ethic and in the purposeful harnessing of human potential, exclaims: "A man should have a job, though; it not natural to be on one long holiday" (20). Stephanie is spiritually poles apart from Bird, the hustler. With their clashing values, they are metaphors of a dichotomized society in transition. She feels betrayed by his obsession with the quick fix of easy wealth and attempts to discourage his materialistic instinct: "But what you want house for? If you get it you going to have to get clothes to go with it and furnitures and a lot of useless things. . . . Money only does bring trouble . . . my life not going to be worth living" – and "a gloom settled over the room" (8–9). Stephanie is simply contented with the experience of being and with her own fragile feelings, especially those that surge whenever Foster visits her: "Her heart was filled with an inexplicable hatred for him and for Bird's stepmother with whom she had had very little contact. Whenever Bird spoke about them she used to fall silent, knowing that whatever she said would only express her dislike. He spoke of them less and less as time went by. Occasionally, when they all met at Ada's, Stephanie would sit in a corner and say little" (22).

For all its mystery and surreal atmosphere, the work remains anchored in realism and Bird's tale that a Water Maid is the source of his wealth only elicits disbelief in Stephanie: "I don't believe you and nobody nowadays would. ... You know what some people saying? They say you thief somebody money" (44), a scepticism shared by Foster: "He must get the money from somewhere. It don't grow 'pon trees" (68). In the face of a strong suggestion that Bird is a thief, the reader is asked to consider his claim of being in the mysterious grip of a Water Maid, which generates a crisis between Bird and Stephanie, for she and the Water Maid are now virtual rivals for the same man, whereas Bird wants to lose neither of them.

The tribute Heath pays to the Guyanese artist Aubrey Williams can aptly be returned to him:

> His inspiration, of necessity, drew largely on the coastal culture into which he was born and brought up, a world of canals and the ever-present sea, of lore figures, like Moongazer who stands at the crossroads and strikes terror into those returning home late at night, of sudden death from malaria, of periodic drought and floods. It is a harsh world that sits on a fertile land, where the trickster thrives in many guises and serves as a model for survival.[14]

Heath explains the relationship between art and myth: "Art is akin to myth and the function of myth is to heighten a culture's awareness of its position in the world."[15]

A Man Come Home exemplifies a notion posited by Joseph Conrad that human existence is underpinned by the bizarre, the irrational, the mesmeric and the absurd, and that the function of art is to engage what is inexplicable and mysterious in human existence.[16] In the event, Bird begins to reap the negative consequences of his feared relationship with the Water Maid:

> "Is not the same. People don't talk to me as they used to. When I go to Ada they don't joke with me. They think I change. And all I want to do is live as I used to."
> "You shouldn't have move from the room in Broad Street, then," Gee told him.
> "What you think I got money for? To live in a hole?" Bird asked harshly.
> "Well . . . is up to you in't it," Gee remarked, showing little sympathy for his friend. (55)

Aside from the ruses of his trickster friend Gee, who "every time he come he ask for money . . . he pick a quarrel" (108), the loss of community is perhaps the more keenly felt by Bird, for even though his newly acquired house on middle-class, residential Brickdam was not far from the Princess Street range-yard "where he was born and grew up . . . he could not get to know the people living in the [new] district" (86) on account of the social segregation in the city, where he now is seen as a social misfit. In a rare moment of self-examination, Bird wonders whether he "could ever recover those tranquil days in [the range-yard in] Broad Street, the noise, the devotion, and above all the peace of mind" (96), and regain the community he knew before he began his strange pursuit of wealth. At the dawn of independence in a former British colony, this loss of community is a symptom of the fragmentation of the society caused by the exodus, not only of the moneyed class, "who sold out during the [recent] political disturbances" (86), leaving the nouveaux riches to occupy their grand Demerara-style houses, but also of the professional class fearful that their freedoms could be curtailed under the native leadership that has replaced the former colonial oppressors. Bird is unable to anchor himself in the social flux even with his newly found affluence.

Caught between his devotion to an illusory Water Maid and the demands of a real woman, Bird exhibits irritability and violent mood swings which cause Stephanie to reject the untenable union and desert him, thus challenging the male authority and asserting her (female) independence. Unable to manage his wounded ego, for "her words cut deep into the sinews of his pride" (74), but eager to assert his male power, Bird grabs an axe in a fit of anger and destroys the expensive furnishings, including the grand piano (75), among his recently acquired possessions. Such destructive and unpredictable behaviour necessitates a second visit to the card-cutter by Stephanie, who senses that her predicament is more than her resilience can manage.

Notwithstanding the exorbitant fees she has already paid on the first occasion of Bird's absence "to make enquiries, see certain people and so on" (29), the card-cutter merely parrots nebulously what is already popular rumour: "Bird does deal with Water People. He married one of them" (89). There, Stephanie, in spite of her otherwise sober outlook on life, finds herself drawn into the surreal workings of a powerful folk culture that purports to challenge the power of the Water Maid. Stephanie yields to the strange power of the card-cutter's séance: "she took the bird before she had time to refuse" (91), drinks the blood of the sacrificed chicken, and joins in a frenzied dance during which she is instructed by an alien voice to "take the chain round his

neck and fling it into the ocean" (92) in order to break the supernatural spell
of the Water Maid.

Myth has a mesmeric impact on the psyche of Heath's characters by
intensifying their dread, while folk figures, such as Bakoo, card-cutter and
obeahwoman, are the suppressed cultural life of the society that Heath now
validates. The rituals of the dark Kali and the white tables laid out to ward off
evil spirits, as well as the Comfa which Mabel dances, the séance to which
Stephanie yields and dances in a frenzy, are all cultural vehicles through
which characters find meaning in their moments of doubt and despair in
their struggle for freedom and survival.

The reader is told that Bird's self-alienation, his transformation into a
stranger he can no longer recognize, haunts him in grotesque dreams, a
device that Heath uses effectively for heightening the inner exile and distress
of characters. Bird's unkempt appearance, his glassy eyes, and his unpredictable moods, all lend credence to the Water Maid because of certain beliefs
we have come to accept: that man is a creature of myth and that human perceptions are shaped by myths, the mystique of which man has no knowledge
or understanding. Bird's puzzling rage, his "access of irrational behaviour
[which] afflicted him from time to time" (99), is most noticeable when he is
searching the beach at low tide to retrieve his gold chain, tossed into the ocean
by Stephanie in defiance of the myth. Tampering with the myth intensifies
Bird's psychological distress. He can make no progress by facing reality and
is now left to face the legendary wrath of a jealous Water Maid.

To compound a tale of dread and incomprehension, the newly acquired
mansion becomes a place of subliminal fear: Stephanie is terrified by the
idea of "a strange woman staring back at her in the mirror" and only pride
"prevented her from going on her knees and begging Eileen [her best friend]
not to desert her" (109). Eileen herself feels "frightened of this house, of what
everybody saying about it" (109). Stephanie, Bird and Eileen are projections
of the enigma and the mystery that characterize human existence. On the
whole, Stephanie is certain of nothing and fearful of the unknown: "When
I go home to see my mother and father I want to leave the house right away,
'cause . . . 'cause . . . I don't know why I want to leave" (108).

Living with her family in a steamy tenement yard whose solitary "fruitless
dunc tree, full of thorns and blight" (41) stands as a testimony to the barren-

ness of colonial existence, Bird's sister, Ada, is involved in the dénouement of the second plot and is a casualty of the myth that completely destroys her in the process. As if driven to an inevitable fate exacted by the myth, Bird takes his sister's children for a drive in his shiny, newly acquired car, which crashes on the East Bank public road, where they all meet tragic ends. The only survivor, Ada's godson, reports the fleeting appearance of a woman in the front seat of Bird's car; the terror of the myth persists: "Stephanie refused to believe the child's account even though it was she herself who unclasped the gold necklace round her dead husband's neck. It was identical to the one she had taken from him while he was sleeping and thrown into the ocean" (118).

Even if one is tempted into the belief that Bird, with unlimited money at his disposal, replaced his necklace, Heath wants readers to accept myth as a credible and potent force in human lives. The author wants us to believe that Bird's involvement with the Water Maid is valid: he wants us to accept the supernatural as a reality we tend to dismiss for lack of rational, scientific evidence. He wants us to believe that the Water Maid is the enabler of Bird's material success, for, if he is a thief, Bird is never caught, and patently thrives on his success. Bird's strange behaviour and tortured state of mind do lend credence to the suggestion that he is in the hold of something more powerful than can be rationally explained.

The Water Maid is Bird's wish to escape the stagnant future that society offers, and the tampering of this myth necessitates that he be destroyed. The myth is psychically more enduring and more terrible than the card-cutter's folk rituals, for the Water Maid gets her revenge in mythical terms. The car crash in which Bird dies, a kind of climax, is somehow liberating for Stephanie, since it allows her to fulfil the revolutionary words she hears in the card-cutter's trance: "throw away everything . . . and begin again" (92). That Stephanie is able to rescue Melda from the stagnant Foster household with its stale, clichéd relationships holds a promise that this new generation of women can work out a new life through art.

Gee's several entanglements with the Foster family allude to an endemic psychic disturbance in the society. Jealous of Bird's unexplained fortune, which he does not share, and not satisfied with his habitual sexual depredation of the Foster women, Gee plots his own way to the wealth. Unlike the traditional trickster figure Anancy, the underdog in society who uses his wiles against the establishment to survive, Gee is a perverted Anancy figure whose diabolical mind is directed against his fellow underdog. Gee routinely cheats Foster of the money that Bird regularly donates to him, but his ultimate aim is to rob Foster of the large amount kept in a bank for his old age – a provision Bird makes from his mysterious largesse. Gee hopes for a large house and a new car to equal Bird's new social success. His rapaciousness is mirrored in this apt imagery: "on the other side of the trench a king vulture was feeding on a dead animal" (130); his contempt for his victims is neatly concealed within the folds of his sinuous mind: "To hell with the whole family . . . Melda's a slut, Foster a fool and as for Christine . . . ah!" (131). Gee, a product of a predatory and directionless society, his mind as crooked as the pillars of his range house; in his self-loathing, he feels the need to cheat and humiliate others to compensate for his own embarrassingly stunted condition. The trickster figure is a recurrent motif in Heath's fictions, but characters like Gee and Fingers are not simply narrative devices used against the middle class; rather, they are metaphors of the degradation endemic in post-colonial societies that are in urgent need of a new order of relationships. As Gee lures his prey, Foster, to his home for a lavish dinner in the hope of cheating him of his money, the thought that he has almost attained his goal makes him tremble with elation:

> He was now on the threshold of a new life. He was about to burst the chains that anchored him to the range yard, to a way of life his parents and grandparents had known as well. No man could live a lifetime in one room and keep his sanity, he thought. Even his reflections died there before he could put them together coherently. It was only when he was walking the streets that he could construct his dreams. . . . The road was his domain, the family room a prison cell. . . . Even as a boy . . . I never did doubt this tomorrow would come. (139–40)

Gee, the predator – "the crooked timber of humanity"[17] – does not count on the possibility of Christine's betrayal or on Foster's self-awakening and uncharacteristic wrath. The novel asks whether individual freedom can be bought on the basis of old habits of opportunism and depravity, of man reduced to his baser instincts, or whether these can be transformed into a new awareness that will allow "a community of valid persons" to cohere. When Foster fails to appear at the bank to transfer the money, Gee becomes desperate, "twisting and turning like an animal in a cage" (142) – a portrait of a base extortioner who "had made up his mind. He would subject Christine to the humiliations Melda had suffered. And in the end he would get the money through her" (142). The naive Foster finally gains a modicum of self-knowledge, waylays Gee and savages him with a cutlass. In striking out against Gee's vagabondage, Foster strikes out against his own weakness and vulnerability, so that this moment of closure reveals Foster's relationship with Gee to be a liberating one.

Too late, Gee comes to realize that his pursuit of wealth is flawed and as he savours precious (almost poetic) memories of the traditional and unchanging way of life in the community before he became consumed by greed, the reader shares Gee's pain when the hunter becomes the hunted and he is forced to flee the town and separate from his wife to escape the wrath of the Fosters:

> His mind began to cloud over with images of shadows and puddles as sleep overcame him. He would, after all, finish his days in the range yard, where he was born, where he learned his childhood games and the games older people played as well. Here he had made his kites in April, fashioned his spinning tops from okari seeds and competed with his round glazed marbles in the games of his district . . . looking on through his window at the goings-on on the door-steps or round the standpipe where the women gathered to wash and gossip. On dark nights he would occasionally trip over a discarded tyre and in the rainy season when the waters from the gutter spilled over into the yard he would have to pick his way from stone to stone if the stepping planks had been moved by some thoughtless child. (146)

The effervescence of yard life is the affirmation of humanity and by this time half of the women in the range-yard were on their doorsteps, "relishing this unexpected contribution to their yard-lore. . . . There was the noise of drawn bolts and one leaf of the door opened. Melda, breathing heavily, entered Gee's room. At this, there was a round of applause from the onlookers" (151–52). Yet it is imperative that an end be put to Gee's depredatory habits. Despite the flaws in human nature and in human relationships and the reality of an existence as mutilated as Foster's flag with "a tear right down the middle" (106), the dismantling of such clichéd forms of human relationships as those depicted in this novel points to the possibility of renewal in a society on the threshold of a new beginning. Bird's self-destruction and Gee's self-exile free Foster, Stephanie and Melda from the "victim stasis" and allow them to function as free individuals and reclaim their humanity, so that Christine's pessimism now seems a thing of the past: "After all these years, the Foster family don't got no luck. Is always something . . . something knocking at the door. And when it come in, it cause nothing but trouble" (149–50).

The Murderer

The Murderer reinterprets colonial society through the dilemma of the anti-hero whose consciousness and perceptions have been shaped by the morality of sexual repression ingrained in him by his mother through the imposed Victorian morality of the mother country. Upon gaining independence the individual and the country find themselves unfree and still tied to this code of conduct.

This is a story of fundamental psychological disturbance, and involving the reader in the peculiar state of consciousness deepens the theme. Frantz Fanon, in *The Wretched of the Earth*,[18] acknowledges the "mental pathology [of the colonized] which is the direct product of oppression . . . and the frequent malignancy of these pathological processes". *The Murderer* explores the psychosis of the colonial subject, the dark workings of the human mind, its compulsion to "right" society (even through criminal act), and its ultimate breakdown to complete mental derangement.[19]

Galton Flood's emotional growth is, in some ways, flawed, and this is mirrored in the relationships he finds impossible to sustain in his adulthood. He is a man on the move, desperately seeking freedom, but everywhere he turns he is faced with duplicated versions of the same old moral patterns from which he is trying to escape. When he gets married and his wife, Gemma, fails to square with his entrenched notion of morality, he deems her unfit to live, murders her, and throws her body in the Demerara River. The work explores the more drastic psychological effects of decolonization and the failure of the freed man to transcend this legacy. *The Murderer* is also a study of female isolation and female victimization by a patriarchal authority.

Set in the late 1970s, *The Murderer* recounts the heightening crisis in the life of one character chiefly through his thoughts and reflections and through his relationships with other characters in the work. The novel is structured in two parts: book one goes up to the murder, while book two traces the fragmentation of Galton's mind into irredeemable madness while time imperceptibly passes: "the months passed, when experiences were scored out with time, like patterns in wet sand" (142).

The reader enters the conscious thoughts of Galton to find a picture of a crippling relationship between mother and son that underpins the tragic drama of his life. Galton's formative years are shaped by a feeling of inferiority and aloneness in the world, by the fear and repression inflicted by his stern mother: "He had, at the age of nine or ten, learned to adapt himself to the bit between his teeth" (9). If the universal image of mother and child ideally infuses the world with hope and love, the reality is that psychosocial growth and development devoid of affection and emotional nurturing leave deep psychological scars the young Galton is unable to overcome.

His earliest memory is of repeated violence and cruelty in the home, traditionally perceived as a haven of warmth and security: "of his mother belabouring his father in a frenzy of anger . . . he looked on, paralysed with fear . . . he wanted the world to come to an end. He was only three then" (87), unable to understand that his father heroically bears the emotional and physical brutalization by maintaining his silence and sublimating his repression in laughter. Galton's impressionable years are marked by humiliation and self-doubt as his domineering mother inflicts her neuroses upon him – "One day when a girl from his school called for him his mother laughed as if it were a big joke. Mortified, he remained inside, his eyes closed tight with shame" (9) – in contrast to his older brother, Selwyn, whose ego is strong enough to resist his mother's will. The most important defect in Galton's personality springs from, as Amon Saba Saakana notices, "the internalization of his mother's neurosis about sex and sensuality".[20] His pride constantly wounded, Galton faces the world with a sense of worthlessness, hardened against emotions and incapable of forming lasting relationships: "He dared not cultivate an affection lest it reared up and attacked him; nor could he express his dislike for a person for fear that the intensity of his disapproval might seem absurd, and with time he brushed away every impulse to display any tender emotion towards the members of his family" (11). Sustained humiliation at his mother's hands "often led him to indulge in fantasies of self-abasement", which leave him with such deep feelings of inadequacy that he imagines himself reduced to the menial labour of driving a dray-cart[21] through the streets while people point at him in ridicule (11).

Galton is nurtured on the Christian outlook that links female sexuality with shame, guilt and sin, and his "disgust is aroused" by what he deems "lecherous gestures" (10) on the day his brother urges him to peer through a chink in their kitchen window to see a neighbour, a former vaudeville dancer, performing by herself with her waist exposed. Shortly after his mother's demise (an event which coincides with the end of colonial rule in the country), he attends a dance but self-consciously "draws back" at the entrance, "seized by a sort of panic", since his rigid indoctrination forbids dancing as "sinful unless the dancers were married" (12).

The reader incidentally gets a sense of social change and of a vanishing landscape in the decade after independence is granted to the former British colony: "He started off in the direction of the railway crossing. The appearance of the parallel steel lines, gleaming under the street lamps, seemed to belie the fact that the railway was closed down. Those trains, day in and day out, bursting with people, dividing the sweltering days with their hissing and hooting, crawling the fifty-odd miles from Georgetown to Rossignol along the flat Guyana coastland like rattling caterpillars, were gone forever" (153–54).[22]

Construing one of Galton's tormented dreams, one comes to understand that his ultimate brutal slaying of his wife is symbolically the subconscious slaying of his mother, an act of the utmost necessity to avenge the brutalization of his father and to free himself from an authoritarian grip whose tyranny continues to dominate him long after her demise:

> He fell asleep in the wicker armchair and dreamt that he was at the edge of the ramp where he had struck Gemma. . . . His eyes were riveted on the water when, suddenly, a hand rose from it, with groping fingers clawing after some object. . . . Galton recognised the apparition as that of his mother. Instead of coming to him it went by, and when Galton looked round it was bringing down a stick with all its might on the head of a man who, streaming with blood, was looking to him for help . . . he recognised him as his father. Galton . . . open-mouthed, stared in terror, sprang forward only to run into a panel of thick glass. . . . From behind the glass, which he began to pound furiously with his fists, he could only remain a powerless observer of his father's distress; and when the latter fell forward into the river his mother pursued him, hacking away with a stick. (186)

The account of the relationship between the antihero and his mother is, on another level, an allegory of Guyana's embedded relationship with the mother country and with varying forms of incapacitating conventions and irrelevant cultural impositions that persist well into the post-independence period and suffocate efforts towards nationhood. The work explores this conundrum by tracing Galton's progress from childhood repression to unmitigated loneliness and isolation until, trapped in a prison of madness, Galton walks the city's streets with the feeling of being corked in a bottle.

Childhood deprivation deepens into adult estrangement, a psychological flaw that corrupts every relationship in his adult life. Emboldened to discover that the patriarchal society, even in the far-flung areas of Linden and Bartica, shares this practised chauvinism – "seriously. Can any man rely on a woman?" (29) – Galton exudes a deep distrust of women and enters marriage with the proverbial worm eating away at the core of his very being. He is then driven to murdering his wife and when he yields to an uncontrollable urge to revisit the scene of the crime, the reader comes to understand, through his reflections, the psychologically damaging effects upon children growing up among the cruelty, repression and fundamentalist ideas of the adult world:

> When he reached the head of the ramp he looked around him once more and then descended into the water's edge. He went down on his haunches and dipped his hand in the cold water, closing his eyes as he did so. . . . It was a rainy night like this, about twenty years ago, when his mother was rocking in her chair . . .
>
> "The world was full of sin once, as it is now," she had said to him. "God sent a flood to cover the earth. Imagine the thousands of people that were drowned, swept away from their gambling tables and places of vice. The earth was enveloped in darkness. Your father is a gambler, Galton. He is steeped in sin and shame and God's mercy is turned away from this house. Kneel down and pray for your father and beg God to spare us and to remember that he was not always like that."
>
> Galton remembered kneeling and praying for his sinful father and secretly begging God that he might at that moment be sheltering from the wind and rain. He imagined him on his bicycle, hatless, making little headway against the wind. (139)

Galton's quandary, of inhabiting a society that still clings to an alien religion that drove the original religions and cultures of slaves (and, less so, indentured immigrants) underground, raises the question of the viability of independence while labouring under an imposed morality. Such is his state of repression that the first time Galton is given voice in the novel is after the death of his parents, when he vows to flee his confused existence in suburban Kitty and seek his freedom and independence in the wider society, at a place far removed from urban deprivation. He heads for Linden, a bauxite-mining town some sixty-five miles up the Demerara River, but there, with his weak ego, he shies away from people, self-consciously hovering on the fringe of the community, around "the cake shops of the arcade near the waterfront" (14), lacking the self-confidence even to make contact with the community. So intensely is this timid character preoccupied with his own internal dread that all social phenomena are excluded from his consciousness. Lodging at the Burroweses at Wismar, on the opposite bank of the river across from Linden, Galton immediately falls in love with Burrowes's daughter, Gemma, "seeing in his passion a release from all the constraints of years gone by" (19). Healing his emotional hurts through the reassuring warmth of love he had never before known seems a distinct possibility for Galton – "he felt at that moment that all the doubts about himself had been washed away" (20) – but, ironically, this possibility is elusive.

A series of parasitic characters feed on Galton's weak ego, intensify his dread and make self-renewal impossible for him. Walk-Man, the first of these, raises Galton's awareness to a common human problem – the lack of self-knowledge – without which the pursuit of self-renewal is improbable: "If everyone else knew that – the impossibility of seeing oneself – we would stop beating our heads against a wall" (24). However, it is for his evil nature that the Iago-like Walk-Man will be best remembered in this novel. He shatters Galton's newly found feeling of security with the malicious innuendo that "Gemma would not marry you even if you asked" (26). Seeds of doubt and mistrust poison Galton's vulnerable ego, "made him sick at heart, each word he spoke withered one of those flowers gathered in Gemma's company in the course of the last few days" (27). Galton is startled by Walk-Man's wife, a double of his own overbearing mother, the ghost that haunts him; this meeting reawakens in Galton feelings of guilt and shame: "his guilt at the pleasure he found in Gemma's company, feelings never far from the surface" (27) and reveals his fickle mind: "Galton cursed his own vulnerability. All the happiness he had accumulated these last few weeks was erased with a few words spoken by someone who evidently bore Burrowes a grudge. Yet, even if the Walk-Man had lied he could not live in that house any longer than was necessary" (28).

From Galton's uncompromising perspective, Gemma "is somehow tarnished" (27) by Walk-Man's innuendo and no longer worthy of his attention. The doubts raised by careless talk "lingered like the taste of aloes, to spoil an appetite he had longed to assuage" (32). Now a misogynist and distrustful of all women, Galton nonetheless experiences an intense aloneness, "as though he was stranded in some vast, unknown country, without money or resources" (29). Despite evidence to the contrary and "his reflections on his own shortcomings" – a small attempt at gaining self-awareness that is cancelled by a paranoia that only allows him to see Gemma and her father as "plotters against his liberty" (28) – Galton flees Linden due to a sadistic desire to make Gemma suffer. Walk-Man embodies the corruption of the adult world and acknowledges his evil ways shamelessly: "When all is said and done only children tell the truth" (32). Galton's quest for freedom is poisoned by both an inner, psychological tyranny and a callous society of stereotypical, malignant misfits that converge to drive him to a complete mental collapse.

Galton is terrified of relinquishing the only moral order he knows, his dilemma an analogy of the newly independent nation clinging to the old colonial order. The following scene vividly describes the inner conflict between Galton's frustrated desire for Gemma and his inhibitions, sublimated in what would seem to be rape of the furnishings and, at the same time, evidence of the damaged psyche of man and nation:

> In the dark room, hung with ancient wallpaper, an absurd idea filled his mind: he must somehow lick the bare walls of its flowers. . . . He began wringing his hands in great excitement and muttering to himself; and then, as if responding to some inner prompting, jumped on the bed and began licking the walls in an attempt to remove the flowers. But when his efforts proved vain he was taken with a violent inclination to smash down the door that connected his room with Gemma's. (29–30)

The flow of time is imperceptible in Galton's consciousness and it is three years before he decides to flee Linden and what seems to him its narrowness. As if fulfilling Walk-Man's verdict that he is "running from himself", Galton

heads for the Mazaruni goldfields, where he works for two years as a diver;
but neither the lure of gold nor the mythical freedom of the vast interior can
bring Galton inner security from the unexorcised ghosts that haunt him.
As in all of Heath's narratives, linear markers are unobtrusive and the only
indication of the flow of time is contained in phrases such as "the first day of
the fourth week" (19) and "the first afternoon of the wet season" (21), and in
the ephemeral flow of the character's thoughts, a style that lends authenticity to the lived experience. And while the freedom of the hinterland remains
an option for Heath's characters, none has ever chosen to remain in the vast
unknown interior of the country. Still, the motif of the journey as a metaphor
of the voyage into the unknown self remains a powerful literary device. His
return to Georgetown to find closure in the festering city and, to the chagrin
of his middle-class brother, to a lowly job as a night watchman at a Lombard
Street sawmill is, in every sense, a necessity.

Back in the family home in Kitty, Galton's mind, anchored to the past and
sealed with bitter memories, is, like the family house itself, only half opened
to let in the figurative light:

> The sun was streaming through a casement window Selwyn must have opened.
> Galton closed one flap of it, the panes of which were thick, patterned glass, to
> reduce the harshness of the sun's rays. He then lay down in the Berbice chair,
> under the Demerara window. This had been his father's favourite resting spot,
> but since his death the window had never been opened, and the bolts that
> anchored its shutters were welded to their stays by a layer of rust. (56)

Where evidence from Galton's consciousness is spare, the narrative admits
his letters to Gemma as first-person testimonies of his psychic insecurity: "If
you realized how uncertain I was about everything you would lose all faith in
me" (49). He is now terrified by the realization that he has returned to Kitty
to face the identical form of tyranny that had repressed him in childhood and
adolescence and from which he futilely sought to flee – his brother, Selwyn,
has replaced their mother as the new authoritarian figure. In addition, Galton
is made more vulnerable by rejection from an "ill-bred and arrogant" (53)
sister-in-law, Nekka, who is jealous of his relationship with his brother. The
officious Nekka is yet another overbearing and negative side of the image
of the woman who compensates for her sense of inferiority by clinging to

petty power. This latest interference causes in him a "profound disgust at his brother's indifference" (55). Through the device of an omniscient narrator, Heath catches the flow of a severely disturbed consciousness: "Everything seemed to come in waves, hatred, fulfilment and even death. From the start there was a certain ebb and flow in his mounting dislike for Nekka, just as there had been a growing and a slackening of everyone's awareness of his mother's impending death. And this longing for Gemma that had to be satisfied, did it not follow a similar pattern, receding from him and submerging him in turn?" (56).

After more than five years of indecision, Gemma marries her "tormentor", albeit the two lovers represent opposing attitudes to marriage. Gemma's liberal approach – "she would marry and if things did not work out, separate" (56) – conflicts with Galton's dogmatic Christian upbringing: "marriage meant a union for life, a certainty beforehand that it would not fail". The notion that marriage is irrevocable is an impossible ideal for her, as certainty about the future cannot be guaranteed. On the other hand, Galton, yearning for the stability he has never known, yields momentarily: "a strange sense of elation had taken the place of his anger. . . . He was tempted to shout out to the men that he was getting married, that he would find another job and leave those damned woodyards" (58). Nonetheless, his old pattern of guilt, shame and inhibitions persists: "he insisted she wear her underclothes in bed" (78). Ever since a revolting encounter with his neighbour's mother in a Lombard Street tenement building when she had pressed his head into her bosom, Galton has kept his puritan distance from women: "not once had he fondled Gemma's breasts, in the belief that he would be engaging in an abnormal practice" (95). Gemma is allowed to voice the woman's dilemma, and it is prescient – "You men lock women up in small places and expect them to be normal" (52) – as it is not long before Galton inflicts similar treatment on her.

The romantic principle is crushed by harsh reality in Heath's narratives and all his weddings are flawed events, none more so than when the atmosphere at Galton's wedding is marred by a puerile argument between his brother and an uninvited guest over the obligations of marriage, the very subject that agitates Galton; thus, "all the gaiety had gone out of the reception" (72). Coming events cast their shadows and that very night, when Gemma confesses to a previous lover, Galton's world comes crashing down, for, in his view, the moral basis of their marriage has been destroyed. He immediately drags Gemma from the hospitality of his friend's house in Peter's Hall to a Lombard Street tenement room behind a dingy cookshop so as to punish and humiliate her, a psychological response earlier observed in some of Heath's characters who feel the urgent need to humiliate someone within their power to compensate for their own injured pride. The one-room dwelling, on the second landing of a wretched tenement building, "lacked bed, dressers, cupboards, running water and the many other conveniences associated with home" (99), a room that overlooks life in all its rawness throbbing in the alleyway: "At night you see a whole procession of people passing there: couples making love, men pissing against the palings, children hiding from their parents, escapees from the police scaling zinc, furtive rubbish dumpers" (113).

Galton's descent into the city slums, "the twilight world of thieves and receivers", the atmosphere of "brittle dreams" (85), is a prelude to his own decline into a "twilight" world of psychological fragmentation. To add to his mounting insecurity, he encounters another Iago figure lurking about, his neighbour and police informer, known to possess "a mind like a cess-pool", to whom he is inexplicably drawn. He attributes this fatal attraction to the enigma and illogic inherent in human behaviour: "People can't explain all their actions. At least I can't" (90). The rare instances of self-knowledge in Heath's works often emanate from the most flawed characters, as in the case of the police informer's awareness of his own perverse nature: "but if they know the filth that lurk in me, just waiting for the first opportunity to break out" (103). Galton acknowledges that this villainous informer is part of the devouring city itself that he is powerless to change, "like an ancient parasite, sucking his blood like some enormous leech, before which he stood mesmerized" (116).

Galton's paranoia intensifies during a passing encounter with the informer's lecherous mother, who awakens his puritanical anguish to the point where "sometimes his heart was filled with such murderous hatred towards women he dreaded the long hours by his wife's side" (95). He is exasperated at his wife's easy acceptance of such conduct, berates her for her own defective morality, how she "came into marriage under false pretences" (94–95) and finds a new reason to torture himself and her. The crisis heightens when the informer, true to his name, informs Galton of a male visitor to Gemma's apartment, exaggerating the facts into many visits, shattering Galton's fragile sense of self-certainty. The informer's role in goading Galton and driving him to the depths of the most destructive emotion must be considered in the latter's descent into madness: "Jealousy's a terrible thing. Every emotion got a value, excep' jealousy" (102), adding for good measure, "Women, they got what men in' got: patience, a deep, voiceless patience; but when they strike! Oh, me God! Is like the floods every ten years that does cover the coast from Rossignol to Parika and lef' a trail of dead cattle in its wake" (103).

Gemma's assertion of freedom – "We could make a go of our marriage but I'm not giving up my freedom" – contradicts Galton's fixed perceptions: "the essential term of marriage could only be the complete subservience of the woman" (107). This challenge shatters his sense of security: "Suddenly, the world seemed a desperately lonely place" (105) at the mention of the word "separation", for he only understands the notion of "subservience": "Before him lay only ghost-like moon shadows between houses of a deserted road and the eyes behind the latticework. He had walked that road a hundred times in his dreams, but only once had found anyone waiting at the end of it: his mother, dressed in mauve" (107).

Galton's paranoia reaches such a pitch that "a feeling of elation" (107) overcomes him and he is driven to dispense brutally with Gemma because she "wasn't fit to live" (180). He lures her to the waterfront almost at midnight on the pretext of visiting a friend, bludgeons her to death and throws her body in the river: "he lifted the length of wood and brought it down on her head with a thud, whereupon all the repressed anger of his boyhood came flooding out like water through a breached koker" (109). Murder is a liberating experience for the deluded protagonist as he descends the ramp and emerges again, devoid of all emotion, convincing himself that he has given Gemma her freedom (in death). Gemma embodies the images of all the women against whom Galton subconsciously rebels. In striking out against her he strikes out against his domineering mother, the repulsive vaudeville dancer, his neighbour's lecherous mother and his nefarious sister-in-law, all of whom must be collectively destroyed since they threaten or offend his inbred morality. Ironically, in his state of mental disorientation, Galton becomes a double of his authoritarian mother and feels justified in victimizing his wife: "She wanted her independence. . . . I gave her it . . . because I don't believe in keeping people by you against their will. You can cause them great damage. Great damage! Oh, yes. *Great* damage. People must be free, you see. If they're not free they can't give of their best" (133).

This is a grim reinterpretation of society that argues that the colonial disorder is deeply embedded and necessitates brutal solutions before independence can acquire meaning and offer viable paradigms for selfhood. We may be quick to attribute this kind of logic to Galton's fundamentalist Christian upbringing, but a similar theme runs through Heath's *One Generation*, where Ramjohn (not a Christian follower) decides that Rohan and Indrani are unfit to live and proceeds to murder them. Perhaps Heath is toying with a frightening fascist philosophy of extermination of the "inferior" as played out in Dostoevsky's *Crime and Punishment*. It is also a proposal in Edgar Mittelholzer's *The Aloneness of Mrs Chatham* (1965), and the reader wonders whether characters are driven to murder due to their social conditioning or because they are flawed in their psychological endowments. Like Ramjohn, Galton is never brought to justice, but in the latter case, Gemma's murder can be read as less a criminal act than the redressing of a historical wrong – a sacrifice to the spectre of colonialism. Galton is a metaphor of a crippled society, a decade into independence, trying to rid its collective psyche of the colonial imprint of irrelevant dogmatic patterns.

Even though there is the sense of the antihero labouring under paranoia and mental fragmentation, this does not prevent us from detecting, in a strangely humanistic way, the interplay between the living natural environment and the character, however flawed he may be:

> Though it was late January the heavy rains had not come. The damp from the river clung to the piles of wood and the air was heavy with the scent of rot and decay. The lights from the nutsellers' stalls, which fluttered fitfully in the light breeze, would be put out by twelve o'clock, after the last ferryboat had come back. He recalled the fireflies in Linden, cleaving the night like shooting stars. It was thus in Kitty, too, over the wasteland opposite their house, where orchids pilfered the sap of the silk-cotton trees. (133–34)

In the same way, Galton realizes that he is losing grip on reality at the moment he confronts the figure of a strange man (possibly his wife's former lover) standing at the head of the ramp, the scene of the murder. Galton experiences terror that leaves him "speechless and numb" and for the first time it occurs to him that he is on the brink of mental chaos, "not, indeed, because he had killed Gemma. He was convinced that any self-respecting man would have done so. Rather, his lack of success at achieving any goal he had set himself and his inability to face up to a situation that had taken him by surprise implanted in his mind that he was progressively losing his grip" (140–41).

Galton's tortured tale does not end there. Faced with the impossible choice of either remaining in the "ugly and degrading tenement" in the city slum or returning to his old home in suburban Kitty "with its barren relationships", he chooses Kitty, with its old "victim" relationship, now with his autocratic brother. Yet the need for companionship urges him to strike up with another young woman, Mildred, a relationship that is crushed through malicious talk by his meddling sister-in-law, Nekka. This new setback devastates Galton: "it was all so sudden, like being struck on the head with a stick from behind" (164), a feeling of desolation that leads him to isolate himself against the inexplicable hurts and the wrecked relationships that have been accumulating around him like driftwood:

> There must be no suffering, no pain. Suffering was in childhood, that unending strand of deprivation . . . all those closest to him had been cut off from him, their relations severed by some incomprehensible act of fate; his father had died suddenly; his brother had got married and Mildred had decided in one night to fall out of love with him. Since those were the terms of living there was to be no emotion. It must be ripped out and put away in some high, inaccessible tree, like the intestines of soldiers wrenched away by the vultures in Li Po's poem. . . . All these words, these reflections, were pointless. They were the haze through which one looked at life. (166–67)

Progressively, the protagonist, no longer his rational self, becomes disconnected from the society he was never in tune with, an empty shell drained of all emotion, for whom "life hasn't got any dreams, success and all that damn nonsense" (172–73). Galton cannot seize the promise implied in independence for he is unable to expunge the bitter memories of his formative years from his damaged psyche: "Ah, brother! That Christmas when our mother tore down the bunting and trampled it under her feet. . . . It doesn't matter, because every Christmas we die a little" (185–86).

Nonetheless, though now dysfunctional and one of history's casualties, Galton struggles to cling to his humanity or whatever is left of it. As he heads home one night, in the direction of Georgetown, he is awash with memories of the community in which he grew up:

> He passed the house where, as a boy, he had spent three weeks while his mother was ill. The backyard, dotted with houses, was full of children in the afternoon. It was there he had learnt to make and spin a buck top which sang and droned until, losing speed, it fell over. There he had got stained with abeer, the red water thrown indiscriminately during the East Indian Phagwah festival. . . . As Galton walked on his thoughts became more sombre. Of late he was dogged by the belief that he was in a bottle and was afraid that if he fell asleep someone would come and insert a cork in its mouth, leaving him imprisoned. (173–74)

Tragically, self-knowledge comes too late for Galton to take his place in the new society, but for him, an ironic freedom lies in a space of madness insulated from society's rules, prejudices and evils: "one gain he had certainly made: he had achieved what he had always longed for, an area that belonged to him alone" (141). Ultimately, Galton, a solitary figure existing on the fringe, roams the streets in a prison of silence, "a night bird in pursuit of brittle dreams" (189–90).

Whereas *A Man Come Home* offers the hope of new beginnings from the ravages of an old plantation culture through radical and revolutionary actions, *The Murderer* demonstrates the more irredeemable aspects of colonialism, as well as the possibility of new beginnings at great cost. Both novels question the existential possibilities of a people mired in centuries of crippling clichéd relationships that have misshaped the psyche. Galton Flood shares a similar dilemma with two generations of the Foster men and their friend Gee, who are all psychologically trapped in the old colonial order with its predator/victim paradigm, its dependency relationships and its Victorian morality, and whose perceptions of self and society are, as a consequence, fundamentally flawed and undermine the quest for selfhood and community.

Heath suppresses specific details of social and historical phenomena in *The Murderer* and concentrates upon the tensions within the family and the vulnerability of the individual. In the minutiae of daily life are revealed the quirks in human nature: the rage, the irrationalities, the self-loathing and self-doubts, in the myriad relationships in which a new and directionless nation drifts futilely in search of self-determination. In *Orealla*, which will be examined in the next chapter, Heath returns to the colonial era to analyse the world of the trilogy from a different perspective in the hope of coming to a deeper understanding of the Guyanese psyche fractured by history.

7

OREALLA
Trapped in the Past

> It was an aching floor on which I crept
> on my hands and knees
> searching the dust for the trace of a root
> or the mark of a leaf or the shape of a flower
> —Martin Carter, "I Come from the Nigger Yard"

In his seventh published novel, *Orealla*, Heath returns to the colonial society of the 1920s, seemingly to examine, from another perspective, the pervasive class differentiation that has shaped human relationships in the colony.

The central character is Ben, a dislocated black man, a product of the plantation. He has lived "in various villages in Berbice and Courantyne, ending up in Skeldon with his grandmother before he came to Georgetown" (*Orealla*, 10). In the city, Ben struggles to be a newspaper columnist, works as a groom, becomes a thief, and is caught attempting a burglary. The theme of class consciousness is elaborated in Ben's relationships with Schwartz; with his wife, Tina; with his common-law wife, Mabel; with Carl, the Amerindian from a riverain settlement at Orealla who has just arrived and is seeking a place in Georgetown; with Edna, the Schwartzes' faithful cook; and with fringe elements of society, including a virago, Violet, and a nameless pavement dweller.

At the centre of the novel is the relationship between Ben and Schwartz, an influential member of the coloured middle class and an employee of the colonial Treasury. Schwartz arranges with the police to have the charge of burglary against Ben suspended, in return for which Ben will be obliged to live in, in a servant's room underneath Schwartz's mansion on Regent Street, Georgetown, and serve as an indentured worker for the rest of his life.

At the time of the attempted burglary, Ben is legally married to Tina, a young woman from a middle-class background, and in addition, he keeps as common-law wife Mabel, a young woman from one of the range-yards of Georgetown. This arrangement does not stop him from being restless and dissatisfied, plagued by "terrible images of torment and cadences of mute despair. It was intolerable to have to go home and listen to bland conversation . . . held in suspension between the poles of two women with entirely different dispositions" (17).

The novel sets up the dichotomy between the urban underclass and the coloured middle class and, this time, the social world is entered through the eyes of a black working-class man. The dilemma of entrapment and subjugation and the struggle for freedom and human dignity among the downtrodden are at the heart of this narrative, which interrogates a condition that Wilson Harris calls "a state of unfreedom in the lives of people".[1]

It is worth noticing that Heath is here commenting on the corruption within the police force and the perversion of justice under colonialism – a feature that seemingly persists into the post-independence years. *Orealla* is also a statement about other forms of exploitation of man by man long after the systems of slavery and indentureship have been dismantled. Ben has been primed by his experiences at the hands of the police to accept the "deal" that has been offered him. When he is taken into custody, Ben is subjected to "two nightmarish days" (18) of interrogation by the limbs of the law, that is, the local police, who are themselves acutely constrained by the hierarchy of colour and class differentiation within the force. Ben is pressured into subjection: "It's the Mazaruni for you . . . and don' say a black man like you didn't warn you. When one of them brown-skin arse-lickers take over from me he'll hand you over to some white man who left school at fourteen and does walk about with a rosewood stick under his armpit to give him confidence. And he'll *do* for you" (19). All of Ben's possibilities seem to be leading to Schwartz, with whom he is destined to spend the rest of his life as a cabman and servant. Schwartz euphemistically "holds an important position" (21) destroying old currency notes at the Treasury.

Acquiescing to indentureship in lieu of a term of imprisonment, Ben resents his master for the "continual blackmail with which he kept him in line. Should Ben misbehave he would be handed over to the police to face the charge from which the master had saved him" (26). Schwartz's arrogance also rouses Ben's anger. He is piqued when the defining moment in the relationship between the two comes and Ben is required "to call him Master, no doubt to emphasize the humiliation of his position" (23). The struggle for power and self in which master and servant are locked fuels the dramatic crises of the work.

The interiorization of experience of a rebellious and tormented servant forms the core of this work and offers a sense of the predicament of the under-class person in early twentieth-century British Guiana, where colour and class dispositions are deciding factors in the pursuit of individual growth and self-realization. Thomas Sutcliffe recognizes this in his brief review of *Orealla*: "Ben's pained introspection, interrogating himself relentlessly, contrasts with Carl's ability to come to decisions with sudden arbitrariness that seems to pre-clude inner debate."[2] It is the argument of this chapter that Heath is rewriting this master-servant relationship as a modern parallel to the barbaric master-slave relationship, features of which persist into the independence period, with its expectations for individual freedom and nation-building.

Ben is a flawed character whose sporadic forays against the law are acts of rebellion against his meagre place in society: "It had more to do with his pride as a man, which could not be satisfied by tending horses belonging to someone else" (26–27). In colonial Georgetown, social discrimination is pervasive. An aspiring black writer like Ben suffers because "only red people can get a good job on the newspaper" (58). Ben's acceptance into the middle class has been made easier on account of his "impressive manner of speak-ing", which inspires Tina's mother to "think highly of him" (8). Through his connection with this family, Ben has achieved the impossible, that is, social accommodation within the fold of the middle class. Tina is a promise to Ben of new beginnings, "to wipe all that mud from his soul", asking in return only the certainty of his love (23). At this time, the coloured middle class in British Guiana is in crisis, and as we earlier noticed in the trilogy, in the case of Gladys Davis, its women must either shift the social parameters and marry out of their class or remain unmarried.

One might say that Ben is psychically stranded in the city. He is anxious not to make his murky propensities known for fear of jeopardizing the relationship with Tina, who "had turned out to be an antidote to his criminal inclinations and a rock upon which he could build an uncertain future" (17). Although he knows that Tina's family is "far removed from the common mob" and insulated from gossip, he lives in fear that their association with him will end abruptly should they come to know the truth about his double life.

Ben's flawed nature betrays him. The impulse to commit another act of theft is presented as the resurfacing of old instincts: "He had to do some evil deed, just one, as an epitaph to his old criminal life. . . . The evil he was most familiar with was theft, simply because it was against the law. He was marked as the dead are, with a blue triangle on his cheek" (17) and one night, on leaving the rum shop, he is overpowered by "a thrill of elation . . . the fascination of evil things", which urges him to make one final assertion of himself, to commit one more rebellious act before he finally yields his freedom and succumbs to the staid order and entrapment of marriage, "before the women appeared from nowhere to domesticate him like a sheep or a hog or a dog wrenched from its freedom on the streets and the alleyways" (17).

It is now the 1920s and some of the old forms of slavery cannot be practised, but Ben is a slave again in terms of Martin Carter's observation that "the institution of slavery [is] the source of our sensibility . . . to live here and have our being here denotes immediately a particular kind of sensibility, derived from the actuality of slavery".[3] Heath recreates not the physical brutalization of slavery in the form of the actual whip, but the daily indignities and, crucially, the psychological bludgeoning endemic in the master/slave encounter.

Locked in mutual hatred with Schwartz, Ben decides to perform his duties while "biding his time" for an opportunity to gain his freedom: "Somehow he had to find a way out of the trap. . . . His humiliating position hardly left him enough time to visit Tina and Mabel", an untenable bondage that hurts his pride and leads him to "walk the streets rather than face the scorn of his women" (26–27). As a slave, and a resentful one at that, Ben adopts strategies for survival that include resorting to acts of sabotage and blackmail, until he is driven to murder his feudalistic master. The power struggle between Ben and Schwartz for dignity and equality is symbolic of the emerging class struggle between the rulers and labouring classes in the colony. The novel traces Ben's determined efforts to define the terms of human freedom and identity within the rigid limitations of his blackmailing master.

Ben's relationships with two women, his legal wife and his common-law wife, complicate his quest for freedom and selfhood. Social status is of such crucial importance in the polarized colonial society that when Ben chooses the offer of servitude under Schwartz, his immediate concern is for Tina and the consequences of the scandal upon their marriage, without sparing a thought for his common-law wife, Mabel, "of the new complications living away from home would bring to their lives, of the way he would go down in her parents' estimation . . . he realized that none of his thoughts had been for Mabel and the children" (21). Tina and Mabel represent contrasting mores and values within the society and Ben feels the need to oscillate between these two polarized worlds. Tina offers Ben a foothold on the social ladder and quells his self-contempt, while Mabel anchors him to his black working-class sensibility.

Through Ben's mediated reflections, it becomes clear that his marriage to Tina hinges largely upon his admiration for the outwardly stable and solid appearance of middle-class values that she and her family represent, a world on a different plane from that of his own uprooted existence and one for which it seems worthwhile to strive:

> The more he reflected on the relationship between Tina and himself the more reasons he found for his attachment. She was born in the house she and her parents occupied. . . . It seemed to him extraordinary that anyone could have enjoyed such stability. The painted shutters that opened upwards as in a salute were old and solid . . . he had never known anything like it . . . the power of louvred shutters opening upwards, of cats asleep in the shadow of a porch, of words in a certain order. (10)

The union between Ben and Tina is based on the expectations of social conventions, while deep and genuine feelings are held in restraint. The British Guianese middle class are so tyrannized by colour and class rules that when Ben informs Tina of Mabel's pregnancy, Tina is more devastated by the social stigma and fear of her mother's snobbish reaction than by her own unexpressed emotions. Tina and Mabel fulfil different needs in Ben. While Tina's childlessness cannot be held against her, it is perhaps (unkindly) used as a metaphor for the sterility of her class and of a union entered into for the wrong reason. She greets Ben with a "long, cold silence, not wishing to discuss the dilemma" because of certain inhibitions that have come to be associated with her class, including a false modesty that does not permit her to state her feelings openly. Words are not used to convey the depth of their feelings for each other but are used euphemistically; thus, Tina "avoided embarrassing suggestions by using words in an oblique way" (14). No intense emotions are shared between these two characters, and in time, "what was once a memory that quickened the blood now drained him of any tenderness for her" (14). Communication strained between them, they go for long walks in silence: "neither of them wanted to go to bed; he, because he had not made up his mind whether he should give Mabel up, and Tina because she was waiting for him to say something" (15). Yet it is Tina who remains faithful to Ben throughout his short, tormented life. In the face of their inability to bridge the gulf between them (the reader will recall a similar crisis in the union of Sonny Armstrong and his middle-class wife, Gladys), Ben falls into a pattern of life that is normal in the colony: "Life went on in more or less the same way, and Mabel bore Ben three children . . . when Tina became accustomed to seeing him as a man who behaved like most other men in town, devoting some of his nights to another woman and dividing his income in two" (16).

Bondage to Schwartz and "the prospect of a life without Ben indefinitely" (27) are found to be infinitely more tolerable options to Tina and her mother than the scandal that a term of imprisonment would incur, even taking into account "his humiliating position in the Schwartz household" (27). Moreover, Tina's father "would die of shame" (22) at the social stigma. However, if Ben could be free – he plans to blackmail his master and extract his freedom – he would go and live with Mabel and their three children, who are his social equals and with whom he enjoys an uninhibited freedom. He would trade the antiseptic orderliness of Tina's middle-class world for Mabel's range-yard in south Georgetown where "coconut husk islands" form "stepping stones across the mud lake" to her tenement door in the rainy season (34), and "clothes lying all 'bout the place" (37) in her one-room dwelling, even though he despises Mabel's mother, who "had six children for six different men and used to knock from pillar to post" (47–48). Mabel's mother, in turn, dislikes Ben because she sees him as "a ship without a compass" (170). Significantly, it is Mabel who has the more fruitful relationship with Ben, evidenced by the children born out of their passion. But Tina, "straight as a locust tree" (1) with "eyes like the forest pool" (9) but conservative by comparison and limited by incapacitating social conventions, is as important an anchor to Ben as the rambunctious, uninhibited Mabel, who unhesitatingly romps with him in the Botanical Gardens, where they frequently take the children on picnics.

Georgetown in the 1920s is a city with no electricity, pure water supply or sewage system, an imperfect citadel for the privileged, and Ben experiences the pervasive gloom while driving his master's cab along the streets: "The denuded silk cotton trees stood out against the background of wooden build-ings. . . . In spite of the sunshine there was gloom in the air, a gloom of people with bent bodies and bloodshot eyes, of buildings in need of repair, of beggars dragging their woes along the dusty side streets . . . a gloom of sodden fruit, of old people dying imperceptibly" (151).

During a period of illness Ben is devastated by news that a rival has dis-placed him in Mabel's attentions and he blames this on the master's hold over him. Violent thoughts invade his mind; he experiences "an unquenchable thirst for the blood" of his oppressive master, vowing, "one of us will destroy the other" (151). The relationship between Ben and Schwartz unfolds in terms of a psychological struggle on the part of the master to maintain his iron grip over Ben and keep him in a state of complete and degrading subjugation. Schwartz's determination to crush his impertinent cabman is captured in the flow of his prejudiced thoughts: "All working people should know their place, because order depended on everything being in its place . . . he had conceived a hatred for Ben that was even greater than his hatred of East Indian beggars whose manner and physical deformities warranted urgent action by the authorities" (68).

On the part of the servant, his struggle is to subvert the unjust power and malice of his master. Ben's problem can be construed by the light of another of Carter's illuminating observations, made in 1955: "Emancipation in the 1830s took the chains off the hands and the feet, but the psychological constitution woven in the gloom of the plantation remained . . . the essen-tial meaning of slavery, the loss of self, the loss of identity and, its inevita-ble consequence, the most shattering, self-concept."[4] In the course of time, the middle-class high-coloured bureaucrat would replace the slave-owning colonialist in the hierarchy of power in British Guiana, and so Carter's statement remains relevant to Ben's struggle for human dignity in the sociopolitical world of *Orealla*. Schwartz's feudal tyranny extends itself in open contempt for the East Indian beggars who he fears "would take over the country one day", representing as they do "a threat" to the status quo: "Ben and those like him were the aggressive aspect of poverty who did not flinch from staring you in the face . . . such people could only be dealt with in a certain way. . . they understood only one tone of voice" (70).

Schwartz's paranoia and his extremist views are projected during private conversations with acquaintances, "in the course of which he elaborated his violent solutions to the colony's problems with a fervour that some of them found repugnant" (69). Schwartz's authoritarian attitude towards "the poor and the powerless"[5] must extend to his cabman, who appears "impertinent and conspicuously lacking in gratitude". When Schwartz discovers, early in the plot, that Ben is not simply an uneducated lackey but an aspiring writer who supplements his income by writing articles for the *Argosy* newspaper, he resolves to crush his servant's aspirations, bring him to subjection and reduce him to the status of a slave: "[H]e imposed extra work on him out of spite. Ben recalled the rage on his face when he asked, 'You wrote this? You? Where did you learn to write like this?' And from then on Ben had to do all sorts of menial jobs and clean the stables in the afternoon as well, when all cab-drivers rested" (28).

The reader is not privy to the tenor of the articles Ben writes for the press, but the image of a thief tacked on to the character of a newspaper columnist and a cab-driver seems as much out of sync as the flow of pruriency encountered in this text, which, one can guess, is an oblique comment on the amorality among the privileged, as well as the pervasive repressed sexuality of Victorian times in which an educated man loses his way.

Schwartz is an evil figure determined to oppress and destroy Ben out of sheer racial hatred; in return, he awakens Ben's rebellious spirit. On the morning when taking Schwartz to the Treasury, Ben provokes the master to anger by going another way, bringing him to a different gate a good fifty yards farther on from the one he is accustomed to using, and as Schwartz shouts and glares at Ben, the cabman grunts to himself, pleased at this small victory over the master and proud that "there was no better way to start the day" (31).

At that moment, Ben resolves that "he and his master had more than their fair share of hatred; they were brothers in hatred, and one of them had to be master" (31). In return, that evening the master pointedly asserts his superiority: "he got out of the carriage pompously, with deliberate gestures, an unfailing sign that something was wrong" (32). Ben's response takes the form of the psychological act of revenge of satisfyingly renaming his master with the name of an animal: "Buttoning up his jacket he turned on Ben, knowing he had violent thoughts about him. And in those minutes of confusion, Ben, feeling humiliated because he had no answer, feeling ridiculous, worse than a mangy dog, thought up of a new name for his employer: Grunt-Hoo. It was the name of a pig in a story Edna once told him" (32).

That night, Ben disobeys his master's instructions not to use the upstairs shower, but, "with Edna's connivance" and sympathy, he does so and, despite his small victories, goes out into the night for a walk with the galling thought of his subjugation, "of his daily humiliation" at having to work for a man "who had a hold over him" (32).

Like a feudal slum landlord, Schwartz rents the dark rooms under his house and ritually collects rent on Friday afternoons. Demoralizing Ben with such names as "villain" and "twisted cretin" (41, 42), Schwartz demands rent from him for keeping Carl in his room downstairs.

Carl is an Amerindian recently washed up from Orealla whom Ben met at a street corner examining birdcages. He invites Carl to lodge in his prison-like room. In defiance of his master, Ben resolves "to use his horse and cab for hire and run the risk of being prosecuted for plying without a licence" (42) to meet the additional rent demanded. Afterwards, he wakes Carl up and tells him that he is "free to show himself" because he is now a legitimate tenant. Ben's pride is injured and his hurts accumulate when Schwartz calls him "a thief and a liar" in front of his wife, "as if . . . as if he were nothing" (43); this was the man "he lived *through*, who preoccupied his thoughts" day and night.

Ironically, Carl gets a new lease on freedom in Georgetown through Ben's courage and sacrifice, even as Ben figuratively "froths at the mouth" (54), condemned to be Schwartz's slave for the rest of his life. In a spirit of defiance, Ben entertains himself with humorous fantasies of eliminating his despicable employer in the most gruesome manner he can conjure up; he plans that one day, to celebrate their freedom, he and Carl "would waylay Grunt-Hoo and

flay him or take him out on the groin by force and throw him into the ocean
... [where] the sharks did for you" (43).[6]

Up to this point, Ben and his master engage in subtle acts of mutual
retaliation and silent warfare. Although Ben's capabilities should make him
a worker to be valued, his master intends to disgrace him, destroy his self-
esteem and his identity in order to reassert his power over him:

> Two considerations had prevented him from teaching Ben a lesson once and
> for all. The first was his wife's disapproval of any harshness towards their
> servants and tenants; the second was Ben's competence. Few people knew
> as much about horses or could cope with repairs that required the combined
> skills of a gutter-smith, carpenter and plumber. But his wife would be away for
> two weeks and he would seize the opportunity to make an issue of the slightest
> impertinence or disobedience on Ben's part. (68)

When his cabman's insolence becomes intolerable, the modern-day slave-
master calculates that "a confrontation with Ben was inevitable":

> As a Civil Servant in authority he knew that a matter like this had to be settled
> once and for all before it got out of hand. Ben was no more than a criminal or a
> beggar with a job, only different. . . . The prisoners who came to weed his yard
> were not paid, yet they dared not look him in the eye. Ben, on the other hand,
> who was paid a wage and given free accommodation, was in the habit of gazing
> at him in a manner that enraged him to the point of distraction. The fellow
> had to be put down and the time to do it was while his wife was away. (69)

On the evening of a going-away party in honour of his wife, Schwartz
humiliates Ben and provokes him to anger by relegating him to a dark corner
of the gallery away from the guests, instructing him to make himself inconspicuous and not to "go on about the *little* pieces you get in the papers" (73),
referring to his journalism. Burning with resentment at Schwartz's attempts
to reduce him to invisibility, Ben "let him have the last word", but retaliates by
slamming the door as the master was mounting the stairs. Everything about
him irritated Ben, "the way he tucked up his balls, and his belief that he had
the right to say whatever he liked to others" (73). Ben's abhorrence at the idea
of being owned by someone forces him to go upstairs to engage the master
in a discussion: "For two years he had had a vague idea of what was at the
bottom of his relationship with Schwartz, but it was while he was standing

alone in the room one morning and caught a brief, imagined glimpse of the master standing before him – that he understood fully. He was possessed by the master" (75).

The cabman's attempt at civilized dialogue, his carefully chosen words and his civility convey the sense that, despite his flaws and his enslaved condition, he is desperately trying to keep a grip on his humanity: "Now, sir, you've got to understand that you only employ me; you don't own me. I'm not your horse or your land. You do not have the right to say what you like to me in front of my friends . . . my pride is awake. . . . I can at least insist that you display good manners when dealing with me" (76).

Schwartz cunningly humours Ben by readily agreeing with him; Ben quakes "at the unexpected victory and the pleasant way in which the demand was conceded" (76) but does not fail to detect the master's ploy and his barely concealed wrath. This defeat emphasizes the deceit and hypocrisy of colonial relationships and causes Ben to reflect on an indelible image from his childhood at Skeldon. In a lengthy excerpt which bears repeating, the servant is caught agonizing over his dilemma of infinite entrapment and a rebellious nature:

> [A]ll of a sudden the flowers in the vases gave off a scent which sickened him and the humidity grew oppressive, and there came to his mind a warm night at Skeldon when the whole family was gathered on the stairs and their attention was drawn to a crowd. Attracted by the children's excited shouting, he had run to join them. In the centre of the gathering a man was belabouring a huge snake, which kept slithering slowly towards the trench. Two other men fetched sticks and added their blows to the assault without seeming to do the slightest harm to the reptile. A man in the group persuaded one of the assault group to lend him a stick, and with a single blow on its head he stopped the snake just short of the water, so that its body kept shuddering. Now why, Ben wondered, should he have thought of that incident at that moment? The blow on that diamond-shaped head came back to him with the clarity of a vivid dream. *Perhaps he was dead and only his body was shuddering, like the snake at the edge of the trench.* Was Carl's indifference to his plight in that house an acknowledgment of his non-existence? *And this personality he attributed to himself, was it the freedom of the slave, who was allowed to wriggle without getting anywhere?* He inhabited a corner of the gallery with orders to be inconspicuous, to show life only when his name was called. He reflected that his life consisted of

tiny, ephemeral freedoms in a long twilight of humiliation. If he had Tina's or Edna's good sense he would not show fight; *but being what he was, like Mabel, he was destined to receive blow after blow* until someone, judging that he had too dangerous an idea of his worth, came and despatched him with a thump on the head. (79–80; emphases added)

Whereas Schwartz plans to double-cross Ben and hand him back to the police while his wife is holidaying in New York, Ben happens to discover Schwartz and his wife's best friend *in flagrante delicto*. Ben enters a new phase in his relationship with his master, and excitedly calculates how he might use this development to blackmail his master and gain his freedom when the mistress returns: "he wanted to go up to the master's room and make him tremble at the knowledge in his possession. But he needed time to decide how to make use of the secret" (93). Then, Ben boldly and impatiently wakens Schwartz in the middle of the night to negotiate his freedom and bring an end to two years of servitude.

Momentarily cornered, Schwartz offers Ben his freedom, a handsome pay-off of thirty dollars and a reference for his silence, but Ben "laughed in his face, a mirthless laugh" (102), hoping to use the information more effectively to destroy his unfaithful master completely. Instead of accepting the offer of freedom, Ben demands higher wages and a waiver of Carl's rent, and Schwartz grudgingly agrees temporarily to appease his servant. Schwartz, a cunning bureaucrat, capitalizes on Ben's fatal error of judgement and soon afterwards withdraws the offer, but, nonetheless, he "slaps Ben on the back" in a mock gesture of friendliness. Then, "holding his arm as they went down the staircase", Schwartz invites Ben to "talk this business over like two edu-cated men" (103) to delude Ben into thinking that he recognizes him as an equal despite everything. Then suddenly, Schwartz "spoke bitterly" and Ben grasps his sadistic intentions: "he was sure Schwartz was thinking of the days when slaves used to be strung up and beaten for minor offences" (104). The tyrant Schwartz seizes the upper hand again and reasserts his power and superiority over his impudent cabman: "He stood looking at his lackey with murder in his eyes. Then in a high-pitched voice he spoke: 'The worst thing we could do in this country is to educate people of your class! You're my servant and, whatever hold you've got over me, you'll remain my servant. If you cut my throat, while I'm dying I'll have the satisfaction of knowing you're my servant. You'll always address me as a servant should'" (104).

From that moment, the psychological war between master and servant intensifies. Schwartz swears that "he would never be at peace until he destroyed Ben" (106), while Ben maintains his civility; although he felt "he had never been closer to knocking out the master's teeth", he smiles before descending to the stables. Late that night Ben sees a light in the upstairs bedroom and knows triumphantly that he has won another victory over his master significant enough to cause the tyrant a sleepless night:

> He could not find peace of mind! And Ben's dejection was immediately trans-formed into an indescribable joy. He saw nothing except the wan lamplight through the panes of the sash window and the open skylight below the eaves. . . . Ben had always dreamed of flattening him, either in the flesh or in the spirit; and here before his eyes was the evidence of his extinguished spirit, a window smudged with yellow light. (105)

Since his flawed negotiations with Schwartz, Ben is able to give Mabel more money, but soon comes to realize that it is a pyrrhic victory. He bitterly regrets his illogical decision, that he did not humbly take Schwartz's offer of the fundamental freedom he craves, instead of deluding himself with the impractical idea that greater glory lies in trying to blackmail and destroy Schwartz when his wife returns:

> He felt like weeping in the shadow of the palms. Suddenly he knew how he lied to himself, even in his sincerest reflections. In bargaining with the master he failed to make the most important demand of all: that he should be allowed to live away from his house. Ben hated being at his beck and call, yet neglected the one demand that would have given him a measure of freedom and, above all, reunited him with one of his women. (130)

At this point the reader can only sympathize with Ben, a character emblematic of the human condition, for Ben himself is uncertain of what he really wants out of life. Paul Binding seems to understand the complex nature of this character: "Ben is the most vivid instance of what for Heath is the truth about mankind . . . that the self is multiple and defies labelling. The Ben who steals, the Ben who loves Tina, who loves Mabel, who loves Carl, who hates his employer, are all equally authentic . . . two impulses of love and hate connect Ben with the ways of life that context the untidy, amorphous, cultureless life of Georgetown itself."[7] The irony of Ben's entrapment and the truth behind his ambivalence is that his quasi-slavery is also a place of refuge, a circumstance that complicates his flawed quest for freedom:

> Edna did not realise that Ben was not permitted to look for another job because the master would not let him, on account of the hold he had on him; and that one side of him liked working there, since at his age he did not care to look for work; that another side enjoyed the hatred he bore the master, and that a third liked the freedom the imposition of living-in gave him from having to account to his women-folk for all his movements. (58–59)

Predictably, in response to Ben's bold attempt at blackmail, Schwartz hardens his resolve to crush his cabman; his reasons were now "twice as strong . . . he would never be at peace until he destroyed Ben". However, Schwartz acts cautiously since he, too, is vulnerable, at risk of being exposed: "Ben's position was unassailable. He need only disclose what he had seen with his own eyes for the clouds of scandal to gather" (106), and, as Heath has earlier stated, "coming down in the world was a kind of death" for the middle class. It behoves Schwartz to flatter and humour Ben to extricate himself from a precarious situation. This he does by deceit and trickery: "If you realized how implicitly I trust you" (122). Ben, for his part, despite his momentary triumph in respect of gaining higher wages, is hardly moved by the flattery. His hatred of his master and desire for revenge are now so compelling that, instead of waiting to blackmail Schwartz, Ben now contemplates murdering him. His greater triumph would be to kill the master, the symbolic oppressor of the working class: "He wanted to take his life and was certain that the violence he aroused in him had nothing to do with the derisory wages he paid, nor his contempt for Carl. If he made over to Ben all his money it would not put out this feeling of hatred and dread he harboured towards him" (122).

One morning, on his way to the Treasury, Schwartz suavely attempts to wheedle Ben into relinquishing his increased wages – "I'll forget the difference in our stations and make a confession: times are difficult . . . I'm lucky having you and Edna and Carl. Yes. I'm not ungrateful, you see. But this drain on my resources" (150) – a beguiling subtlety that fails to impress the cabman, who "drove off when Schwartz had barely taken his seat and began turning over his employer's words, slowly, slowly, like a portion of garlic pork served up at Christmas, musing, 'One of us will destroy the other'" (151). To show his contempt for his deceitful master, Ben drives so recklessly that he knocks over a cyclist, so that when they arrive in front of the public buildings, Schwartz is so unnerved that he "jumped out and fled up the stone steps" (151) without remonstrating with his cabman. That day, to continue his assault on Schwartz, Ben takes Carl and the two drive about the town in the master's cab in celebration of this small victory, "drinking from a big bottle of rum he had bought for the occasion" (151). In the afternoon, to register his defiance, Ben fails to appear at the public buildings to ferry his master home. Living in Schwartz's house, Ben "had discovered what a certain kind of freedom was – that it was a beast with head and feet and arms and eyes" (155) and he resolves to wrestle with the beast.

The next day, Schwartz appears humbled, "as circumspect as a pupil in the teacher's presence", allowing the servant to delude himself that he had won another battle in the war:

> He played his part well, not wanting to drive him [Ben] into a corner. He said not a word about the day before, nor did he leave Ben at the Public Buildings as if he did not exist but gave a quick dignified wave before climbing the short staircase. Ben had set out to squeeze every advantage he could from his hold on him and, as Ben saw it, yesterday was only the beginning. (158)

Ben believes that he is mentally equipped to deal with his antagonist. He had learned from his "grassroots" childhood about negotiating the harsh realities of life. Once, as a boy, his grandmother had taken him to the sugar factory at Rose Hall – the great learning institution of the colonized – and "as he walked along the catwalks, high above the thundering machinery, she said to him: 'You have to know where to negotiate the cat-walks. One slip and you'd be mangled'" (161). Determined "to break every convention and hack his way towards a condition of the certainty of happiness" because "inaction was not in his nature" (161), Ben stands in sharp contrast with Sonny Armstrong, in the first volume of the trilogy, whose traumatic encounter with the middle class emasculates him and renders him powerless to rise above his apathy in the paralysed era of the 1920s. All of Ben's conscious thoughts are dominated by the desire to act to be free. His mind flashes back to the time when he had gone to the lighthouse and looked down at the birds below "manoeuvring on the currents like threads in the sunlight, with a freedom that made him envious" (162). At heart, Ben is a freedom-lover who had "vowed never to marry because he was the sort who was liable to wake up one morning and clear off in the direction of the trade wind" (5). He had succumbed to marriage to serve his social aspirations, but now class prejudice and servitude are galling experiences he must resist in his pursuit of selfhood.

In anticipation of yet holding his adulterous master to ransom and gaining his freedom, Ben notifies Tina of "his intention of moving in with Mabel" (179) and, in spite of his dread and the uncertainty and restraints of his circumscribed existence, exhibits a spirited desire for life: "He laughed to be alive and to feel the night air on his neck and hear the mewing gulls and know that the rain would fall as it did the year before, reviving the parched grass and the wild daisies at the roadside and filling the long trenches to the brim" (183).

Ben's exhilaration is short-lived, his plan about to collapse like a house of cards at the news of the mistress's illness. Faced with this crisis, he is vulnerable:

> [S]uddenly Ben stopped, arrested by a terrible thought. Suppose the mistress went and died, where would he be with his blackmail of the master? He would no longer be able to threaten him . . . he would never be at peace until the mistress recovered. . . . Ben was distraught. He felt as if he were in a garden full of scorpions. . . . How often he had dreamt of finding himself naked or half-dressed in some public place with long avenues between him and his room, and the sun rising majestically over the houses to expose him to every gaze. (185–86)

Sobered by reality, Ben is most respectful to his master the next morning, "calling him 'Sir', doffing his hat and bowing slightly", he waits until he "had been sitting for a good half-minute before he drove off at a respectable pace" (186). He believes he sees in the master's face "an odd expression" as he gets out of the cab and knows instinctively that Schwartz has been reassessing their precarious relationship in light of his wife's impending demise (211). If earlier Ben deludes himself that he has been winning with his rebellious strategies, it now occurs to him that Schwartz has been playing a waiting game, "like a jaguar that had cornered its prey", and Ben feels compelled to "admire him for his cunning and ruthlessness" (211). He comes to realize that blackmail is a wasted idea, no longer a viable weapon against his cunning master and yet, against all reason, he refuses to "relinquish my grip on my new rights", rights that are no longer valid. Nonetheless, not prepared to yield to his antagonist in the face of evidence to the contrary, Ben resolves to do the minimum, to get the mistress's prescriptions filled and to "do nothing else, at least not that day" (213). That day, Ben whiles away his time with Carl in more defiant acts, breaking in the new foal on the foreshore, and heedlessly neglects to fill the prescription. When it appears likely that the mistress will succumb to her illness, Ben is devastated, as if mocked by fate: "A chill ran through Ben's body and even had he wanted to speak he could not. It was as if a screen separating one side of his life from another had been drawn back to reveal a company of grinning dwarfs" (221).

The sudden death of the mistress throws Ben into a state of deep distress and primeval grief, his last hope of freedom cruelly shattered:

> It was a grey, ugly day, as if the world had grown old. . . . The uncertainty of his situation tortured him more than any quarrel he had had with the master in the past. . . . He was like a man who had lost a limb and stood apart helpless, while others settled his future. . . . His independence, so important to his way of life, suddenly appeared like a burden he was not permitted to lay down. He was at war with a man who had begun to toy with him as a cat with a bird fallen from its perch. . . . The urge to rush upstairs and kiss the hands of the mourners and beg them to help him, to plead for his children, was so powerful he could have cried out. (227)

His inner security shattered, Ben is overcome by a "desolate aloneness" and remembers a surreal and frightening image from his childhood – "a half-alive bird being devoured by sweat bees under the afternoon sun" (228) – a metaphor for his own impending fate.

Following his wife's death and the removal of her sanctions, Schwartz is now free to act upon his desire "to avenge himself on humanity". Revenge is urgent, as it will compensate him for the sudden loss of his wife, and Ben, with "his insolence and ingratitude", the embodiment of all the contemptible poor who offend Schwartz's sense of superiority, is in the direct line of fire: "All his confusion, his bewilderment and grief now flowed into one channel, directed to his cabman. . . . The poor *must* know their place and Ben's fate would serve as a lesson to all those who took charity for granted and regarded equality as a right" (230).

Not unexpectedly, the master summons Ben and humiliates him with reminders of his wretched status as "a lackey. You begin the day cleaning horse dung" (231), before reducing his wages and all his privileges. This provokes a violent reaction in Ben, who "grabs him by the collar and pushes him against the wall, while Edna stood aside, aghast" (231). Ben walks out into the street, conceding defeat, *"I have played and lost . . . of the game itself I had an insufficient knowledge"* (233). The coloured middle class remains a fearful force in twentieth-century Guyanese society, and characters such as Ben and Sonny Armstrong encapsulate the emasculation of the working class in their separate struggles to negotiate the treacherous class divide.

Even so, Ben's resolve to humble himself, make peace with Schwartz and "try to salvage as much of his pride as possible" (233) comes too late and is meaningless, since he again naively underestimates the superior force of the antagonist. In conspiracy with the police once again, Schwartz lays a trap for Ben and gets him imprisoned for two years on a false charge of theft. When Ben is released from jail, he is incited by a perceptive pavement-dweller to murder his Machiavellian master and, in so doing, exorcise the ghost of the oppressive slave-master. The rootless women in the boarding house opposite Schwartz's mansion provide the weapon Ben uses to murder Schwartz and assuage his sense of injustice. Together with the beggars, the women represent all the elements of discontinuity and dispossession with whom Ben shares an unwilling affinity. Ben is the first of Heath's murderers to face justice as an example of the underclass knowing their fixed boundaries. Schwartz's slaying is a symbolic attempt to bring to an end a cruel old order of power and human degradation practised by the influential urban middle class who have emerged as the new oppressors.

Orealla offers glimpses into the widely varying value systems prevailing in the multicultural society. As family and friends gather around the dying Mrs Schwartz, Ben is acutely aware of the social gulf that separates him from the mourners and sympathizers: "the yawning gap between his way of life and theirs was unbridgeable" (219). He reflects on the contrast between the spontaneous community of genuine relationships he left in rural Berbice and the contrived manners of the city folks:

When his grandmother was dying her relations wailed so loudly and persistently that the fowls started flapping their wings in the trees and the cocks started crowing as at morning time, and the little birds flew away to the wild courida bushes. That was mourning for you, a deep resonant celebration of relationships. . . . Watching the mistress's friends broach bottle after bottle, he saw that they respected nothing except outward appearances and the fetish of skin-tone. (219–20)

Whenever Ben's mind settles "on the peaceful recollections of his own childhood at Skeldon", he recalls an idyllic place of innocence and tranquility, a lost paradise that cannot be regained in colonial Georgetown, with its alienating divisions: "the fish-seller blowing his conch to call the women; the far banks of the Courantyne side of Surinam, a passing corial on the river with an aboriginal Indian paddling at the back and his wife and children sitting in front. . . . Those becalmed afternoons were made of boats and cottages and hammocks all drifting gently up and away to that calm the aboriginal Indians had always known" (50).

In this novel the Amerindian enters the narratives of Roy Heath, and perhaps the real meaning of *Orealla* lies in the relationship between Ben and Carl, who share an affinity, each in desperate quest of his own "Orealla".[8] Just as Ben is marooned in the city since his displacement from Skeldon, with its enduring communal values, so Carl is stranded in the intrigues and sterility of city life since his dislodgment from Orealla, an Amerindian community that has in place a predictable and equitable value system: "Aboriginal Indians never went to jail except for crimes against those who intruded into their territory, money was for them a useless commodity, and the absence of any regime of their own dispensing punishment made revolt unnecessary" (246).[9]

If Carl is the agent for Heath's experiment with the integration of the Amerindian into mainstream society, he is also a device for allowing the city-dweller to enter the world of the Amerindian, however obliquely. In this way, the coastal dweller gains an awareness of the precarious existence of Amerindians and their devastating encounter with the New World, the exploitation of their womenfolk, and their struggle for survival at the turn of the century, a picture that gives the lie to the stereotype image of the indolent Amerindian languishing in an Edenic space in the "bush": "[Carl's] mother's clan had to disperse when they were being wiped out by influenza; he was then six. His family travelled along the Courantyne River until they came to Orealla where there was an Arawak settlement and the Indians were protected" (30–31).

Prior to his meeting with Carl, Ben had held a stereotypical view of Indians, as he had never heard of the Macusi tribe: "All Ben knew about aboriginal Indians at that time was that they drank paiwari, the cassava beer" (27). Ben undergoes a transformation of consciousness, in the same way he realizes that, after his mistress's death, he and the master "would not be the same after that night. But how he would be different he had no idea" (223). If Schwartz does not grow through his "inferior" cabman, Ben grows in self-awareness and self-knowledge through his brief encounter with Carl, and feels a new respect for him: "Suddenly Ben was in the throes of a boundless joy and glimpsed the futility of trying to judge Carl's personality from his conversation or his behaviour in the company of people so different from himself" (215). One of the virtues of Heath's novels is their attempt to cultivate an empathy with the cultural forms and traditions and the humanity of the downtrodden elements of the society.

Carl trades the freedom of Orealla for urban entrapment and dependence, for the isolation of the city, where he is either confined to the black hole of Ben's cell-like quarters, "pacing up and down in a cage adorned with windows" (108), or to the upstairs room of a ramshackle Regent Street boarding house across the road, "living mostly in rags" with the virago Violet, and "looking out the window in the backyard, where they in' got nothing 'xcept latrines and the backs of shops" (194). In a city overflowing with [East] Indian pavement beggars shunted out of the sugar estates with tattered clothes and sick bodies, no longer able to toil and dying like flies without pensions or benefits, even the beggarman knows that Carl "can't get a job in this rat-hole of a town" (197).

Except for the fellowship that develops between Ben and Carl, Carl remains unaccommodated in mainstream society. The integration of the Amerindian into city life is improbable because there is no community into which he can integrate, as symbolized in the poisoned and fractured relationship between Schwartz and the underdog, Ben. Schwartz's contempt of Carl, derogatorily labelling him "buck-man", as well as his indignation that Ben finds "the time to cultivate these strays" (28), ironically exposes not his superiority but the savagery and primitiveness of the upholders of Western culture that Schwartz represents.

The Georgetown society of this novel is an impoverished world comprising either the powerful or the powerless, victor or victim,[10] and, in a sense, Georgetown is an open prison and Ben's indentureship to Schwartz is a metaphor of psychic entrapment in the city. Carl, Violet and her powdered-up women friends "knocking from pillar to post" (100), and the yellow-haired beggar man, are all disconnected elements of a non-existent community, social misfits connected by a common sense of revolt in a peculiarly postmodern condition. All the characters of this novel are trapped in the "peculiar distress that town life bred" (93): Ben and Schwartz are trapped by human frailty, one by his weakness for crime and his rebellious spirit, the other by his tyrannical disposition and his infidelity. Violet and her colleagues are trapped by poverty and by their choice of making their living by prostitution, which makes return to their community impossible; Carl is trapped by "his isolation in town, by the distance between him and Orealla" (106) and by an irrational hope of a better life in the city.

Although he is "cast out" of Eden, Eden remains in Carl's head. In the end, he rejects his "narrow dependence" in the city and quietly returns to Orealla, to a pattern of life "in the bush where he and his family and friends meet at least once a month, when the men drink paiwari and the women have to restrain them from fighting" (59), in an innocent, idyllic community. Heath adopts poetic language to describe the communal values of the Amerindian community, where "nothing was done in haste, where rain-birds sang in the wake of storms and children collected the pink eggs of giant snails" (91).

Ben's relationship to the interior lies in his dreams of the tantalizing freedom of Carl's Orealla up the Courantyne River, a place "at once real and legendary". And yet Orealla is a device for emphasizing Ben's entrapment in the soulless city, "thinking of visionary journeys, the lairs of jaguars, blackwater creeks and whistling anacondas dragging themselves along the banks of dried-up rivers. Carl's world, at once real and legendary. . . . He could be there next week, but now he was here in Georgetown, which paraded its precisely measured avenues, where animals were harnessed and people no longer needed to be harnessed, being so docile" (60).

If Ben's stance against his master can be deemed to represent the voice of the black man in the upsurge of black rights movements in other parts of the globe, an unsuccessful attempt at freedom given the time frame, perhaps the ultimate meaning of *Orealla* lies in the invincibility of the human spirit, evidenced in Ben's determined silence and his characteristic spirit of defiance and unrepentance during his trial for murdering a man he considered evil and oppressive, thus striking a symbolic blow at all oppressors: "When the verdict of guilty was pronounced, Ben experienced a curious indifference, as though his last stay in jail had irreparably damaged his instinct of self-preservation. . . . He had become indifferent to death. . . . What he had told the beggar in anger was true: prison had indeed made him free . . . had made not the slightest impression on him" (254–55).

Ironically, just when Tina's mother leaves her house for Ben to enjoy without her intimidating presence, the rebellious servant is led to his inevitable fate on the gallows, his life a sacrifice to the possibility of a new order in the relationships of the British Guianese society that will hopefully begin again from innocence: "the voices of children in the failing afternoon light, sunset on the Courantyne River" (255).

It should be noted at this point that in the next chapter, which analyses *Kwaku* and *The Ministry of Hope*, Heath goes on to show the growing authoritarianism of local rulers, walking in the footsteps of Schwartz, after independence.

8

KWAKU AND THE MINISTRY OF HOPE
Community in Chaos

> In this foul age of a new
> and recurring despair, I
> keep working for a storm, some
> kind of fury to write new dates
> in our vile calendar and book.
>
> —Martin Carter, "Some Kind of Fury"

A confidence trickster named Kwaku is the central character of both *Kwaku* and *The Ministry of Hope*. The two narratives represent the penultimate works of an oeuvre that attempts to reinterpret the psychosocial and cultural reality of twentieth-century Guyana and its tortuous transition from colonialism to independence. In sequence, the two novels crystallize the picture of man adrift in a deformed society, a picture which first emerges in Heath's two earlier, ironically deemed "independence" novels, *A Man Come Home* and *The Murderer*. *A Man Come Home* opens with Foster gleefully examining the new Guyana flag, full of expectations of change in the lives of ordinary people. However, the narrative unfolds to reveal Foster and his circle of family and friends trapped in postures of dependency. Foster's son Bird meets a tragic end pursuing instant wealth, while his friend Gee prepares to exile himself from family and community. Political independence has been granted to the former colony, but the structures through which a free people might subsist are not yet in place. With no viable possibilities for economic independence, the characters of this novel are driven to exist through flawed schemes and hopes. In *The Murderer*, Galton Flood is freed by the deaths of his parents to pursue an independent life, but finds it impossible to jettison the entrenched Victorian morality that defined colonial life. Galton's outcome parallels the newly independent country still fixed in old postures of dependency. Galton ultimately succumbs to madness, walking the city streets thinking he is corked in a bottle.

Together, the two later novels, *Kwaku* and *The Ministry of Hope*, seek to deepen the reader's understanding of the meaning of independence and freedom in post-independence Guyana. They provide a frame for further discussion of the implications of constitutional freedom and offer an instructive critique of the political class in a society under the new dispensation of native leadership. George Lamming is perhaps the most political West Indian writer, but whereas Lamming's allusions to politics are more direct in his novels, Heath examines the political establishment in the place of his birth through a psychopathological study of the ordinary working man and his futile efforts to negotiate survival.

Heath has used the same character, Kwaku, in both works to be able to trace his psychosocial development, as he becomes a more mature adult and as his personality changes. Kwaku of the earlier novel, *Kwaku*, is a man adrift, like a colony cut adrift from the towline of the motherland and directionless at independence. Pushed and pulled by the vicissitudes of life, Kwaku becomes utterly impoverished and ends up a figure of scorn by the end of the novel. The Kwaku of *The Ministry of Hope* is essentially a transformed character, wiser to the ways of the world, especially in a place where democracy is being varied. It is the argument of this chapter that *The Ministry of Hope* is a continuation of *Kwaku*. Where the rural world of *Kwaku* seems innocuous and society is left to its own devices, Kwaku has graduated to the centre of power in *The Ministry of Hope* and the reader is able to trace the pathological change in his actions and the choices he makes to negotiate survival. He has learned what it takes to survive and is a survivor in *The Ministry of Hope*.

This chapter examines Kwaku's social and emotional progress and his rebellion against his fixed place in the scheme of things through his relationships with his wife and children, his employer, his fellow villagers, his gullible clients in *Kwaku*, and, later, in *The Ministry of Hope*, through his friends, family and acquaintances in the ruling political party.

In *Kwaku*, the protagonist is a father of eight, a miscreant and village buffoon who flees the village when he mischievously breaches the Conservancy Dam and causes crops to flood. He arrives in a secondary town, assumes a new identity and, posing as a herbal healer, makes a thriving income before circumstances reduce him to poverty. This work goes up to a low point in Kwaku's life when he loses his clients, has no means of livelihood and has become a figure of scorn. After completing this novel, Heath then saw the chance to develop the malleable Kwaku character to mirror the developing progress of the society; in *The Ministry of Hope*, Kwaku goes further in demonstrating his ability to exploit the environment. To this end, he travels to the city, the heart of opportunities, and graduates into a hardened impostor.

The Ministry of Hope is more overtly political and brings Kwaku directly into contact with conditions where, according to the critical narrative voice, the "condition of the national economy provided the base from which Kwaku's fortunes were resurrected" (5). When Kwaku learns in a rum shop in Berbice of a "promising trade in painted chamber pots which gullible tourists are buying as souvenirs", with the prospect that "there is money to be made in hard times", his trickster instincts are aroused. He is confident he can use his cunning and "superior intellect" to capitalize on an unsuspecting clientele with this ridiculous scheme. The psychological exploration of the mind of the trickster is the triumph of *The Ministry of Hope*: "What mystified Kwaku above all was the gap between his own view of himself and those that others entertained of him. Apart from his tendency to exaggerate he gave no cause for offence. He would even describe himself as considerate and, without doubt, the possessor of an unusual intelligence" (7–8).

In each work, Kwaku's progress demonstrates how the psyche in some ways adjusts to the social environment. It is the argument of this chapter that a relationship exists between the flawed evolution of the main character, his tragicomic struggle for selfhood and the condition of the society.

Guided by the all-knowing voice of an omniscient narrator, we follow Kwaku's drift into uncertain territory. Through the character's introspections we become aware of the formlessness of the society and experience the palpable question of the promise of independence. On the surface, *Kwaku* is the tale of a clownish, picaresque buffoon. Kate Cruise O'Brien sees the Kwaku in *Kwaku* simply as "the village idiot, reduced to poverty and failure, trying to find dignity in a new identity",[1] while another review puts him in social context: "a wonderful comic novel about an irrepressible hustler and the culture that spawns and sustains him".[2] On a deeper level, Kwaku is one of history's casualties; he embodies an endemic sense of dysfunction in a free society that appears to have lost its way.

To enter the world of *Kwaku* and *The Ministry of Hope* one must at least be aware of the nature of the society upon which the fiction feeds and the history that underpins that world. The society inhabited by Kwaku in both novels in every sense resembles a newly independent Guyana. In preparation for the 1964 elections, the British moved to completely outmanoeuvre the Marxist Cheddi Jagan by altering the electoral boundaries and changing the electoral system from "first past the post" to proportional representation. The People's Progressive Party gained more seats (twenty-four) than other contestants; however, the People's National Congress, led by lawyer Forbes Burnham (twenty-two seats), and the United Force, led by businessman Peter D'Aguiar (seven seats), were invited by the governor to form a coalition government. Burnham soon tired of his coalition partner and was then courted by the imperial powers to lead the nation into independence in 1966. Guyana was declared a cooperative republic in 1970, and Jagan remained in the political wilderness for twenty-eight years, a period that sociologist Ken Danns famously called "the militarization of Guyana".

Novels create enough of their own background to make a work intelligible to readers, but should a reader wish to enlarge his knowledge of the evolving course of the social setting depicted, relevant works on Guyanese history exist.[3]

In 1970, Martin Carter resigned as Burnham's minister of information with these poetic words: "the mouth is muzzled by the food it eats to live",[4] when, as Rupert Roopnaraine, co-founder of the Working People's Alliance, reflects, "the regime took its first step on the road to absolute power".[5] On 13 June 1980, the Working People's Alliance leader and historian Walter Rodney met his death in the heart of the city that Heath seeks to recreate in *The Ministry of Hope*. As a result, the cruelty of the colonial plantation culture seemed to have been replaced, and a society that had looked forward to freedom and redemption from colonialism found itself floundering from unfolding events.

There were many consequences of the ensuing exodus for the society: fundamentally, the splintering of the family unit and the breakdown of community – two pillars of society – in addition to the drawing away of skills and human capital. It has to be said that there are two opposing views of this period of Guyanese history: those who see Guyana as a failed state of cooperatives replacing free enterprise, and those who revere and admire Burnham as a leader with a vision of a self-sustainable nation. This study only seeks to examine the world depicted in Heath's novels.

The condition of Guyana in the second half of the twentieth century is reflected in much of the imaginative literature that later appeared. Martin Carter's revolutionary poems (*Poems of Resistance*) speak eloquently to imperial subjugation, poverty and the subversion of the colony's attempt at self-determination. Carter was a budding poet when the constitution of British Guiana was suspended in 1953. His "Black Friday 1962"[6] gives a sense of heightened crisis in the colony, while Grace Nichols's *Whole of a Morning Sky*[7] offers, in narrative form, vivid scenes of the same disorder. Andrew Morrison's *Justice: The Struggle for Democracy in Guyana, 1952–1992* aims to "chart the Odyssey of a small nation in search of its soul as it struggles to find an identity after a history of borrowed meanings and alien cultures", but, instead, offers a picture of disorder, "long series of clashes . . . while the country gradually sinks into civic disarray".[8]

The literary response to the political anxiety in the state conveys a sense of the emotional disturbance caused by public events. The senseless slaying of Father Darke is the subject of Carter's celebrated poem "Bastille Day", while his "Assassins of conversation / they bury the voice" came after the shock of Rodney's death.[9] Bernard Heydorn's *Walk Good Guyana Boy* recreates one of the most vivid instances of psychic trauma: the novel's protagonist, Stephen Sleighton, is rescued in a life raft off Barbados after fleeing Georgetown following an inferno at the home of his girlfriend when at least four members of the family perished: "The news sent shock waves through the city and country. Stephen was numb and his family spoke in whispers."[10]

For more overt examinations of the theme of ontological insecurity that characterized the times one can go to Harischandra Khemraj's *Cosmic Dance* and Narmala Shewcharan's *Tomorrow Is Another Day*.[11] The reader has much to learn from these two novels about Guyana during a period of anxiety.

Shiva Naipaul's *In a Hot Country* also speaks to the period, and his *Black and White* relates the horrors of the Jonestown holocaust, in which Jim Jones, an American cult leader and megalomaniac, chooses the Guyana hinterland to establish his fanatical religious commune which goes horribly wrong.[12] This God-figure mirrors the flawed quest for power by a deluded individual and we submit that the lessons learned from this episode are instructive for Guyanese. Lakshmi Persaud's *For the Love of My Name*[13] seeks to visualize the period as a reign of disorder and offers a mine of details.

Three of Heath's novels traverse the same territory as the works mentioned above, but they do so indirectly until *The Ministry of Hope*. In a fictional work any resemblance to actual people is usually refuted by its author, but Heath's work contains scarcely veiled allusions to the state of Guyana (318) and to well known events of the period (312). However, this study emphasizes that even though *The Ministry of Hope* has all the features of a post-independent Guyana, the work transcends the mundane details of history and retains its value as a work of fiction through its psychological depth of character. Perhaps the most memorable scene of this novel is of a government minister luring an erstwhile party man to his death in the Conservancy canal. It is a study in psychology, a well-created fictional scene and worth quoting in full:

> He stepped aside and remained standing on the edge of the path.
>
> And in the moment when the two men were side by side on the dam, at that very moment the purpose of their proximity high above the water came home to Correia with such clarity he remained rooted to the spot convinced by some quirk of time that what was about to happen had already happened, perhaps many years before. And while he stood, so paralysed by fear he had no thought of defending himself. . . .
>
> Walking along the dam, the Minister became obsessed with the idea of the side on which he would allow Correia to go past; should it be on the right- or left-hand? The success of the undertaking seemed to depend on the choice. Yet when the moment came to invite Correia to step ahead, he lost his head and allowed him to approach on the right, the side he decided should be barred at all costs. In the dark he could only stare at the immobilized figure of his former employee who, he believed, had stopped because he did not care to lead the way. And this last act of apparent defiance drove him into such a rage he conceived Correia as the embodiment of all the opposition he had encountered during his rise to the top.

Suddenly, the night was rent by a piercing shriek, and a flock of birds flew up from their roost beneath a nearby clump of trees.

By the time the Minister's car was back in town the tyre treads that had come in contact with the muddy village path had long shed their clods of earth, and when it turned into the driveway and moved slowly between the tall pillars of the mansion, only the most observant onlooker would have noticed anything unusual about its wheels. (*Ministry*, 256–57)

Unlike Khemraj and Shewcharan, who give a sense of racial tribalism at work in their novels through numerous characters, Heath's reinterpretation of this period in Guyanese history is sustained by exploiting the conscious-ness of a single character whose graphic details of the period – "mixed Creole and Indian villages became exclusive ramparts of a single race overnight" (217) – reveal the polarization of the society. It would seem that Kwaku has always lived in a society in some kind of crisis: "He was a small boy when British soldiers landed from a warship anchored beyond the lightship [in 1953]" (217) and the colony's constitution was suspended shortly afterwards.

At the heart of the two fictional works under consideration is the drift of the eponymous antihero, Kwaku, to uncertainty and loss of self. In the absence of manuscript evidence it is difficult to speculate why Heath did not keep the simple title *Kwaku* for both works, or why he felt obliged to name the sequel ironically *The Ministry of Hope*.

In *Kwaku*, the antihero is an inveterate liar, would-be photographer, near-bigamist and father of eight. A semi-literate buffoon, Kwaku gets mar-ried, builds a house with the help of the community, raises a large family on the meagre salary of a shoemaker's apprentice and makes regular party contributions to be assured of favours. He has learned the value of posing as an idiot to shirk responsibility: "intelligence was like a plimpla palm, bearer of good fruit, but afflicted with thorns" (*Kwaku*, 7), and among his many flaws is a reputation as "the man who could not keep his mouth shut" (the subtitle of *Kwaku*). However, government thugs menace him for allegedly making disparaging remarks against the administration and cause him to go into hiding, so that political victimization adds to the complexity of Kwaku's psychological predicament in his futile struggle for survival in this novel.

Kwaku must be seen for what he is, a flawed individual as well as an Anancy figure who both subverts the status quo and is set to exploit his fellow men in a society in transition. Although he gains self-esteem from his work – "his employer praised him highly and even claimed that the care and skill he brought to half-soling his clients' shoes had earned him the sort of reputation that attracted custom from villages miles away" (20) – the fact is that he cannot manage on his meagre salary as he grapples with the responsibility of marriage and home. Kwaku labours under delusions of grandeur, believing that he is bigger than his place in the village and that he is "made for better things" (121); hence self-deception and a false self-image cause him to shun his uncle's offer of an acre of land aback to grow crops and augment his income by honest toil, deeming it backbreaking work. The fact that he feels "a vague distress . . . an indefinable unease at his place in the life of the village" (28) does not prevent him from refusing a salaried job as a bus driver that his lover, Blossom, organizes for him, as he believes "in his superiority over other men, in a destiny that went beyond driving a bus-load of unthinking passengers past endless clumps of courida bushes to the end of the world. . . . No, he could not end his days at the wheel of a bus, the hero of small boys" (8). Kwaku is desperate to rise above his inferior station in life, but on his own terms. The possibilities for social and economic stability by honest toil do not appeal to him, and he flounders blindly when he can avail himself of no opportunity for self-realization and self-determination.

When a locust plague causes crop failure, retrenchment and destitution in the villages on the east coast of Demerara and "everywhere there is despondency" (58), two of his children are despatched to his wife's parents – the symbolic start of the breaking-up of the family unit that was typical of the period Heath attempts to discuss – yet Kwaku is prevented by a false pride from going aback to hunt or fish, as other villagers are doing to survive. Instead, he deceives his wife, Miss Gwendoline, by hanging on at the shoemaker's without pay or idling at nearby houses during working hours. Even though he spends sleepless nights frightened about his future and agonizing over "how he has failed his family and how thin his children have become", Kwaku, as head of a family, is a pathetic creature who lacks the will to act and instead spends his time evading responsibility.

Having two women in his life complicates Kwaku's quest for social mobility. Clinging to her moral values at a time when such values seem under erosion, Miss Gwendoline is outraged by the offer of charity from Kwaku's "sweet-woman" and orders Blossom to "take her money somewhere else". Kwaku's pride is injured, "ashamed that he could not provide for his family", but, coward that he is, he "dared not intervene" (60). Kwaku is trapped by his infidelity. To escape his wife's scorn, he flees his home and wanders aback, where, either out of defiance of the government or sheer mischief, he breaches the Conservancy Dam, thus flooding the cultivated lands and adding to the chronic poverty in the villages. A crisis develops when Blossom's husband, with his "well-developed civic consciousness" (78), informs on Kwaku and five burly men hunt him to punish him.

Barely escaping the hands of the law, the emasculated Kwaku abandons his family and takes flight from the village, ostensibly to seek work – "on the face of it he was leaving the village to find a means of maintaining his family; but at bottom it was his inability to deal with his wife's unspoken scorn that was driving him away" (96) – leaving Miss Gwendoline to head a household of children without tangible means of support. Instead of heading for George-town, where everyone flocks in search of work, Kwaku heads to New Amster-dam, a "dump town" in the county of Berbice, where he stumbles upon a new identity as a herbal healer, ready to exploit any situation, the more obscure the better: "Kwaku shrugged his shoulders for an answer. . . . He would have liked to reveal that that was precisely why he was going there. In fact he knew perfectly well why he was going to New Amsterdam instead of the capital, with its unlimited opportunities for *freelance work*" (96–97; emphasis added).

It seems that the author is using Kwaku, a weak figure who cannot manage his home and therefore flees his village, as an analogy of flight in the fictional world of the novel. Across the country's blighted landscape, scenes of "long queues fighting for scarce food items" (199) are duplicated and "contraband goods are sold openly" (199), offering a picture of a society uncertain of its rules. In the first novel, *Kwaku*, Kwaku's struggle to keep his place in society can be read as the people's struggle for survival in lean times.

Although Kwaku is involved in a number of outrageously hilarious and bizarre episodes, Heath is really essaying a disturbing psychological study of the underdog, the drifter in the fictional society whose rules are breaking up. On the day Kwaku sets off for New Amsterdam, he first goes to collect his last wages from the old shoemaker, but ends up jumping atop his employ-er's counter and lewdly relieving himself on the latter in his outrageously mischievous style. This is a crude form of justice against his malicious employer, whom Kwaku suspects of informing on him, but in the society of the novel there is no redress for such obscene behaviour.

Kwaku is an impostor who, upon arrival at the New Amsterdam stelling, passes himself off as an islander whose wife, a doctor, and children have been blown out to sea by a hurricane. This trickery is in keeping with Kwaku's character, but the episode opens up into one of those bizarre happenings in which Heath's novels characteristically comment obliquely on the irregular in society. A woman at the stelling, who would appear to be as much a trickster as Kwaku, invites him to her home, gives him a meal and forces him into a weird marriage ceremony with her dead daughter, whose decomposing body dressed as a bride is lying in a coffin. Although it is difficult to exhaust the meaning of this morbid development, the reader can be sure that this grotesque realism at least points to the irregularity of the social world that Heath is writing about.

Heath satirizes a credulous society in which Kwaku, a nonentity without a past, is allowed to drift from obscurity to fortuitous fame. Quite by accident, Kwaku recommends simple but effective herbal remedies to gullible neighbours in New Amsterdam, where he is in self-exile, and, "quick to discover the advantages of his popularity" (118), he moves to exploit their naivety and reinvent himself:

> The transformation of Kwaku's condition, coming out of the blue as it did, took him unawares, so much so that he was not certain how he should conduct himself. The face he presented to the world was no longer appropriate; of that there was no doubt. On the other hand he was unwilling to relinquish the bearing to which, at least, he was accustomed. But one night the matter was decided for him by the shoemaker, who remarked that he could not maintain his reputation in clothes that would disgrace a beggar.
>
> So Kwaku bought several lengths of cloth and gave instructions to a tailor to dress him like a gentleman with a reputation to maintain. And four weeks from then he strode into Winkle [a section of New Amsterdam] bearing a new walking-stick and a brand new appearance. (118)

As a poseur, Kwaku conducts himself "as befitting a healer . . . the days when he could be himself were over" (124–25). The image of a village buffoon must be suppressed to allow a new, tentative identity to take its place.

Kwaku opportunistically widens his knowledge of herbs by speaking with credulous clients who are themselves already familiar with the common, everyday remedies and rituals he prescribes, and which he then embroiders with esoteric meaningless details, for instance, "an infusion of burra-burra *at the start of the full moon*" (119, emphasis added). In his newfound role of faith healer, Kwaku travels up and down the Corentyne coast exploiting a gullible clientele, his evolution from anonymity to confidence trickster a close parallel to the absurdity related in the world of the novel when "people long dead voted and returned to their places in the cemeteries and ballot boxes" (*Ministry*, 251).

Kwaku, surviving by trickery behind his impostor's mask, calculates: "at a stroke, his fortunes had changed . . . his chances of an assured future might well lie with him. . . . If he knew how to harness chance, what ambition was capable of resisting him? What freedom would he not conquer? His pride, constantly under attack, would become unassailable" (*Kwaku*, 121). Brashly, he savours the security of the white-painted paling surrounding his rented cottage and revels in his fraudulence:

> He experienced, for the first time, the full satisfaction of his new-found position as healer and the security it brought him. . . . If he accepted money from sick people without having been trained to cure them, most of them were nevertheless cured. Besides, guilt never flourished in his soul. . . . Those who dispensed drugs from a surgery smelling of carbolic soap and indifference were no better than he was. His patients made their own diagnosis and compared them with his. (121)

An outwardly transformed Kwaku discovers himself importantly "standing with his hands behind his back, involuntarily adopting the pose of those accustomed to success" (121). Swelling with pride, he feels vindicated to have rejected Blossom's offer of work as a lowly bus driver and is eager to seek her out and show her that "he was made for better things" (121). Kwaku is at once seduced by his own deceit and overwhelmed with his newly created image and unexpected financial success:

> He awoke to the singing of birds. . . . Through an open window the sky stretched away to an invisible horizon beyond the roofs of the low houses. . . . He thought with satisfaction that he would soon be able to buy his own house and keep it in good repair. . . .

Kwaku loved his work, the freedom it had brought him and the respect bestowed upon him by people who had no idea what he was really like.

He was tempted to sing out loud but until his neighbours got to know him he would conduct himself as befitted a healer, a man of the people. (124–25)

The truth is that Kwaku remains a vulnerable creature, cowering behind his mask, afraid of being discovered and exposed for the fraud he is. If he does not acknowledge his duplicity in his conscious thoughts, it surfaces in his subconscious, in nightmares in which a troop of monkeys appear and menace him: "Grimacing through the panes, one was trying to open the window while two others were searching in a hysterical, preoccupied way for an aperture . . . having managed to raise the window, they stood on the ledge grimacing and watching him. Then, without warning, they threw themselves on him in a body and began devouring him" (124).

If the thought ever crossed Kwaku's mind that he should find a way out of his false pretence and fraud before his psyche is destroyed by it, the truth is that he has long dreamed of "escaping poverty" and has no intention of self-examination. Emboldened by his so-called success, his ambition knows no bounds, for now he is "driven by some unquenchable thirst to be rich . . . his reputation was everything; it enveloped him like a luminous garment, drawing people's attention to him, covering the nakedness of his character" (130). In his euphoria, he crosses the Berbice River to meet Blossom on its other bank at Rosignol, but is disappointed and "annoyed because she had not said or done anything to show that she recognized him as a new man, a healer of repute" (147). Brazenly, he demands respect, but Blossom "sucks her teeth in derision" (146), certain that Kwaku is a fraud. In his delusion, Kwaku wants to shout at Blossom: "I am the healer of New Amsterdam. Dozens of people does recognize me when I walk past the market and the post office and the fire station. You come and meet me, just as if it was years ago when I was a laughing stock and every crab-dog did wash their mouth 'pon me" (147). The tale of Kwaku is a satire of the delusions of grandeur and excesses of self-confidence of men whose outward pomp and ceremony are incongruent with the aspirations and anxieties of underdeveloped societies.

Kwaku's libidinous nature, his sexual affair with Blossom in a Rosignol restaurant, his one-time sexual demand of an indigent woman from Corentyne that takes place hurriedly in an open field, under a bridge near a rum

shop (and, in the next novel, *The Ministry of Hope*, his ravaging of Mrs Correia in his office), all emphasize the nature of the trickster, the urgency of
base instincts and the perversion of values which make the society degraded.
Kwaku suggests that the citizen no longer exists at the intellectual level to
pursue knowledge and enlightenment, but, rather, now uses his intellect to
exploit his fellow men and pursue other vain self-seeking endeavours.

When the successful trickster returns to "C" village in a triumphal mood
to visit his family, his status as a "professional" is undercut. As a returning
exile, he is a misfit among his former neighbours, who have maintained
the closeness of village life and who converse with facility on every subject,
however trivial, from "the mass murders at Jonestown to the arrival of a ship
with a cargo of garlic" (154). Kwaku becomes increasingly disconnected and
alienated from the everyday concerns that unite the community, although in
the underdeveloped villages of the country at this time there is an impoverishment of intellectual curiosity – intelligent exchanges are now reduced to
the anticipation of scarce commodities such as garlic, flour and other mundane items necessary to exist. The Reverend Jim Jones, who has taken close
to a thousand lives in a suicide pact in a reserve in the Guyana jungle, is
yet another version of the trickster abounding in a society where values are
shifting in the aftermath of empire. Wrapped up in his own delusions, Kwaku
fails to grasp the relevance of the Jonestown tragedy to his own falsity, lust for
success and power, or impending alienation.

At this point, the place where the fictional Kwaku lives is a haven for swin-
dlers. A fellow villager, Mr Gordon, who returned from overseas a wealthy
man and now lives in a majestic house, enlightens Kwaku on the finer points
of dishonesty: "Where I was working everybody was on the fiddle. So I went
straight ahead and did in London what the Londoners do. And here? I pay my
Party dues and grin with everybody . . . but you, you're so damn self-centred;
you're a blabberer and a misfit" (223). Even though Kwaku wonders "why a
calculating man like Gordon should choose him to confess that he is a thief"
(222), Gordon strengthens Kwaku's confidence that he can make his way in
the world through cunning and deceit, so that by the time we meet Kwaku in
The Ministry of Hope he is less of a "blabberer" and a more focused swindler.

Still in his home village, the protagonist offers to use his so-called magical powers to help a village fisherman find his lost sister, but he returns to

New Amsterdam without honouring his promise. The vengeful fisherman menaces Miss Gwendoline, who goes blind from hysterical fear, necessitating Kwaku's return to the village and forcing him to go back and forth with all his paraphernalia of herbs, bottles, and jars between New Amsterdam and village "C", where his wife is no longer able to manage the growing family. As he prepares for the journey he is again mocked by the monkey whose existence, delineated by a length of chain, is the perfect metaphor for the limited circumference of Kwaku's life of mimicry: "He could hear the jangling of the monkey's chain as it abandoned its itinerary and slid down its pole to stand on the ground, and then again when it clambered back up to its perch, where there was enough room to resume its fruitless journey to the limits of a circumscribed world" (191).

As an adulterer and work-shy drifter, Kwaku is known in his village more for his buffoonery than for his fame as a healer. His fellow villagers slight him and he is reduced to destitution, while his two teenage sons have grown unruly in his absence. The family drifts apart, floundering in the pervasive disorder all around them, while Kwaku cannot summon the will to do anything by honest means to keep his family intact:

> No one gave him custom, and he sat all day at Blossom's window, silent and morose . . . and took to spending a couple of hours each day in the new beer-shop, where unemployed young men were in the habit of passing much of the day playing pool as the weeks and months went by. . . . Each morning he had to get up with the birds, just like everyone else, dress as if he had a destination, and then finally take his place at the window to welcome clients who never came. (193–95)

His futile journeys between New Amsterdam and his village parallel a society going around in circles under a wily leader. As Kwaku's image as a "professional" collapses, he vents his frustration on his sons and brutalizes them: "the frenzy of the attack took the lad by surprise" (193). It is left to old Barzey, the moral voice of the work and the one who had provided an alibi for Kwaku when he was being hunted for breaching the Conservancy, to remind him that "dignity is the only thing worth living for" (199); however, Kwaku lacks the self-knowledge necessary for such a struggle towards human dignity and renewal. Barzey's wise advice to Kwaku to return to New Amsterdam with his wayward sons and salvage their empty lives through honest toil opens up complications, for when Miss Gwendoline, suspecting him of adultery, announces that she and the entire family intend to accompany him to New Amsterdam, Kwaku is plunged into the depths of despair: "he had peered into an abyss", as his false hope of "taking up again a lifestyle that had brought him a measure of dignity" evaporates (210).

Kwaku's notion of redemption is to find shortcuts to instant wealth, fame, and self-promotion. Forced to come to grips with the daily responsibility for a family he has so long neglected, the intransigent Kwaku "could not suppress a new surge of resentment" (216). To compound his predicament, back in New Amsterdam, where he has preceded his family, his clients have found a new healer, and, faced with utter destitution, Kwaku exchanges his posh rented cottage for a hovel and begins once again to knock from "pillar to post".

Kwaku is rescued temporarily by an old shoemaker, from whose workshop he writes a grandiose letter to Miss Gwendoline purporting to be a successful photographer with an opinion on public affairs: "If I had to live my life over I would buy land, land, land. Now that people standing in line all over the country to buy food is people with land that laughing" (116). Since the real world holds no satisfaction for Kwaku, he seeks refuge in the world of fantasy, so much so that his lies "did not strike him as being odd. Indeed they were no longer lies, but necessary additions to the dull fare of day-to-day living" (116).

In his self-delusion, Kwaku takes no responsibility for his own adulterous behaviour, which precipitated the upheaval and crisis he now faces, shifting blame onto his children for his coming down in the world – "If the twins did know how to behave we would've be rich by now" (218) – and hesitating to square with the truth that "sooner or later, he would have fallen a victim of Blossom's shameless intrigues" (233). Even his favourite daughter, Philomena, has lost sympathy for him; her pressing questions remain unanswered: "A year ago she had felt deeply for him; today she found it almost impossible to contain her irritation at his behaviour, his indolence, his very presence. Why did he lack the authority of their neighbour, Barzey? Why had his role in the business with the fisherman been so passive?" (219). Kwaku, possessing a weak ego and now a product of a society with few possibilities, can creatively find no avenue to self-realization through honest means. He turns his energies to dubious schemes, thus perpetuating the pervasive culture of the trickster in society. Such figures thrive in the gap between the absence of possibilities and their own flawed quest for self-fulfilment.

Miss Gwendoline's blindness is a symbol of her refusal to be a witness to Kwaku's wiliness and his failure as husband and father. When Blossom bears his love-child, the intractable Kwaku rocks the child in his arms in full view of both his unsuspecting children and Blossom's husband (who believes it to be his), "whispering endearments into its porcelain ears . . . he wanted to shout out his claim to the little creature with clenched fists" (246), at the very moment when, ironically, his precocious sixteen-year-old daughter, Philomena, makes the devastating announcement that she is pregnant. Apart from the tragedy of children being born to children, one more mouth to feed must necessarily put more strain on Kwaku's impecunious circumstances. While Kwaku is wrapped up in a fantasy world of his own, the real world of his family and their very real needs come crashing around him. Kwaku's adultery with Blossom and the child she bears him only serve to complete the picture of a society where man is led by passion rather than reason, to his own peril.

The work mourns the loss of community that village life offers – "the sound of wet garments being beaten against wood" – as well as the simple sight of modest village girls "placing their hands against their thighs with the other on their head to prevent their hats from being blown away" (176); at the same time, Miss Gwendoline, in her state of literal and figurative darkness, laments their fall to a sterile backwater town and its "terrible isolation" (243): "We not make to live in town. We's village people. . . . Look at it; it like a snake with red eyes, calling you, calling you and whistling like a comoodie snake. . . . And when you wake up you see the snake love you so much he squeeze you till you guts come out slow, slow, till you got no pride" (241). All of Heath's texts speak to a sense of loss in the movement from village to urban centre, the loss of community values and spirit, and Miss Gwendoline's feeling of insecurity echoes Ben's scepticism of the soulless city in *Orealla*: "Mark my words, the town will be our downfall" (*Orealla*, 211).

The protagonist's tragic fall is as swift as his meteoric rise to fame and money. Driven to the ground, the bright light of his success suddenly extinguished, he lives in literal darkness: "The electricity had already been cut off; and when night came the family gathered at the front to talk or brood by the light of the street lamp" (*Kwaku*, 230). To increase his distress, the bailiffs levy on Kwaku's scant possessions, the family further disintegrates as the teenage children desert the home one by one, and he and his wife are offered shelter on the fringe of the town, to share the old shoemaker's hovel at Winkle. Kwaku is drawn to the "areas of refuge" – the rumshop, "a private world of boredom and despair" (244) – and otherwise reduced to scavenging through dustbins for vegetable peelings to resell to pig-farmers for money to buy rum. Yet Kwaku has enough humanity left in him to feel "the urge to weep, on account of his impotence in the face of a fate he could not control and the growing hostility of his sons" (234).

The last image in *Kwaku* is of the protagonist tottering into a rum shop, a figure of ridicule. A mortified Miss Gwendoline endures terrifying night-mares that mirror her desolation: "an army of worms crawling from her mouth as she lay prostrate on the floor" (254). Miss Gwendoline's feeling of psychic dread is not different from Ben's in *Orealla* when, overcome by a "desolate aloneness", Ben remembers a surreal and frightening image from his childhood – "a half-alive bird being devoured by sweat bees under the afternoon sun" (*Orealla*, 228) – a metaphor of his own impending fate. It is hardly surprising that Miss Gwendoline is "glad of her blindness", saved from witnessing the public scorn of Kwaku's wretchedness: "The night when he had danced in the rum shop with two one-dollar notes sticking out of his trouser pockets like paper-wings was her enduring image of his humiliation" (*Ministry*, 80–81).

In *The Ministry of Hope*, Kwaku, trembling with excitement at the possibil-ity of rebounding to fortune, prepares to enter the festering city from which he had previously shied away. A tropical storm outside is matched by a storm of anger inside his household as volatile emotions erupt at the thought of Kwaku once again abandoning the family in their state of impoverishment: "Angrily he got up and opened the door, intending to go down to the rum shop. But it was wrenched out of his hand by the force of the wind, which threw everything into confusion. Philomena leapt up to help her father close and bolt the door, but it resisted with a violence . . . while the two used all their strength to subdue the door Miss Gwendoline remained impassive" (37).

The trickster exists at several levels of society: the government official to whom Kwaku is sent for assistance is as much a trickster as Kwaku. He steals Kwaku's seemingly lucrative business idea and offers Kwaku a lowly job as assistant to a messenger in the ministry. Through the consciousness of a thirty-eight-year-old semi-literate fake healer and his various social relationships with family and society, Heath critiques a dark moment in the social history of his fictional country and the response of a foundering society in its struggle for survival. In thirty-eight rapid chapters, the narrative imposes order upon the inner and outer anarchy of man and society and traces Kwaku's evolution from an uncertain drifter to a convincing fraud.

This chapter argues that the Kwaku of *Kwaku* and the Kwaku of *The Ministry of Hope* are the same character. The seeds of the older, fraudulent Kwaku seen in *The Ministry of Hope* are already sown in the earlier novel, except that the later Kwaku becomes a more conscious and seasoned impostor. If the earlier Kwaku drifted into the role of faith healer accidentally, the older Kwaku is now a hardened and calculated confidence trickster, conscious of being "the same fraud as when I used to practise in New Amsterdam an' did treat people with nothing but garlic . . . how frighten I used to be that people goin' to find me out" (*Ministry*, 301). Kwaku is a caricature of the "new man" and, in a sense, a version of the wily leadership of this fictional work.

One can see the shapings of a similar character in the fictional figure of the Honourable G. Ramsay Muir, MBE, in V.S. Naipaul's classic *The Mystic Masseur*.[14] Ganesh Ramsumair has progressed from a self-styled pundit to the position of an important government functionary through his wiliness and willingness to be a toady, flaunting his falsely elevated position when he is met at a London train station by an aphasic Oxford student, one of his early "patients" who knew him in Trinidad simply as Pandit Ganesh – the mask and the wearer have now become indivisible. Whereas Naipaul's acerbic insight leaves no hope of redemption for his flawed characters, Heath's depth of compassion for his characters guarantees their fragile humanity.

The fictional political directorate that Kwaku encounters in the city, with a flawed electoral machinery, causes the character to take note of certain irregularities: "they had things their own way for more than two decades with their falsified registers and mysterious resurrections of the dead who appeared at polling stations, voted and promptly returned to their resting-places in cemeteries all over the country" (312). Thinly veiled allusions are made by the author to figures who feature in the turbulent history of Guyana, for example, an American felon evading justice whose band of religious zealots regularly terrorizes dissenters, and also a Jesuit priest who dies at the hands of just such a fanatical band, ironically outside the courts of justice. Kwaku is a product of this society of self-imposed authority, but he is no longer hanging loose on the periphery. In *The Ministry of Hope*, Kwaku has arrived in the city hopeful of a niche from which to practise his idealism. His philosophy for survival is clearly defined – it is one that dispenses with the necessity of struggle and toil: "Life seems to accommodate certain people, while others are forever kicking against the pricks and end up by cursing fate for its unbending attitude". Kwaku belongs to the first group – "however low he sank, circumstance would conspire to raise him up again" (5) – as, by nature, Kwaku is a man of no quality, always willing to compromise himself.

Kwaku's induction into the city and his links with the nameless Minister of Hope are, typically, a matter of sheer chance. Years ago, while practising as a herbal healer on the Corentyne coast, Kwaku had come across a youth of unusual intelligence. Limited by his own "meagre education" (30), he seeks to co-opt the lad for the new venture in chamber pots but discovers that, by a stroke of intrigue, this character is now the permanent secretary to "a Minister without Portfolio" in the Ministry of Hope. Another chance event, a scribbled note from the minister's mother, Miss Rose, with whom Kwaku has had a one-night stand, suffices for his entry into the surreal urban arrangement.

Kwaku and Mohun Biswas from V.S. Naipaul's *A House for Mr Biswas*[15] have much in common, both foundering in formless societies in their tragicomic struggles for self-esteem and social mobility, although their aspirations are poles apart. Biswas only wants a simple house, a simple family life, and acceptance into the "moneyed" class of the society, while Kwaku is "driven by some unquenchable thirst to be rich" (*Ministry*, 130) and famous. Both characters embody the suggestion that man is a creature of illusion, for Biswas's ostensibly simple quest is no less complex than Kwaku's dubious ambitions. In many ways, Kwaku's relationship with his wife bears similarities to that of Biswas with his wife, Shama. Both women are anchors to drifting men: "He knew nothing about keeping books and it was Shama who had suggested that he should make notes of goods given on credit on squares of brown paper. It was Shama who suggested that these squares should be spiked. It was Shama who made the spikes."[16] Similarly, Kwaku is astonished to discover in Miss Gwendoline a humanity that respects him even "when he was incapable of protecting her" (*Ministry*, 191). Both Biswas and Kwaku represent the desire for individualism, while Shama and Miss Gwendoline represent the traditions of family and community, two impulses often impossible to reconcile.

Kwaku's relationship with a hopelessly corrupt government functionary, the ironically named Minister of Hope, captures a sense of the underlying perversity of the social world Heath engages. This nameless official has been hastily promoted to the post of minister on account of his being the right-hand man of "top brass" and feared by his colleagues as "the embodiment of ruthlessness" (21). He had begun "as a creature of a government minister", performing such menial tasks as "spying on the minister's mistress, and on people suspected of being disloyal to the ruling party" (20). Heath critiques a morally bankrupt administration that can be found anywhere in the world where ability is no longer a criterion for gaining office, and, most instructively, he offers glimpses into the psychopathology of its fictional leaders. For his compliance in these shameful activities, the "Right Hand Man" gains rapid promotions, "until he reached the point where he came to be recognised as the most brilliant star in the galaxy of young pretenders to ministerial responsibility. When, finally, he was appointed a Permanent Secretary, leaving behind him older and more experienced men with a solid academic education, he boasted that behind ambition lurked a sinister companion who eschewed morality" (20).

All the while Miss Rose naively believes that her son's success is due to "an ability to read well", but Amy Correia discovers the dark forces beneath the surface of the man she has linked herself with as her employer and lover:

> Week by week, Amy discovered something new in the Minister of Hope, and her own weakness for attributing to him qualities he did not possess. His sophistication, conspicuous to acquaintances and those who worked in the ministry, was a veneer that covered a solid foundation of a different kind laid down, no doubt, in his formative years. . . . [T]he conclusion was forced upon Amy that the carefully contrived separation of his real Self from the public figure could have only been achieved by a person with no pretensions to morality. (166–67)

A lackey-turned-minister embodies the perversity of rulers in Heath's scalding novel. Through various shenanigans, this functionary has amassed "a not inconsiderable sum of money since his political appointment. . . . He owned a part-share in an airline, a tract of land . . . a special account that accommodated bribes he had not sought, but had been foisted on him for real and imagined favours. After all, his countrymen had become so bribe-conscious, they thrust money into an official's back pocket if he even blinked at them" (45) – barely disguised corruption that makes a mockery of the mean-ing of independence. Ironically, this is the man under whose wing Kwaku, the opportunist, intends to "nestle while nurturing his own unbounded ambi-tion" (46), matched by a well-concealed contempt for the self-made man who, after all, "was the son of Miss Rose, who used to frequent New Amsterdam rum shops and rub shoulders with down and outs". The rise of a party thug to the echelons of power both repels and fascinates Kwaku and further boosts his confidence that he too can somehow bluff his way to wealth and fame: "All things considered, he was impressed by the official's demeanour, a model worthy of emulation" (47).

Kwaku arrives at the Ministry of Hope in a mood of optimism that matches "the sun, high in a cloud-free sky" (39) only to find a freakish, upside-down world unfolding before him: a typist who behaves like "the Queen of Sheba", and a lack of regard for punctuality from the very top official, in addition to ineptitude and affectation. In an atmosphere that appears to him to spawn freaks and frauds, Kwaku is inspired to put his trickery into practice. In order to be taken seriously, he boldly announces himself as a cousin of the minister:

> He resolves to revive his habit of lying extravagantly. After all . . . he had come home! He had found his level at last! In the village and in New Amsterdam he had passed for being a freak. . . . There could be no doubt that the town was full of Kwakus, better educated than he, no doubt, but branded with the unmistak-able mark of the peculiar breed. . . . Since he was among people who made a profession of misbehaving, he must make of misconduct a fine art. (41–42)

Kwaku, the confidence trickster masquerading as idiot, is the means through which the urban chaos and corruption unfold. Kwaku is deemed a "nincom-poop" by his co-workers, some of whom do not conceal their contempt for the lowly assistant messenger, but the fact is that, typical of other tricksters we have encountered in Heath's corpus, Kwaku's naive manner is a mask:

> Having had much practice since childhood . . . he had become the Prince of

dissembling and the Fool who flaunted his flawed literacy, while taking in everything that went on around him. . . . It had not taken him long to realize that the people who got on were the virtuosos of manipulation. He saw himself as an apprentice in this city of Sodom where strange growths spring up in a manner of fungus on decaying wood . . . the reality of living in the capital was altogether stranger, and Kwaku listened and waited while feathering his nest. (63)

Face to face with a dysfunctional civil service, an "unserviceable electricity generating unit acquired at a great sum" that is a national joke, a hundred Public Corporation vehicles unaccounted for, the country going to the dogs, the currency now worthless, the police force above the law, to name a few in a long list of woes (118), Kwaku does not fail to see that he too could be a successful fraud in a society where fraudulence is the norm. He gains an awareness of the Machiavellian nature of the regime from the canvases of a mad artist, Surinam, one of which immortalizes all the people murdered in the race riots tacitly presided over by the same Minister of Hope.

The quest for freedom and dignity is at the heart of the human condition and this struggle for dignity is evidenced in some of Heath's most flawed characters. As a conscious choice, Kwaku accommodates the regime with his silence and compromises his dignity, all for the lure of wealth and status in a dubious setting. Rather than settle for less than freedom, a large part of the society chooses exodus. The older Kwaku is no longer the buffoon; rather, he is learning to be more manipulative in his relationships. Aware of the vendetta society he inhabits, he addresses Shakespeare's famous question "to be or not to be" when he resolves to be not one of the regime's statistics but a survivor by any means.

The Minister of Hope, tireless in his ploys, sends Kwaku to Lethem, on the Brazilian border, ostensibly to spy on his illegal currency dealer, Correia, whereas his real motive is to keep Kwaku away from Georgetown and from discovering that he has cheated Kwaku of his euphemistic business idea "in antiques" (76). There, even the caretaker of the guesthouse notices Kwaku's shiftiness and opines that he cannot enjoy the peace of the Rupununi savannahs "cause you got frenzy in your soul"; with his flawed self-image, the trickster is convinced that "the frenzy was in the world around him, not in *his* soul" (89–90; emphasis added).

In a dramatic turn of events, Correira absconds with the currency and disappears in Lethem, but the minister, determined to ensnare Kwaku "before he entertained inflated ideas about his independence" (125), offers him Correia's job. However, Kwaku intuitively refuses to accommodate his benefactor, who intends to crush him "like a matchstick" and, with a rare show of moral strength, threatens to expose the minister's corrupt currency dealings (126). With this uncharacteristic display of courage in his crooked struggle for freedom and identity, Kwaku resists the minister: "I'm grateful for the way you help me, sir. I want to repay you. But you don' own me" (127). In the world of dictatorship, it is to Kwaku's credit that he chooses not to be used as fodder for a ruthless machinery.

Kwaku's show of independence stems from textual evidence that he is no longer dependent on a government patron, but has formed a new relationship with Heliga, his intended son-in-law and amateur acupuncturist, with a new practice in the city where all tricksters seem to converge. Heliga, a man "of unbounded ambition who reminds Kwaku of his own callow youth", and whom the blind Miss Gwendoline intuits to be like "a malignant scorpion scurrying to an underground nest with its tail curled up" (227), is another underworld creature of a lawless society. Where the pair is deficient in expertise, they impress their clients with the superficial suavity that Heliga adopted from his short sojourn in America: "Kwaku cultivated *style*, unashamedly copying Heliga" (134). Kwaku's veneer of transformation is so convincing that the minister's mother, Miss Rose, is taken in on a visit to his "modern surgery . . . scarcely believing her ears, for not only did he speak with a different voice but he seemed to have acquired a different vocabulary" (173). In the hardening regime of the novel, Kwaku becomes a more refined impostor and professional fraud and the tragedy is that society believes the mask it sees.

To Miss Rose's anxious queries about her son's involvement in the fall of Correia, the party's fire-raiser and illegal money-changer, Kwaku simply replies: "I don' know, Miss Rose" (174). Kwaku knows everything, but he knows nothing; he no longer blabbers idiotically and no one would suspect "what a heroic effort he made to keep his tongue in check" (132) or how much he "longed for his old status as buffoon; like the gilded butterfly of a fantastical tale that hankered after the pristine home of its tomb-like cocoon" (314). And when the minister swiftly dispenses with Correia in the Conservancy canal, Kwaku's knowledge of the murky world of party politics "guaranteed his silence" (263). The reader is alerted to the degree of political naivety in a party minion who allows himself to be lured to his death.

By this time, the fictional despot has died unexpectedly, but the administration remains in power and to what extent it will perpetuate the legacy of corruption and abuse of power is left to be told. Kwaku's awareness of the treacherous terrain was raised earlier by a co-worker who has since been eliminated – "he opened his eyes to the reality of politics as a cess-pool" – and made no secret of his revolutionary vision: "burn everything to the ground and start all over again" (230).

Kwaku is threatened with the same fate as Correia, ironically, by the minister in whom he had placed his hope of salvation: "When Kwaku's turn came that would be the way" (255). *The Ministry of Hope* can be read as a narrative of Kwaku's emotional and psychological response to a despotic government and his quest for survival and identity in a treacherous environment.

In this work, role-playing becomes second nature to Kwaku and his son-in-law, Heliga, two villainous impostors: "For Kwaku the experience was a kind of rebirth. Like the silk-cotton trees that lose their leaves and appear to die in the season of drought only to recover their vigour with the April rains, all his confidence returned" (129).

Kwaku's dismissal from his post as assistant messenger in the Ministry of Hope is in his favour, as it allows him to devote himself fully to the role of fraudulent talk therapist while imitating Heliga and his "unctuous tone" (177). Kwaku, "who keenly felt his inadequacy" (179) in the presence of influential clients, embarks on the road to knowledge, or rather, the illusion of it. He takes English lessons from his former co-worker Suarez, and proves himself "an exemplary pupil" (182). In the process, he imports books and pretends to be an educated man, builds up a library and has shelves put up in his rooms at the new East Bank surgery to display his collection: "nothing gave him greater pleasure than a chance remark by a client about his distinguished collection of books . . . harbouring excessive pretensions to intellectual distinction" (183). Kwaku is a symptom of the widespread illiteracy in the society on account of the neglect of the education system under skewed leadership and of the illiterate's awe of the written word. Barely managing "to dispel the shadow of poverty" (185), Kwaku thrives in the capital city as he had on the

Corentyne coast, "achieving the ambition he had always aimed for" (206) of wealth and social status, however fraudulently acquired.

Amy Correia, the minister's secretary and lover, whose act of betrayal sends her husband to his death, is herself a victim of the ruthlessness and the depravity of both the administration and Kwaku. In her confusion, she turns to Kwaku for help, but the fake doctor takes advantage of her vulnerability and sexually exploits her during, euphemistically, a consultation in his surgery.

The façade of moral rectitude and worldly wisdom adopted by Kwaku is modelled upon the tactics of his patron, the Minister of Hope, for both Kwaku and his mentor are impostors and masqueraders:

> Originally driven by ambition alone, he had become contaminated by the ruthlessness and self-seeking of his superiors . . . one minister in particular who made a fine art of courting popularity. . . . He filed away every ploy, copied every posture that might contribute to an eventual success, so that in the end the person he moulded for himself, far from being the result of some unwitting process, became the finely wrought end product of a deliberate crafting . . . cultivating the appearance of an uncommonly pleasant man whose morals were never in doubt. (79)

Behind the illusion of knowledge he gains a greater sense of security, no longer afraid of exposure; his audacity grows to the point where "he could look upon the world around him with a tranquility that suited ill his old character" (229).

As Kwaku speaks at his sons' wedding with the authority of a self-made professional, he is brutally reminded that, in reality, he is a fraud and a failed father, but neither self-awareness nor the pangs of conscience can induce Kwaku to relinquish his fraudulent course:

> The twins sat staring at him with baleful eyes . . . one had never worked and the other had filled many temporary posts since his first job at the post office, but no one had ever managed to discover how they managed to survive. On noticing the way they were staring at him, Kwaku faltered and quickly brought the speech to an end . . . feigning a hilarity impossible to achieve in the twins' presence. (316)

Kwaku's sympathy for his patients is a crucial development: "He came to accept his patients' fractured lives as a kind of norm, refusing to sit in judg-

ment against them. Every impulse, every feeling was a manifestation of life"
(319). This growth in Kwaku suggests the possibility of renewal and comes
over as a human positive. In the event, the redemption of Kwaku never takes
place in the novel, on account of his incorrigible habit of self-deception. Even
though his sympathy for his patients may be read as an indirect plea for the
reader's sympathy for the character himself, ultimately Kwaku is one of society's tricksters. As Donald Newlove notices, there is "a quality of wiliness in
this Kwaku who comes up like a cork each time, his foxiness a natural force
. . . such characters live by guileless guile".[17]

Heath perhaps leaves us with the sad but harsh truth that the trickster
figure is the survivor, so that although there are no heroes in this work, he
at least induces us to make the distinction between the impoverishment of
society and its facile success stories, for Kwaku's chicanery is society's tragedy.

9

THE SHADOW BRIDE
A Passage from India

As a Guyanese, Heath would be conscious of the presence of people of Indian origin in the society and one would expect that they would float into his work, even though Edward Brathwaite reminds us: "Few non-Indians know much about Indians . . . although Indians make up a large percentage of the population in the Caribbean, their customs and ceremonies remain quaint and even exotic."[1]

Olive Senior's short story "The Arrival of the Snake Woman"[2] raises the issue of this seeming lack of knowledge of the Indian in Caribbean society more than a century after Indians first began to arrive as indentured workers on British West Indian plantations and, except for small numbers returning, stayed on as settlers. Earl Lovelace, in *The Dragon Can't Dance*, attempts to assimilate the Indian into West Indian creole society by transferring Tiger from a sugar estate in Trinidad to the multiracial village of Barataria, in the suburbs of Port of Spain, so that Tiger can reach towards social mobility. Derek Walcott, in his acceptance speech to the Nobel Prize Trustees in 1992, declares: "Deities were entering the field. What we generally call 'Indian music' was blaring from the open platformed shed from which the epic would be narrated. Costumed actors were arriving. Princes and gods, I supposed. What an unfortunate confession! 'Gods, I suppose' is the shrug that embodies our African and Asian diasporas. . . . While nobody in Trinidad knew any more than I did about Rama, Kali, Shiva, Vishnu, apart from the Indians, a phrase I use pervertedly because that is the kind of remark you can still hear in Trinidad: 'apart from the Indians'."[3]

Heath, however, had more than a passing acquaintance with Indians, and, in his unfinished autobiography, recalls a significant leap in his awareness when he began to commute between his genteel Queenstown world and an Indian village at Pouderoyen, on the West Bank of Demerara, where he worked at the commissary's office: "If in Forshaw Street I did my apprenticeship in the ways of the Creole world, in Pouderoyen I became initiated into East Indian society" (*Shadows*, 57). Heath's particular connections with Indians in the community[4] provided raw material that later enabled him to pursue an in-depth treatment of Indian experience in his eighth published novel, *The Shadow Bride*.

The Shadow Bride opens with Dr Betta Singh in retirement in the 1980s, remembering and reflecting on his childhood and growth and contemplating the unresolved issue of his India-born mother, who remained an eternal puzzle he failed to fathom all his life. Whereas on the social level Dr Singh has made significant progress, on the psychological level he is plagued by inner conflict, and in the final scene of his narration, it comes to him that he is in some way responsible for his mother's tragic fate: "he was jolted into the realization that his was a private grief, for his mother was a stranger to the community . . . she had lost an identity nurtured in the wake of her marriage and voyage across the ocean. . . . Her death was his doing, but he could not have acted otherwise" (437).

The Shadow Bride can be read on two levels: as a particular account of Singh's social evolution, and as a three-generational account of the evolution of the Indian in a setting that is recognizably early twentieth-century British Guiana, depicting a period of social history earlier than Mittelholzer's *Corentyne Thunder*. The narrative structure would suggest that it is Singh who is the main character, but as John Spurling argues, there is another dominant presence in the work:

> Having focused on the wealthy Singh family whose only son, Betta, is an idealistic doctor devoted to the health of the poorest people, Roy Heath gradually reveals another reality. The doctor's relatively straightforward struggle with malaria and exploitation, his happy marriage, his comfortable home, his reputation as a good man and his own constant desire to be one – these cover an

abyss he is not aware of himself. His mother, the "shadow bride" of the title, brought from India by his father but never fully accepting her exile, grows more and more demented and destructive.[5]

Singh's widowed mother plays such a central part in the entire drama that unfolds, and her story is so compelling, that she wrenches away the role of main character from her son. This examination of the experiences of the Indian woman takes into account that Mrs Singh was born in India (like thousands of Indian women who came to British Guiana among the indentured immigrants from 1838–1845 and 1854–1917); but she has not been brought to the colony under the auspices of indentureship. Nonetheless, one can argue that Mrs Singh's struggle for cultural identity is convincingly that of Indians lured to the colony to serve on sugar plantations even if this character adopted extreme methods to preserve Indian culture, and even if some cultural customs of Indians before her had been diluted with time, there is evidence of the proliferation of Hindu temples of worship and a strong desire among them to cling to Hinduism.

The novel is convincingly about the Indian woman, her dislodgement from India, her cultural dispossession, her crucial struggle for identity and her evolution into becoming Guianese in a patriarchal society. The broad theme of Indians is enriched and made more complex by Heath's exploration of the experiences of the Singh family in British Guiana. This chapter analyses the dilemma of female displacement in a New World colony by focusing on Mrs Singh's relationships with other characters in the work.

People of Indian origin generally owe their presence in the Caribbean to the indentureship system that was adopted in 1838, ostensibly to counter a labour shortage in the aftermath of emancipation. Numerous scholarly works of history, sociology and cultural anthropology have traced the arrival of Indians in the Caribbean, their condition of bondage, their presumed assimilation into the dominant creole culture, and the implications of their presence for the nature of society and politics, particularly in Trinidad and British Guiana, where they form a substantial part of the respective populations.[6]

The regional novel has not been neglectful in attempting to reinterpret Indian experience in the multicultural Caribbean,[7] and, as is rightly claimed, it is in imaginative literature that "one finds the best (sometimes only) insights into Indo-Caribbean female experience".[8]

Indian immigrant workers were the last addition to the heterogeneous society of the British West Indies and John La Guerre in *Calcutta to Caroni* argues: "the new (Indian) migrant who enters a changing social structure with creolization broadly at work" occupies "a precarious position".9 Patricia Mohammed notes that the nature of existence within Indian migration is further complicated by "a period of flux and rapidly changing boundaries" within the Hindu cultural system itself.10 The crossing to a new world saw a certain erosion of the strict lines of caste, a dilemma of adjustment and accommodation that V.S. Naipaul comments on more extensively in *The Middle Passage*.11

Merriman, an African-Guyanese character in *The Shadow Bride*, is invested with sufficient awareness of the plural society to detect that Indians have been in limbo since their historic crossing: "They had lost caste in their journey across the water, a constant complaint of those who claimed to be Brahmins, and the swift dismantling of the caste system that delighted many had left others bewildered and confused" (21). This issue was first raised in Harold Ladoo's fictional work *No Pain Like This Body* (1972), where a priest who performs a funeral rite capitalizes on the situation and claims that his father was a Punjabi Brahmin, but the Indians of Tola Trace in Trinidad consider him a "*moderass* chamar".12 This ambivalence is again evidenced in the character of the Pujaree in *The Shadow Bride*, who claims to be a pandit of high Brahmin caste, but, in his manifest lack of spiritual values, comes across as representing the practice of Hinduism by degenerate and self-promoted individuals in the wake of migration.

The Shadow Bride is perhaps the first work that not only grapples intensely with the psychological consequences of dislocation but also does so from an essentially female perspective. Ladoo's *No Pain Like This Body* perhaps offers the earliest fictional reinterpretation of female Indian displacement and fragmentation in the New World; however, it is driven by the vision of an innocent child narrator.

We intend to examine Mrs Singh's evolution into becoming a Guianese in the context of cultural dispossession and fractured identity, but, before we do so, we must map out the social progress of her son, Dr Betta Singh. It is useful to contrast Singh, a Guianese-born Indian, with his father. The older Singh – also born in British Guiana in the 1870s to indentured parents who had chosen repatriation and had returned to India without him – had come to unexplained wealth: he had found "a chest of Dutch guilders, gold coins in mint condition which had lain hidden at the base of a silk-cotton tree" (*Shadow Bride*, 5, 6) and that had allowed him to travel to Kerala, bring back a beautiful wife and build a mansion capped with a weather vane in Vlissengen Road, where he retired rather prematurely (5, 6). Coming to wealth by easy money rather than by struggle and toil, he was content to retire to his mansion, which, with its lofty water tank, "represented the summit of his ambition" (7). He passed his time drinking spirituous liquors with exotic names until one night, when he had locked himself away with his bottles and his hoard of gold and jewellery, he fell into "a drunken stupor" and passed away into oblivion. Betta Singh was four years old, and his father an isolate who failed to claim a place in the Guianese society of his time.

This analysis must look at this woman from Kerala, a stranger, married to a man living on the periphery who plays no part in his wife's induction into the new society or in her process of adjustment and accommodation, while she, on the other hand, is shocked to discover that her husband is "a nobody" in the country where he was born and did not even toil to acquire his wealth (7). She is then left to find ground for herself in an alien country, and so her struggle for identity and self must take into account her alienation from Kerala, where her father owns a prosperous coconut-rope-making business and where she was privileged to have had private schooling. We find a good description of a progressive community with its matrilineal traditions of the type the fictional woman has left behind in Kerala in Elisabeth Bumiller's *May You Be the Mother of a Hundred Sons*.[13] That the entrance of Mrs Singh into the social world of *The Shadow Bride* has not been under the auspices of indentureship, ironically, makes her doubly an outsider, for not only is she unaccommodated in the wider society on account of being a stranger, but she also stands outside the predictably rigid structure of estate regulations by which indentured Indians in the society define and understand their existences, however repressive the system may be. This adds complexity to her struggle for accommodation and identity in the new land.

In Guiana, Mrs Singh suppresses her vitality and submits to the role of dutiful, invisible wife in a patriarchal society, taking no pride in being a "shadow" to an unheroic husband. Her strong sense of self is eclipsed by a man who has no standing or connections; his inability to give her any kind of social location leads to her intense loneliness and isolation. If, in his lifetime, his wealth "separated him from the humble estate Indians", and if each succeeding house "was larger and more sumptuously appointed than its predecessor", the truth is that he had lost the crucial connection with community: the villages he lived in were to him "stations in the journey to isolation" (*Shadow Bride*, 7). When passers-by stopped to admire the wide driveway and the shuttered mansion near the train lines so far back from the asphalt road, "he would smile bitterly to himself. Some inner force had obliged him to make the journey and now he could not return to a village" (8).

The isolation of the Singhs is not entirely of their own disposition. Their segregation is also directly related to the nature of the society presented, where racially diverse groups live side by side but do not integrate to form a community of shared values, beliefs, and customs.[14] The meeting of Dr Singh and the African-Guyanese pharmacist, Merriman, springs from a more humanistic impulse that argues for the integration of the major strands that comprise the colony in a holistic vision of the concept "Guianese".

This analysis takes into account the psychic difficulty experienced by the alien Indian woman in severing ties with India, her tragic struggle to adjust to the existing heterogeneous disorder, her isolation within isolation. Having arrived in the British colony outside the indentureship system makes her rejection of indentureship, with its scornful treatment of Indians, all the more poignant and convincing. Finding herself "worlds away, across the Indian and Atlantic oceans", in a Demerara tropical landscape which bears a striking resemblance to Kerala, with its coconut trees and the sea never far away, "never once did she speak of her loneliness so far from home" (*Shadow Bride*, 7); her isolation remains unrelieved by the wealth inherited from her husband. As a widow, she cannot project her felt superiority; her husband did not grant her that superiority in his lifetime, and now her idiosyncratic attitude perhaps causes society to view her as an outsider. However, marooned on an alien shore, this Indian woman compensates for her state of dispossession and powerlessness by remaining fixated on her place of origin, to the authenticity of the culture, traditions and customs of the ancestral homeland she has left behind. It is the only certainty she knows, and she feels she must cling to its authenticity. Stranded in Guiana, Mrs Singh is a psychically divided character, "certain she had left some part of herself on the other side of the sea, something that might have come to terms with this endless journey in which she was doomed never to arrive" (371) but, particularly for the widowed Indian woman, because of her blood ties with the new land, return is impossible: even as "Kerala never ceased haunting her", she "could not return, for she had given birth here" (101) – the decision of many Indians who came from Uttar Pradesh and Madras under indentureship.

We are likely better to understand the plight of the Indian woman by the light of a psychoanalytic study of society in India that posits that the Indian concept of identity integrates cultural, historical and psychological data which underlie the network of social roles, traditional values, customs and kinship regulations with which the threads of individual psychological development are interwoven. It is useful to quote Sudhir Kakar at length:

> An exploration of the psychological terrain of the Indian inner world must begin with the cluster of ideas, historically derived, through which Hindu culture has traditionally structured the beliefs and behaviour of its members. At the heart of this cluster of governing ideas is a coherent, consistent world image in which the goal of human existence, the ways to reach this goal . . . are conveyed . . . values and beliefs which percolate down into the everyday life of the ordinary people and give it form and meaning.
>
> The world image of traditional Hindu culture, like those of other societies, provides its members with a sanctioned pattern, a template which can be superimposed on the outer world with all its uncertainties and on the flow of inner experience in all its turbulence, thus helping individuals to make sense of their own lives. Shared by most Hindus and enduring with remarkable continuity through the ages, the Hindu world image, whether consciously acknowledged and codified in elaborate rituals, or silently pervading the "community unconscious", has decisively influenced Indian languages as well as ways of thinking, perceiving and categorizing experience. This image is so much in a Hindu's bones he may not be aware of it. The self-conscious efforts of westernized Hindus to repudiate it are by and large futile based as they are on substantial denial.[15]

A preconscious, primary and instinctual belief system – cultural baggage carried by her as a guarantee of her identity – underpins Mrs Singh's perceptions of womanhood, motherhood, and her struggle for selfhood. A psychic dilemma fuels the work and is sparked off by the sudden death of the elder Singh, who had wanted his son to be more than he was, and to attend Queen's College, the most prestigious secondary school in Georgetown. However, his widow has assumed control of her son's life and rejects the idea, citing racial inequality in the colonial schools: "white boys sit in the front and the East Indians at the back" (*Shadow Bride*, 6). Mrs Singh speaks with the cultural certainty of an Indian who has not endured the indignities of indentureship and "has no intention" of allowing her son "to suffer, either directly or vicariously, the humiliations heaped on the children of estate workers" (6). Her real motive is to overlook the creole society, which is steeped in an inbred Victorian morality, including its education system, and to groom her son to the cultural purity and distinctiveness from which she derives. She sets out to subdue those around her, to change the world to her views rather than allow the world to change her, and these intentions are vividly translated in her relationships with four men in her life – her son, the doctor; the Mulvi Sahib, a spiritual mentor; the Pujaree, a Madrasi priest; and Sukrum, a derelict ex-indentured hanger-on. We note that in casting the character of Mrs Singh, Heath seems to be critical of her desire to retain her cultural authenticity.

Mrs Singh's isolation is increased by the scorn of her fellow Hindus when she secures for her son the services of a Muslim priest as private tutor, the Mulvi Sahib, whom she orders to maintain the distinctions of the Hindu/Muslim divide and forbids him to impart Islamic teachings to the youth. At this time, private colleges in Georgetown are linked to the Christian church and not worth Mrs Singh's consideration. In opposing her son's entry into Queen's College, linked as it then was to the planter class, Mrs Singh effectively attempts to subvert his evolution into a British Guianese person, even though, ironically, one of the suggestions of the work is that it is only through immersion with the mixed society, by becoming a part of it, that Indians can hope to overcome the daily humiliations and indignities of indentureship. Mrs Singh is viewed as an enigmatic character, her motivations diametrically opposed to any ideals that link her to the general herd of colonial Indians. She is now determined to distinguish herself ethnically as the orthodox Indian without the stamp and stain of indentureship, rejecting any identity of womanhood based on colonial subservience. She is also bent on keeping her son in her possessive grasp and constraining him within a self-referring Hindu enclave patterned on the rich Indian civilization in which her own socialization took place. To this end, she invests emotionally and financially in her son's education so that her own status and authority as a Hindu mother will be guaranteed. This plan, however, has implications for the psychosocial growth and development of her son, who is Guianese-born.

Traditionally, Indian female identity is valorized through the roles allotted to wife and mother, and, typically, in this work the main character is known only as "Mrs Singh" or "Dr Singh's mother". "Mrs Singh" is a social mask through which her identity is validated through her husband's wealth, and even though he turned out to be "a nobody", what is important in the patriarchal society is the fact of being married. As "Dr Singh's mother" she wears a cultural mask that guarantees her identity through the high esteem attached to Hindu motherhood and its traditional authority and power. As a result, nothing short of the complete submission of her son to her worldview would satisfy this uprooted Indian mother.

Mrs Singh enters the most challenging phase of her existence after her husband's death, for it liberates her to strike out for independence, but hers is an ironic freedom linked to impossible expectations. Whereas she was voiceless and faceless while indentured to an uninspiring husband, she must now translate her newly found freedom into purpose and meaning in a dying colonial society. Instead of seeking creative ways to self-realization, Mrs Singh resorts to the outward trappings of independence. She cuts her hair short and takes "to wearing trousers like a man" (*Shadow Bride*, 6), a mask she considers necessary to counter the inbred sexist attitudes in the patriarchal society where many people think, "there's something disgusting about a widow. She's like used cloth. . . . A woman without a man" (75). Ironically, were she still in India, Mrs Singh would have derived power through her veil, since mothers and matriarchs are held in the highest esteem as a *dharmic* right. At this time in its evolution, the British Guianese creole society is a hodge-podge of derivative values and customs, a polyglot society lacking a mythology of its own and without the institutions and traditions from which the psyche might take strength.

In his quest to reinterpret the dilemma of the first-generation Indian, Heath creates a character in Betta Singh who, in spite of a deliberate cultural nurturing, privileges patriotism over cultural heritage – even though the embrace of one's cultural heritage does not invalidate one's love of country, culture being the bedrock of human civilization and the essence of self-certainty. But such is Dr Singh's predicament, for in Dublin, Ireland, where he studied medicine, he questioned his attachment to India and decided that, as an Indian in the New World, it is necessary for him to make the distinction between patriotism and cultural identity: "He discovered something else, something about himself, about the gulf between himself and the students from India he knew, and his soul's longing for the country of his birth" (80).

As a Guianese, Dr Singh returns home at twenty-nine with certain idealistic beliefs about himself and his people that are in direct contradiction to his mother's cultural ideals. It would seem that the "secure arrangements" she had made to guarantee her standing in society come to nothing for, ironically, Betta is influenced by the Mulvi's life and his humanistic philosophy of "service to others – sacrifice at the very heart of human experience" (17), the very teachings his mother had forbidden the Mulvi from teaching her son. Betta Singh's return to the colony coincides with the political awakening of Indians in Guiana and the emergence of an Indian professional class that would contribute to the social and intellectual progress of the colony of their birth. The crisis of the work begins just before the labour unrest of the 1930s, which would bring working-class Indians directly into the struggle for freedom from the shackles of colonialism. It is worth mentioning at this point that Indians developed their own version of a creole society in the process of readjustment and accommodation, and so there exist two "creole societies", each with distinctive features, within the multiracial colony. Moreover, the notion of an all-embracing "Indian" community is flawed in view of the wide variety of cultural and religious traditions represented by ethnic indentured Indians from the wide geographic spread of colonial India.[16]

Just into the second chapter, crisis develops that shatters Mrs Singh's sense of ontological security: "Dr Singh's mother was angry when he declared that he intended remaining in private practice for no more than two years", after which he would seek a post "as an estate doctor to help in the fight against malaria" (12), which continued to ravage the ill-nourished immigrants. Her understanding of existence rooted in Indian customs, whereby a mother's cultural identity is tied to her son's social success, is now undermined. Mrs Singh is a vulnerable woman whose preoccupation with her Indianness and with the value system of India becomes a crucial issue in her struggle for cultural identity and survival in the New World.

The clash between mother and son is symbolic of the generational gap between indentured Indians, marooned with the weight of cultural baggage, and their offspring with fresh aspirations and idealisms in the New World, as articulated by Dr Singh in his initial confusion: "I don't know whether I'm an Indian or a Guyanese . . . you did all you could to prevent me mixing with other children and now I'm a freak. . . . You are from India, and I was born here and have as little attachment for Kerala as for the moon" (57–59). The plight of the Indian caught in a cultural limbo is recounted in Ismith Khan's *The Jumbie Bird* (1961), where three generations of an Indian family try to understand their place in early twentieth-century Trinidadian society and, crucially, how to sever ties with India, in the same period traversed by *The Shadow Bride*, where Dr Singh rejects the cultural baggage of the motherland and is driven to pursue an identity as a British Guianese. For choosing his own road to self-realization, Dr Singh incurs his mother's wrath and triggers the crisis of the work.

Dr Singh's desire "to lose himself on a sugar estate", to serve his people unconditionally and, also, to mix with the wider creole society, is an artistic vision of assimilation in a society that has all the characteristics of a plural society. His meeting with the creole pharmacist, Merriman, and their genuinely shared compassion for the disadvantaged Indian masses, give the impression that acceptance and assimilation are generally easily achieved, whereas racial antagonisms that remained latent at this time would come to a head in the early sixties and virtually polarize the country. On account of sharp social differentiation existing in the colony, integration of the two major racial elements as proposed in this novel would prove difficult, and the reality is palpably different. The lifestyles and values of each strand of the multiracial society vary widely: the Merrimans' middle-class household, copied from the pseudo-European model, is so very different from Dr Singh's that "every visit was like crossing a frontier into another country. It was a household of tie-pins and linen jackets and books on shelves" (20). The reader is surprised to note that in the home where Dr Singh grew up, "there was not a single book, except a copy of the *Mahabharata*, his old school texts and medical books", even though Dr Singh has had a solid Western education and his mother had the benefit of a private education in the progressive state of Kerala.

Whereas the older Singh lacked a sense of commitment and failed to see himself as part of the community, Dr Singh belongs unequivocally to the society and gains self-fulfilment and recognition through service to its people, even though Heath casts him as a stereotype of the pagan Indian who lacks the trappings of the pseudo-European world of literature and art. This in itself separates him from Merriman, even though the intention is to see them as compatriots, kindred spirits and equals in a mixed society. It is worth mentioning that the *Mahabharata* is virtually a library in its own right, containing treatises on Eastern philosophy, arts, culture, religion, ethics and other relevant areas of man's spiritual growth, so that Dr Singh's home is not culturally bare as is perhaps suggested. Dr Singh is the first and the only one of Heath's characters to strive towards a sense of belonging, and succeeds in becoming a Guianese by struggle and toil, a prerequisite defined by a character in Michael Gilkes's post-independence drama *Couvade: A Dream-Play of Guyana* (1974): "There are still some misguided souls who cling to the old myth of El Dorado. The myth that says you can get rich without hard work. But you and I know different. We know that without honest, hard toil there can never be an El Dorado. That if we want to have an El Dorado we must create it ourselves, out of our sweat, our own tears, our own dreams."[17]

At the time of narration, Dr Singh's two daughters are qualified physicians who have migrated to Canada, while he remains in Guyana in his frail old age, with his wife and their handicapped son, whose story remains to be examined in this analysis.

Dr Singh's sympathy for the malaria-stricken labourers and their destitute families huddled in the estate *logies*[18] incurs the wrath not only of his mother but also of colonial planters, who persecute him and cause him to flee Anna Catherina after three years on the west coast of Demerara. As a first-generation Guianese of Indian ancestry, Dr Singh struggles to transcend the identity of the transported Indian, but all his efforts are qualified by his complex relationship with his mother. V.S. Naipaul, in *The Middle Passage*, remarks on the cultural imperatives by which transplanted Indians are bound: "More important than his religion was his family organization, an enclosing self-sufficient world absorbed with quarrels and jealousies, as difficult for the outsider to penetrate as for one of its members to escape. It protected and imprisoned, a static world, awaiting decay."[19]

Hence Dr Singh's achievement is a willed achievement, consciously worked for against the stratagems of his mother, who, "clinging to the accoutrements of a vanished past", wishes his profession to be an enhancement of her own status and vanity, as obtains in India (437).

As a young doctor, Dr Singh is driven to leave the family home and head for Anna Catherina. Stung by her son's abandonment of her and no longer certain of the basis of her identity and of her place in the world, Mrs Singh retaliates by severing all ties with him. For crossing his mother's will, Dr Singh comes to experience the seething cauldron of her mind: "She turned her back, leaving him to face the reality of a rift he had long thought to be inevitable" (60). At the same time, the recognition of his mother's determination to have her own way "came as a surprise to him" (60), and, in spite of his maturity and education, Dr Singh's understanding of his mother's character is as imperfect as when he was a child.

He recalled that as a small boy he used to associate her with the colour blue, after an illuminated print of the goddess Durga, in her benevolent aspect, "but now he sees her transformed into an unrecognizable entity". Through a dream he has of his mother (as Durga in her more destructive aspect), he was convinced even as a youth that her emotional manipulation, masked as maternal love, the unconscious suggestion of a mother/son fixation, "could not fail to bring in its train the most terrible consequences" (77) for both of them:

> Then, one night after she had petted and fondled him while putting him to bed, he dreamt of her with staring eyes and a long tongue which hung over her lower lip. And soon afterwards, among the numerous old calendars she kept in her camphor-wood chest, he discovered a picture of Durga in her terrible aspect, the devourer of children. The picture was red and baleful. And what remained of the experience, what lingered until his childhood was overtaken by his youth, was the ascendance of red over blue. Now he felt pity for his mother, realizing that her power was illusory, that he no longer cared to explain in detail why he was obliged to leave as soon as he could, before he was overcome by a complacency which . . . in him would be a kind of death. (57–58)

Shocked into recognition of this duality in his mother, Dr Singh resolves to flee her manipulative grasp and their prison-like home, with its irrelevant internal laws. On the afternoon Betta is due to leave the home to assume his appointment at Anna Catherina, Mrs Singh suddenly becomes ill, with a vague fever and "bad feelings" (82). He is convinced that "his mother's indisposition was a contrivance" (84) either to detain his going or to arouse guilt. This scene recalls the histrionics of the Indian matriarch Mrs Tulsi, in V.S. Naipaul's *A House for Mr Biswas*, whenever she perceives her authority challenged. Dr Singh lacks the subliminal cultural attachment to India that his mother presumes him to possess, and his departure from her mansion is a symbolic rejection of the self-referring fortress of Hinduism. By the time of Mrs Singh's death, the mansion is a mere shell, a symbol of a low point for Hinduism in the New World in the early twentieth century.[20] That this artistic dismantling of Hinduism can be interpreted as a necessary denial of cultural values in order to claim a Guianese identity is a worrying development, since the reader will argue that, inherently, man is a cultural entity and a sense of cultural certainty is crucial to one's sense of a national identity and belonging.

Labouring under a delusion as to her strong cultural hold over her son, Mrs Singh "secretly felt she was capable of persuading him to remain; she did not believe he could abandon the camphor-wood chairs" (13), while Dr Singh meets his mother's fury "with the gentle firmness he had adopted from abroad, driven by the impulse seven years of independence had kindled in him" (13). When she fails to dissuade him from abandoning her, she is inconsolable: "she wanted to howl with impatience at her impotence in the face of events she could not control" (33). Mrs Singh has no identity other than that derived from the bond of motherhood, and her son's cutting of this line leaves her in a state of aloneness, psychically shipwrecked on an alien shore, her sense of ontological security shattered. As she reflects on her life and ponders her options, she considers going back to India: "If Betta let her down, she would go back to India, to the place of longboats. . . . It was he who had anchored her to this land where the sand burnt your feet. . . . Now she feared its interminable coastline and above all the poverty of those who came and would not go back" (16).

But return to India is impossible for Mrs Singh. The agony of the Indian woman echoes that of Galton Flood in *The Murderer*, both characters subjugated to the morality of a mother country irrelevant to their existence, and the "purity" of its values so ingrained that to jettison this fixation would incur irreparable psychic damage.

As Mrs Singh's flawed progress continues to be traced in the novel, one will notice a complicated sense of the society emerging through the workings of a series of ill-fated arrangements she makes with certain other characters. Her relationships with her household staff also have to be taken into account. During what seems to be her son's abandonment of her, Mrs Singh yields to a desire for power over her servants and hangers-on to compensate for her loss of power over her son and her sense of rejection and also to assert her authority as head of a family: "Then, with a gesture of desperation, she went off to her room, reflecting as she went that as a girl she never defended herself, that as a wife she never raised her voice, that soon after her husband's death she had her long hair cut, took to wearing trousers and discovered the tumult behind her expressionless face and a terrible desire to exercise power over Aji and her husband's hangers-on" (34–35).

The anguished Indian woman might have been dismissed as an irrelevance by society but for her mesmeric personality and her seeming generosity to a number of minions she cultivates, who boost her sense of power: "People Betta had never seen before began visiting them . . . the coming and going of countless friends who, impressed by her hospitality, dared not criticize her freedom" (6–7). Mrs Singh needs the sycophantic throng and its "exaggerated show of respect" and flattery to validate her existence, even if they serve "to emphasize her loneliness" (15). In order to gain the recognition she craves in the New World, it is crucial for her to recreate the sense of community and the way of life that gave her identity in Kerala:

> Rarely was a request to hold a fete or build a tajah in her yard refused. In fact, on the occasion of the Mohammedan festival of Hussein and Hassan, the tradition was all but established that the tajah was to be built in her ample yard, and when the glistening structure set out from the grounds of the house, followed by a crowd of hundreds of people from all sections of the community, small children who were not permitted to follow it through the streets were in the habit of occupying her staircase, believing it to be communal property. At other times, on finding strangers squatting under the samaan tree, she had no thought of asking them to leave, for that was the way of her parents in Kerala, whose compound was never empty . . . she had brought from her homeland a tradition so firmly implanted in her character that any enquiry into the extent to which it was a part of her natural bent would have been pointless. (77)

Early in the novel, as Mrs Singh strives to be a dutiful mother, she wears around her neck "a medallion with the image of the goddess Lakshmi on one side and that of Ganesha, the elephant-headed god on the other" (222). This work opens for us a door to Hindu cosmology and its relationship to the individual struggle for freedom and identity: Lakshmi, the goddess of light, purity, and goodness, is the feminine aspect of a loving and benevolent god, while Ganesha represents the search for knowledge, the awareness that the human mind is limited by its incapacity to know the unknowable or to comprehend the incomprehensible. Every Hindu religious ritual is prefaced by an invocation to Ganesha in recognition of man's frailties and limitations, and of the dualities and the polarities which man blindly encounters in everything he does and everything he says. We note that as the plot develops and Mrs Singh becomes mentally distressed by the fractured relationship with her son, she comes under the influence of Pujaree, a Madrasi priest, and she yields to the rituals devoted to the goddess Kali; thereafter she descends into psychosis and fragmentation. The Madrasis of southern India ritually worship and make sacrifices to Kali, but this departure from mainstream Hinduism throws Mrs Singh into deeper psychic confusion than that already presented by her condition of shipwreck. Just as Kali, with her aggression, destruction and blood sacrifice, is a shadow of Lakshmi, so the besieged Mrs Singh is transformed into a shadow of herself. The work resonates with the traditions of India, now largely blurred in the New World, but by which Mrs Singh understands her existence, since she finds it impossible to jettison the collectivity of her culture.

Mrs Singh's separate associations with two religious leaders, the Mulvi Sahib and the Pujaree, apart from offering glimpses into the Hindu/Muslim polarity and the rituals of Hinduism, affect her process, or lack thereof. After Betta leaves for university in Ireland, the Mulvi Sahib "thought it proper" to cease his contact with Mrs Singh "because we're separated by our religions" (105) – the Mulvi's function in the Singhs' household ceases, for Mrs Singh only intended to use the Mulvi as a tutor to shape her son into becoming an educated and important person in society. In her state of loneliness, Mrs Singh might have turned to the Mulvi for solace, but refrained, for, wilful as she is, she is not interested in the Mulvi's spiritual guidance; she recognizes that she cannot wield her power over him in the way she might be able to do with the fawning Pujaree, who steps in to fill the void, not as mentor, but as financial and sexual exploiter.

Betta's decision to work on a sugar estate upon his return to the colony coincides perfectly with the Pujaree's ambition, and, in the three years he spends as estate doctor at Anna Catherina, the Pujaree supplants Dr Singh in his mother's affection. The Pujaree's motive stems from an incorrigible materialism and a greater predilection for the pleasures of the body than of the spirit. He assumes the role of guardian of a vulnerable woman, ironically depriving her of that power and independence she herself craves, while he seizes the opportunity to cohabit with her under the guise of "spiritual partners" (159). Mrs Singh's relationship with the Pujaree exemplifies the altering conditions of womanhood under the new dispensation of migration. In gaining the freedom to behave licentiously, she simultaneously loses her traditional power of Hindu motherhood and thus unwittingly contributes to the dilution of Hinduism in the New World at that time and place. Her living arrangements with the Pujaree would have been deemed untenable were she still in India, where she would have gained power through the renunciation of earthly pleasures after her husband's demise.

The Mulvi's asceticism and moral authority stand in direct contrast with the Pujaree's trickery and his false claims to the spiritualism of Brahminical Hinduism. Emasculated by the indentureship experience, the Pujaree seeks to salvage himself through leeching off Mrs Singh. He is one of those migrants who benefited from the erasure of the caste distinction under indentureship and was able to pass himself off as a pandit of the more popular Hinduism, even though he remains steeped in Madrasi customs. He begins the relationship by demanding that Mrs Singh "promise to prostrate herself before Durga's image" (44), thus inducing her to become a version of the goddess Durga. Durga and Kali appeal to the more aggressive and destructive aspects of self, and the reader witnesses the irruption of inner disorder and negative tendencies in Mrs Singh since her association with the Pujaree and the Kali rituals he imposes on her. In retrospect, Dr Singh's feelings of guilt and regret, with which the work opens, spring from the thought that somehow he allowed his mother to fall prey to this degenerate character, that his absence created the space for the Pujaree to move in and exploit her, and for her further degradation at the hands of the rum-sucker Sukrum; but, in view of his own ambitions to become a Guianese, "he could not have acted otherwise".

The Indian ethnic differentiation represented by the Mulvi and the Pujaree is brought into sharp focus in a confrontation between Mrs Singh and the Mulvi, who is incensed at her spiritual decline at the hands of the semi-literate Pujaree and his distortion of Hinduism: "Did he teach you that your troubles were the wretchedness of the Kali Yuga and that you should not worry about your present or future? I also live my life submitting to the cosmic order, but I'm also responsible for myself" (291). This line of questioning only intensifies Mrs Singh's psychic confusion. As a Hindu, she subscribes to the notion of existence in terms of cosmic cycles, of which the Kali Yuga is the current and final cycle lasting a few thousand years, and the one in which man is helplessly in his most profound state of darkness and degeneration. Hindu philosophy teaches her that life is Maya or Illusion, and that reality is God, the ultimate truth, but this should not preclude her from dealing with the reality of daily existence and from assuming responsibility for her actions from a position of relative truth. The Mulvi, on the other hand, believes that his destiny is linked to a predetermined struggle in the here and now, however chaotic the present world may be, wherein service to mankind is only one prerequisite for entry into paradise. The choice between the trickery of the Pujaree and the moral authority of the Mulvi places certain pressures on Mrs Singh to make an impossible choice, and this precipitates her state of divided consciousness.

The Pujaree next exceeds his authority and forbids Betta to enter his mother's house to take refuge from planter persecution, and so widens the rift between the estranged mother and son: "The Pujaree's word was law in the house. He settled quarrels, made prohibitions, distributed gifts and generally behaved as if he were Mrs Singh's lawful husband" (238) and man of the house, leaving Mrs Singh's son to take shelter with the Mulvi, who is outraged that the villainous Pujaree, "a man he had known as a wayfarer priest . . . wandering the suburbs of Georgetown with his brass lotah and a cloth thrown over his shoulder . . . a disreputable opportunist who gave East Indians a bad name" (278), now pretends to have moral authority and "exercises a fatal influence" on a vulnerable woman. Mrs Singh, in the Mulvi's eyes, is no longer the woman whom he had schooled in the need for self-denial. He has watched the

change in her "as a child would watch something transformed into its opposite in the hands of a magician, at once fascinated and bewildered" (277–78).

The Pujaree is a study in perversity. Another trickster figure, he is overwhelmed by his sinister ambitions and unexpected good fortune of parasit-
izing on vulnerable people. He no longer resents the memories of "his years
of poverty, his perpetual anxiety, walking barefoot along the suburban road"
(231). As he gazes over the samaan tree in the Singhs' yard, the impostor is
pleased that he has successfully subverted the social hierarchy: "This was *his*
yard now, its trees were his and he would have them cut down soon" (278).
He seizes the chance to reinvent himself in the wake of migration by preying on Mrs Singh's fragile ego, assuming complete control of her affairs, her
mind, her body, and her soul. Heath offers a graphic portrait of the predator:

> For the first time he had been roused to exercise his full rights as her spouse
> and protector. Standing at the head of the stairs he listened and was surprised
> at the spirited way she had carried out his orders.
>
> The Pujaree had been working quietly towards this end for years. All his
> actions had been regulated by his ambition, so much so that it would have
> surprised him had he been accused of pursuing the very thing that consumed
> him. Hardly had he taken in the fact of living by her side, in the house that had
> dazzled him for so many years then he found himself in a position of being able
> to make of it whatever he chose. He was familiar with every piece of furniture
> in the drawing room. . . . If life was change then he would change everything
> around him beyond recognition. (295)

The Pujaree belongs to a band of people who exploited Hinduism in the
New World and practised a perverted version of it. He shamelessly exploits
Mrs Singh under the pretext of religion: "He decided there and then to install
in the centre of the drawing room a glazed earthenware model of Shiva, Par-
vati and Ganesha" (295) to create the impression of deep religiosity, under the
cover of which he extracts from her "substantial contributions" towards the
building of a temple in Kitty for his own self-aggrandizement. In an unexpected flash of self-awareness, Mrs Singh feels "ashamed of having given in
to her mentor's plan to install an image of the goddess of destruction [Durga]
in her house [because] Betta would not approve if he found out, nor would the
Mulvi Sahib" (102), but in spite of this moment of recognition of the Pujaree's
skewed influence, she remains in the stranglehold of the trickster and is led

to evil: "In exchange for her undertaking to convert the lower storey of her house into a temple, he agreed to harm Betta's infant son as a punishment to Betta. . . . The Pujaree had instructed her what to do when she approached the infant" (357). In the first chapter of the novel we meet Dr Singh's son, made an invalid from infancy by this evil act. However, society believes the façade it sees, and the Pujaree grows so much in authority in Mrs Singh's social circle that someone had made him a present of a thousand-year-old *veena* (341). When he learns of Meena's visit to her mother-in-law, he is indignant, his power exceeding his false place in the house. However, just when the Pujaree thinks that "his control over her soul was so complete" (379), Mrs Singh unexpectedly awakens to the realization that she "needed the illusion of an identity", which he cannot provide (380), and attempts, albeit futilely, "to plot her extrication" from his influence and regain her freedom. The intensity of Mrs Singh's needs and her rebelliousness throughout the work guarantee her greatness as a literary character.[21]

At the moment when Mrs Singh replaces the idol of Lakshmi (the goddess of goodness, love, and fertility) with that of Durga (the goddess of destruction) at the Pujaree's command, she releases a negative energy: "a fire burned intensely in her and she was transformed into an opposite quantity" (278). In the reformulation of the impossible struggle of the Indian woman to find a place in the New World, it is worth mentioning that Hinduism in its Brahminical aspect is a pure form of religion that is beyond the reach of the Pujaree – it is a puritan equivalent to the Muslim asceticism that the Mulvi represents; it is spirituality that dispenses with the need for idols and images and blood sacrifice, as in the Kali Mai puja rituals that the Pujaree embraces. Perhaps some Madrasis are drawn to the dark forces of Durga and Kali and to the worship of idols – practices that cannot be reconciled with mainstream Hinduism.[22] The Pujaree can only be seen for what he is, a villainous impostor who is able to outwit a vulnerable woman in spite of her own crucial desire for power and control.

The self-willed woman finally flees the mansion in a state of confusion over her identity and her inner motivations: "The Pujaree said I was generous, but my generosity is not mine. Keralans are hospitable *as a people*, so I don't know what I'm actually like. The Mulvi Sahib said I was own-way and wanted to be a man, yet the Pujaree saw me as the most feminine woman . . . I don't know what I am." The Pujaree, too, flees the irrelevant mansion and seeks refuge at the temple, leaving the "empty shell" of failed idealism, its yard, "overgrown with weeds", suggesting its decline (435). This is a time when many Indians in the colony are converting to the Christian faith in order to obtain jobs and educational opportunities with such institutions as the Canadian Presbyterian Mission. Indian culture and religion were revived from around the middle of the 1930s with the large-scale introduction of Indian movies to the colony and the progress of an Indian Renaissance represented by a number of visiting scholars from India, both Hindus and Muslims.[23]

Even though the truth of his mother's complex mind unfolds by degrees before Dr Singh, he is powerless to stop her degradation in the face of her wilful and irrational ways:

> yet another piece in the jigsaw of her personality. . . . The discovery that she believed she was entitled to her own way in everything . . . had disclosed hidden features of a landscape . . . like a familiar contrivance that bursts open unexpectedly to reveal an alarming complexity . . . her strength, her ability to persuade people to do what she asked them "because I'm a widow" . . . qualities which gave him security earlier but which he now despised intensely. (76)

Mrs Singh's dishevelled state and her intemperate display at the wedding of one of her protégées occasion an awakening of self-knowledge in Dr Singh, causing him to reflect more sympathetically on the underlying reason for her desolate condition:

> He reflected on his shame, on the chaos in his former home; yet now he was over-whelmed by a feeling of relief. His animosity at his mother's earlier behaviour passed away at the discovery of her loneliness . . . he examined his discovery from every angle, astonished that he had missed what lay before his eyes. She was an exile from marriage and from her country, and the last link with both had been severed at Aji's death, leaving her stranded on the shore of an unrelenting loneliness. (291)

While displacement and exile are not in themselves the villains, they provide the stresses that aggravate the dilemma of the flawed character. Near the end of the work, Mrs Singh reveals her own surprise at her deviant nature: "The flower from Kerala that closed modestly in the dark was only part of a plant. But when the root became exposed it was a revelation not only for my husband, but for me" (430). Mrs Singh's psychological problems can be measured by the weight of her cultural baggage, under which she is unable to adjust and adapt to the new dispensation.

In the event, Dr Singh only momentarily escapes the unpredictability of his complex mother, even though the Mulvi has cautioned him of the dark recesses of her personality – "your mother punishes and rewards like Kali Mai herself" (303), for the rebellious mother feels "the affront of her son's abandonment deeply enough to seek revenge on someone closely related to him" (99). Mrs Singh's personality undergoes morbid changes such that she is convinced that she "had arrived at the point where the road forked, where good and evil separated. And she had no doubt that it was Betta's conduct that obliged her to take the one leading to the destruction of herself at the moment when she was about to embark on the other" (100). These diabolical words echo those of the rejected Satan in book 4 of Milton's *Paradise Lost*: "All good to me is lost. / Evil, be thou my good", and also recall Heathcliff's vows of revenge when he is faced with rejection in Emily Brontë's *Wuthering Heights*. Freud's findings on the anarchic id that inhabits the irredeemable depths of the human mind help to explain the inner tyranny and the chaos that overwhelm the minds of some of Heath's psychically frail and vulnerable characters. The literary tradition is replete with characters who do not commit errors of judgement but errors of the will – free will taken to extremes, as we see in some of Shakespeare's characters, notably Macbeth and Iago. This error deforms and diminishes those who succumb to it. A feature common to all these literary creatures is the manic energy, the half-civilized ferocity with which they pursue their goals, the patient scheming and manipulation they employ in their premeditated revenge. Mrs Singh is driven to evil and revenge as an ill-conceived response to a frustrated will.

Debarred from the family home since his return from the west coast, Dr Singh is only invited to visit his mother when his wife is expecting their third child, and now detects in her voice "that underlying strength that reminded him of forces that have yet to be described" (342), that is, the dark side to his mother's nature that he hesitates to confront. Intent on revenge and power, she drugs his cup of tea and extracts from him a promise to hand over to her his first-born son to mould in pure Indian values (something she had failed to achieve with Betta): "the [evil] Pujaree wants a boy he can guide . . . someone he can make a pandit among pandits" (348). When Betta fails to keep his promise, of which he has no memory, his mother conspires with the Pujaree to harm the infant, leaving him permanently disabled.

This brings us to Mrs Singh's tortuous relationship with her daughter-in-law, Dr Singh's wife. In awe of her mother-in-law's ethnic superiority, "the overpowering presence of the distant continent in Mrs Singh's white sari and pictures that decorated the walls" (366) and of the power and authority she appears to wield, Meena pays her a conciliatory visit, but instead enters a surreal world of terror at the Singhs' lonely mansion that can only be construed as a projection of the chaos in the mind of the psychologically disturbed Indian woman:

> All of a sudden the dogs reappeared at the entrance of the door. Meena, gripping the arms of her chair, closed her eyes and waited. And just as suddenly as the animals had appeared, so their gasping filled the room and Meena, unable to restrain herself any longer, uttered a piercing shriek which resounded throughout the house, accompanied by the bellowing of the dogs. . . . She then remembered that her mother-in-law had replaced her shrine to Lakshmi, goddess of prosperity, by one to Durga, the destroyer. And just thinking of the name struck terror in her heart. (367–68)

To Mrs Singh's surprise, the terrorized woman "knelt before her, then bent her head forward until it touched the ground" (369), doing homage as an Indian woman to her mother-in-law, hardly suspecting that the psychotic Mrs Singh has already carried out her evil act of revenge on their infant son. As Mrs Singh descends into madness, she seeks refuge at her son's home, where she extends her perceived ethnic superiority over the common herd of post-indentured Indians, which includes Meena and her family: "you and your mother and your vulgarity . . . who grew up with the jabbering of the illiterate and half-illiterate in your ears . . . but every day I hear your mother bawling like a market woman and your children rampaging through the house" (434). In her mad rage, she terrorizes the young woman, threatening to chop off her hair and "cut out your tongue and feed it to the carrion crows" (434).

Mrs Singh's instinct for power and revenge brings us to examine her relationships with Rani and Lathi, her two "protégées". Mrs Singh is yet another of Heath's frail and inflexible characters who experience difficulty in understanding their own illogical minds or in accepting the place allotted them in society. In the following scene Mrs Singh feels "ashamed of the absurdity of a charge" she has laid against one of her young protégées:

> She broke off in the middle of the tirade . . . astonished by her own conduct, by the realization, after all these years, that her husband was really dead and by all that had befallen her since her marriage as if it had happened to someone else and she had just heard tell of it. She listened to the silence created around her by her dictatorial voice and was ashamed that Rani's irresponsible smile had vanished and that Lathi seemed cowed by her outburst. (34)

Through Rani, Lathi, Sukrum, and Bai (an innocuous straggler), Mrs Singh reconstitutes a family of sorts over which she wields power and control. The latter two occupy the surgery room left vacant by Dr Singh. Lathi and Rani had come to Mrs Singh through the informal trade in small girls "that had wrenched them away before they were of age to give their consent", a form of indentureship and child slavery "not regarded as exceptional" in the colony (108). Mrs Singh resolves that the worst fate she can ultimately inflict on Rani is to yoke her to a husband with whom she has "little in common"; hence her scheme of revenge is "consummated" in a hastily arranged marriage between Rani and Tipu (99), a jeweller's assistant and a spineless creature glad of the security of the widow's mansion. The reader is taken to new depths in Mrs Singh's increasingly psychotic state of mind as she routinely manipulates the couple and undermines the authority of the young bride by ingratiating herself with Tipu, in addition to making it known that her influence must also extend to Rani's newborn child and, "fortified by her growing influence over Tipu . . . curiously enough, the discovery of her intentions caused her neither embarrassment nor guilt, only a hardening of the resolve to bend the couple to her will" (99–100). She calculates that economic circumstance will oblige Rani to be seduced by the opportunities afforded to her offspring, "as one succumbed to the influence of a debilitating drug that seduced before it destroyed" (99). However, self-awakening comes to Rani, who detects in Mrs Singh "a flint-like hardness" (108), and, piqued at having been robbed of the right to name her son, sees the necessity of fleeing from the euphemistic "protection" and possessive grasp of her benefactress.

Interwoven into her scheme of domination is a degenerate hanger-on, Sukrum, psychopath and agent of Mrs Singh's wilful plans. Sukrum is a casualty of indentureship who has drifted from the estate to being an inmate of a poorhouse before drifting further into Kitty and into Mrs Singh's plan of revenge on Lathi. A derelict who ended up "knocking from pillar to post, weeding one person yard for six cents, carrying some lady bunch of plantains for four cents and sleeping all over the place like a Lombard Street stray dog" (231), is the way the malevolent Pujaree describes Sukrum. Castrated by indentureship, his "dignity eroded by the long sojourns in the dosshouse" (227), Sukrum fits Mrs Singh's evil plan perfectly. A scathing portrait of this predator prepares the reader for the inevitable tragedy that awaits Lathi, a granddaughter of the older Singh by a previous marriage, whom the widow despises, though she cleverly masks her hatred with solicitousness and generosity:

> The Sukrums he had met in New Amsterdam. They were only found in towns, just as a certain type of rats was found inhabiting the area around the wrought-iron-fenced markets of Bourda and Stabroek and Kitty. They scavenged on discarded vegetables and rotting fruit and the offal and dried blood of butchers' stalls. They were to be seen lurking in the gardens and yards of houses several hundred yards away, brash, grey inhabitants of a secret underworld that occasionally penetrated the compound of an unsuspecting home. (230)

At this time in the colony, indentured immigrants at the end of their labour contracts offer a desolate image of poverty as they flock to the city and its suburbs, even sleeping on the pavements, "the army of beggars whose indenture was at an end and who came to Kitty and Newtown, often scantily dressed, in search of work. One of them, a woman wearing no more than a flimsy skirt and a joolah, came to the temple to beg for food, sharing a room with eight others, six of them men" (231).

Discovering Lathi in Sukrum's room one night, Rani suspects that Mrs Singh has engineered Lathi's depravity and degradation. Perhaps, in sending Lathi out to apprentice with a creole seamstress, Mrs Singh had already begun Lathi's alienation from the fold of Indians. Perhaps, too, it was Dr Singh's long absence from the family home that permitted Sukrum's "corrosive influence" (229) over Lathi: "Her clandestine abortion appeared [to Rani] to be the direct result of Betta's departure . . . an atmosphere had descended on the house like an enveloping cloud" (90). Rani, "until then unwilling to acknowledge the destructive impulse in Mrs Singh, once believed that she had allowed Sukrum and Bai to occupy the old surgery out of generosity", but is now convinced of Mrs Singh's grand design; she comes to the realization that Lathi's brazen conduct "could not be explained simply by her ability to slip downstairs to the men's room when the rest of the house was asleep" (95–96) were it not for Mrs Singh's calculating mind. Mrs Singh unleashes her masked hatred in premeditated revenge against Lathi, a plan in which the debased Sukrum will be encouraged to ruin the young woman with his sexual depredations, necessitating for Lathi the "indescribable terror" (144) of repeated and risky abortions.

Both protégées had always held Mrs Singh in deep respect, not only for her wealth, but also for her defiance of colonial morality, "at a time when they had never yet met a woman who had so completely defied the conventions of subservience to men" (91–92). Their admiration for their benefactress's "ability to suffer while behaving like someone untouched by suffering" is unfailing, even though she remains an enigma and they "had never managed to understand her" (48). Lathi, offered a chance at social mobility through her dressmaking apprenticeship, is unable to escape her cultural bondage: "The world began and ended in Mrs Singh's house and yard where many of its festivities were echoed. . . . Lathi came from a poor East Indian family of numerous children who competed for the right to eat and be educated. Only a fool would leave the sanctuary that was Mrs Singh's home of her own free will. She had resolved to live and die there as a kind of celebration of perpetual immaturity" (92).

Wealth and status often serve to muzzle society, so that however much of an enigma Mrs Singh appears to be, the fact is that she "has so much prestige people see her conduct in a different light" (179). She gives Lathi free rein to consort with Sukrum, until, during one of her mad rages, she drives them both out of the mansion at a time when Lathi is once again pregnant, physically ravaged and weak, with no place of abode. Succumbing to Sukrum's viciousness, Lathi knocks from "pillar to post" and dies in a deserted field, to Mrs Singh's indifference and, by now, her state of madness.

Another significant figure in Mrs Singh's crumbling household must be taken into account. It is the ancestral figure, Aji – the "ancient voice intoning disaster" (45) – who holds up a mirror to Mrs Singh and exposes the fiction of her life. Dr Singh's mother exists as a shadow of her real self behind her masks, her authentic self overpowered by the dark forces of her mind. Her masks succeed through the mystique of her foreignness: her underlings, who exist in a glamourless colonial society, are captivated by the aura of wonder in the ethnically superior image of an authentic India that she projects. It is left to Aji to unmask her: "You pretend you so kind and generous when all the time you frighten of an empty house" (240). What Mrs Singh is actually afraid of is an empty *self*, a spiritual void that threatens to engulf her since the loss of her cultural anchor, her son. The villainous Pujaree fails as a spiritual anchor and only emphasizes her desolation. The only cultural certainty Mrs Singh is left with is Aji, and when Aji dies, Mrs Singh becomes an exile, "stranded on the shore of an unrelenting loneliness" (291), drifting towards a void.

Mrs Singh, with her psychopathic tendencies and her lack of remorse, is a self-willed character bent towards evil to compensate for frustrated primary desires. She is now feared even by the perverse Pujaree, who "takes care not to advise Mrs Singh to expel Sukrum", for he comes to detect the depths of her chaotic mind, "her curious need to give Lathi as a sacrifice", but can never confront Mrs Singh, because she is unpredictable, "a woman whose character he could never fathom" (230) and, moreover, because he is scared of losing his own tenuous position in her mansion and affections. It is impossible for Lathi to escape the combined evil forces of Mrs Singh, the Pujaree and Sukrum, all of whom preside over her inexorable doom.

Even though Sukrum mingles in the band of destitute ex-indentured labourers existing on the fringe and left to complain bitterly of their uprootedness and the idea of "compulsory repatriation to India", he is really a second-generation Indian and, notwithstanding his parasitical nature, Sukrum's sense of identity as a Guianese is intact – he declares his Guianeseness at his marriage ceremony and although he does nothing to capitalize on this increase in self-awareness, the reader comes to appreciate that Heath often puts flashes of truth into the mouths of his most flawed characters.

Ironically, Sukrum, harboured for the purpose of effecting Lathi's degradation, is also the agent of Mrs Singh's final destruction. The disintegration of the Singh family witnesses another change in the social order as the rootless vagabond Sukrum establishes himself as the man of the mansion in Vlissengen Road after Mrs Singh severs relations with the Pujaree. He invites his derelict friends to the mansion, "an assortment of vagrants drawn from the afflicted parts of Kitty" (409), and, in what seems like an act of poetic justice, climbs the stairs and rapes Mrs Singh, who entertains a curious sense of retribution and "felt obliged . . . to remain in the house, offering herself to Sukrum as a sacrifice to her past [evils]" (426) – a *coup de grâce* to the pursuit of selfhood of a vulnerable woman dislocated in the New World.

Weary of an existence of manipulating others, and driven over the brink since her rape, the prodigal mother goes to her son's home, where she commits suicide among "a carnage of mutilated dolls" (437) she had collected in her insanity; she thus releases herself from the bondage of being entrapped in a false self. This traumatic event undercuts Dr Singh's struggle for selfhood and leaves him with feelings of guilt only resolved through the telling of this narrative: "He was jolted to the realization that his mother was a stranger to the community . . . she had lost an identity nurtured in the wake of her marriage and voyage across the sea. Incapable of coming to terms with his desertion, she had installed herself in his house with defiant gestures. Her death was his doing, but he could not have acted otherwise" (437).

In this work, Mrs Singh is a metaphor of female displacement and speaks for all women unceremoniously ejected from India under the auspices of indentureship and left to find accommodation in the New World. Heath's decision to make her India-born is to illustrate both the urgency and poignancy of her cultural needs when juxtaposed with Indian women already in the colony, whose cultural customs were blurred and distorted during accommodation, when Indian customs were decried as pagan.

The journey across the dark waters culminates in cultural and physical suicide for the Hindu woman who finds the psychic stresses of female displacement too overwhelming and the process of adjustment too threatening. R.D. Laing's *The Divided Self* offers insights into Mrs Singh's adoption of masks to survive the reality of the New World with which she could not identify. His study suggests that the outsider, estranged from society, invents a false self with which to confront both the world around him and his inner despair: "The tragic paradox is that the more the self is defended in this way, the more it is destroyed. The fragmentation of the real self coincides with the growing unreality of the false self until the whole personality disintegrates."[24] Laing argues that an understanding of this psychic split is based upon the recognition of "distinctiveness and differentness, separateness, loneliness and despair. Lack of a sense of an autonomous identity results in ontological insecurity, despair, dread and panic in the individual."[25] A definition of madness by Lillian Feder in *Madness in Literature* corroborates Kakar's theory that one's cultural system is deeply ingrained in the unconscious infrastructure, "a state in which unconscious processes predominate over conscious ones to the extent that they control them and determine perceptions of and responses to experience".[26] These theories do much to illuminate the dilemma of the alien Indian woman stranded in a New World colony. The motif of madness allows Mrs Singh (as it did for Galton Flood in *The Murderer*) to evade society's corrupted morality by isolating herself in a prison of insanity. The despair of the introspective antiheroine is mirrored in her subconscious mind as she descends into madness, "haunted by a dream of a flock of birds watching the house from the telephone wires" (278). The separate appearances of the ghosts of her husband and her servant Lathi in her dreams are devices to intensify Mrs Singh's desolation (276, 426).

By choosing a first-generation Indian who arrives in the New World with her cultural certainty intact, the writer is able to throw a spotlight on the process of adjustment and accommodation into creole society from its initial stages of contact and change. Through the schizophrenic response to dislodgement from the ancestral land, the work comments on the sea change that Hinduism undergoes in the New World, as evidenced in the compromise of Hindu values and the loss of Indian cultural certainty in the early twentieth century. The tragic life of Mrs Singh is a metaphor of East Indian displacement, of the unanaesthetized truncating of the Indian from his or her roots and of the cultural schizophrenia and fragmentation in the initial years of Indian immigration. This dilemma appears to have been resolved in this work for the second-generation East Indian, as both Dr Betta Singh and the despicable psychopath Sukrum declare their "Guianeseness" with certainty. By the end of the work, the Indian family has reconstituted itself on different terms: Betta's natural father dies; Betta's surrogate father, the Mulvi, dies; Meena's father (the upholder of Indian customs in his village) dies; and the ancient voice of Aji is silent; leaving Betta and his wife, Meena, to continue life in Plaisance with a Creolised outlook in raising their two daughters and handicapped son in a British colony. Society will always have to be wary of the tricksters, Pujaree and Sukrum.

This chapter has examined Mrs Singh's progress in four phases, taking into account her dilemma of being a Hindu struggling to sever ties with India: her Kerala phase and her uprootedness; the experience of her marriage and disillusionment; the period after her husband's death and her alienation from her son; and the phase of her fragmentation, final degradation and tragic end. While Mrs Singh's traumatic experience is not entirely the story of indentureship, nonetheless, her narrative is valid, since the struggle for independence and cultural certainty of all indentured women is contained in her. She is both a Kerala woman and an indentured woman, and however flawed she may be in her wilfulness, her courageous struggle for identity, individual freedom and independence from the ambivalences of colonialism stands out.

Appendix

REVIEWS IN CHRONOLOGICAL ORDER

D'Costa, Jean. "A Critical Review: *A Man Come Home*". *Jamaica Journal* 9, nos. 2–3 (1975): 53–58.

Harris, Wilson. Review of *The Murderer*. *World Literature Written in English* 17, no. 2 (1978): 656–58.

King, Francis. Review of *The Murderer*. *Spectator*, 8 April 1978, 24.

Vaughn, Stephen. Review of *The Murderer*. *Observer*, 7 May 1978, 33.

Bhabha, Homi. "Uncorking the Bottle". Review of *The Murderer*. *Times Literary Supplement*, 19 May 1978, 564.

Wordsworth, Christopher. Review of *The Murderer*. *Observer*, 17 December 1978, 36.

Naughton, John. Review of *From the Heat of the Day*. *Listener*, 13 December 1979, 825.

Lee, Hermione. Review of *From the Heat of the Day*. *Observer*, 16 December 1979, 39.

Batchelor, John. Review of *One Generation*. *Observer*, 29 March 1981, 32.

Naughton, John. Review of *One Generation*. *Listener*, 16 April 1981, 517.

Eley, Holly. Review of *One Generation*. *Times Literary Supplement*, 17 July 1981, 820.

Rumens, Carol. Review of *Genetha*. *Observer*, 20 December 1981, 21.

Eley, Holly. Review of *Genetha*. *Times Literary Supplement*, 1 January 1982.

Mellors, John. Review of *Genetha*. *Listener*, 14 January 1982, 25.

Sutherland, John. Review of *From the Heat of the Day*, *One Generation*, and *Genetha*. *London Review of Books*, 21 January 1982, 15.

Review of *Genetha*. *Times Educational Supplement*, 26 February 1982, 30.

Review of *One Generation* and *Genetha*. *Publishers Weekly*, 25 June 1982, 104.

Review of *Genetha* and *One Generation*. *Booklist*, 1 September 1982.

O'Brien, Kate Cruise. Review of *Kwaku*. *Listener*, 11 November 1982, 27.

Bold, Alan. Review of *Kwaku*, *Times Literary Supplement*, 12 November 1982, 1243.

Blishen, Edward. Review of *Kwaku*. *Times Educational Supplement*, 28 January 1983, 26.

Review of *Kwaku. Kirkus Reviews* 51 (1983): 900.

Review of *Kwaku. Publishers Weekly*, 9 September 1983, 50.

Review of *Kwaku. Booklist*, 1 October 1983.

Larson, Charles L. Review of *Kwaku. New York Times Book Review*, 15 January 1984, 11.

Munro, Ian. Review of *One Generation* and *Kwaku. World Literature Written in English* 24, no. 2 (1984): 383–85.

Lee, Hermione. Review of *Orealla. Observer*, 15 July 1984, 20.

Sutcliffe, Thomas. Review of *Orealla. Times Literary Supplement*, 27 July 1984, 847.

Review of *The Murderer. Observer*, 29 July 1984, 21.

Binding, Paul. Review of *Orealla. Listener*, 2 August 1984, 27.

Mackay, Shena. Review of *The Trilogy, The Murderer* and *Orealla. Times Educational Supplement*, 22 February 1985, 22.

Review of *Kwaku. Observer*, 5 May 1985, 24.

McDowell, Robert E. Review of *Orealla. World Literature Today* 59 (1985): 310.

Review of *Orealla. Publishers Weekly*, 17 October 1986, 59.

Review of *Orealla. Observer*, 26 October 1986, 29.

Haggie, David. Review of *Orealla. Times Educational Supplement*, 16 January 1987, 30.

Spurling, John. Review of *The Shadow Bride. Observer*, 17 April 1988, 43.

Review of *The Shadow Bride. Observer*, 19 February 1989, 45.

Dasenbrook, Reed Way. Review of *The Shadow Bride. World Literature Today* 63 (1989): 151–52.

Robinson, Jeffrey. Review of *The Shadow Bride. Journal of West Indian Literature* 4, no. 1 (1990): 63–64.

Blishen, Edward. "As Thrilling as Fiction". Review of *Shadows Round the Moon: Caribbean Memoirs. Tablet*, 9 June 1990, 733.

Schaeffer, Susan Fromberg. "Comedowns". Review of *Shadows Round the Moon: Caribbean Memoirs. London Review of Books*, 12 July 1990, 19.

Jaggi, Maya. "Promising Secrets". Review of *Shadows Round the Moon: Caribbean Memoirs. Times Literary Supplement*, 14 September 1990, 979.

McLeod, A.L. Review of *Shadows Round the Moon: Caribbean Memoirs. World Literature Today* 65 (1991): 753–4.

Review of *The Murderer. Kirkus Reviews* 60 (1992): 10.

Review of *The Murderer. Publishers Weekly*, 6 January 1992: 48–49.

Seaman, Donna. Review of *The Murderer. Booklist* 88, no. 11 (1992): 1009–10.

Heany, Patricia. Review of *The Murderer. Library Journal*, 1 March 1992, 117.

Harris, Michael. Review of *The Murderer. Los Angeles Times*, 12 April 1992, 6.

Begley, Adam. Review of *The Murderer. Boston Review*, 17 May 1992, 38.

Polk, James. Review of *The Murderer*. *New York Times Book Review*, 23 August 1992, 9.

Review of *From the Heat of the Day*. *Kirkus Reviews* 60 (1992): 1325–26.

Review of *From the Heat of the Day*. *Publishers Weekly*, 9 November 1992, 73.

Snapp, Joanne. Review of *From the Heat of the Day*. *Library Journal* (December 1992): 186.

Seaman, Donna. Review of *From the Heat of the Day*. *Booklist* 89, no. 10 (1993): 877–88.

Rubin, Merle. Review of *From the Heat of the Day*. *Christian Science Monitor*, 17 February 1993, 15.

Dabydeen, Cyril. Review of *The Murderer*. *World Literature Today* 67 (1993): 427–28.

Review of *The Murderer*. *New York Times Book Review*, 28 March 1993, 24.

Ruta, Suzanne. Review of *From the Heat of the Day*. *New York Times Book Review*, 27 June 1993, 19.

Dorsey, Michael. Review of *The Murderer*. *American Book Review* 15 (1993): 25.

Dabydeen, Cyril. Review of *From the Heat of the Day*. *World Literature Today* 67 (Spring 1993): 876.

Review of *From the Heat of the Day*. *New York Times Book Review*, 5 December 1993, 60.

Review of *The Trilogy*. *Kirkus Reviews* 62 (1994): 234.

Love, Barbara. Review of *The Trilogy*. *Library Journal*, 1 April 1994, 131.

Rubin, Merle. Review of *The Trilogy*. *Christian Science Monitor*, 1 July 1994, 10.

Thelwell, Michael. Review of *The Shadow Bride*. *Washington Post*, February 1996.

Dyer, Richard. Review of *The Shadow Bride*. *Boston Globe*, 22 February 1996.

Review of *The Ministry of Hope*. *Kirkus Reviews*, 1 December 1996.

Childress, Mark. Review of *Kwaku* and *The Ministry of Hope*. *New York Times Book Review*, 16 May 1997.

Schaeffer, Susan Fromberg. "The Murderer". *Persea Books Newsletter* (n.d.).

NOTES

Preface

1. Jeffrey Robinson, "The Guyaneseness of Guyanese Writing", *Kyk-Over-Al* 31 (June 1985): 47.
2. Roy Heath, acceptance speech, Guyana Prize for Literature, University of Guyana (typescript, 1989), 2.
3. Josef Conrad, letter to *New York Times*, 2 August 1901, 460, cited by Keith Carabine, introduction to *Nostromo* (Oxford: Oxford University Press, 1984), viii.
4. Roy Heath, *Genetha* (London: Allison and Busby, 1981), 155. Subsequent references are cited parenthetically in the text.
5. Roy Heath, *One Generation* (London: Allison and Busby, 1981), 58. Subsequent references are cited parenthetically in the text. Walter Rodney's *A History of the Guyanese Working People, 1881–1905* (Baltimore: Johns Hopkins University Press, 1981) describes the struggle of the labouring class to humanize the narrow coastal strip, below sea level and under constant threat from the Atlantic fury, and records the constant battling with the sea of the planter, Quintin Hogg, who is eventually driven to abandon his Bel Air estates along the Atlantic coastline. This challenge to keep the ocean from flooding the land continues up to the present and has even increased in the face of global climate change.
6. Roy Heath, interview with Ameena Gafoor, London, 24 July 1998.
7. Susan Fromberg Schaeffer, "Comedowns", review of *Shadows Round the Moon: Caribbean Memoirs*, *London Review of Books*, 12 July 1990, 19.

Introduction

1. See the section "Primary Sources" in the selected bibliography.
2. Amon Saba Saakana, *Colonialism and the Destruction of the Mind: Psychosocial*

Issues of Race, Class, Religion and Sexuality in the Novels of Roy Heath (London: Karnak House, 1996).

3. See Anne Walmsley, *The Caribbean Artists Movement, 1966–1972* (London: New Beacon Books, 1992) for a comprehensive account of the struggle of Caribbean artists, writers and critics in Britain, in the second half of the twentieth century, for space to define a distinctive West Indian aesthetic.

    Heath was never a member of the Caribbean Artists Movement, never attended its meetings and congresses, and started publishing his novels after the movement's groundbreaking period. His novels, nonetheless, articulate the very issues about the colonial status of Guyana that the members of the Caribbean Artists Movement engage.

    In a telephone conversation with Ameena Gafoor (26 February 1993), Heath said that he had little interest in the Caribbean Artists Movement, as he had embarked on a teaching career and also wanted space to concentrate on creative writing. He said he started work on the trilogy in 1966 but it was published much later.

4. Heath died on 14 May 2008. A tribute by his son Royston Heath affords a precious glimpse into his early years in London. See *Arts Journal* 4, nos. 1–2 (2008).

5. Louis James, "Dark Muse: The Early Fiction of A.K. Heath", *Wasafiri* 3, no. 5 (1986): 26–27.

6. Anthony Boxill, "Penetrating the Hinterland: Roy Heath's Guyana Trilogy", *World Literature Written in English* 29, no. 1 (1989): 103–10.

7. For each novel, title, facts of publication, time setting, place setting, brief summary of text, main characters and main issues and themes are provided.

8. C.L.R. James, "Triumph", *Trinidad* 1 (Christmas 1929), reprinted in *Stories from the Caribbean: An Anthology*, ed. Andrew Salkey (London: Elek Books, 1965), and cited by Kenneth Ramchand, introduction to *Minty Alley* (London: New Beacon Books, 1971), 8.

9. Jean D'Costa, "A Critical Review: *A Man Come Home*", *Jamaica Journal* 9, nos. 2–3 (1975): 53–58.

10. For example, *Trinidad*, followed by *Beacon* in Trinidad; *Bim* in Barbados; *Focus* in Jamaica; and *Kyk-Over-Al* in British Guiana.

11. Heath recalls the beginning of his Marxist consciousness, his close friendship with Martin Carter around mid-century (Heath, conversation with Gafoor, London, July 1998). Phyllis Carter confirmed Heath's visits to the Carters' home on Anira Street, Georgetown, up to about 1950, when he left for England, their shared socialist and radical anti-colonial beliefs, their embrace of the Marxist philosophy and their imbibing of Marxist classics (Phyllis Carter, conversation with Ameena Gafoor, September 1998).

12. The flaws of Marxist theory and communist ideology were exposed by later philosophers, notably Karl Popper (*The Open Society and Its Enemies* [London: Routledge, 1945] and *The Poverty of Historicism* [London: Routledge, 1957]) and Polish thinker Leszek Kolakowski (1927–2009), who termed Marx's theory "a romantic ideal of social unity" (*Toward a Marxist Humanism* [New York: Grove Press, 1968]) as evidenced in the collapse of the Soviet Empire in the late twentieth century, about 150 years after Marx prepared the *Communist Manifesto* with Friedrich Engels in 1848, and further elaborated it in *Das Kapital*, the first volume of which appeared in 1867. After Marx's death, Engels completed the second and third volumes and published them in 1885 and 1894.

13. Heath and Gafoor, a conversation centring on the influences that shaped his writing (London, 24 July 1998).

14. "Quest for an Ideal Social Order", in *Sociology: Man in Society*, by Melvin L. deFleur, William V. D'Antonio, Lois B. deFleur (Illinois: Scott, Foresman, 1971).

15. Heath, conversation with Gafoor, London, 24 July 1998.

16. Michael Gilkes, *Racial Identity and Individual Consciousness in the Caribbean Novel*, Edgar Mittelholzer Memorial Lecture (Georgetown: Ministry of Information and Culture, 1974).

17. Throughout Mittelholzer's novelistic explorations his chief preoccupation was of a psychological nature – the attempt to resolve the inner conflicts of his divided blood – but Michael Gilkes faults the author for the "superficiality of the psychological theme" and for failing to deliver "genuine psychological drama" (*The West Indian Novel* [Boston: Twayne Publishers, 1981], 41–85).

18. Garth St Omer's short story "Syrop" stands out as an evocation of grief unrelieved by the imagery of the indifferent propeller blades of a ship from which tourists watch in delight as little native boys dive to the bottom of the sea to retrieve the coins thrown at them. St Omer's novels that follow are explorations of man's frail understanding of self and his tenuous relationships, all underscored by a sense of loss and sadness.

19. Saakana, *Colonialism*.

20. Ibid., 5.

21. Notably, Kenneth Ramchand, *The West Indian Novel and Its Background* (London: Faber and Faber, 1970); Gilkes, *West Indian Novel*; Sandra Pouchet Paquet, *The Novels of George Lamming* (London: Heinemann, 1982).

22. This list is not exhaustive.

23. For instance, *Savacou, Caribbean Quarterly, Kyk-Over-Al, Journal of West Indian Literature*.

24. Saakana, *Colonialism*, 5–6.

25. Ibid., 175.

26. Ibid., 102; emphasis added.

27. Saakana relies on John Bowlby, *Attachment* (London: Penguin, 1978) to support his argument that the "social environment is principally responsible" for human behaviour: "Not only does the new term (environment of evolutionary adaptedness) make even more explicit that organisms are adapted to a particular environment but it draws attention to the fact that not a single feature of a species' morphology, physiology, or behaviour can be understood or discussed intelligently except in relation to that species' environment of evolutionary adaptedness. Given constant reference to man's environment of evolutionary adaptedness, the vagaries to which human behaviour is liable become, it is held, much less incomprehensible than they are when the nature of man's environment is ignored."

28. Edward Said, *Humanism and Democratic Criticism* (New York: Columbia University Press, 2004), 21–22.

29. Heath, telephone conversation with Gafoor during which he states emphatically that England has held no appeal for him and that he has never seen himself as a British citizen but rather as an exile (26 August 2006, his eightieth birthday).

30. D'Costa, "Critical Review", 56.

31. *Times* (UK), 2 December 1978.

32. Winner of the Guyana Prize for Literature 1989 in the Best Book of Fiction category.

33. "Judges' Report: The Second Guyana Prize for Literature", University of Guyana, 1989.

34. Schaeffer, "Comedowns", 19. It is worth noting that by 1990 Heath had lived in the United Kingdom for at least four decades.

35. See the section "Secondary Sources" in the selected bibliography. A survey that evaluates the existing criticism on Heath's texts informs this work: we have analysed ninety-eight pieces of writing that represent the body of critical responses to Heath. Of these, sixty-seven are reviews appearing in newspapers and magazines either in the United Kingdom or the United States. Seven critical articles and two reviews have appeared in refereed journals and one unpublished essay has been presented at a regional conference. The novels have been reviewed singly and in groups and one critic has conducted three interviews with Heath in an attempt better to understand the world of the writer and the views and beliefs that underpin his writings.

Some of Heath's novels have attracted more critical attention than others. *The Murderer* has been reviewed fourteen times and examined in three critical articles. The trilogy has been reviewed seven times in a cluster, while *From the Heat of the Day* has been reviewed thirteen times as a single novel, *One Generation* ten times singly, *Genetha* six times singly, and seven critical essays have examined these three texts in various groupings. *Orealla* and *Kwaku* have been reviewed and critiqued nine times each and *The Shadow Bride* seven times. *A Man Come Home* appears to have attracted the least attention (with one review and one critical article) while *The Ministry of Hope* has recorded three reviews so far, all from the American side.

We considered the coverage the novels have received, the extent to which they have been discussed, the literary and critical conventions to which they have been assigned, the ways in which the existing criticism may be enriched, whether there are emphases to be developed and false (misplaced) impressions to be modified, whether there have been serious omissions or whether a new approach to reading Heath has been suggested. The criticisms range from mere announcements to tenuous critical efforts to thoughtful assessments.

36. Mark McWatt, "Wives and Other Victims: Women in the Novels of Roy Heath", in *Out of the Kumbla*, ed. Carole Boyce-Davies and Elaine Savory Fido (Trenton, NJ: Africa World Press, 1992), 223.

37. Ibid., 223–24.

38. D'Costa, "Critical Review", 54; McWatt, "Wives and Other Victims", 223.

39. John Naughton, review of *From the Heat of the Day*, *Listener*, 13 December 1979, 825.

40. Robert E. McDowell, review of *Orealla*, *World Literature Today* 59 (1985), 310.

41. Ian Munro, review of *One Generation* and *Kwaku*, *World Literature Written in English*, 24:2 (1984): 383–85.

42. Holly Eley, review of *One Generation*, *Times Literary Supplement*, 17 July 1981, 820.

43. Francis King, review of *The Murderer*, *Spectator*, 8 April 1978, 24.

44. Stephen Vaughn, review of *The Murderer*, *Observer*, 7 May 1978, 33.

45. Cyril Dabydeen, review of *The Murderer*, *World Literature Today* 67 (Spring 1993): 427–28.

46. D'Costa, "Critical Review", 56.

47. Thomas Sutcliffe, review of *Orealla*, *Times Literary Supplement*, 27 July 1984, 847.

48. Northrop Frye, *Anatomy of Criticism: Four Essays* (Princeton: Princeton University Press, 1957), 36.

49. McWatt, "Tragic Irony: The Hero as Victim – Three Novels of Roy Heath", in *Critical Issues in West Indian Literature: Selected Papers from West Indian Literature Conferences, 1981–1983*, ed. Erika Smilowitz and Roberta Knowles (Parkesburg, IA: Caribbean Books, 1984), 56.

50. Ibid., 50.

51.   Jeremy Poynting, "African-Indian Relations in Caribbean Fiction: A Reply", *Wasafiri* 3, no. 5 (1986): 15.

52.   Landeg White's *V.S. Naipaul: A Critical Introduction* (London: Macmillan, 1975), Michael Gilkes's *Wilson Harris and the Caribbean Novel* (London: Longman Caribbean, 1975) and Paquet's *Novels of George Lamming* are all introductory studies of single West Indian authors that situate the writer through a close reading approach without engaging theoretical arguments in the first instance.

53.   Said, *Humanism and Democratic Criticism*, 62–64.

54.   George Lamming, "The Negro Writer and His World", *Caribbean Quarterly* 5, no. 2 (1958): 110–11.

Chapter 1

1.   Roy Heath, telephone conversation with Ameena Gafoor, 26 February 1993.

2.   Roy Heath, *Shadows Round the Moon: Caribbean Memoirs* (London: Collins, 1990), 124. Hereafter referred to as *Shadows*; subsequent citations appear parenthetically in the text.

3.   Michael Gilkes, correspondence with Ameena Gafoor, 6 September 2000.

4.   James Crosby was the first immigration agent general, who held office in British Guiana between 1858 and 1880 as the British-appointed mediator between indentured Indians and the colonial administration. However, the office itself and all subsequent office holders came to be known as the "Crosby", while hearings became known as "Crosby Courts".

5.   Heath, conversation with Gafoor, London, 24 July 1998.

6.   A literary culture was by then in the making in British Guiana, for *Kyk-over-Al* was founded in 1945 by A.J. Seymour as editor; Heath was one of the group of young artists and budding intellectuals (including Seymour and Gilkes) that frequented the Woodbine House, home of the Taitts, where Dorothy Taitt was a patron of the arts and culture. In addition, the organ of the People's Progressive Party, *Thunder*, gave space and voice to young writers and thinkers, notably, the emerging revolutionary Martin Carter.

By 1953 universal adult suffrage would be introduced to British Guiana, after the 1938 Royal Commission of Enquiry, whose report was published in 1945, after World War II.

7.   From the United Kingdom, Heath contributed to *Kyk-Over-Al* 6, no. 19 (Year-End, 1954), which carries a poem by him entitled "The Peasant".

It is noteworthy that A.J. Seymour was connected by marriage to Guy DeWeever, a young teacher who wrote *The Children's Story of Guiana* (Georgetown: Education Department, 1932). Guy DeWeever was uncle to Roy Heath (his mother's brother).

The celebration, in 1931, of the centenary of the establishment of the colony of British Guiana (that is, the union of the colony of Demerara and Essequibo with the colony of Berbice) led to a welcome revival of interest in the history of the colony. A one-volume history of the colony suitable for use in schools was lacking and DeWeever's publication filled that void. The needs of the general reader had been met by the publication of A.R.F. Webber's *Centenary History and Handbook of British Guiana* (Georgetown: Argosy, 1931), which analysed the economic development of the colony in its first century of existence. Webber died suddenly on 30 June 1932 at age fifty-two. This is the shaping of a literary culture in the colony that Heath was heir to.

8.   Reissued by Macmillan Caribbean, 2003.

9.   Reissued with an introduction by Selwyn R. Cudjoe and an afterword by Wilson Harris (Wellesley, MA: Calaloux, 1988).

10.   Reprinted by Dover (New York, 1989).

11.   Reprinted by Peepal Tree (Leeds, 2003). See also Joel Benjamin, "The Lesser-known Tradition of Guyanese Fiction: A Preliminary Bibliographical Survey – Part 1", *Kyk-Over-Al* 30 (1984), and "The Lesser-known Tradition of Guyanese Fiction: A Preliminary Bibliographical Survey – Part 2", *Kyk-Over-Al* 31 (1985).

12.   Gilkes, *Racial Identity*, 6.

13.   Heath, telephone conversation with Gafoor, 26 February 1993.

14.   In Guyana the term "coloured" is used to describe people of mixed African and European ancestry.

15.   Heath, telephone conversation with Gafoor, 26 February 1993.

16.   Heath, acceptance speech, Guyana Prize for Literature.

17.   Georgetown (in the county of Demerara) is the capital city of Guyana (then British Guiana). Mittelholzer was born and raised in the small town of New Amsterdam in the county of Berbice; Harris was born there but moved to Georgetown in his early adolescence; and Carew was born in Agricola – a few miles from Georgetown, on the east bank of the Demerara River, where the Heaths lived briefly in the early 1930s – but spent his adolescent years in New Amsterdam. Harris and Carew are connected by marriage.

18.   Sheila Thorpe, conversation with Ameena Gafoor (Barbados, June 2000). Thorpe was Jan Carew's sister, and sister-in-law to Wilson Harris; she grew up in New Amsterdam.

19.   Guyanese historian James Rose, conversation with Ameena Gafoor (Georgetown, June 2000). Rose grew up in Canje along the Berbice River.

20.   Edgar Mittelholzer, *A Swarthy Boy* (London: Putnam, 1963), 43. Subsequent citations appear parenthetically in the text.

21.   Gilkes, *West Indian Novel*, 41.

22. Michael Gilkes, conversation with Ameena Gafoor, Georgetown 2000.

23. A.J. Seymour, *Edgar Mittelholzer: The Man and His Work*, Edgar Mittelholzer Memorial Lecture (Georgetown, Guyana: National History and Arts Council, 1968), 28.

24. Gilkes, conversation with Gafoor, Georgetown, 2000.

25. Robinson, "Guyaneseness", 50.

26. Gilkes, *West Indian Novel*, 72.

27. Ramchand, *West Indian Novel*.

28. Martin Carter, "Not Hands Like Mine", in *Selected Poems* (Georgetown: Demerara Publishers, 1989), 52–53.

29. Readers who are unfamiliar with the setting may gain from a sense of the Guyana landscape from which the texts are mined. Geographically, Guyana's landmass of eighty-three thousand square miles is divided into three zones: the coastal zone bordered by the Atlantic; the savannahs, and the dense and haunting rainforest that extends from the Orinoco in Venezuela to the Amazon in the south. Almost 95 per cent of Guyana's heterogeneous peoples occupy a mere five per cent of its expansive physical landscape. Village settlements are concentrated mainly along the narrow coastline from Morawhanna, where the north-western tip of the country borders Venezuela, stretching eastwards for more than four hundred miles into the far reaches of the Corentyne River beyond Orealla to the Brazilian border.

   Townships are settled at the estuaries of the country's main rivers: the city of Georgetown is at the mouth of the Demerara River; Bartica is spread out on the Essequibo River at its confluence with the Mazaruni and the Cuyuni tributaries, while New Amsterdam sits at the mouth of the Berbice River. The bauxite-mining town of Linden is located deep along the Demerara River and the tropical forests and savannahs are home to Guyana's aboriginal tribes.

30. Homi Bhabha, "Uncorking the Bottle", review of *The Murderer*, *Times Literary Supplement*, 19 May 1978, 564.

Chapter 2

1. Heath, telephone conversation with Gafoor, 26 February 1993.

2. Roy Heath, *A Man Come Home* (London: Longman, 1974). Subsequent citations appear parenthetically in the text as *Man*.

3. Roy Heath, *The Murderer* (London: Allison and Busby, 1978). Subsequent citations appear parenthetically in the text.

4. Heath, conversation with Gafoor, 26 February 1993. Roy Heath, *From the Heat of the Day* (London: Allison and Busby, 1979), *One Generation* (London: Allison

and Busby, 1981) and *Genetha* (London: Allison and Busby, 1981). All references in this work are to the UK editions and citations appear parenthetically in the text.

5. Roy Heath, *The Armstrong Trilogy* (New York: Persea, 1994).

6. Webber, *Centenary History*, 203.

7. Rodney, *History*; Basdeo Mangru, *Indenture and Abolition: Sacrifice and Survival on the Guyanese Sugar Plantations* (Toronto: TSAR, 1993).

8. The *Argosy* was the mouthpiece of the planter class, but Uncle Stapie's (a pseudonym) column "Uncle Stapie Pon de People", was generally written in Creolese. It appears that it was not beneath the middle class to read the Creolese once the image of themselves was enhanced in it and their social boundaries re-emphasized.

9. S. Lebovici, "Psychoanalytic Theory of Family", in *The Child in His Family*, ed. E. James Anthony, MD, and Cyrille Koupernik, MD (New York: Robert E. Krieger Publishing, 1979).

10. Webber, *Centenary History*, 219.

11. Elsa Goveia, "The Social Framework", *Savacou* 2 (1970): 7–15; Kari Levitt and Lloyd Best, "Character of Caribbean Economy", in *Caribbean Economy: Dependence and Backwardness*, ed. George Beckford (Kingston: Institute of Social and Economic Research, University of the West Indies, 1975), 34–60; George Beckford, *Persistent Poverty: Underdevelopment in Plantation Economies of the Third World* (New York: Oxford University Press, 1972); Clive Y. Thomas, *The Poor and the Powerless: Economic Policy and Change in the Caribbean* (New York: Monthly Review Press, 1988).

12. W.M. Macmillan, *Warning from the West Indies* (London: Penguin, 1935), cited by Cheddi Jagan in *The West on Trial* (London: Michael Joseph, 1966), 61.

13. Ibid.

14. Wood Commission, 1922; the Royal Commission, 1927; the Moyne Commission, 1938.

15. Michael Gilkes, *Creative Schizophrenia: The Caribbean Cultural Challenge*, Third Walter Rodney Memorial Lecture (Coventry: Centre for Caribbean Studies, University of Warwick, 1986).

16. Frantz Fanon, *Black Skin, White Masks* (London: McGibbon and Kee, 1968).

17. Derek Walcott, "A Far Cry from Africa", in *In a Green Night* (London: Jonathan Cape, 1962), 18.

18. Heath, telephone conversation with Gafoor, 26 February 1993.

19. E.R. Wolfe, "Specific Aspects of Plantation Systems in the New World: Community Sub-Cultures and Social Classes", in *Plantation Systems in the New World: Papers and Discussion Summaries* (Washington, DC: Pan American Union, 1959), 136.

20. Raymond T. Smith, *British Guiana* (London: Oxford University Press, 1962), 36.

21. Jay Mandle, *The Plantation Economy: Population and Economic Change in Guyana, 1838–1960* (Philadelphia: Temple University Press, 1973), 47–53.

22. Webber, *Centenary History*, 257.

23. Edgar Mittelholzer, *The Life and Death of Sylvia* (London: Secker and Warburg, 1953). Subsequent citations appear parenthetically in the text as *Sylvia*.

Chapter 3

1. Roy Heath, *Art and Experience*, Edgar Mittelholzer Memorial Lecture (Georgetown: Ministry of Arts and Culture, 1983).

2. John Sutherland, review of *From the Heat of the Day, One Generation*, and *Genetha, London Review of Books*, 21 January 1982, 15.

3. Wilson Harris, "Art and Criticism", *Tradition, the Writer and Society* (London: New Beacon Publications, 1973), 7.

4. Heath, telephone conversation with Gafoor, London, 26 February 1993.

5. Sigmund Freud's *Interpretation of Dreams* might have been an influence on Heath's portrayal of characters.

6. John Rickman, ed., *A General Selection from the Works of Sigmund Freud* (London: Hogarth Press, 1953).

7. Michael Gilkes, telephone conversation with Ameena Gafoor, 3 May 2000.

8. J.P. Sartre, *Existentialism and Human Emotions*, trans. Bernard Fretchman (1957; New York: Philosophical Library, 1985), 15.

9. Dr Rafael Gafoor, consultant psychiatrist at King's College Hospital, conversation with Ameena Gafoor, London, 23 December 2002.

10. Frantz Fanon, *The Wretched of the Earth*, trans. Constance Farrington (1961; repr., New York: Grove Press, 1968).

11. Isaiah Berlin, *The Crooked Timber of Humanity: Chapters in the History of Ideas*, ed. Henry Hardy (1959; repr., London: Fontana Press, 1991).

12. "The difficulty faced by Christian thinkers in this regard follows from their doctrine of the Nazarene as the *unique* historical incarnation of God. In Judaism, likewise, there is the no less troublesome doctrine of a universal God whose eye is on but one Chosen People of all in his created world. The fruit of such ethnocentric historicism is poor spiritual fare today." Joseph Campbell, *Myths to Live By* (New York: Bantam, 1972), 262.

13. It is interesting to note that the Russian writer Leo Tolstoy, in "The Kreutzer Sonata" (in *The Kreutzer Sonata and other Stories*, trans. David McDuff [London: Penguin, 1985]) and set in nineteenth-century Russia, similarly questions the moral dilemma of marriage and its condition of bondage: "Marriages nowadays

are set like traps. . . . We were like two prisoners in the stocks, hating each other, yet fettered to each other by the same chain, poisoning each other's lives and trying not to be aware of it" (47, 75).

14. John Rickman, ed., *A General Selection from the Works of Sigmund Freud* (London: Hogarth Press, 1953) affords an insight into Freud's investigation of the unconscious mental processes of man.

15. One of whom is the writer Albert Camus, who spent his childhood years in Algeria and who meditates on the subject in *The Myth of Sisyphus*, trans. Justin O'Brien (1942; London: Penguin, 1986).

16. Martin Carter, "Do Not Stare at Me", *Selected Poems* (Georgetown: Demerara Publishers, 1989), 6.

17. Carter, *Selected Poems*, 6.

Chapter 4

1. In 1946 the Jagans formed the first nationalist political movement in Guyana, the Political Action Committee. They were joined, in 1950, by black nationalist Forbes Burnham when the People's Progressive Party, headed by Cheddi Jagan, was formed. This alliance did not last, an occurrence that is widely documented in accounts of the country's political history and can be seen as a symptom of enduring racial antagonisms.

    The most instructive insights into African-Indian relations in the multiracial societies of the West Indies are to be found in our body of imaginative literature. Kenneth Ramchand critically examines fictional accounts of the meeting of the two racial composites in "Indian-African Relations in Caribbean Fiction: Reflected in Earl Lovelace's *The Dragon Can't Dance*", *Wasafiri* 1, no. 2 (1985): 18–23, and in "The Theatre of Politics", *Twentieth Century Studies* 10 (1973): 20–36. Poynting's "African-Indian Relations" also analyses some works of contemporary Caribbean fiction that depict the meeting of the racial "other".

    The 1957, 1961 and 1964 general elections in British Guiana were each seen to be determined by race and not class cleavages, an indication that race has superseded class in the plural society. Paul Singh's definition of a plural society as "one of discrete units, where races live side by side, rather than an integrated society" helps us to understand the segmented nature of Guianese society into which Rohan rushes headlong around the middle of the century. *Guyana: Socialism in a Plural Society*, Research Series no. 307 (London: Fabian Society, 1972), 1–3.

2. C.L.R. James, "Discovering Literature in Trinidad: The Nineteen-Thirties", *Savacou* 2 (September 1970): 56.

3.   Earl Lovelace, *The Dragon Can't Dance* (London: Longman, 1979), 147.

4.   The reader will recall that similar social inequality exists between the coloured citizens, the working-class blacks and professional Indians in New Amsterdam; see Mittelholzer's confession in *A Swarthy Boy*.

5.   Clem Seecharan remarks on the racial jealousies of the society at the time: "The 1940's were marked also by an ominous rise in racial consciousness – a situation that was accelerated by the establishment of the Indian middle-class with a base in rice, cattle, and commerce who were ready to challenge the superiority" of the coloured middle class. "The Shape of Passion: The Historical Context of Martin Carter's Poetry of Protest", in *The Art of Martin Carter*, ed. Stewart Brown (Leeds: Peepal Tree, 2000), 24–47.

6.   A phrase made famous by Samuel Taylor Coleridge's description of Shakespeare's Iago.

7.   Harris, "Art and Criticism", 7

8.   Herbert Marcuse, *Eros and Civilization: A Philosophical Inquiry into Freud* (London: Sphere Books, 1972), 29.

9.   Poynting, "African-Indian Relations", 22.

10. In reality, cross-racial marriages and mixed-race children are commonplace but have never been a guarantee of racial unity in the society in Guyana and the Caribbean.

11. Wilson Harris, *The Whole Armour and The Secret Ladder* (London: Faber and Faber, 1973), 115–16.

Chapter 5

1.   On this occasion, protesting sugar workers (now known as "Enmore Martyrs") were gunned down by colonial police.

2.   One hundred and thirty-three days into a new government, Britain acted in collaboration with America to depose Cheddi Jagan, leader of the majority party, citing fear of a threat of communism taking root in the colony – effectively cheating the colony of its right to self-determination.

3.   McWatt, "Wives and Other Victims", 223–35.

4.   A term first used by critics to speak of Antoinette in Jean Rhys's *Wide Sargasso Sea*.

5.   Sibyl is a literary allusion to the women in ancient times who, acting as mediators of gods, uttered prophecies and oracles, hence a Sibyl is a pagan prophetess or fortune-teller.

6.   Carol Rumens, review of *Genetha*, *Observer*, 20 December 1981.

Chapter 6

1. D'Costa, "Critical Review".
2. Francis King, review of *The Murderer, Spectator,* 8 April 1978, 24.
3. Stephen Vaughn, review of *The Murderer, Observer,* 7 May 1978, 33.
4. Dabydeen, review of *The Murderer,* 427–28.
5. Goveia, "Social Framework".
6. Clive Y. Thomas, *The Poor and the Powerless: Economic Policy and Change in the Caribbean* (New York: Monthly Review Press, 1988). This argument has also been offered by other regional socio-economists, including William Demas, *The Economics of Development in Small Countries* (Montreal: McGill University Press, 1965) and Norman Girvan, "Notes on the Meaning and Significance of Development", in *Gender in Caribbean Development,* ed. Patricia Mohammed and Catherine Shepherd (Kingston: Women and Development Studies Project, University of the West Indies, 1988).
7. Martin Carter, "University of Hunger", in *Poems of Resistance from British Guiana* (London: Lawrence and Wishart, 1954), 8–10; also in *Selected Poems* (Georgetown: Demerara Publishers, 1989), 45–46; and in *Selected Poems* (Georgetown: Red Thread Press, 1997), 77–78.
8. Martin Carter, "A Free Community of Valid Persons", *Kyk-Over-Al* 44 (1993): 30.
9. The American equivalent of the "ghetto". See the introduction of this work for notes on depressed areas of the city.
10. Wilson Harris, review of *The Murderer, World Literature Written in English* 17, no. 2 (1978): 656–58.
11. Heath, conversation with Gafoor, 26 February 1993.
12. D'Costa, "Critical Review", 53–58.
13. The obeahman or -woman is now someone of any race and consulted by all races in West Indian societies. This character in Ismith Khan's *The Obeah Man* (London: Hutchinson, 1964) has "no race, no caste, no colour; he was the end of masses of assimilations and mixtures . . ." (11).
14. Roy Heath, "A Tribute to Aubrey Williams", opening of an Aubrey Williams exhibition, Whitechapel Art Gallery, London, June 1998.
15. Heath, *Art and Experience.*
16. Josef Conrad, letter to *New York Times,* 2 August 1901, in Keith Carabine, introduction, *Nostromo* (Oxford: Oxford University Press, 1984), viii.
17. Berlin, *Crooked Timber.*
18. Fanon, *Wretched,* 251–52.
19. A treatment of this symptom in fiction was first noticed in Dostoevsky's *Crime and Punishment.*

20. Saakana, *Colonialism*, 66.
21. An open cart with a long wooden tray drawn by mules or donkeys and used by ordinary people for transportation of goods. The more affluent would use a motor vehicle. Driving a dray-cart is considered a demeaning occupation in the class-structured society.
22. The Guyana East Coast Railway – Georgetown to Rosignol – was scrapped in 1974.

Chapter 7

1. W. Harris, review of *The Murderer*, 656.
2. Sutcliffe, review of *Orealla*, 847.
3. Martin Carter, "Sensibility and the Search", *Argosy*, 26 January 1958.
4. Ibid. (Collected in "A Martin Carter Prose Sampler", special issue, *Kyk-Over-Al* 44 [May 1993]: 78.)
5. A phrase borrowed from Thomas, *Poor and the Powerless*.
6. Groin: a low broad wall extending into the ocean to break the force of waves and prevent erosion of the beach.
7. Paul Binding, review of *Orealla*, *Listener*, 2 August 1984, 27.
8. Nicholas Laughlin writes: "Guyana's writers and artists have been especially keen to demonstrate some kind of continuity between Amerindian culture and contemporary creativity. From A.J. Seymour's poem "The Legend of Kaieteur" to the Timehri motifs in Aubrey Williams's paintings to the intricate allusions in Wilson Harris's novels, an Amerindian presence haunts Guyana's modern art and literature." In "As It Was in the Beginning: A Review of Denis Williams's *Prehistoric Guiana*", *Sunday Stabroek*, 25 September 2005.
9. For an account of the highly structured indigenous society at Orealla on the Berbice River, see Andrew Sanders, *The Powerless People* (London: Macmillan, 1987).
10. The dichotomy of powerful/powerless and victor/victim is corroborated in Heath's trilogy and in Mittelholzer's *Sylvia*.

Chapter 8

1. O'Brien, review of *Kwaku*, *Listener*, 11 November 1982, 27.
2. Richard Dyer, review of *The Ministry of Hope*, *Kirkus Reviews*, 1 December 1996.
3. For example, Jagan, *West on Trial*; Rodney, *History*; Jai Narine Singh, *Guyana: Democracy Betrayed: A Political History 1948–1993* (Kingston Publishers, 1996); and newspapers at Guyana National Archives.

4. Carter, "A Mouth Is Always Muzzled", *Selected Poems*, 97.

5. Stewart Brown, ed., *All Are Involved: The Art of Martin Carter* (Leeds: Peepal Tree, 2000), 53.

6. Carter, *Selected Poems*, 81–82.

7. Grace Nichols, *Whole of a Morning Sky* (London: Virago Press, 1986).

8. Andrew Morrison, *Justice: The Struggle for Democracy in Guyana, 1952–1992* (Georgetown: Morrison, 1998), xi.

9. Carter, "For Walter Rodney", *Selected Poems*, 210.

10. Bernard Heydorn, *Walk Good Guyana Boy* (Toronto: Learning Improvement Centre, 1994), 208–9.

11. Harischandra Khemraj, *Cosmic Dance* (Leeds: Peepal Tree, 1994); Narmala Shewcharan, *Tomorrow Is Another Day* (Leeds: Peepal Tree, 1994).

12. Shiva Naipaul, *In a Hot Country* (London: Penguin, 1983) and *Black and White* (London: Hamish Hamilton, 1980).

13. Lakshmi Persaud, *For the Love of My Name* (Leeds: Peepal Tree, 2000).

14. V.S. Naipaul, *The Mystic Masseur* (London: Andre Deutsch, 1957).

15. V.S. Naipaul, *A House for Mr Biswas* (1961; repr., Penguin, 1969).

16. Ibid., 147.

17. Donald Newlove, *Philadelphia Enquirer*, 13 April 1987.

Chapter 9

1. Edward Kamau Brathwaite, *Contradictory Omens: Cultural Diversity and Integration in the Caribbean* (Kingston: Savacou Publications, 1974), 50.

2. Olive Senior, *Arrival of the Snake Woman and Other Stories* (London: Longman, 1989).

3. Derek Walcott, "The Antilles: Fragments of Epic Memory" (Nobel Lecture, 7 December 1992), http://www.nobelprize.org/nobel_prizes/literature/laureates/1992/walcott-lecture.html.

4. Refer to chapter 1. Heath's grandparents lived at Forshaw Street.

5. John Spurling, review of *The Shadow Bride*, *Observer*, 17 April 1988, 43.

6. Among these, Hugh Tinker, *A New System of Slavery: The Export of Indian Labour Overseas, 1830–1920* (London: Oxford University Press, 1974); Keith O. Lawrence, "Immigration into Trinidad and British Guiana, 1834–1871" (PhD diss., University of Cambridge, 1958); Rodney, *History*; Reddock, *Women, Labour and Politics in Trinidad and Tobago*; Patricia Mohammed, "A Social History of Post-Migrant Indians in Trinidad from 1917 to 1947: A Gender Perspective" (PhD diss., Institute of Social Studies, 1994); Michael Angrosino, "Sexual Politics in the East Indian Family in Trinidad", *Caribbean Studies* 16, no. 1 (April 1976); Bridget Brereton,

"Foundations of Prejudice: Indians and Africans in Nineteenth-Century Trinidad", *Caribbean Issues* 1, no. 1 (1974): 15–28; Michael Cross, *The East Indians of Guyana and Trinidad* (London: Minority Rights Group, 1972); Morton Klass, *East Indians in Trinidad: A Study of Cultural Persistence* (New York: Columbia University Press, 1961); Alan Adamson, *Sugar Without Slaves: The Political Economy of British Guiana, 1838–1904* (New Haven, CT: Yale University Press, 1972); Dale Bisnauth, *The Settlement of Indians in Guyana 1890–1930* (Leeds: Peepal Tree, 2000); Dwarka Nath, *A History of Indians in Guyana* (London: Nelson, 1950); Peter Ruhoman, *A Centenary History of East Indians in British Guiana, 1838–1938* (1946; repr., Georgetown: East Indians 150th Anniversary Committee, 1988); David Chanderbali, *A Portrait of Paternalism* (Georgetown: Guyana National Printers, 1994); Jay Mandle, *The Plantation Economy: Population and Economic Change in Guyana, 1838–1960* (Philadelphia: Temple University Press, 1973); Edward Jenkins, *The Coolie, His Rights and Wrongs* (New York: Routledge, 1871); David Dabydeen and Brinsley Samaroo, *India in the Caribbean* (London: Hansib, 1987); John Gaffar La Guerre, ed., *Calcutta to Caroni* (St Augustine, Trinidad: University of the West Indies, 1974); Clem Seecharan, *Tiger in the Stars: The Anatomy of Indian Achievement in British Guiana, 1919–1929* (London: Macmillan, 1997); Clem Seecharan, *Mother India's Shadow over El Dorado: Indo-Guyanese Politics and Identity, 1890s–1930s* (Kingston: Ian Randle, 2011).

7.   Among such works are Sam Selvon, *A Brighter Sun* (London: Alan Wingate, 1952), *Turn Again Tiger* (London: MacGibbon and Kee, 1958) and *The Plains of Caroni* (London: MacGibbon and Kee, 1970); Naipaul, *House for Mr Biswas*; Ismith Khan, *The Jumbie Bird* (London: Longman,1961); Harold Ladoo, *Yesterdays* (Toronto: Anansi, 1974); Earl Lovelace, *Dragon Can't Dance*; and Rooplall Monar, *Jhanjat* (London: Rooplall Monar, 1989) and *Backdam People* (Leeds: Peepal Tree, 1985).

Among those works that pay particular attention to the condition of Indian women are: A.R.F. Webber, *Those That Be in Bondage* (Georgetown: Daily Chronicle, 1917); Edgar Mittelholzer, *Corentyne Thunder* (London: Eyre and Spottiswoode, 1941); Ian McDonald, *The Humming Bird Tree* (London: Heinemann, 1969); Harold Ladoo, *No Pain Like This Body* (Toronto: Anansi, 1972); James Bradner, *Danny Boy* (London: Longman, 1981); Jan Shinebourne, *The Last English Plantation* (Leeds: Peepal Tree, 1988), and, more recently, books by a crop of female writers including Narmala Sewcharan, *Tomorrow Is Another Day* (Leeds: Peepal Tree, 1994); Lakshmi Persaud, *Butterfly in the Wind* (Leeds: Peepal Tree, 1990), *Sastra* (Leeds: Peepal Tree, 1993) and *For the Love of My Name* (Leeds: Peepal Tree, 2000); Shani Mootoo, *Out on Main Street and Other Stories* (Vancouver: Press Gang, 1993) and *Cereus Blooms at Night* (Vancouver: Press Gang, 1996); Ryhaan Shah, *A Silent Life* (Leeds: Peepal Tree, 2005); Peggy Mohan, *Jahajin* (Noida,

India: HarperCollins, 2007); Ramabai Espinet, *The Swinging Bridge* (Toronto: HarperCollins, 2003); and Ameena Gafoor, "From a Forthcoming Novel", *Arts Journal* 4, nos. 1–2 (2008): 159–67.

8. Jeremy Poynting, "East Indian Women in the Caribbean: Experience, Image and Voice", *Journal of South Asian Literature* 21, no. 1 (1986): 133; Verene A. Shepherd, *Maharani's Misery: Narratives of a Passage from India to the Caribbean* (Kingston: University of the West Indies Press, 2002); and Ameena Gafoor, "The Depiction of Indo-Caribbean Female Experience in the Contemporary Novel of the Anglophone Caribbean" (MA research paper, University of the West Indies, 1988).

9. La Guerre, *Calcutta to Caroni*, ix.

10. Mohammed, "Social History", 85.

11. V.S. Naipaul, *The Middle Passage* (1962; repr., London: Penguin, 1978).

12. A label given to a Hindu on the lowest level of the social hierarchy.

13. Elisabeth Bumiller, *May You Be the Mother of a Hundred Sons: A Journey among the Women of India* (New York: Random House, 1990), 275–81.

14. As British economist J.S. Furnivall points out: "A plural society is one which owes its existence to external facts; it is a unit of disparate parts, and lacks a common social will. There is a medley of people who mix but do not combine" (*Colonial Policy and Practice: A Comparative Study of Burma and Netherlands India* [Cambridge: Cambridge University Press, 1948], quoted in Singh, *Guyana*, 1). Or, as Philip Singer puts it: "It is presumed that the process of 'Creolization' is the new, dominant cultural pattern shaping emerging, or emerged, Guyanese personality. This presumption is doubtful" ("Caste and Identity in Guyana", in *Caste in Overseas Indian Community*, ed. B.M. Schwartz [San Francisco: Chandler, 1967], 95).

15. Sudhir Kakar, *The Inner World: A Psychoanalytic Study of Childhood and Society in India*, 2nd ed. (Delhi: Oxford University Press, 1981), 15.

16. See, for example, Dale Bisnauth, *East Indian Settlement in British Guiana* (Leeds: Peepal Tree, 2007), 178.

17. Michael Gilkes, *Couvade: A Dream-Play of Guyana* (Coventry: Dangaroo Press, 1990), 29.

18. A small unit in range-type housing accommodation for estate workers – the former dwellings of the enslaved.

19. Naipaul, *Middle Passage*, 88.

20. Following a low point of Indian culture and sense of identity in the colony, a renaissance of Indian arts and culture began to occur from the 1930s with visits from Indian missionaries and the introduction of Indian films.

21. As in Gustave Flaubert's *Madamme Bovary*.

22. For an account of Hindu rituals and the reformist steps of the emerging Arya Samaj in the 1930s (against pandits of the old school), see Kusha Haraksingh, "Aspects of the Indian Experience in the Caribbean", in *Calcutta to Caroni*, ed. John Gaffar La Guerre (St Augustine: University of the West Indies, 1985), 164. My thanks to Bernadette Persaud for insights into the practice of Hinduism and the perversion of this religion by the Pujaree.

23. My thanks to Paul Persaud (also known as Paul O'Hara) for conversations that gave me a sense of early-twentieth-century Georgetown and the place of East Indians in it.

24. R.D. Laing, *The Divided Self* (1960; repr., London: Penguin, 1986), 77.

25. Ibid., 38.

26. Lillian Feder, *Madness in Literature* (Princeton: Princeton University Press, 1980), 5.

SELECTED BIBLIOGRAPHY

Primary Sources

Camus, Albert. *The Myth of Sisyphus*. Translated by Justin O'Brien. London: Penguin, 1986.

Carew, Jan. *Black Midas*. London: Longman, 1969.

———. *The Wild Coast*. London: Secker and Warburg, 1958. London: Longman, 1983.

Carter, Martin. *Selected Poems*. Georgetown: Demerara Publishers, 1989.

Gilkes, Michael. *Couvade: A Dream Play of Guyana*. London: Longman, 1974. Coventry: Dangaroo, 1990.

Harris, Wilson. *The Whole Armour and The Secret Ladder*. London: Faber and Faber, 1973.

Heath, Roy, A.K. "According to Marx". In *So Very English: An Anthology*, edited by Marsha Rowe. London: Serpent's Tail, 1991.

———. *The Armstrong Trilogy*. New York: Persea, 1994.

———. "Da Costa's Rupununi". In *Border Lines: An Anthology*, edited by Kate Pullinger. London: Serpent's Tail, 1993.

———. "The Cage". BBC Short Story Series, London, 1995.

———. *From the Heat of the Day*. London: Allison and Busby, 1979. Reprint, New York: Persea, 1993.

———. *Genetha*. London: Allison and Busby, 1981.

———. *Inez Combray*. Staged at the Theatre Guild, Georgetown, 1989.

———. *Kwaku*. London: Allison and Busby, 1982. Reprint, New York: Persea, 1997.

———. *A Man Come Home*. London: Longman Caribbean, 1974.

———. "Masquerade". BBC Short Story Series, London, 1996.

———. "The Master Tailor and the Teacher's Skirt". In *Colours of a New Day: An Anthology*, edited by Sarah Lefanu and Stephen Hayward. London: Lawrence and Wishart, 1990.

———. "The Matriarch of Den Amstel". In *Telling Stories 4: A BBC Anthology*, edited by Duncan Minshall. London: Hodder and Stoughton, 1995.

———. *The Ministry of Hope*. London: Marion Boyars, 1997. Reprint, New York: Marion Boyars, 1997.

————. "Miss Mabel's Funeral". In *New Writing in the Caribbean*, edited by A.J. Seymour. Georgetown: Guyana Lithographic, 1972.

————. *The Murderer*. London: Allison and Busby, 1978. Reprint, New York: Persea, 1992.

————. *One Generation*. London: Allison and Busby, 1981.

————. *Orealla*. London: Allison and Busby, 1984.

————. *The Shadow Bride*. London: William Collins, 1988. Reprint, New York: Persea, 1996.

————. "Tomorrow". In *Smoke Signals: An Anthology*, edited by London Arts Board. London: Serpent's Tail, 1993.

————. "The Wind and the Sun", *Savacou* 9–10 (1974): 55–64.

————. "The Writer of Anonymous Letters". In *Firebird 2*, edited by T.J. Binding. London: Penguin, 1983.

Heydorn, Bernard. *Walk Good Guyana Boy*. Toronto: Learning Improvement Centre, 1994.

Khemraj, Harischandra. *Cosmic Dance*. Leeds: Peepal Tree, 1994.

Lovelace, Earl. *The Dragon Can't Dance*. London: Longman, 1979.

Ladoo, Harold. *No Pain Like This Body*. Toronto: Anansi, 1972.

McWatt, Mark. *Interiors*. Coventry: Dangaroo, 1988.

————. *The Language of Eldorado: Poems*. Coventry: Dangaroo, 1994.

Mittelholzer, Edgar. *Children of Kaywana*. London: Peter Nevill, 1952. (Reissued as two volumes, *Children of Kaywana* and *Kaywana Heritage*. London: Secker and Warburg, 1976.)

————. *Corentyne Thunder*. London: Eyre and Spottiswoode, 1941. Reprint, London: Heinemann, 1977.

————. *The Harrowing of Hubertus*. London: Secker and Warburg, 1954. Also as *Hubertus*. New York: John Day, 1955. Reissued as *Kaywana Stock*. London: New English Library, 1959.

————. *The Life and Death of Sylvia*. London: Secker and Warburg, 1953.

————. *A Swarthy Boy*. London: Putnam, 1963.

Naipaul, Shiva. *Black and White*. London: Hamish Hamilton, 1980.

————. *In a Hot Country*. London: Penguin, 1983.

Naipaul, V.S. *In a Free State*. London: Andre Deutsch, 1971. Reprint, London: Penguin, 1981.

————. *A House for Mr Biswas*. London: Andre Deutsch, 1961. Reprint, London: Penguin, 1969.

————. *The Mystic Masseur*. London: Andre Deutsch, 1957. Reprint, London: Penguin, 1980.

Nichols, Grace. *Whole of a Morning Sky*. London: Virago, 1986.

Persaud, Lakshmi. *For the Love of My Name*. Leeds: Peepal Tree, 2000.

Rhys, Jean. *Wide Sargasso Sea*. London: Andre Deutsch, 1966.

Shewcharan, Narmala. *Tomorrow Is Another Day*. Leeds: Peepal Tree, 1994.

St Omer, Garth. *A Room on the Hill*. London: Faber and Faber, 1968.

Secondary Sources

Beckford, George. *Persistent Poverty: Underdevelopment in Plantation Economies of the Third World*. New York: Oxford University Press, 1972.

Berlin, Isaiah. *The Crooked Timber of Humanity: Chapters in the History of Ideas*. Edited by Henry Hardy. London: Fontana, 1991.

Bisnauth, Dale. *The Settlement of Indians in Guyana 1890–1930*. Leeds: Peepal Tree, 2000.

Boxill, Anthony. "Penetrating the Hinterland: Roy Heath's Guyana Trilogy". *World Literature Written in English* 29, no. 1 (1989): 103–10.

Boyce Davies, Carole, and Elaine Savory Fido, eds. *Out of the Kumbla: Caribbean Women and Literature*. Trenton, NJ: Africa World Press, 1990.

Brown, Stewart, ed. *All Are Involved: The Art of Martin Carter*. Leeds: Peepal Tree, 2000.

Bumiller, Elisabeth. *May You Be the Mother of a Hundred Sons: A Journey among the Women of India*. New York: Random House, 1990.

Chaudhuri, Nirad. *To Live or Not to Live*. New Delhi: Orient Paperbacks, 1971.

Coomaraswamy, Ananda, K. *The Dance of Siva*. London: Hamilton, Kent, 1924. New York: Dover, 1985.

Danns, Kenford. "Decolonization and Militarization in the Caribbean: The Guyana Example". Center for Inter-American Relations, New York, 1978.

Demas, William. *The Economics of Development in Small Countries, with Special Reference to the Caribbean*. Montreal: McGill University Press, 1965.

Fanon, Frantz. *Black Skin, White Masks*. 1952. Translated by Charles Lam Markmann. London: MacGibbon and Kee, 1968.

———. *The Wretched of the Earth*. 1961. Translated by Constance Farrington. New York: Grove Press, 1968.

Feder, Lillian. *Madness in Literature*. Princeton: Princeton University Press, 1980.

Freud, Sigmund. *Civilization and Its Discontents*. Translated and edited by James Strachey. New York: W.W. Norton, 1961.

———.. *Historical and Expository Works on Psychoanalysis*. Volume 15, edited by Albert Dickson. London: Penguin, 1986.

———. *Totem and Taboo*. London: Routledge and Kegan Paul, 1950.

Freeman, Lucy, and Marvin Small. *The Story of Psychoanalysis*. New York: Pocket Books, 1960.

Frye, Northrop. *Anatomy of Criticism: Four Essays*. Princeton: Princeton University Press, 1957.

Furnivall, J.S. *Colonial Policy and Practice: A Comparative Study of Burma and Netherlands India*. Cambridge: Cambridge University Press, 1948.

Gilkes, Michael. *Creative Schizophrenia: The Caribbean Cultural Challenge*. Third Walter Rodney Memorial Lecture. Coventry: Centre for Caribbean Studies, University of Warwick, 1986.

————. *Racial Identity and Individual Consciousness in the Caribbean Novel*. Edgar Mittelholzer Memorial Lecture. Georgetown: Ministry of Information and Culture, 1974.

————. *The West Indian Novel*. Boston: Twayne Publishers, 1981.

Girvan, Norman. "Notes on the Meaning and Significance of Development". In *Gender in Caribbean Development*, edited by Patricia Mohammed and Catherine Shepherd. Kingston: Women and Development Studies Project, University of the West Indies, 1988.

Goveia, Elsa. "The Social Framework". *Savacou* 2 (September 1970): 7–15.

Haraksingh, Kusha. "Aspects of the Indian Experience in the Caribbean". In *Calcutta to Caroni*, edited by John Gaffar La Guerre. St Augustine, Trinidad: Extra Mural Studies Unit, University of the West Indies, 1985.

Harris, Wilson. *Tradition, the Writer and Society*. London: New Beacon Publications, 1967.

Heath, Roy, A.K. *Art and Experience*. Edgar Mittelholzer Memorial Lecture. Georgetown: Ministry of Arts and Culture, 1983.

————. Acceptance speech, Awards Ceremony, Guyana Prize for Literature. Ministry of Culture, Georgetown, 1989.

————. "Criticism in Art: A View from the Diaspora". *Ariel* 24, no. 1 (1993): 163–72.

————. "The Function of Myth". In *Caribbean Essays: An Anthology*, edited by Andrew Salkey. London: Evans Bros, 1973.

————. *Shadows Round the Moon: Caribbean Memoirs*. London: Collins, 1990. Reprint, London: Flamingo, 1991.

————. "A Tribute to Aubrey Williams". Exhibition of the Paintings of Aubrey Williams. Whitechapel Art Gallery, London, June 1998.

Jagan, Cheddi. "Poverty: Cause and Cure in Developing Countries". People's Progressive Party pamphlet, 1972.

————. *The West on Trial*. London: Michael Joseph, 1966.

James, C.L.R. "Discovering Literature in Trinidad: The Nineteen-Thirties". *Savacou* 2 (September 1970): 54–60.

James, Louis. "Dark Muse: The Early Fiction of A.K. Heath". *Wasafiri* 3, no. 5 (1986): 26–27.

Jung, Anees. *Unveiling India: A Woman's Journey*. New Delhi: Penguin, 1987.

Jung, Carl Gustav. *Modern Man in Search of a Soul*. London: Routledge, 1933.

———. *The Undiscovered Self*. Boston: Little, Brown, 1957.

Kakar, Sudhir. *The Inner World: A Psychoanalytic Study of Childhood and Society in India*. Delhi: Oxford University Press, 1981.

Laing, R.D. *The Divided Self: An Existential Study in Sanity and Madness*. London: Penguin, 1960. Reprint, London: Penguin, 1986.

Levitt, Kari, and Lloyd Best. "Character of Caribbean Economy". In *Caribbean Economy: Dependence and Backwardness*, edited by George Beckford. Kingston: Institute of Social and Economic Research, University of the West Indies, 1975.

Macmillan, W.M. *Warning from the West Indies*. London: Penguin, 1935.

Mandle, Jay. *The Plantation Economy: Population and Economic Change in Guyana, 1838–1960*. Philadelphia: Temple University Press, 1973.

Mangru, Basdeo. *Indenture and Abolition: Sacrifice and Survival on the Guyanese Sugar Plantations*. Toronto: TSAR, 1993.

Marcuse, Herbert. *Eros and Civilization: A Philosophical Inquiry into Freud*. 1955. Reprint, London: Sphere, 1972.

McWatt, Mark. "Tragic Irony: The Hero as Victim – Three Novels of Roy Heath". In *Critical Issues in West Indian Literature: Selected Papers from West Indian Literature Conferences, 1981–1983*, edited by Erika Smilowitz and Roberta Knowles. Parkesburg, IA: Caribbean Books, 1984.

———. "Wives and other Victims: Women in the Novels of Roy Heath". In *Out of the Kumbla*, edited by Carole Boyce Davies and Elaine Savory Fido. Trenton, NJ: Africa World Press, 1992.

Mohammed, Patricia. "A Social History of Post-Migrant Indians in Trinidad from 1917 to 1947: A Gender Perspective". PhD dissertation, Institute of Social Studies, 1994.

Morrison, Andrew. *Justice: The Struggle for Democracy in Guyana, 1952–1992*. Georgetown: Morrison, 1998.

Naipaul, V.S. *The Middle Passage*. London: Andre Deutsch, 1962. Reprint, London: Penguin, 1978.

Poynting, Jeremy. "African-Indian Relations in Caribbean Fiction: A Reply". *Wasafiri*, no. 5 (1986): 15–22.

———. "East Indian Women in the Caribbean: Experience, Image and Voice". *Journal of South Asian Literature* 21, no. 1 (1986): 133–80.

Ramchand, Kenneth. "Indian-African Relations in Caribbean Fiction: Reflected in Earl Lovelace's *The Dragon Can't Dance*". *Wasafiri* 1, no. 2 (1985): 18–23.

————. "The Theatre of Politics". *Twentieth Century Studies* 10 (1973): 20–36.

————. *The West Indian Novel and Its Background*. London: Faber and Faber, 1970.

Reddock, Rhoda E. *Women, Labour and Politics in Trinidad and Tobago: A History*. London: Zed Books, 1994.

Rickman, John, ed. *A General Selection from the Works of Sigmund Freud*. London: Hogarth Press, 1953.

Robinson, Jeffrey. "The Guyaneseness of Guyanese Writing". *Kyk-Over-Al* 31 (June 1985): 47–51.

Rodney, Walter. *A History of the Guyanese Working People, 1881–1905*. Baltimore: Johns Hopkins University Press, 1981.

Saakana, Amon Saba. *Colonialism and the Destruction of the Mind: Psychosocial Issues of Race, Class, Religion and Sexuality in the Novels of Roy Heath*. London: Karnak House, 1996.

Sanders, Andrew. *The Powerless People: An Analysis of the Amerindians of the Corentyne River*. London: Macmillan, 1987.

Sartre, J.P. *Existentialism and Human Emotions*. Translated by Bernard Fretchman. New York: Philosophical Library, 1957; 1985.

Seecharan, Clem. "The Shape of Passion: The Historical Context of Martin Carter's Poetry of Protest". In *The Art of Martin Carter*, edited by Stewart Brown. Leeds: Peepal Tree, 2000.

Seymour, A.J. *Edgar Mittelholzer: The Man and His Work*. First Edgar Mittelholzer Memorial Lecture. Georgetown: National History and Arts Council, 1968.

————. *I Live in Georgetown*. Georgetown: Labour Advocate, 1974.

Singer, Philip. "Caste and Identity in Guyana". In *Caste in Overseas Indian Communities*, edited by B.M. Schwartz. San Francisco: Chandler, 1967.

Singh, Paul. *Guyana: Socialism in a Plural Society*. Research Series no. 307. London: Fabian Society, 1972.

Smith, Raymond T. *British Guiana*. London: Oxford University Press, 1962.

Thomas, Clive Y. *The Poor and the Powerless: Economic Policy and Change in the Caribbean*. New York: Monthly Review Press, 1988.

Walmsley, Anne. *The Caribbean Artists Movement, 1966–1972*. London: New Beacon, 1992.

Webber, A.R.F. *Centenary History and Handbook of British Guiana*. Georgetown: Argosy, 1931.

Wolfe, E.R. "Specific Aspects of Plantation Systems in the New World: Community Sub-Cultures and Social Classes". In *Plantation Systems in the New World: Papers and Discussion Summaries*. Washington, DC: Pan American Union, 1959.

Interviews

Birbalsingh, Frank. "An Interview with Roy Heath". *Kyk-Over-Al* 43 (1992): 81–98.

———. "Roy Heath: A Conversation". *Kyk-Over-Al* 48 (1998): 223–39.

Gafoor, Ameena. Personal interviews with Roy Heath. London, February 1993; June 1998; July 1999.

INDEX

ACKNOWLEDGEMENTS

I am deeply indebted to many people without whose generous assistance this work might not have been completed.

First, deepest gratitude to Emeritus Professor Kenneth Ramchand, who gave of his time selflessly in supervising the dissertation, made invaluable critical contributions to the text, and to whom I dedicate this work.

I am deeply grateful to Dr Mark Tumbridge of the University of Warwick and the University of Guyana for sparing valuable time to review the manuscript in preparation for publication and suggest valuable improvements to the text.

I am also deeply indebted to Professor Michael Gilkes, Dr Rupert Roopnaraine, and Dr Adeola James for their valuable critical comments on an early draft of this work; to Dr James Rose and Sheila Thorpe, whose brains I picked for a sense of the New Amsterdam society where Heath's contemporaries lived; to Phyllis Carter (Martin Carter's widow, herself now deceased) and her family, who provided information on the early literary gatherings at their home in Georgetown; to Professor David Dabydeen for encouragement always; to Jan Shinebourne for love always; to Bernadette Persaud for her wry wit and her sharp critical opinions, and for her gracious permission to use her painting *Kali's Necklace* for the cover of this work; to Professors Mark McWatt, Evelyn O'Callaghan, Elaine Fido and Roydon Salick of the University of the West Indies at Cave Hill, who laid the foundations of a literary sensibility for me.

I thank the numerous staff members of the University of London Library; the Colonial Records Office at Blackfriars, London; the University of the West

Indies Libraries at Cave Hill and St Augustine; the University of Guyana Library; the National Library of Guyana; and the National Archives of Guyana for their unfailing courtesy and efficiency when approached for material.

My gratitude also goes to Roy Heath Jr for providing the photograph for the frontispiece and to Roy A.K. Heath's widow, Aemilia Heath, for her kind permission to use the photograph.

Deepest gratitude to my husband, Sattaur, who financed my studies; to my children Omar, Arif and Reaud, who gave me love and encouragement even when they themselves were at various stages of their own studies and needed encouragement; to my brothers and sisters, Nisha, Hamid and Nazreen; I remember my two dear brothers, Farouk and Mustapha, who passed away while I was completing this work; to all my nieces and nephews, especially Ayube, Rosean and Jennifer, Ian, Nika and Asha for their loving support.

I hope this work will inspire my grandchildren, Alia and Asher, who were infants and a great source of joy when I was working on this project, to keep alive the spirit of critical inquiry in the years to come.

Thanks are inadequate.

CPSIA information can be obtained
at www.ICGtesting.com
Printed in the USA
FFOW03n1820250218
45229359-45814FF

9 789766 406363